THE DRAGON'S TEETH

David Fraser, biographer of *Alanbrooke*, historian of the British Army with *And We Shall Shock Them*, social commentator in *The Christian Watt Papers* and novelist with *August 1988* and the *Treason in Arms* series, was once one of Britain's most senior generals. He is married, has five children and lives in Hampshire.

Four of the five novels in the *Treason in Arms* series, depicting the turbulent and dangerous period in Europe from the First World War up until the aftermath of the Second, are now in print:

The Killing Times
The Dragon's Teeth
A Kiss For the Enemy
The Seizure (to be published in
   Fontana 1989)

KU-208-728

DAVID FRASER

The Dragon's Teeth

FONTANA/Collins

Contents

Part I

1932

CHAPTER I

The rain had been driving across the flat Brandenburg plain ever since they had left the port of Stettin. All the way to Berlin torrents swept by the April wind had struck the glass of the train windows, struck and cascaded down as if the express was being subjected to some almighty cleaning process, devised with Teutonic thoroughness by a German God. The water had impeded their view, but it didn't look as if there was much of a view anyway, Desmond Dillon had thought, peering through the streaming windows at a featureless, grey-green landscape. And then the rain had been beating on the roof of the railway station in Berlin, mixing its remorseless sound with the sharp cries of the arriving travellers.

'Pförtner! Pförtner her!'

'Taxi!'

They had found a taxi. Theo, always a move ahead of the crowd in any circumstance of life, had secured the taxi, not without difficulty. Desmond smiled at Theo's success. Theo could always see at a glance what systems existed to regulate the small or large matters of life, could appraise them and exploit them – instantly. Desmond's instinct was always to jump over fences, to do things the hard way, often to rebel. Theo was adept at finding a way through.

They had not yet had time to gossip about the peculiar encounter they had experienced on the Stettin train and Desmond thought this could wait. He was unsure how much their words to each other could penetrate through the heavy neck to the mind of the taxi driver, upright in front, peak cap set very straight, who was now steering them through the rain towards the eastern suburbs of Berlin. Not much, probably – there was a partition although it was ajar; and the odds against the man understanding English were presumably high. Besides, what did it matter? But something decided Desmond to postpone discussion of the train journey just concluded, and Theo was particularly silent.

Desmond had given the taxi driver his instructions. The man had nodded.

'*Jahwohl.*'

He had looked sulky. Desmond, climbing in, had said to Theo, 'It's quite a way. Almost out of the city. Herr Fischer was apologetic about not meeting us.'

'So you said.'

'He said, "I don't believe you'll have any difficulty", rather as if we were about to penetrate a jungle. But it's not as far as all that. I've a vague idea – rather like taking a taxi to Hounslow. From Victoria.'

'Not bad. But expensive, doubtless. Still, why should Herr Fischer drive through this weather into the centre of Berlin to collect two Englishmen he's never met and is being good enough to put up at the suggestion of a third, elderly, Englishman he's not seen for some time? A taxi is the least we can do.'

'Of course. Anyway, I believe he's a charming man. For that matter he may not own a car. I think he's fairly hard up.'

'That thought depresses me,' said Theo Tate. 'I need rather generous hospitality just at the moment. This weather lowers the spirits.'

It was getting dark and the rain was coming down as hard as ever.

A policeman's hand halted the traffic at a major intersection and the huge letters on three separate hoardings were illuminated by street lamps. '*Hindenburg*', read one, beneath an enormous picture of the venerable, moustachioed Field Marshal, President of the Republic, eighty-five years old, a candidate for re-election in this month of April 1932. '*Hindenburg*'; the crude portrait, the vast, simple, heavy lettering, the impression of solidity, continuity, sheer *mass* which that name conjured up, thought Desmond. Hindenburg! And on two hoardings on the other side

10

of the street he read '*Thälmann*' in red letters, and, in Gothic script beside another picture, a picture in shadow while the name was strongly illuminated, '*Hitler*'. The policeman waved them on.

'When do they vote?'

'Tomorrow. 10th April. It's the second ballot. You know – there was no clear-cut result from the last one, in March, and they have to go through it all again! Wonderful time to be here. And our host, Christoph Fischer, has the reputation of being a really sharp political journalist. He's bound to be interesting.'

Theo said nothing. He, too, was looking forward to meeting Christoph Fischer of whom he, like Desmond and independently, had heard a good deal. He preferred, however, to hold the initiative with his friend in any conversation which touched politics. Theo had political ambitions. Politics were his study, his concern, his field of expertise – at least in company like that of Desmond Dillon. Desmond, charming though he was, danced through life without much political commitment, Theo reflected. Desmond was something of a buccaneer, and Theo enjoyed that, enjoyed the sense that in Desmond's company anything could happen, enjoyed vicariously Desmond's taste for doing unpredictable things, his taste for activity, mystification, sudden change. Desmond liked life to be a blend of excitement and enigma. To Theo this was immaturity – but agreeable immaturity.

Theo looked at his friend's narrow, rather swarthy face, dark hair, brown eyes, handsome alertness. Desmond intended to write a book, a novel, set against the background of this Europe they had been spending a few weeks touring together. He was observant, articulate, good with a telling phrase, romantic and susceptible, thought Theo. He had been a pleasant companion; days of Cambridge friendship easily revived after some four years. But did Desmond really understand anything much behind the surface of events? Theo doubted it, and was content to doubt. He hoped Herr Fischer would appreciate that he, Theo Tate, possessed sufficient background knowledge of European politics to understand the nuances of what Herr Fischer should, at a time

11

like this, be in a position to convey. Desmond's novel might, or might not, flower in due course. Theo had other fish to fry. The next year – even, perhaps, this year – might see him short-listed as a candidate for a constituency in the south of England, the safe, Conservative south. Perhaps a man who could speak with experience and authority on some aspects of foreign affairs might hold a card denied to others; even if not a particularly high one, Theo appreciated, English insularity being notorious. He sighed in what was now the darkness, street lights being less numerous. They had been driving, it seemed, for a long time.

'Desmond, we must be half way to Poland!'

Desmond grinned. He liked the sensation of being transported through darkness, into the unknown.

'He said it was the outskirts, Theo – *"In der Umgebung, lieber Herr Dillon."* We've not come as far as you think. Distance always seems greater in a strange place.'

'If you say so.'

Ten minutes later their driver braked sharply. Beneath a street lamp ahead they could see two halted vehicles, a knot of people, torches swinging and flickering outside the lamp's circle of light. They seemed to be in a broad curving avenue, with houses of substantial size set back from the road behind low garden walls. Desmond could make out a number, white against a blue background, on the nearest gate. They were still in Berlin, or its suburbs. Its *Umgebung*.

'What's this, I wonder? A breakdown?'

The rain seemed almost to have stopped and they saw two men carrying torches approaching the taxi. The driver wound down his window.

'*Guten Abend.*'

The tone of the leading man was sharp and confident though not unfriendly. Desmond and Theo could see a peaked cap with strap under chin, a black belt with shoulder brace, and tall boots: some sort of uniform, colour hard to define beneath the street lamp. On the man's left sleeve was an armband.

12

The torch was shone perfunctorily into the interior of the car. The taxi driver's response, his '*Guten Abend*', sounded deferential. Nobody seemed disposed to accost Desmond and Theo. In a quiet voice the leading man seemed to be asking the driver his destination. Several uniformed companions now strolled towards them and Desmond saw that over the shoulder of each a rifle was slung. He couldn't make out much of the exchanges with the driver, but they culminated in the taxi moving slowly forward once again and the two uniformed men who had appeared at the window signalling it on with something between a wave and a salute. Nobody seemed in a hurry. The whole incident had lasted about three minutes. When the taxi had rounded a corner, some quarter of a mile further on, the driver accelerated sharply, as if glad to put behind him as far and as quickly as possible the experience just undergone. Yet, Desmond reflected, his tone had been wholly unresentful – respectful indeed. He opened the partition glass wider and said to the man's back, '*Polizei?*'

No answer. And Desmond said, speaking louder and more sharply – '*Ich fragte! Polizei?*'

'No,' the driver said, without turning, eyes on the road, grunting the answer over his shoulder, 'No, not police.' Then who? Desmond wanted to know.

'*Sturmabteilung –*'

'SA,' Theo said softly. 'Röhm's lot, isn't that his name? Hitler's crony, his strong-arm man, Röhm.'

Desmond nodded. He had found confusing the kaleidoscope of personalities in and out of the news in the German Republic, and had not identified names with parties or causes sufficiently to remember them at all times. But he had read a certain amount before leaving England and he reckoned Theo was right. Röhm. Captain Röhm. Leader of the Brown Shirts, the uniformed militia of the National Socialist German Workers' Party, NSDAP. The Nazis. The 'Storm Troopers', as the British press described them, using inverted commas to explain and apologize for the term, bizarre to English readers.

'They seemed perfectly friendly. Theo, did you notice those

people simply standing on the platform at Stettin, standing quite still, obviously not travelling, not porters or employees?'

'I did. Their faces were grey.'

'Yes,' said Desmond, 'grey. Grey faces. Motionless, grey people.'

'They were hungry. One saw the same in Leningrad. It's the hungry look.'

'I suppose so.'

'Everyone here is hungry,' said Theo conversationally, 'I talked to a man on the boat, he told me that it's like it was immediately after the War once again. Like the time when we kept on the blockade until they signed the Peace Treaty. After that was the inflation. Then foreign investment and boom. And now, after the American crash, disaster again.'

'And no work.'

They had seen the headline in a paper bought at Stettin station. Unemployment, it screamed, was approaching five million.

'And no work,' agreed Theo. 'No work, and not much food, I expect, for those without jobs.' There is crisis everywhere, of course, Theo thought. We are seeing the German version of a certain, inevitable phenomenon.

At that moment, and in a voice politer than he had used hitherto, the driver told them that in two minutes they would arrive at their destination.

The week in Leningrad had been, on the whole, a disappointment. Desmond had been set on it for months. The opening scenes of his novel were planned to take place in St Petersburg. Desmond had throughout 1931 fancied himself in love with a Russian girl whose family, after extraordinary adventures, had got away from Odessa in one of the last ships to leave before the Bolsheviks finally took over. Katya had then been nine years old: they had, she and her mother, ultimately reached Ireland, and her father, long presumed dead fighting with Denikin had, astonishingly, turned up in 1920. Desmond found Katya fascinating and her changes of mood, her tempers, even her violence all part

14

of a delicious experience. Katya was fair-haired and smooth-skinned; Katya was emancipated and had fought and won her independence from the austere standards by which her impoverished parents still lived; Katya was fun. In due course, however, Katya had proved altogether too difficult and Desmond knew that she resented the fact that he was elusive, emotionally hard to pin, appeared to take too little seriously. Desmond was twenty-six, and his restless itch for novelty and adventure worked against constancy in any affair. But something of Katya would always remain with Desmond, he thought; not least her descriptions of St Petersburg.

'I long to see it. Couldn't we go there together, and you'd show me?'

'I? Desmond, my name alone would get me shot! Besides, it is all a slum now, horrible! That world is over.'

'I don't believe that's entirely true. Some echoes, I'm sure – and it must be nonsense about them shooting you! You were only nine years old!'

'You don't know them! Did youth save the Romanov girls?'

When Desmond and Katya had finally decided to avoid seeing each other again, perhaps for a long time, they managed neither to quarrel, nor think with bitterness. Much later Desmond came to appreciate this for the achievement it was. Later, too, he understood that it had been made possible only because real feeling had been waning for some time. Desmond's body was still sharply aware of the memory of Katya but his heart was almost completely whole once again. He felt grateful.

But Katya's vivid descriptions of Peter the Great's glittering northern capital by the Neva had sown the seeds of at least one book in Desmond. When he and Theo Tate, taking up the threads of friendship again, had decided to spend a month abroad in the spring of 1932, Desmond had been decisive.

'I must go to Russia, Leningrad.'

'But I need to go to Germany! The political situation there – '

'Leningrad features in my book – or rather Petrograd does. I must see it. We'll do both!'

Theo had talked of the difficulties. A Soviet visa could take years – and when one got there one would be watched, conducted everywhere by officials, spied upon. You couldn't, said Theo, live like an ordinary tourist in Russia, everybody knew that. And the place was bankrupt, destitute, nothing was functioning, their ridiculous economic plans had subsided in chaos and misery: everybody knew that too. Why not spend longer in Germany? Or Hungary, perhaps?

Desmond said, 'You don't want to go to Russia because you're such a crusted Tory, you disapprove of their experiment! You're irredeemably hostile!' Theo made no attempt to deny his hostility to the Bolsheviks. He was aware of his reputation. It was a careful artefact, cherished. He raised his eyebrows.

'Well – do you approve?'

Theo knew nothing from Desmond of Katya. Desmond said, 'No, from what I've heard the horrors have been unbelievable. But I want to see.' He produced a trump card. 'Adrian Winter's going to get us fixed up. His contacts are excellent.'

Adrian Winter, a Conservative Member of Parliament, was a name to subdue Theo, as Desmond knew well. Adrian had met Theo and told others that he had been very favourably impressed. And Adrian was contemplating giving up his seat. His second wife had died in tragic circumstances in Germany in 1923. She had been a cousin of Desmond's mother, and Adrian had always nourished the connection. A large, generous man, he had promised Desmond that if he really wanted to go to Russia he, Adrian, knew how to fix it up.

And so they had spent a week in Leningrad, and although Desmond had not confessed it, the week had been a disappointment. He had known that the young Soviet State was probably no place for romantic adventure or casual encounters, that it was likely to be grim, without the sort of colour and vitality which were, for Desmond, the essentials of life. He had been ready for drabness – these people were living in the aftermath of revolution, civil war, famine – but the real disappointment had been with the faces of the Russians. Desmond supposed that he had, at least subconsciously, peopled the Petrograd of his imagination with Katyas – and, indeed, with Annas, Natashas, Vronskys, for Katya had induced a mood in which he had for months read little but translations of the Russian novelists. Instead he had found a sort of solid charmlessness, a lack of grace, something supremely *uninteresting*, he admitted to himself, in almost every face he passed in the street. It was as if an evil fairy had waved a wand and removed all distinction from these people's characters and countenances. Desmond did not discuss with Theo how despondent the place made him feel. It had been his idea, after all, and he concentrated on the undeniable beauties of Czar Peter's great buildings, peeling and alienated though they now appeared. Theo took it all very well, secretly relieved to find his ebullient friend somewhat subdued. He kept his own reactions to himself. He looked at Leningrad through a different lens. Desmond supposed that Theo was, as he was, breathing more freely on reaching Germany, disturbing though the atmosphere there too might prove to be.

They had travelled by a Swedish ship from Leningrad to Stettin, the Baltic gleaming beneath an ever-changing sky, with small white clouds driven by a cold wind, eternally, it seemed, in the east. At Stettin it had been raining for the disembarkment and raining ever since: yet even for so noble a spirit as Desmond's there was something consoling about the cleanliness, the rather old-fashioned comfort, the sheer sense of efficiency which pervaded the Berlin train, despite the silent, grey, hungry look on the faces of those people without motive or hope it seemed, standing waiting on Stettin platform. The train was uncrowded and they had found corner seats opposite each other. Each had previously paid one visit to Germany as an undergraduate, in 1927. Each could speak a halting, careful German. Each supposed his mastery of the language was superior to that of the other.

Then, irrupting into the compartment like a battering ram, there had been the Pole.

No doubt whatever about his nationality. His opening move

after bursting unsteadily into the carriage, staring at them, and sitting down was to declaim in English –

'Two Englishmen! Listen – I am Polish!'

He accompanied this with a smile of great charm. Then he shook Theo's hand and Desmond's. He smiled at them as if they had all just stumbled on the most enchanting coincidence. English reserve was under assault. The scent of strong spirits, too, was powerful in the compartment. Desmond said with a grin, disengaging his hand, 'How do you do? You speak very good English.'

The Pole accepted this compliment with a nod, perceiving that it was based on small evidence and had correspondingly little value. He said, 'My name is Rodoski.'

They told him theirs, and Rodoski explained that he was a journalist based for the time being in Berlin.

'We Poles are interested in what is happening in Germany. It is important for us, you see, the politics of this neighbour of ours. So our newspapers wish to be well informed.' Rodoski had been visiting a friend in Stettin, a retired sea captain, he said, and half Polish. Theo eyed him.

'We've just arrived from Leningrad.'

Rodoski had produced a flask and handed it round: a fierce liquor. At the mention of Leningrad he rolled his eyes upwards. Conversation had been in a mixture of German and Rodoski's quaintly pronounced English.

'Leningrad! Well, what did you think of the Bolsheviks?'

'A sad atmosphere,' said Desmond, 'it feels like a prison. I mean leaving it is like leaving prison. When there one was chiefly conscious of apathy, I think.'

Rodoski pursed his lips and took a swig.

'Twelve years ago, not long, they tried to invade us, to force their filthy ideas on us with bayonets, you know that?'

'Certainly.'

Theo and Desmond had been schoolboys when Marshal Pilsudski drove the Red Army back from the gates of Warsaw, but the story had penetrated even English schoolboys' consciousness.

'And you know something else? These people here' – he jerked with his thumb at the Brandenburg plain beyond the rain-streaked windows – 'they preferred the Reds to us! We had enemies behind as well as in front. Of course.'

Theo raised his eyebrows and Desmond, wishing he could recall clearly more of the complexities of central European history in the decade just past, said, 'Why?' He warmed to Rodoski and his brown eyes sparkled. He couldn't remember the part Germany had or had not played in Katya's occasional and dramatically expounded history lessons. Rodoski, thought Desmond, was fun, whatever the accuracy of his prejudices.

'Why? Surely not many Germans felt like that? I know Communism was strong in Berlin – and – and in Saxony, wasn't it?' He was fumbling a little and Rodoski, slightly tipsy but unsmiling, was watching his face with a frown. 'But,' said Desmond, 'the revolution here was put down and the Communists have been getting quite a small vote – surely nobody else would have backed the Russians, the Bolsheviks, at the expense of Poland?'

Rodoski, eyes still on Desmond, thrust out the flask to him. Desmond took a gulp and the Pole handed it to Theo. Then he said, 'Wrong! Twice wrong!'

'Why?' Theo, echoing Desmond, chipped in. He wore the courteous, not-enormously-interested, good-tempered expression of the Englishman discussing another nation's affairs. 'Why?'

'Twice wrong! I tell you why. First because you say the German Communists have been getting a small vote and you think they not very important' – he held up a hand as Desmond opened his mouth to remark that he'd not advanced that opinion.

'Please! I think you mean that Germany quiet, democratic country, the Communists not very important, eh?'

'Well, we've just arrived, I don't know. The English papers don't seem to regard them as a very strong electoral force. *The Times* – '

'Electoral!' said Rodoski. 'Maybe not electoral! But they are a force! They have strong arm' – and he bent his elbow and clenched his fist – 'Like in Russia, they don't count numbers, they don't think they'll win election! A friend of mine – half

Polish, the friend I've visited in Stettin – he's got a workshop. Understand?'

They nodded. *Werkstatt.* Presided over by a retired sea captain. They could not exactly envisage it.

'Employs twenty-five men. You know something? He has to have two of them all night with a gun. In the workshop! And he does it himself, too. Takes his turn. So that he can defend it if the Communists come.'

'Why would they come?'

'To take it over. Declare it belongs to the people.'

'Isn't that something for the police?'

'Police look the other way. Police don't want to offend the Communists too much. Bad condition this country, I tell you. You'll see.' He drew on the flask again, wiped his mouth, and replaced it in his pocket. He was nodding, almost complacently it seemed, as he contemplated the distressing condition of the German Republic. Then he smiled at Desmond and Theo, as if enchanted to find so much innocence ready for enlightenment.

'And I tell you another reason you wrong, when you say not many Germans prefer the Reds to us. Wrong! They hate us! You know what Lenin said?'

They shook heads, uncertain what particular light Lenin had cast on the matter.

'Lenin said, "Germany wants revenge. We want revolution. For the moment our aims are the same."'

'"For the moment",' said Desmond, enjoying the argument, aware of getting rapidly more out of his depth, 'but not for long, surely? And what Germans could agree?'

'Most of them. You heard of General von Seeckt? He made their new little Army. Conservative. Monarchist.' Rodoski mimed the twisting of a monocle into the eye and stiffened his back to a semblance of the military man he intended to convey. 'Old school,' he said, 'clever man, General von Seeckt. He said, "The existence of Poland is more intolerable for Russia than ourselves." And he said, "The restoration of the frontier between Russia and Germany is necessary." You knew that?'

'No.' Nor were they sure they believed it. Rodoski looked satisfied. He added, 'And he said that Poland must collapse. And will collapse, given collaboration between Russia and Germany. Von Seeckt. Conservative. Monarchist. That's what he says.'

'A long time ago, perhaps.'

Rodoski shrugged.

'A few years, maybe. But that doesn't change. And now he's a deputy.'

'You are saying,' Theo remarked carefully, 'that although the leadership of the German Republic has been liberal –'

'I was speaking of the *Reichswehr*. The Army.'

'Very well. But it has been serving a liberal, democratic regime. And you are saying that in spite of this regime being liberal and democratic they would – or some of them would – be prepared to cooperate with the Bolsheviks to bring about the collapse of Poland?'

Rodoski shrugged his shoulders and said, 'Cooperate? Yes. Why not? They cooperate plenty already. And the Bolsheviks want the same. You know what Radek said – ' Radek and his words were unknown to Desmond. He looked impassive.

'Karl Radek said, about the German Nationalists and the Bolsheviks, "We have a common enemy, the victors of Versailles." I tell you something –'

But at that exact moment, Desmond always remembered afterwards, the compartment door had opened and a tall man in a brown suit carrying a briefcase with a raincoat over his arm had come in, glanced at them and sat down. And had then leaned forward and tapped Rodoski on the knee.

'Herr Rodoski!'

'Correct!' said Rodoski, looking cautious, 'I think we met – '

'We met at the Kornitz house. Langenbach.'

'Yes, yes,' said Rodoski, 'Herr Langenbach, I remember well. We had many friends. These two gentlemen,' he waved his hand over Desmond and Theo, 'are English.'

'English, eh?' said Herr Langenbach. 'Travelling from where to Berlin, may one ask?'

'From Leningrad.'

Langenbach gave Theo a very straight, hard look followed by the offer of a cigarette case. He remarked that he had found the rear part of the train crowded and guessed, correctly, that the front portion, where they were, would be emptier. There was a silence in the compartment as Langenbach lit a cigarette. Rodoski was obviously disinclined to continue his dissertation on German politics or attitudes to Poland. Langenbach and Rodoski kept up a largely social exchange about mutual acquaintances: Desmond and Theo were content to sit back, relax, and feel a certain relief at the pause in Rodoski's ruthlessly informative stream of conversation. When they had steamed into Berlin, Langenbach shook the hands of all three and vanished. And before Rodoski left them or Theo found his taxi, the Pole, breath spirit-laden but smile still warm and attractive, took their arms.

'We will meet again. I will show you Berlin. And you must meet my friend.'

'What friend?'

Rodoski smiled –

'My Sonja. A very close friend. She and I will show you Berlin. You will remember our conversation?'

'Of course.'

'That other – Herr Langenbach – I can tell you – '

Rodoski had suddenly drawn Desmond's face near to his own, his hand at the back of Desmond's neck. Desmond thought, without pleasure, that he was about to suffer an embrace.

'I can tell you, we speak of cooperation! Germans! Bolsheviks! But that one!' And Rodoski had rolled his eyes upwards, a favourite trick, accompanied by a sardonic smile and succeeded by a belch. He had obtained the Fischer address and telephone number from them and seemed determined to renew contact, to show them Sonja, and to show them Berlin.

'*Siebzehn!*' the driver grunted, and moved round to open the door. They had, it seemed, arrived at the house of Herr Christoph Fischer.

'It is monstrous,' said Kitzi Fischer. A Silesian, he had lived long years in Bavaria before moving to Berlin in 1930 and had acquired the diminutive 'Kitzi' in the southern manner. He disliked it at first but it had stuck, and even the dour, sceptical Berliners used it. Kitzi Fischer. He was a tall man, lamed for life in the fighting in France in 1916 as an officer in a Landwehr battalion, a man with independent views, with a sharp wit and a clever pen. A brave man, a man of passionate principle. A man found by most to possess exceptional charm. He had instantly taken to these two young Englishmen, introduced to him by a letter from Herr Winter, that Adrian Winter whom he had befriended after Mrs Winter's death – death in a Munich street, death in 1923. A beautiful, gallant, quixotic woman as he thought of her, and remembered her in his prayers: and her husband, Adrian Winter, Member of the British Parliament, had made friends with him, kept in touch with him, always showed generosity and kindness. Kitzi had only twice been to England but he thought of it with affection now and he had taken pains, late in life, to learn to speak very passable English – some sort of tribute, he felt, to Veronica Winter of noble memory. Kitzi was forty-three. He looked at Desmond and Theo sitting at his supper table and said again, 'Monstrous. Monstrous. I'm ashamed that you experienced that.'

'Herr Fischer, everyone was perfectly polite, there was no trouble.'

'No. But the shame is that we have these gangs of uniformed louts, acting as if they were authorized police. As if they had the power of the State behind them. They have no authority. None.'

'What were they up to? And who exactly – '

'As to who,' said Kitzi, 'they were undoubtedly the SA. I have heard from other people tonight – you've arrived on an interesting evening for Germany! The SA have cordoned Berlin. Set up checkpoints and blocks all round the city, with reserves ready to march. Thousand upon thousand of them. They are the Nazis' street troops. All organized from the early days of our National Socialist German Workers' Party! They are under the authority of a Captain Röhm.'

Desmond and Theo nodded pleased recognition to each other. They had got this right.

Kitzi said, 'He really is a captain. He was an officer in the Army. And he then devoted himself to politics. Street politics. The organization of the Movement. The SA – *Sturmabteilung* – are very numerous, they are everywhere. And they have arms.'

'They're out tonight because of the election?'

'There's no secret about that. They suppose Herr Hitler, their leader, will be elected our President. And they imagine, or pretend to imagine, that there will then be trouble – from those who dislike the idea of Herr Hitler being elected our President! Then they, the SA, will deal with this trouble and all will be well.'

Theo said, 'Are the SA the only organized Party fighters? Have they any equivalent rivals in the other parties?'

'Certainly. The Communists have produced what they call their Workers' Militias – strong in the early days. Sometimes they even joined with the SA against the police! More often they tried to wreck each other's meetings. Röhm would tell you the SA were necessary to protect National Socialist meetings from organized violence and disruption – I don't dispute that. But the point, I think, is that the Republic can't survive unless these private armies are, somehow, destroyed, disbanded. We have seen worse violence, especially here in Berlin, in these last weeks, in this election, than I ever remember since the Revolution itself, in '18 and '19.' Seeing their questioning faces, he smiled and said, 'Oh yes, we had our own little revolution. Nasty while it lasted.'

'And this present violence – ?'

'Is mainly created or provoked by the Nazis. They want an atmosphere of crisis.'

Desmond frowned and shook his head.

'I'm still uncertain why the Nazis have so much support. They were pretty well seen off eight years ago, weren't they?'

'They were, Herr Dillon, they were – '

'Please, Herr Fischer, call me Desmond. And this, as you know, is Theo.'

'And you,' said Kitzi, bowing, 'should call me "Kitzi". Everyone does, and I know you English like to be informal. Now, the Nazis were, as you say, "seen off". Hitler was put in prison after that Munich *putsch* – I was there, as it happens.' His mind went back to the tramp of marching Nazi feet, the shouts, 'Ludendorff! Ludendorff!' the police volley, the panic-stricken, fleeing marchers. 'Yes, I was there,' he said , 'and they, the Nazis, were beaten, scattered. And then for a while things, here in Germany anyway, got better. Our economy was helped to recover, as you know. The inflation was beaten although many had been ruined, there was food again, jobs again. The Nazi vote was small, the Communists not strong. But since this economic crash which has hit us all, your country too, I know – since that, all the earlier resentments and despairs have become popular again.'

'Resentments? Despairs?'

'Resentment at the Treaty of Versailles. Resentment at second-class status for Germany. You may think that's got nothing to do with economic hardship, but believe me, all these things are linked up in people's minds, and the Nazis, above all parties, do the linking! Weakness abroad means poverty at home, it's not an unnatural association of ideas. And poverty at home means hunger. So there's resentment at our armed forces being held to a tiny figure and not allowed mechanized vehicles, or anti-aircraft artillery, or submarines or aircraft even. Aircraft! People say, "Obviously aeroplanes will dominate warfare in the future. So if Germany is forbidden to fly she is defenceless." And so on.'

'Despair – ?'

'Despair!' said Kitzi. 'Ah, despair, that's different. Excuse me, we will have some more wine.' He raised his voice – 'Günther!' Günther was Kitzi's sole servant, except for a woman who cooked in the middle of the day and was seldom seen. Günther had met Theo and Desmond when they had arrived two hours earlier, when the rain was beginning to come down more heavily, had seized their suitcases, accompanying his greeting with a small bow, picking up the baggage as if handling feathers, muttering

'*Bitte, Bitte*,' nodding, smiling. Günther was a huge man. Knowing exactly what was required of him he now came into the dining room again with an equally huge smile on his face and a second bottle of Mosel in his hand.

He said, 'Ah, Herr Kitzi, wine,' and drew the cork. Kitzi smiled back at him.

'Still raining, Günther?'

'Still raining, Herr Kitzi.'

'Günther, these two gentlemen, Herr Dillon and Herr Tate, drove through an SA road block in their taxi. Only a mile from here.'

'That's correct, Herr Kitzi. The Browns have got every main road blocked. They're checking, it seems.'

Kitzi looked hard at him. 'You're not going out tonight, Günther?'

'I thought, when you'd finished, Herr Kitzi, I –'

'No, Günther. Give the *Bierstube* a miss, tonight. Stay in.'

'*Befehl*, Herr Kitzi? An order?'

'An order, Günther.' Kitzi was still smiling. When the man left the room Kitzi said, 'He was my servant in the Army, wounded the same day as me. He came to see me after discharge, rather lost. The shell knocked his mind about a bit, under-- stand?'

Theo nodded. 'You've told him to stay in!'

'Yes, Günther's a Silesian, like me. He's a gentle, charming fellow, very strong. Once an SA man hit him – he says for no reason but I expect Günther sounded rude, he can be misunderstood, it's really he's a little simple. Anyway, this fellow hit him, and Günther took them both on – there were two, I gather – and left both in rather a bad way. Günther's a noticeable chap with that size, and he's developed, ever since, a sort of allergy to the SA in uniform! I don't want him wandering round the streets when Röhm's boys are out in strength, and no doubt in a rather excited state. Now you must have more wine.'

Kitzi refilled their glasses. He said, 'Despair! I said that former despair as well as resentment has been re-awakened and the Nazis thrive on it. You've had enough supper?'

'Thank you, Kitzi. Excellent.'

It had been simple, somewhat frugal. Adequate.

'Not many Berliners will have had as good a supper. This country is experiencing real privation again.'

They had heard of it. They both remembered the grey faces at Stettin station.

'There's no work,' said Kitzi. 'There's no economic activity or nothing like enough. We're exporting nothing, and there's not enough money or initiative to stimulate our domestic market. Hitler says the Nazis would change all that. He says he'd create jobs directly, and indirectly produce a mass of others. Do you know how high our unemployment is?'

'One has heard a figure of five million.'

'And rising. Rising! Hitler says the power of the State will be used, must be used, to solve this. But to make this acceptable he also says that Germans must recover pride in themselves. He tells them that they can go anywhere – anywhere – if they believe in themselves. He tells them that the Nazis will produce work, food, and self-respect. No more being trampled on and kept down by the victors of Versailles.' Kitzi's voice was objective, cool, ironic.

Theo said, 'It's obviously an attractive package. But why should anyone believe the Nazis can deliver it?'

'They are not without skill, believe me,' said Kitzi. 'If it was just bombast they would not be the force they are. And they will increase their strength in the Reichstag, I suspect, in next year's elections.'

'And will Hitler be elected President tomorrow?'

'I think not. I think not. He was seven million votes behind in second place last time, but there was no absolute majority, you see. It will, anyway, suit Hitler better to try and bring the Nazis to power under the respectable aegis of Hindenburg. I believe Germans will elect our venerable President again tomorrow, although he's in his dotage! Many Conservatives and many Liberals and so forth will vote for him. Socialists too – it's quite a paradox that our old Field Marshal has become almost the darling of the democratic Left these days! He didn't want to stand for re-election, of course. But the alternatives to Hindenburg are the Nazi, Adolf Hitler, and the Communist, Thälmann.'

Desmond said, 'Are Hitler's followers all thugs, Kitzi? You spoke just now of the despair and resentment they exploit, and you spoke almost with sympathy.'

'I have no sympathy with the Nazis,' said Kitzi very sternly. 'They have turned their backs on morality. They practise a sort of politics wherein every brutality is legitimate if the object is good – good by their standards. Good, I will admit very often, by all our standards. But ends do not justify means, we all agree on that, do we not?'

They were silent as he poured more wine. He looked at his two English guests with approval. They were contrasting physical types – Desmond Dillon, a dark-haired man, with brown, dancing eyes and a wide, mobile mouth, a mouth that smiled often: when he laughed, Kitzi noted, he laughed with his whole being, he abandoned himself to laughter – and was then quickly serious, even stern, again. The other, Theo Tate, was altogether different – very fair hair, a pale skin of almost feminine smoothness, blue, blue eyes which, Kitzi noted, held one's own with almost hypnotic force. A cold young man, perhaps: an intelligent young man certainly. Both were handsome – very handsome. There was no doubt in Kitzi's mind that young Tate was the more impressive, although perhaps the less agreeable of the two. Kitzi had noticed how every question or comment of Theo's had been carefully phrased, mind moving behind those devastating eyes, no emotion or reaction betrayed. Dillon, thought Kitzi, is spontaneous, a natural creature, a charmer. No fool, but without instinct for subtlety or dissimulation. But this other one!

He said, 'I have written articles condemning the National Socialist movement.' He said it with his chin stuck out, breathing deeply. It was curious, Desmond thought, to see so much emotion in describing a political stance. What was politics but talk, after all?

'I have condemned them,' said Kitzi, 'and they have called me a Jew-lover and an anti-patriot. But I know some of them personally and they are not all bad men. Especially the young ones. In fact some are very idealistic young men. They believe devoutly in their war-cry – "*Deutschland erwache!* Germany awake!" That's the paradox. Of course it will be increasingly difficult for a devoted National Socialist to acknowledge that he knows me socially! One day it may even be dangerous! But I don't think about that. You are to meet my nephew, Wieland, the day after tomorrow, by the way. My sister's son. He still visits his uncle – my sister is dead and Wieland's father is in some sort of a home, a mental home after his wounds in the War. He was in Galicia. The poor fellow – ' Kitzi shrugged and looked melancholy. Then he said, 'Wieland will interest you. In spite of everything he's a very charming boy. Slightly younger than you, I think.'

'In spite of what, Kitzi,' asked Theo, 'is he a very charming boy?'

'Wieland joined the SS – *Schutz Staffel*. The Elite Guards, they called themselves, a very select branch of the Nazi Party. A sort of Praetorian Guard.'

'I thought that was Röhm's SA.'

'Quite different. Röhm's lot are largely bully-boys, street fighters, roughs. Very loyal to him personally – he's a notorious homosexual, by the way. Wieland's lot are austere, disciplined, dedicated. Black uniforms. The Jesuits of the Nazi church,' Kitzi observed with a sour smile, taking a large mouthful of wine, 'but utterly devoted to Adolf Hitler. They are not only the Praetorian Guard, they're the theoreticians. Or some of them are. Of course there's a hierarchy – thinkers and doers. Bosses and others. But all bound together by a very close inner loyalty. Oaths and so forth. A freemasonry.'

'A freemasonry!' said Theo. 'A Praetorian Guard, and a Jesuit order! Secrecy, discipline, loyalty and intellect in one body! You make them sound formidable!'

'They are formidable. But, as in most organizations, some people are more formidable than others. And Wieland is not formidable. He is, perhaps, not formidable enough to survive. In that atmosphere. But he is charming, and I have asked him to meet you, and he will be here to *Mittagessen* on Friday unless his duties demand otherwise. He still is brave enough or foolish enough to visit his old uncle, his old anti-National Socialist uncle. It may not always be so. I am afraid it will not always be so.'

Next day Kitzi was looking rather tense. He was as charming as before, suggesting how Desmond and Theo should travel to the centre of Berlin, making light of their previous night's experience of an SA cordon, chuckling and full of advice.

'Not like your election days in England, I expect!'

But they guessed he was on edge for the result, on tenterhooks to learn who would be Germany's next President. The President, the Head of State, possessed certain monarchical functions which, in the wrong hands or unwisely used, could sink the fragile ship of German State. Would it be Hindenburg? Would it be Hitler? Might it even be the Communist, Thälmann? Kitzi was murmuring to himself, frowning, leafing through several morning papers. Günther came into the room and stood to attention.

'Herr Dillon!'

Desmond looked up in surprise.

'*Telefon*, Herr Dillon.'

Desmond nodded. The telephone was in the hall. He failed at first to recognize the voice which said, indeed seemed almost to whisper, 'Mr Dillon?'

'Dillon here, yes.'

'Mr Dillon, it is Casimir Rodoski. We are going to have dinner together, my friend and me and you two gentlemen. And we will show you something of the city, yes?'

Rodoski sounded sober, as was reasonable at nine o'clock in the morning. He also sounded, as he had the day before, conspiratorial.

'Mr Dillon, could it be Saturday? In two days' time, I mean?'

'I think so, Mr Rodoski. It's very kind of you. But I'm – we're staying with a friend, you know. This is Herr Christoph Fischer's house. I shall have to ask him about plans.'

But Kitzi nodded amicably to the news of the invitation and Desmond returned to the telephone to confirm.

'Mr Dillon, that is Herr Fischer who writes books and articles?'

'Yes, that's right.'

'He is well known. That is very interesting. Well, we will see you on Saturday evening. Sonja will be glad, very glad. And Germany will have a new President by then. Later today, in fact.'

'Or, perhaps, an old one still, Mr Rodoski.'

'Perhaps. Perhaps.'

CHAPTER II

Sturmführer Wieland Breitfall had certain physical characteristics in common with young Tate, Kitzi thought as he looked down the luncheon table to his nephew with affection and the usual disquiet. Wieland was in a grey suit of decidedly inelegant cut – sad to reflect, Kitzi reflected with honesty, how much better the boy looked in that black uniform of his, that regrettable black uniform which would, with luck, soon be banned. For it was public knowledge that with the Presidential election behind him, old Hindenburg would yield to the demands of his Chancellor, Brüning, and his Defence Minister, Gröner, and ban these Party-uniformed organizations for good and all.

Hindenburg had been re-elected on the previous day, with over fifty per cent of the vote, to Kitzi's unsurprised relief. It was known that Brüning had declared it impossible to govern while the streets of Berlin were dominated by rival bands of louts in uniform: and Gröner, ex-General Gröner, a quiet, efficient, high-principled *Würtemburger*, had made it plain that unless these private armies were put out of action by decree he could not continue in office. The Prussian State Police had, on the whole, behaved bravely and with an admirable sense of duty but the situation was intolerable. Both the Communist Red Front and the SA must be made illegal. The Reichswehr, the Army itself, had once taken the same line: but recently, Kitzi knew, the leaders of the Reichswehr had been ambivalent. General von Schleicher, a clever, charming, untrustworthy man, no friend of Gröner now although once his favourite protégé, had the ear of the old President. And von Schleicher had persuaded plenty of his Army colleagues, it was said, that the Nazis wanted many of the same things as they did – renunciation of the Versailles Treaty, an end to the keeping of Germany defenceless, a tough settlement of the Communist threat.

As to the rest of the Nazi programme, the exaggerations, the promise to solve unemployment, the shrill denunciations, the hyper-nationalist rhetoric – all that was containable, Schleicher was telling people with nods and winks; containable and useful in its way. The Nazis had popular appeal, they made sense to the young – they made sense, for that matter, to many of the young officers of the Reichswehr itself, although Nazis had been excluded from their ranks so far. If the Nazis were anchored, as it were, by the Reichswehr and by some of the respectable, conventional, conservative elements in Germany, their enthusiasm and popularity would produce a dynamic and their political allies would ensure decency and continuity. So the argument ran. Then Germany would have a chance of getting on course again after the misery and alienation of the last fourteen years. Kitzi knew many people – honest, patriotic, agreeable people – who nodded their heads to that. And one should never forget, such people said, the appalling possibility that the Nazis might join with the Communists and swamp everything – it had already happened once. These National Socialists weren't too bad, people said – 'the Nazis' had matured since their early, brash, revolutionary days. And, for God's sake, something had to be done, with unemployment moving towards six million, widespread hunger and a state not far from civil war in many cities. Something had to be done, they said, and that something needed popular support and decisive leadership. The Nazis could drum up popular support. As to leadership – Schleicher and his friends shrugged their shoulders. They observed that the time was past for the liberal scruples of a man like Brüning. And if the Nazis were to be conciliated and tamed how could one start by disbanding their organizations, like the SA, the old faithful of the Movement? And the SS, the Elite, formed in 1925? It would be a declaration of war, and the National Socialists must regard it as such. But it looked as if Brüning and Gröner had persuaded the old President, and almost immediately, it was rumoured, Wieland Breitfall's black uniform was to be outlawed.

Kitzi watched his nephew – perversely, his favourite relative despite his loathing of the boy's politics – and saw how these two Englishmen, especially young Tate, were enjoying the company of this youthful Nazi, no doubt the first such animal they had ever met. Wieland was a good-looking, animated, enthusiastic young man, with fair skin, like Theo Tate, fair hair, and a charming, serious expression. He spoke good English but the two seemed to be getting on all right in their hesitant German which they clearly wished to practise: and sometimes Kitzi tossed in an explanatory word or phrase. They were talking politics of course – how not? And why not? It was what they had come for. Kitzi avoided the topic with his nephew now; Wieland was so heart-breakingly like his mother, Kitzi's sister, who had died when he was a child. Kitzi knew that their minds could never meet, now, on what was best for Germany. When he had, in the early days, thrown a savage accusation or two about Nazi behaviour at Wieland the young man had always courteously, carefully, answered the charge, explaining the exceptional circumstances, the conspiracy by the Left – and not only the Left – to suppress the Nazis because they told the truth, gave hope to the poor, and loved Germany in a way which degenerates had temporarily made unfashionable. Where Kitzi had countered with more examples – including his own recollections of Bavaria ten years before – Wieland explained that the situation was different now. Of course some of the SA were a coarse lot –

'But Adolf Hitler, *Onkel* Kitzi, realizes that, and has given strict instructions about these things. He deplores excesses, but of course he has affection for many of the SA, they were loyal in the early days. He had a breach with Röhm for years, as you know. He's forgiven him now, it's not in his character to bear a grudge, but it's not easy for him – '

Kitzi would speak with bitter words of traditional morality, of God as the touchstone of all things, of the false gods the Nazis sometimes preached: and Wieland would patiently, gently, protest that his own Evangelical Christian faith was absolutely consistent with his belief that in National Socialism lay Germany's future.

'Purity, unselfishness, sacrifice – our Party really believes in these things, without humbug. But we also believe in action, in man's ability to right wrongs if he is brave and has faith.'

Kitzi avoided such talk now. He realized that Wieland was blindingly sincere and it made him want to weep. He was content, today, to listen to the talk between his nephew and the two Englishmen and to say little. There would be time for his contribution later. One day, perhaps, Wieland and he would be such liabilities to each other, the SS officer and the liberated Christian writer, that their ways must part, their relationship of blood be rejected, their friendship lapse. With luck, Kitzi thought, I'll be dead by then – or it won't happen, the tide will turn. For he had loved his sister: and he loved her son.

'We believe,' said Wieland, in his slow, careful, exact way, 'that more employment can be given, straight away, by a large programme of public works. That the Government must finance that.'

'How?' said Desmond. 'How – without leading to the sort of inflation you've suffered before? How do you pay for it?'

'We believe it can be done. Germany is more self-sufficient than Germans have been led to suppose and by employing large numbers of people on these works we would increase spending on the home market. Carefully, of course – no runaway issue of money, you are quite right about that. But also we believe that Germans can be encouraged to work more, produce more, earn more and live better – even within the present system.'

'How?'

'By being given a society which they will feel is truly theirs. By being joined together with Government, employers, everybody as fellow workers. Each playing his part for one –' Wieland felt for the word which would make clear his meaning to these Englishmen, ' – one *ideal*,' he ended, unsure whether they could understand and connect.

Theo said, 'What ideal?'

'The ideal of a National Socialist Germany, united, respecting itself and respected by others.'

Theo pressed the economic point. State intervention within an ostensibly free society had generally led to inflation, incompetence and disaster. Did Wieland really suppose that these objections could simply be answered by saying that fiscal affairs would be handled 'carefully'? Yes, Wieland did, although it was clear that he was rehearsing arguments with which he was not particularly at home. How had Kitzi described the SS? Desmond remembered – Freemasonry, Praetorian Guard, Jesuit Order. He thought Wieland was probably more at home in the Praetorian Guard.

'What's your actual *job* in the Party, Wieland?'

'I'm responsible for a security section,' said Wieland, perfectly naturally. 'The Movement has many security problems. Adolf Hitler's life has been threatened often. And there are other matters. But we all try to think, and read, and learn,' he added with a smile, 'and talk, of course, talk to others, explain the Movement. I welcome it. It is good to have the chance to talk to friends from England.'

'From England,' said Desmond agreeably. 'From one of the hated Versailles Powers, who created the conditions you're determined to alter. Conditions which left Germany artificially weak.'

'Of course. And it is not only National Socialists who are determined to alter that – the difference is that the others talk and do nothing. But we don't blame England. We think many people in England sympathize with us about the Treaty, the reparations and so forth. Adolf Hitler, our leader, greatly admires England, he always has. He teaches that Germany and England need each other.'

Kitzi said softly, 'Perhaps you will explain to our friends Herr Hitler's opinions on the Jewish question. I don't think we've mentioned it but it features a great deal in his writings and speeches – the so-called Jewish problem.'

'Yes, the Jews,' said Wieland, turning his palms upwards and raising his eyebrows as if addressing a painful and universal problem, 'the Jews. As my Uncle Kitzi says, Adolf Hitler is very concerned about the Jews. No doubt there are many Jews in England, too.'

'Certainly,' Desmond answered forcefully, 'but I don't think of them as a problem. Some people like them, some people say they find them unattractive – generally people who've hardly met a Jew. Jews have been among the most gifted people in English life – in politics, commerce, the arts. They are not "a problem", Wieland. Why should they be?'

'Here it is different. Here there are Jews in all the most powerful positions, you see, in business, in – in certain other fields. And they all help each other, you see; and Germans suffer because of that.'

'Really?'

'Yes, it is so. There are things which must be corrected. People here demand it.'

Desmond thought there was a puzzled, even an uncertain note in Wieland's answer. Kitzi had, however, decided that it was an occasion which at last might be improved by an intervention of his own, and he called out –

'The truth is that there is anti-Semitism in Germany, like in many European countries – a popular, mediæval, nonsensical inherited prejudice. And because we've had a hard economic time and the Jews are clever, shrewd people, many of them have done well, so Germans are jealous. And that jealousy feeds the ancient prejudice and turns the Jews into a "problem". Then the Nazis come along and decided that to blame a lot of our troubles on this non-existent problem will be popular. And it is. So now the Jews are indispensable to Herr Hitler and his Movement. Hatred of the Jews is like glue which helps stick all Wieland's friends together! That is the Jews' function, eh, Wieland?'

'No, *Onkel* Kitzi,' said Wieland, shaking his head. 'It is not like that. Not like that at all. But it is true that in a National Socialist Germany, German interests will be considered first. Is that wrong? Don't people think like that in England?'

There was a silence. Theo smiled at Wieland and said, 'Yes, they certainly do.' He was entertained by the way these exchanges

37

were going, but if there was irony in his voice it was lost on Wieland. The moment was lightened by the entry of Günther, a broad grin on his face, whose antipathy to the *Sturmabteilung* did not, apparently, extend to SS *Sturmführer* Breitfall: whom he had, indeed, known since he was a little boy, of whom he was fond, as if Wieland was one of Herr Kitzi's valued possessions, and to whom he now advanced with a proffered bottle of liqueur brandy, known to be a favourite with Herr Wieland and not now refused.

The small dance floor was deserted. Two couples had been moving around it slowly, almost mechanically, while a dark-haired woman murmured her song into a microphone and a piano hesitantly tinkled. The melody was enchanting, Desmond thought – haunting, sentimental; but not one to get the feet itching to dance.

Irgendwo auf der Welt
Gibt's ein kleines Bisschen Glück –

'It will become more amusing,' said Rodoski, nodding his head with confidence. 'More people come soon. They have a performance at half past nine. Then every half hour I think.'

Desmond smiled at him, bored by the smoky dimness of the atmosphere but considerably intrigued by Sonja. He was alone with the two of them. He had made Theo's excuses.

'It was difficult. Our host had planned our evenings, you see – '

Rodoski had looked hurt. The fact was that Theo had been invited to dinner by Wieland Breitfall.

He'd said, 'Bizarre as it may seem, I think our little blond, black-jacketed boy is going to be more informative company than the Pole and his girl. Poles are so predictable. Everyone's about to do them down, and sometimes, wicked though it is, one has a tiny bit of sympathy with everyone. Black-jacket is at least different.' Not that they had yet seen Wieland in uniform.

Desmond was glad. One cannot hunt in a pair for too long at

a stretch, and he had felt Theo's irritation with Rodoski. Now that he had met Sonja he was gladder still.

Sonja was, to say the least, striking to the eye. She had black hair and near-black eyes, very white skin and a long, slender body. She was wearing a short-skirted black dress which showed excellent legs. Round her head was a dark red silk band. She was heavily made up, her fingernails tinted to match her head-silk and her eyes emphasized by skilful painting. Desmond looked at her, startled at first and then appreciative. Appreciation had grown as the evening extended and Sonja had shown every sign of liking him, while Rodoski drank heavily and with a free hand stroked Sonja's arm.

Desmond had had some warning what to expect. Kitzi had known Rodoski's name.

'He is correspondent for several Warsaw publications. He's been about a year in Berlin. Was he agreeable?'

'I'm not sure. Friendly, but perhaps not entirely agreeable.' Kitzi nodded to the distinction, saying, 'He has a girlfriend, a rather flamboyant lady, I believe. She is some sort of a journalist too.'

'I think she's going to be at our dinner. He's going to show me Berlin.'

'My poor boy! It will disgust you! Perverts! Voyeurs!'

'Is the girlfriend German, Kitzi?'

Kitzi was unsure. 'I think a German citizen, he found her here, yes. But a mixture of races, I rather suspect – an exotic background, one might say.'

Looking at Sonja, Desmond thought that was probably accurate. As the piano tinkled he said, 'You are wholly German, Sonja? Through and through, a hundred per cent?'

Rodoski laughed and fingered Sonja's skin.

'Not she! Percentages now – twenty-five per cent Hungarian, twenty-five per cent Rumanian, twenty-five per cent Pole, right, Sonja?'

'About right, but the Rumanians and Hungarians were mixed up. But I've both Latin and Magyar blood, yes. Rumanians are Latins.'

'And Poles are Slavs,' said Rodoski. 'Sonja is a little piece of the old Habsburg Empire, all brought together in one body. One body!' His hand wandered over her dress.

'And the last twenty-five per cent?'

'Ah,' said Rodoski, 'that's German. And she's a German citizen, a true Berliner now.'

Sonja had a very clear, deep, musical voice. She said, 'Yes, I'm quarter German. But that quarter is half Jewish.' She said it calmly and precisely, blowing a little wisp of smoke from her cigarette towards Serge Rodoski. Somehow, Desmond had the clear impression that Rodoski disliked her Jewish blood and that she was taunting him with his dislike. Or, perhaps, it intrigued him, added spice to his desire for her but the spice annoyed him. Whatever it was, Desmond was sure their relationship was uneven. A man in a dinner jacket moved forward on to the little dance floor in a pool of light as the rest of the club was plunged into near darkness. The new show, new this week, he said, was about to begin. Two girls ran forward and began to perform a dance with many kicks and wriggles of the bottom. They wore black underclothes, black stockings revealing a lot of thigh and black top hats. They sang as they danced, in rather breathless, throaty voices. Desmond couldn't follow the words. He thought the show disappointing so far.

'A new couple,' said Rodoski. 'There was that blonde with a whip last week, to start it off. Much better!' He spoke loudly and Desmond thought he heard a murmur from a neighbouring table, unfriendly. Rodoski filled their glasses, spilling some wine in the process. As on the Stettin train he was far from sober.

The two dancers were now miming erotic movements with each other, keeping somewhat disjointed time to the music. One, starting to fumble between the other's thighs, pretended to give a cry of astonishment, and both lifted their hats in the air and then broke into a more energetic dance, with some high kicks.

'They're men, you know,' said Sonja, 'men, of course.'

Desmond had not known. The music had changed and the pianist struck up a tune familiar to most people, who started singing words, joining the two dancers in a raucous, rather incongruous chorus, the melody infectious. When the top hats waved themselves off stage with many bottom wriggles the applause was protracted.

Desmond had found it boring and disagreeable. He wanted to stretch his limbs, make some violent gesture, be active rather than watch without pleasure or amusement, let alone titillation. He smiled at Sonja and said, 'What next?'

'You didn't think much of that, did you?'

'No, not much. Are many Berlin shows like that – men dressed like girls and vice versa?'

'Yes, very many. But often with more talent, and some wit. Those two were vulgar without being amusing. Could you understand the words?'

'Not much.'

'There were some jokes in the song, *double entendre*, about this Presidential election of ours – not very funny. Serge, we should have more wine.'

'I agree,' said Rodoski. When the waiter came he said, 'You can tell the manager that we hope the next show will be an improvement. That was – ' He made a face and a rude gesture. The man looked at him with evident dislike and moved away to bring another bottle. Rodoski said again, very loudly, 'Rotten! Berlin at its worst! But at its best it can be something special, I can tell you – '

At that moment Desmond became aware of two large young men standing by their table looking down at them. The lights were still low. One of the young men said softly, 'You didn't like the show in this club, Herr Rodoski?'

'No,' said Rodoski, not looking up, 'not yet. Not as good as last week. Agree?' His voice was quieter than it had been and not very steady.

The other young man said, 'You expressed your opinion loudly and rudely. That gives offence to other guests. It is uncultivated.'

'It is particularly uncultivated, Herr Rodoski,' said the first young man, 'if – '

Rodoski said, 'You have my name, do you? How?' He was frowning angrily. Sonja was smoking, looking at the pianist and

41

taking no notice whatever of the aggressive little scene being played a few feet from her. Desmond sat very still. It looks as if it's coming to a fight, he thought; and slightly wished the two young men were less large. That apart he felt rather happy. The evening was waking up. Rodoski said again, 'How do you know my name? Eh?'

The two young men stood, impassive, and the one who had spoken first said, 'You write for Polish newspapers. You are a Pole. And if you live in Berlin there is no reason why you should not be polite about Berlin. Including, even, its night shows.'

'They *are* somewhat degenerate,' said the other young man reasonably, 'I think that's true, Pole. But the reason you're disappointed, Pole, is that they're not degenerate enough. True, Pole?'

'And if you don't like anything here,' said the first, still in a soft, reasonable tone, 'then why not leave Germany, Pole? Taking your Jew girl with you, preferably.'

'You!' said Rodoski, standing up and pushing his chair back behind him with such force it fell over. 'You!' and he swung his right fist at the first young man but hit the air. The young man had stepped backward smartly. Several people at adjoining tables cried out and two men in dinner jackets could be seen hastening towards them. Desmond made a sound between a chuckle and a yelp and stood up quickly, loosening his shoulders, eyes alert. Then he felt Sonja's fingers gripping his forearm tightly.

'Say nothing!' hissed Sonja. 'Say absolutely nothing.'

The manager and his assistant came up, expostulating.

'Herr Rodoski! What – '

The two young men had distanced themselves a few feet from the Rodoski table. One of them said to the manager, 'No problem. Herr Rodoski doesn't like your show and became a little violent. It's all over.'

'Herr Rodoski!' said the manager, turning half-indignant, half-beseeching to Rodoski, 'Herr Rodoski, please, we know you well –'

'Yes,' said Rodoski, breathing unevenly, 'you know me well.

42

I don't know if you also know well these two gentlemen – these two perfect, pure-bred German gentlemen!'

But the two young men had given short bows, muttered a brief word to the manager and withdrawn into the shadows. Soon thereafter Desmond, with a certain perverse disappointment, saw them leave the club. He was not unused to late-night brawls, from Cambridge onwards, and the truth was they tended to stimulate him, adolescent though the reaction might be. There had, however, been something especially disagreeable about this one. He'd not, he reckoned, cut a very heroic figure. Perhaps he and Rodoski should have pitched into them, started a fight, wrecked the place, seen off those two smooth-voiced thugs; or at least gone down in bloody glory. The trouble was that Rodoski was so aggressive; and, somehow, so unpredictable. Desmond felt sorry for him and said, 'You were very good. You kept your temper longer than most people, and – '

Rodoski scowled. It was not a compliment he relished.

'What you mean, kept my temper? They insulted me.'

'They were louts,' said Desmond, 'of no importance. There are always people to start trouble in nightclubs. When the drink and the darkness mix. Same in England.'

'Not the same in England. You don't have that sort. You know what they were?'

'No idea.'

'Brown Shirts. Nazis. SA out of uniform. I can smell them a mile away.'

None of this was said quietly. The pianist had been joined by fiddle, drummer and saxophonist and people began to dance.

They drank, watched another show which was more suggestive, more obscene but slightly more skilful than the first. Rodoski muttered about it but there was no more trouble, and Desmond noted, too, that Rodoski was one of those curious men who became more sober at a certain stage of drinking. Having been noisy and quarrelsome he had turned serious and informative. He had beckoned their heads together at the table so that the three, sitting, sipping, smoking, were communicating by whispers. Desmond thoroughly enjoyed the nearness of Sonja. Her

43

scent was delicious, and the slight smell of her skin mingled with it was even more so.

Rodoski now murmured to him, 'You remember what we talked about on the train?'

'I think so.'

' "Cooperation". You remember I used that word?'

It came back to Desmond. German Army cooperation with Bolshevik Russia. The arch-Conservative von Seeckt and the Bolshevik, Lenin. He remembered. He didn't believe it, or all of it. He had reflected on Rodoski's remarks and had concluded that they arose from the pathological antipathy of the Pole to both Russian and Prussian. Rodoski had surely exaggerated.

Desmond said cautiously, 'I remember you said that both – both the nations who share a frontier with your country dislike you. And that dislike is a bond between them.'

Rodoski said, ' "*Cooperate*", that was my word, you remember? Now, you ask Sonja! Sonja is a very good journalist. She has contacts in many countries. She finds things out, eh, Sonja? Sonja will tell you – '

Sonja was frowning. She said, very quietly, 'Not here, Serge. Stop it.'

'Sonja, tell him a little. You know a lot. Anyway, a lot of it's quite well known, one hears jokes about it in these cabarets, one understands if one has the key. Go on, Sonja, tell us, tell England! For instance, the noble Kurt Langenbach was on the train, came into our apartment. They met him, our Desmond here and his friend. And where was he travelling from? From Russia, of course!'

Sonja looked at the smoke of her cigarette, narrowed her eyes and said, again almost inaudibly, 'Not here, Serge.'

But Rodoski was in garrulous mood by now, although quiet.

'Desmond, this Herr Langenbach on the train, he's one of the most skilled young aviators in Germany. You know the Germans aren't allowed military aircraft?'

'Of course. It's one of their chief resentments. And I understand that resentment.'

'They've been building military aircraft for years! And they've trained a whole generation of pilots. In Russia. Factory near Moscow – Junkers, you know the name?'

Desmond didn't, and Sonja frowned while Rodoski said, 'Big people! And this Langenbach was one of the first – and since then he's been a key man in the training system. He's also heir to a big estate somewhere near Hanover, as it happens.' Rodoski belched. He pursed his lips and said, 'Brilliant flying man. So you see – '

Something came back to Desmond, from Cambridge days. Had there not been some sort of revelation in the *Manchester Guardian* at that time, in about 1926? Soon after the British General Strike, whose conduct and aftermath had so dominated the English news as to drive such trivial foreign affairs stories from most people's awareness, including Desmond's? A story about German evasion of the provisions of the Versailles Treaty? About the Bolsheviks – fellow outcasts – conniving at it? It had seemed farfetched and uninteresting, and almost certainly exaggerated by some foreign correspondent short of a story. War was over, had been ended for ever. Mankind was awakening to sanity.

Now he said, 'I think there was once something in our papers – '

'There was,' said Rodoski, 'and not only in yours. But none of them understood the scale of the thing. Or its implications. And now – '

'And now,' said Sonja, still almost inaudible, but hissing, 'Now you will *hold your tongue*, Serge. That is quite enough.'

Rodoski took this surprisingly well, winked at Desmond, said, 'We'll talk more some time. Excuse me,' and moved towards the entrance, to the lavatory. He had drunk a good deal by now, although he was surprisingly steady on his feet. Alone with Sonja, Desmond smiled at her.

'Sonja, will Serge mind if we dance?'

She stood up instantly and put both hands on his shoulders. A few minutes later he found his body more aware of hers than of any other with which it had had contact, ever. She swayed into his arms and he felt her thigh firm against his. The music was

45

perfect, Desmond thought. He hoped Rodoski would spend a long time in the lavatory.

Sonja's hand caressed the back of his neck. She whispered, 'Serge talks too much. The Poles have charm but no discretion. Whether in love or politics – no discretion.'

'They've a brave history.'

'Of course. But to survive one needs more than courage. They are always being destroyed, divided, occupied. When your people made Poland again at Versailles – '

'Not only my people, Sonja. The Americans. The French. Self-determination was the watchword, remember?'

Her fingers moved at his neck with great delicacy and she moved her nose so that it stroked the lobe of his ear. Sonja was a tall girl. The place was still in half-darkness. She whispered, 'Yes. Self-determination. And all the wise old men who knew their European history said, "Don't create Poland. If you create Poland there is always trouble." '

'Perhaps they did. But it had to be done. If for Czechs and Hungarians why not for Poles? And Poland was, after all, one of the ancient kingdoms of Europe. Why not again?'

'I don't say not,' murmured Sonja, 'I just say how much trouble has often followed.'

'And you think will again?'

'It all depends. It all – '

She sighed. They swayed on to the music, bodies communicating, talk now tedious. A blonde girl began singing. The words were unfamiliar to Desmond, the tune cloying but irresistible. Suddenly he felt Sonja stiffen in his arms as if expecting a blow. Her head turned and he turned his own to see the manager, who appeared to be bustling and busy. He seemed to be muttering to the band and looking about him. Then they saw him speaking to a waiter near their table. Next moment he was weaving his way through the dancers and Desmond, half-disengaging from Sonja, found himself looking directly into the manager's eyes. The man was saying, undoubtedly to him, 'Please. One moment, sir. Please.'

Desmond steered Sonja to the edge of the dance floor. He had a disagreeable premonition. The manager addressed both of them together.

'Excuse me, you are the friends of Herr Rodoski?'

'We are.' Desmond decided to do the talking.

'He has had an accident. The police are here.'

Sonja made a noise, 'Ah-h-h', an outrush of breath, and Desmond said, 'What sort of accident?'

'He made a disturbance. Will you come, please?'

They followed him towards the exit. In the small foyer, off which a lavatory door gave, there were several people standing round the walls. In the middle were two policemen, their long green coats indicating that the April night was still cold. Each wore a black belt, a revolver holster, tall black boots, and a green shako. One, who seemed the senior of the two, had a heavy moustache and was addressing the assistant manager, notebook in hand.

On the floor was stretched a very still Serge Rodoski. He was lying on his face but there was no doubt about his identity.

The manager spoke, politely, beseechingly, to the police officer.

'These are the friends of Herr Rodoski.'

Desmond said, 'What's happened?' and the police officer said, 'An ambulance is already on its way. You are friends of Herr Rodoski? Whom should we contact? Has he a family?'

Sonja said sharply, 'It is me you should contact, only me. Is he badly hurt? Is there not something to do, now, before the ambulance comes?' She sank to her knees beside Rodoski. The second officer darted forward and took her arm.

'Madam, please – '

'Let me alone!' said Sonja. 'What's wrong with him? Is he concussed?'

'He is dead, Madam.'

Sonja looked at them, looked at Desmond, said, 'Oh! Oh!' and fainted clean away. Desmond and the manager lifted her to a sofa which extended along one wall. The senior police officer said to Desmond, 'Herr Rodoski, it seems, attacked a group of guests. They defended themselves.'

At that moment, Desmond noticed for the first time four young men in the shadows near the street door, standing with the second policeman. One of them, certainly, was one of the pair who had marched to their table earlier in the evening. Of another he was unsure; and the remaining two were in uniform – the same uniform which had first hit him at the road check between the railway station and Kitzi's house, the brown uniform which in the last two days he had seen everywhere speckling the streets of Berlin. The uniform which was, Kitzi said, about to be banned, with many others. SA.

Desmond said to the policeman loudly, 'Do you suspect that our friend attacked those men there? One against four?'

'It appears so. He was drunk. They defended themselves.'

'And killed him.'

'Herr Rodoski fell heavily. He struck his head. Several people saw it.'

Desmond had a habit, which could appear alarming, of raising his chin so that it jutted and then edging his way forward by tiny steps towards an opponent in argument. The gesture, imitated by friends to his surprise for he was invariably unconscious of doing it, held the implication of menace, of physical violence only just restrained: and the contrast between this and the usual, essentially friendly and easy Desmond, reflected in his narrow, handsome face and brown, dancing eyes – this contrast was formidable.

Now, as he glared at the policeman, his chin was out and he inched nearer and nearer to him.

'The several people standing there, perhaps? The same several people whom you say he attacked?' Desmond was controlling his voice carefully, speaking slowly, taking a good deal of trouble with his grammar. His temper was rising and he knew that he had to keep it well in hand and that it was going to be difficult. They were all staring at him. As calmly as he could he said, 'You say Herr Rodoski struck his head. On what?'

There was a sharp interchange in German Desmond did not catch. He was further aroused when the manager changed to halting English.

'That is a matter for the police, sir.'

'*Das ist wahr!*' Desmond angrily switched their talk back to German. The policeman now addressed him.

'May I now see your papers? And take your particulars? As well as those of this lady?'

'I am an English visitor. My name is Dillon. I have no papers. My passport is at the house of a friend with whom I am staying. Herr Fischer.'

'Herr Fischer. Herr Dillon.' The policeman wrote in his notebook. At that moment the sound of an ambulance siren was heard, and a minute later two large men appeared at the street door. The second police officer took charge and soon the body of Serge Rodoski was on a stretcher and moving to the door. One of the ambulance men covered the face as they turned the body. Desmond had never seen a dead man before, and was himself feeling a sense of shock. Before Rodoski's face was hidden Desmond took in a mass of caked blood covering most of the skin between eyes and lips, with nose sticking obscenely from a mass of congealed, crimson jelly. They must have laid into him with more than their fists, thought Desmond, his stomach turning. These wounds were frightful, although no doubt the blood made things look worse than they might be. Sonja was a few feet away from him. He sensed her movement and knew that she had come round. There had been no way to help or support her: or shield her. It had all happened very quickly – the summons, the shocked and ill-tempered exchanges, the police officer writing down his name, the ambulance's arrival. He glanced at Sonja. She was motionless, her face in shadow. As Rodoski's body was carted out one of the young men in uniform spoke sharply to the senior police officer. Desmond heard the reply – names were recorded, there would be a need for formal statements, would all four please report as soon as possible to the police station in Friedrichstrasse. The police officer's voice was calm but supplicant.

Desmond felt disgust but no surprise when he heard the tall young man, the one whom he recognized as the originator of the earlier quarrel, say, 'That will be in the morning. We have an

49

appointment now. We will make full statements in the morning, right?'

'Very well.'

Desmond heard the hesitation, the wretchedness in the police-man's voice. Law was not sovereign tonight in Berlin. Desmond said, very sharply, doubtful whether the form of address was correct but showing no lack of confidence: aggressive. He knew it was right –

'*Herr Polizei Offizier!*'

The man turned. 'Herr Dillon, I shall ask you and this lady to give me statements about the deceased person, your knowledge of him. In one minute. Now, please – '

'By all means,' said Desmond sticking out his chin, knowing that his foreignness made them uncertain, speaking carefully, grimly. 'By all means, but I want to tell you one thing before these gentlemen leave us. I believe you should be informed that Herr Rodoski had a quarrel, earlier this evening, with one of these gentlemen, and a friend of his who is not here. Rather a violent quarrel.' He indicated with a stabbing forefinger the tall young man. The police officer looked wary. Then he raised his eyebrows to the tall young man and said to him, 'Herr Schmidt?'

Schmidt said '*Nein!*' very forcibly. He said, 'I remember the Pole making a noise inside the club. No quarrel.'

'The manager,' said Desmond, 'can, I know, confirm what I say.' But when the police officer turned to him the manager shrugged his shoulders.

'No quarrel, as far as I know. I don't allow that sort of thing in my club. Certainly no violent behaviour.'

'It appears,' said Schmidt, smiling most unpleasantly, 'that this English gentleman is mistaken in his recollection.'

'The lady with us,' said Desmond, 'this lady here, will tell you that Herr Schmidt had violent words with Herr Rodoski. I believe you should be aware of the fact.'

The policeman looked at Sonja.

'Fraülein?'

Sonja said very softly, 'It was dark. Some sort of an argument. I really can't be sure.'

'Thank you,' said the police officer. 'I would like to take down your statements in full at the police station. Tonight, if you please. And full statements from you gentlemen tomorrow, please. There will be an inquiry, naturally. This is a very serious matter.'

A gruff voice answered 'Hullo!' Desmond recognized Günther. It was two o'clock in the morning.

'Günther, this is Herr Dillon. Listen, is it possible to speak to Herr Tate? It is important.'

A pause, and then Günther's voice said, '*Moment.*'

And three minutes later a sleepy Theo said, 'What den of vice are you in now? Are you telephoning to explain exactly what you're doing to someone's body, as you talk? I believe some people enjoy that. Or what? It's rather late.'

'I know it's late. Theo, something ghastly has happened. Serge Rodoski, the Pole – well, you know, the one I've been dining with – '

'Yes, yes. Him and friend.'

'Well, he's dead. There was a brawl, a row, and some Nazi thugs killed him. At least it looks certain they did – they're saying he attacked them first. Anyway, he's dead.'

There was a silence. Then Theo's voice said, 'Desmond, are you all right?'

'Yes, I'm perfectly all right. But I've just spent an hour at the police station, and I've had to take Sonja home. You can imagine how appalling this has all been for her. Sonja's Rodoski's girl.'

'Where are you now?'

'In Sonja's flat. Just arrived. I want to make sure she's all right. There may be a friend she can get round. Perhaps I'll be able to go and fetch a friend. Something like that.'

'I see. Well, I suppose there's nothing I can do. Shall I knock up Kitzi and tell him?'

'No. Now we've got clear of the formalities, statements and so forth, I don't need any help. Tell him in – if I'm not back, tell him in the morning. Don't worry, I'm pretty caught up but I'm all right, everything's under control.'

'I suppose, dear boy, I'd better have your address and telephone number.'

Desmond gave it. When he put down the receiver he found Sonja pressing a large glass of brandy into his hand. She sat down beside him, holding another. Theo had been calm, rather comfortingly calm. Desmond fixed his eyes on her.

'Are you all right, Sonja?'

'All right, yes. I'm strung up, shock I think.'

'You loved him. I don't know what to say.'

'I don't know if I loved him or not. I was used to him. At the moment I feel absolutely nothing.'

Desmond took her hand and kissed the palm very gently.

'What can I do for you?'

Sonja smiled at him. She had taken off the silk bandeau round her head and her hair, longer than worn by most women that year, fell over her shoulders. Her arms were bare and very white. She said again, 'I'm in a state of shock.'

'Is brandy a good idea?'

'I expect so. Have you any other?'

Desmond heard himself saying, 'I'm not sure', as if he were listening to a third person. He found his eyes were on Sonja and that she was staring at him very intently and breathing deeply.

Desmond whispered again, 'I'm not sure.' Then, 'But nearly sure.'

Next moment Sonja said something abrupt, stood up, put down her glass and left the room. Desmond put his glass also on a small table by the sofa's arm. He found that nothing at all was happening inside his head. Five minutes passed. He wondered, dully, whether Sonja had fainted again, or was having some sort of seizure. Then the door opened and she walked in. She was absolutely naked.

Hours later Desmond said, 'I feel I've known you all my life.'

Sonja smiled. 'That's not long. You are very young – deliciously young.'

'I'm twenty-six. Very, very old.'

'You are impulsive, you act before you think, you are a dangerous sort of person, all that I could feel immediately we danced. The body cannot lie. Now I don't know what I think about you, Desmond.' She gave equal stress to both syllables.

He stroked her shoulders and buried his face in the cleft between her breasts.

'Sonja, you didn't want to say that that young Nazi thug had quarrelled earlier with Serge, did you?'

'Certainly not. You remember what he said in the nightclub? "Clear off and take your Jew girl with you." I'm only a small part Jew, but it's enough to make those people have a down on one, I can tell you. If they were ever in power they'd start to push the Jews around. Even part-Jews like me. One-sixteenth Jews.'

' "Push them around"? You mean actually discriminate against them?'

'Probably. They pretend to think Jews should leave the country. If the Nazis won an election I expect a good many would. Otherwise they might find themselves facing special taxes, or something hideous like that!'

Desmond yawned and started kissing her again.

'Darling, I shall make some coffee. It is seven o'clock.'

When she had done so, Desmond said sleepily, 'Sonja, this business of the Germans rearming secretly, helped by the Bolsheviks – you're meant to know all about it – ' He held his tongue. This was tactless. It brought recently murdered lover Serge to mind. And it was the wrong sort of conversation at the wrong time and in the wrong place. Still –

Sonja was busying herself with coffee and called out through an open door, 'Well?'

'It's an odd story. I suppose it's a pretty closely guarded secret

– presumably it's all in breach of the Treaty of Versailles and all that. Did it go on much?'

Sonja looked at him.

'You should ask *does* it go on much! It is still continuing.' She brought a cup of coffee over to the bed.

'You think so?'

'I know so. And of course it's a secret, although everyone knows there's undercover rearmament, there are jokes about it in Berlin cabarets, as Serge said.' She mentioned his name with a slight tremor but without awkwardness. Her face was serious.

'Desmond, you must be careful about this, and so must I. I said it's fairly widely known, but there are certain people who would kill me – or come near it – if they heard me talk. It's been a very important part of a lot of people's lives.'

'What sort of thing has been happening?'

And Sonja started speaking, very quietly, while Desmond gently caressed her body, and yawned and felt enormously at peace; and only half-listened. But then found himself listening with ever greater astonishment. This might be pillow talk, but it was pillow talk of an extraordinary kind.

After a while Desmond said, 'Do you suppose other governments know all about this?'

'Maybe,' she said, stroking his hair. 'Maybe, but not for certain, I think. And Desmond, love, you should not say, ever, to anyone, that I say these things. I would never try to write them. No editor in Germany would dare print them. There would be trouble. Very much trouble. But it is good, I think, that some people in other countries should know.'

CHAPTER III

Theo had been instructed to meet Marcus. He had not seen
Marcus for some months. Marcus would be interested in Theo's
travels in Russia, in Germany, in his impressions, whom he'd
met, whether he had plans for future meetings with them. And
Marcus would be eager to learn, too, whether Theo's political
prospects had matured or altered in any way since last they'd
talked. 'Contor,' he would say – Theo was always 'Contor' to
Marcus – 'Contor, you are right not to hurry these things. A
political career in England takes time to establish. We understand
that perfectly.' But, as it happened, Theo reckoned that there
were indications of advance in that direction also. Marcus – Theo
knew no other name – was an excellent listener, a most intelligent
companion. They were to meet on Barnes Common.

It had all started with The Tapir.

Alaric Playfair, Professor of Mediæval English Literature, was
known throughout Cambridge as The Tapir because of his long
nose which seemed permanently pointed towards the ground by
a forward inclination of the head: a head on which thinning hair
straggled forward over his very tall, receding forehead. The Tapir
was no beauty. He had, however, a considerable following among
intelligent undergraduates. He observed them with care. He
informed himself about their tastes and activities. He spoke of
one to the other with calculated and entertaining malice – malice
seldom applied to his fellow dons, whose proclivities would, he
rightly assumed, bore his younger friends. But to undergraduates,
gossiping about undergraduates, as well as commenting with

scurrilous enjoyment on the seamy side of public affairs, he was excellent company. The Tapir had, during his second year, brought Theo into his inner circle. Desmond Dillon was excluded from first to last. 'Your friend Dillon,' The Tapir would remark, 'is very much a type, isn't he! Such a nice, clean-limbed fellow, I think. Likes playing the bandit, doesn't he! A taste for immature violence. That sort of character, once one sees through it, is rather dull, of course. Benthall tells me he wants to write one day. I can imagine the sort of thing, too! Claret, my dear?'

Theo had, like most of the circle, been simultaneously flattered, charmed and repelled by The Tapir. But when, as sometimes happened, others drifted away from some party in Playfair's rooms and they were alone, he always found his host more stimulating company than any other man in Cambridge. When the gossip, the banter, the scandal was put aside, The Tapir would completely change his mood, even his voice. He would talk penetratingly about modern society, modern European society, in terms which were both awful and compelling.

'Things have got to change, of course. Violently, completely. They will – it's historically inevitable – but the open question is at what pace and exactly how. And, naturally, who is going to be sufficiently perceptive to discern the historical current and catch it rather than be drowned by it.'

Theo found that, more and more, he would take every problem, every impression of life, to The Tapir for comment. Playfair encouraged his political ambition.

'It's a sort of game in this country, my dear. Those who play it greatly enjoy it and I'm sure you'd excel. There are, of course, other ways, if one is really interested in having influence on events – '. And Theo would say, lightly, 'What other ways?' and The Tapir would smile, and pour wine, and say, 'You could do anything if you chose, my dear Theo. You could be a man of history – there are very few about.' And Theo would laugh as if at the absurdity of The Tapir's flattery: but he would be warmed.

One day The Tapir remarked, 'You attract both sexes, my dear Theo. Nor, I suspect, is that simply your youth. You have a dangerous gift. And, perhaps, a dangerous weakness. You'll have to watch it – to use it rather than be used by it.'

Theo was silent. It was no good saying 'Nonsense' to The Tapir's shafts. He was too well informed.

At a later session, during his second summer up at Cambridge, they'd discussed Theo's future. It had always been accepted between them that politics was Theo's dominant interest, that in a political life his ambition lay. The question, of course, was how to further it. It was 1928 and Theo was surprised to hear The Tapir observe that Labour would probably be the largest party in the House of Commons if a General Election came soon.

'Alaric' – they called him The Tapir behind his back, by his first name to his face – 'Alaric, I suspect one should join the Labour Party. They've at least got ideals.' Theo inclined to throw at others intentions of this kind, as much to observe effect as because he meant it. There was always a touch of sincerity at the least, a half-intention, but he wanted to try ideas on others, the more disapproving the better, before committing himself in any direction, whether emotional, spiritual or political. Not that Alaric Playfair would ever be disapproving, however bizarre the suggestion. The Tapir, Theo found, was the most companionable of creatures on whom to test a mood. 'Ideals,' Theo said. 'Some sort of vision, even if it's half-baked! Something more than ease, comfort and security!'

'Ideals!' said The Tapir. 'Maybe! But to put ideals into effect you need sharp knives and strong arms. And nerves. Ideals are about transforming society, not reforming it at a snail's pace, wouldn't you say?'

'Perhaps. But I think I might be more at home with them – '

'I doubt it. Bores. And incompetent. And if they *do* form a government it won't last. You'd much best stalk a Tory seat, my dear. Bother ideals – you get into the circles of real power, Theo. Then you can actually *do* things. Besides – '

'Besides?'

The Tapir was silent for a little and then said, obscurely, 'What better protective colouring in the world is there than membership of the British Conservative Party? You can think what you like, say little, do as you please, and wait your moment. Conform, drift upwards, act in the shadows. You can be like an invisible man.'

'How very dull, Alaric!'

'Not *necessarily*,' said The Tapir, dwelling on the word. 'Not necessarily dull. I know you care about things, Theo. I know you don't want mediocrity. But achievement can come in different forms.'

'It's not only dread of mediocrity, Alaric. I really want to change things. The materialism, the vulgarity of a lot of England repels me. And the heartlessness. We are run by sleek old men in the interests of sleek old men.'

'I know,' said The Tapir, with no banter in his voice at all. 'I know you're sincere, my dear. It's a foolish superficiality to think that because a man has personal ambition – and you have – he can't also give himself to a cause. A man like you needs a cause, Theo, or your desire for greatness, influence, power, whatever you like, would be ultimately fruitless. It would satisfy you not at all. You need not only achievement but also belief – I know, my dear. It is the mark of any real high-flyer. Cynical opportunists constitute life's third eleven.'

Theo was not displeased to hear it, for when The Tapir had said, 'I know you're sincere', he had been accurate. Theo Tate was a battlefield on which opposed forces and instincts warred. His good looks, his easy wit, his reputation for a certain rather elegant languor, the facility with which undergraduate cynicisms – better than the attempts of most in that genre – came to his tongue: all this was consistent with social success, popularity with young people aspiring to fashion, an agreeable life. Allied to a quick brain, a retentive memory and a gift of articulacy with both voice and pen, these talents bid fair, also, to bring prizes in that world of politics to which he was temperamentally drawn.

But the smarter sort of undergraduates with whom he spent most of his time – and even those less smart, more serious and intellectual youths against whom he sometimes enjoyed sharpening wits in argument and who felt for him a reluctant but acknowledged respect – would have been surprised to a man or woman by knowledge of another Theo, kept close-locked within. For Theo was at heart deeply unhappy. He was guilty at his comparative good fortune. He was ashamed at the comfort and apparent heartlessness of his style of life. And he felt, without always being able to analyse why, a sense that the world was out of joint, that Europe was teetering on the edge of some huge, unimaginable disaster.

Once, during the Easter vacation of 1928, Theo had been dining in London before a dance. It was a large, rather grand dinner party but someone had dropped out at the last minute and Theo, most unusually, found himself sitting next to his hostess. She was a large, rich lady whom he had only met once before. Her daughter, a spoiled, insipid girl, was somewhere around the middle of the table bubbling inanities to neighbours. Theo sat quietly. His left-hand neighbour was talking across the table and his hostess was initially absorbed to her right. They were already eating cutlets when she turned to him, a penetrating, appraising look. Her name was Mrs Brinkney.

'I was telling Bobby here about the trouble we had in Scotland last year. We always go up at the end of the first week in August, to get things ready, before people arrive.' She did not think it necessary to explain, so obvious must it be, that they took a Perthshire grouse moor and shooting lodge in the summer of each year.

'When we arrived we found the under-keeper incapacitated because his wife was having a baby and it had all gone wrong! And the head man had done nothing about a temporary replacement – simply let MacKenzie go off without a second thought! The place *has* to have two men – it doesn't work otherwise. Greig, the head keeper, hardly apologized, although the result was a very disappointing fortnight. In fact, when my husband told him what he thought of his management the man was downright offhand. We were furious!' She smiled, pretending apology for the weakness which had led to such forgivable anger. Her eyes were hard.

'My husband wrote to – ' (she mentioned a Scottish name, unknown to Theo) 'and said he thought he deserved an explanation, and that anyway he supposed he'd see a new team of keepers if we ever take it again. A stiff letter, I can tell you!' She took a bite at her cutlet.

Theo said politely, 'Has your husband had an answer?'

'Of course he has – he wrote straight away in September. The upshot was we're not going there again.'

'Your landlord – I didn't get his name – '

Mrs Brinkney disliked the superiority implicit in the word 'landlord'. She said brusquely, 'Hugh Drummond – Braerowan is one of his best moors if it's decently run. Of course he's very hard up, as everyone knows. We've taken it for years. I've got on well with Hugh, but he wrote back – '

She looked searchingly at Theo. He was too insignificant to deserve such personal confidences, but also too insignificant to matter.

'Hugh wrote back something about Greig and MacKenzie being loyal, good men whose service he valued more – well, whose service he valued. Perfectly polite, he said he was sorry we'd had a disappointing season, all that. But he backed them up, idle though they'd been. I'd never do that. I believe in high standards, and if I let a place and there was mismanagement like that I'd not let anybody get away with it. I'm afraid that's the way I am.' Her mouth was set like a rat trap.

Theo gave a sympathetic nod and asked, 'The under-keeper's wife – was she seriously ill?'

'That's got nothing to do with it.' Mrs Brinkney did not welcome examination at her own table. She added, 'As a matter of fact, it made me even angrier, because Hugh – Hugh Drummond – said in his letter that we'd be glad to know Mrs MacKenzie was now better, having been very bad, or something like that. Nasty!' she said, fixing Theo with a fierce eye. 'Nasty! It was clearly meant as a dig, implying we'd been practically responsible for the wretched woman's condition! And also implying that we are the sort of people who don't care! In fact my husband and I have been brought up to look after that sort of person, as if they were – ' she waved away the butler who had been offering to fill her wineglass – 'as if they were, well, anybody! As Hugh well knew! I don't like sarcasm of that kind. Are you going up this year?'

Theo said it was unlikely.

'Do you know Scotland?'

'Yes. But I've never shot there. I don't.'

Mrs Brinkney raised her eyebrows, said that she didn't know people went to Scotland for any other reason but that they would of course be taking a different moor this year, that sort of thing was insufferable, it was a pity as they'd had good times at Braerowan. Theo knew that her grandfather-in-law had made a considerable fortune in condensing milk, a pioneer of the art; and Theo also knew that she would not recall his own name in the future.

As he walked home from the dance in the small hours of the following morning he thought about Greig and Hugh Drummond and Mrs MacKenzie and was surprised to find his head still throbbing with such anger that he would have enjoyed making a detour and smashing a window or two of the Brinkneys' house in Eaton Square where he'd dined. They were untypical, he thought, untypical although possible. There were, he said to himself, also plenty of the sympathetic, the impecunious Hugh Drummonds. But the Brinkneys had power and it made him sick with an anger which he only half-mocked when he recalled it on waking.

At a dinner party a short time later, Theo had found himself sitting over port for a few minutes with older men when the women had left the dining room. He generally found such sessions tedious, but endured them with his usual quiet good manners. On that occasion a man was talking about the British economy, which was slumping.

'Lot of nonsense talked,' said Theo's fellow guest, 'people forget what goes up has to come down. Seen it all before. There were the 'eighties in our fathers' time, remember?'

There were several murmurs of assent and the same man said, 'Thing is to provide against the bad times in the good times. Remind oneself nothing goes on for ever. Don't be greedy.'

Theo heard himself, unusually bold, say, 'I suppose, sir, it's a bit hard to provide for the bad times if one's – well, say, a labourer, isn't it?'

The other examined him over the tip of his cigar and said, 'Of course. But those fellows tend to be improvident, you know. Spend as they get.'

Theo told himself that the vulgar indifference of the Brinkneys, the brutal acceptance of others' misfortune implied by this conversation, all were out of the ordinary, exceptions, caricatures. Increasingly, however, he found himself listening for such notes in conversation with a certain bitter familiarity. A lot of people, he came to feel, are exactly like that: and perhaps, the world being organized as it is, cannot be otherwise. But, he uneasily and honestly admitted, I still enjoy the dinners they provide, enjoy them very much indeed.

It was during Theo's last year at Cambridge, 1929, that The Tapir said one day, 'I'm fascinated by Headley's Communism. He's so enthusiastic, it's like talking to one of the early Bolsheviks ten years ago, when they were making the world afresh every day! Headley's still got that intoxicated feeling, as if spring is about to burst out in a completely new way. Absurd and endearing.'

'Headley?'

'Headley – ah, you don't know Headley. Headley works on a literary review in London, none of you know it, it's rather specialized and dull. Not much seen in Cambridge common rooms, I fear. But Headley himself is a charmer. He's coming to see me in a few minutes. He's in Cambridge.'

So Theo had met Headley, and been charmed, as predicted, by his energy, his enthusiasm and his idealism. Headley was a huge, shaggy man with a loud laugh and a strong handshake. He paid any companion the compliment of giving careful attention to his or her every word. With Headley heart seemed to speak instantly to heart, even at first meeting. When he shook Theo's hand to say goodbye he had said, '*You* are the sort of man we need!'

'I rather think – '

'Yes, you're unconvinced, Alaric told me, you don't see it

yet. But you will, believe me. Come and dine in London next vacation!'

Theo lived in London with a widowed mother. He was an only son. Like Desmond Dillon's, like many of them, his father had been killed in the War.

'I'd like that.'

Meetings with Headley had become regular. And Theo read and read, diving for the first time into a very different philosophical and political corpus of written work. Headley, with his infectious warmth, advised. Headley never hectored. Theo, through some instinct, kept this part of his intellectual adventures to himself. He didn't discuss it with friends like Desmond Dillon. When Headley's name came up in undergraduate conversation as it sometimes did, instinct kept Theo silent. He didn't discuss it with The Tapir. And, oddly, The Tapir seemed seldom to probe now, seldom to say, 'Well, my dear, what are we reading, what are we thinking?'

And one day Theo had said to Headley, 'There's a lot I find absurd. But the main thrust makes sense.'

'Of course there are absurdities. The jargon, the naivety – I agree. But, you're absolutely right, the main point, the central overriding historical point, if you like – '

'What does one do?' Theo felt himself an improbable Nicodemus. Headley had looked more serious than Theo had ever seen him.

'Everyone has a different part to play. It needs patience, dedication. History moves jerkily, you know that already. Somebody like you – no, not someone like you; *you*, Theo – could be enormously important.'

Theo had said again, 'What does one do?' and Headley had said, 'I'd like you to meet someone. Leave it to me. Meanwhile I think it better to wait a bit, and keep this completely between ourselves.'

Then what seemed an age passed without incident, without contact with Headley. And during this time Theo continued to read and to think, and found that he could at last set the disturbed experiences of the nineteen-twenties in a historical context which made sense. He could even comprehend the unfeeling reactions of others, the sort of thing which had so infuriated him in the conversation of such as Mrs Brinkney, the casual unkindness which regarded economic disaster to the individual as of little consequence provided it wasn't oneself, and provided the system ran free from interference – he could explain all this now, saw it clear. It wasn't the imperfections of single human beings which outraged him, he realized. These people could not do otherwise. They were playing parts which history had absolutely dictated, they were behaving as they had to behave. Until all was changed.

Thus Theo came to know – at first incredulously, then with increasing fervour, and at last with an extraordinary sense of peace – that he would become a Communist. Theo had for a while, two years previously, flirted with the idea of embracing Catholicism. He had admired the assurance, the sense of living under an all-comprehending discipline, being part of a mighty and timeless structure which his Catholic acquaintances conveyed. The Tapir, an unabashed sceptic, had smiled sympathetically.

'You'd feel enormously happy, my dear. Anyway at first. There's emotional release, I've seen it often, of course. And intellectually it's bliss, at least until you get uneasy. And that doesn't come for ages,' The Tapir added maliciously, 'Not until full maturity, if then! I'm sure you'd make an excellent Catholic, Theo. Why not take it further?'

'You believe it's all nonsense, don't you, Alaric?'

'Of course, my dear.'

Now, after that first rather breathless exchange with Headley when he had said, 'What does one do?' Theo had felt the same sort of benefaction which he guessed would have followed conversion to Catholicism. He longed to serve, to demonstrate belief, to suffer, to obey. He had at about this time found himself one morning walking through Trinity Great Court with Adler, an unpopular, eccentric undergraduate with a shock of hair and dirty fingernails. Adler professed Communism. Theo was mindful of Headley's injunction – 'keep this between ourselves', and Adler undoubtedly regarded Theo with loathing as a mindless young fashionable, a wealthy, frivolous irrelevance in the stream of history. But Theo felt now a tenderness for Adler. He longed to confide in Adler, to see Adler's hostility change to incredulous complicity. He found a few agreeable words about nothing much, and Adler looked at him with suspicion as they walked. Theo said suddenly, 'What do you think of the Vorontsov Trial?'

The trial in Moscow of some alleged traitor had received a good deal of coverage in the Western press, in which there was plenty of comment on the shameless barbarity of what passed for Bolshevik justice. It was clear, reports said, that Vorontsov had been tortured before his wholly incredible confession.

Adler grunted. Then, reluctantly, as if ashamed of wasting words on a creature so obviously incapable of understanding them, he said, 'He's guilty of course. The bourgeois press are working themselves up about what they call the facts of the case. That's entirely mechanistic – absurd. Vorontsov is a traitor *because* his case is used by the forces opposed to the Revolution, if you like. His supporters abroad condemn him by the fact of their support. I'm afraid you wouldn't understand.'

Theo smiled and said nothing. He knew, by now, that although Adler was a rather stupid man he was on the right side in this and any similar argument, because he had come to terms with the fundamental principle that the Party embodied the irresistible, active force of history and that only by submitting judgements, so-called facts, to the test of Party philosophy and Party discipline could they be seen truly as correct or erroneous judgements, as facts or lies. And it was too much to hope that the Party would only be served by people of intellectual subtlety. It needed – the Revolution needed – its foot soldiers. It needed its Adlers. And he longed to stand with Adler, with stupid, fervent, bigoted Adler, submitting to the same order, fist raised in the same cause. He was frustrated by his own inaction. It seemed a long time before his next meeting with Headley; and when it happened he said, this time with a frown of impatience, 'What does one do?'

'In due course I'd like you to meet someone.'

'So you said. But I imagine I can join?' Headley gave him a long, serious look; a look of great affection.

'Theo, Party members are organized in cells, known to each other and operating, under discipline, for mutual support.'

'I know that. It is what I want.' Theo felt a passionate need for acceptance, for sharing. All this time he was living, outwardly, his usual, agreeable, social life among those he could not stop regarding as his friends. It was a strain and he needed to ease it by membership of another circle, a circle whose eyes had been opened to dialectical truth, a circle dedicated in fact and name to the Party.

Headley was still looking at him fondly but seriously. After a pause Headley had said, 'Party members come in all shapes and sizes, Theo. Some understand – well, not much. They need jargon, simplistic reactions expressed in easy, memorable formulae. The bourgeois often call these lies. They're not, because they serve a higher truth, which you and I understand. A historical truth.'

Theo thought of Adler. He said, 'Well?'

'Well, it is the duty of some – of a select cadre – to keep membership secret. Not to join a cell. Not to voice these inspired opinions, which are necessary but, as I've said, are sometimes simplistic and open to bourgeois criticism of a mechanistic kind. It's the duty of some, instead, to work within the enemy system. Even to rise high within the enemy system. The capitalist enemy.'

Theo felt a thrill of excitement at the word 'enemy'. He stared at Headley, who continued, gently.

'That is a very arduous duty. It requires great character, imposes great strain. It is only appropriate, obviously, to members whose talents are considerable. It means that an outer life must be lived, if possible a highly successful outer life. That, indeed, is the point. But there is also an inner life. An entirely secret inner life.'

Theo said, hardly breathing, 'An inner life!'

And Headley said, very softly, 'The Party. Contact with those who can direct, advise and be informed. I'd like you to meet someone. Leave it to me.'

And then, several weeks later, Theo had met someone. And later again – by which time he was approaching his final term, contemplating a post-Cambridge future – he'd met Marcus for the first time. Three years ago. Theo would always recall their first encounter, with a twinge of recollection that was almost romantic, like the first mutual recognition of love. He had, during his first year at Cambridge, written a certain amount of verse. He now regarded it as immature and derivative but he had not thrown it away. The man to whom Headley introduced him, with extraordinary perception, said, 'You have written poetry?'

'A little. Poor stuff.'

'Could you write something of it for me from memory? Something short – a stanza, perhaps.'

Theo had stared at him and then written a few lines on a piece of paper. The man had thanked him without expression, and asked him to go to a particular glass house at Kew Gardens on a Saturday afternoon ten days hence.

Theo had done so. After a few minutes he was aware of a figure in a dark coat inspecting the same plant as himself. The figure quoted gently the first two lines of Theo's verse, paused and smiled at him. Theo completed the stanza, heart beating, and the other said, 'Exactly so. Exactly.'

It had been Marcus. And Marcus had explained, lightly, that they'd probably see a certain amount of each other and that their method of communication would always be curious, clandestine, exactly devised by Marcus and followed by Theo, without deviation. And that Theo would be known as Contor.

'Socialism in one country,' said Marcus, 'the principle which must guide us in the present phase of history, as you know, means great vigilance. The socialist revolution is still enormously vulnerable to external attack: as well as to subversion from within. It is particularly important that in this country, in England above all, the forces of reaction are checked, watched, balanced by people who are on the side of progress. Of course that needs dissimulation – how not?'

It was 31st May, 1932. Theo and Desmond had returned from Germany a month before.

Theo said, 'Adrian Winter's seat is bound to be vacant by the next election.'

It was not the first time he had mentioned this, but they had not met for a little and the outlines of this prospect had become clearer.

'He's been in Parliament, off and on,' said Theo, 'since the 'eighties! He would have left at the last election, in '31, but he pretended that there was a national crisis and it was his duty to stay on. They all fool themselves it's their duty to stay on! But he's told a great friend he's definitely going next time. Might even go before, depending on his health. He's over seventy.'

'And Winter's seat – '

'Safe Conservative seat. Sussex. He wants to find a successor and then push a name at his constituency association. They'd take it from him, he's got a lot of standing, as an old stager.'

It had always been accepted as Theo's part that he should make a career in politics in the Conservative interest. Others, Marcus hinted, had assumed other roles, equally impeccable. A man in the House of Commons, with Tory colouring and the sort of gifts which could bring advancement, perhaps soon – such a man could, Marcus said, bring novel and important benefits to the cause: of an exact kind which only time would show.

Marcus now asked, 'You reckon he might accept you? You thought, I remember, that you had made a good impression.'

'Yes. And since then he's talked about it to Patsy Dillon. That's Mrs Dillon, mother of Desmond Dillon who's been on this trip with me. Winter's fond of her – she's a cousin of his second wife whom he adored and Patsy reminds him of her, it appears; anyway, he's always asking her impressions, and Desmond told me that Winter had brought up my name. Asked her view of me. Her word carries a lot of weight with him.'

'She knows you, this Mrs Dillon?' Marcus's English was flawless, his very slight touch of a foreign accent attractive, his usage of the language occasionally a little more precise than native slovenliness made usual. He was smiling.

'She knows me slightly. Desmond told her, of course, how splendid I am. And industrious!'

Theo was certainly hard-working. He had left Cambridge with a good degree and had joined a firm of discount brokers, a family firm with whom his own family had a connection. The entire system was doomed, in a way his City colleagues could not begin to suspect, and their innocence amused him. Meanwhile, a man must live. Theo had a certain amount of money derived from his father, killed at Loos seventeen years ago. His mother lived carefully but comfortably in Albion Street and he had a bedroom and sitting room in her house, although planning soon to find rooms of his own. Materially, life was comfortable. His firm approved his political ambitions.

'No doubt,' said Marcus, 'you can improve your acquaintance with your friend's family. It sounds promising.'

'I know his sister. The mother slightly, as I say.'

'My dear Contor, it would be better if you observed the – shall we say little conventions – of our association. And spoke the truth. You know Mrs Dillon a great deal better than slightly. I applaud it. Why disguise it?'

Theo smiled, a slightly twisted smile, shrugged and said, 'Very well. As a matter of fact I'm staying at the same house as them next weekend. It's all coming together I hope.'

But a picture of Emma Dillon flickered momentarily before his eyes as he spoke and he wanted to erase it. He said again, 'All coming together,' and tried to sound indifferent, calculating. Marcus looked at him shrewdly and said, 'Good. Now tell me about Germany. You met a young man in the National Socialist Party's SS, I understand.'

'Ah, you have heard that!'

'I have heard that.'

Of course, Theo reflected, Marcus had heard that. Absolutely dedicated now to this curious, exciting, sometimes agitating double existence, it still often irritated him to feel how entirely open to their scrutiny every aspect of his private life was. And would always be. Everywhere. He knew Patsy Dillon more than slightly. He had dined and talked, dined and talked with Wieland

Breitfall. They knew. And it was his duty to tell them, whether they already knew or not. They have to be perpetually vigilant, he said to himself, unconsciously and silently using the jargon phrase, perpetually vigilant. They have enemies everywhere. But it made him quiver with annoyance at times.

Yet Theo had by now entirely accepted that certain behaviour, much subterfuge, many sacrifices were absolutely necessary because of the supreme, the overwhelming importance of Cause and Party. Theo had, finally, been convinced and had, he realized, accepted a faith which he no more queried and jibbed at on points of detail than the loyal Catholic he might have become examines each tenet of his beliefs because of a periodic uprush of intellectual curiosity. Doubts must come and go, but there was an answer to everything, the faith was a seamless robe, authority and discipline alone could keep it from tear and destruction, personal qualms were eradicable weaknesses, since 1917 the world was new and the Revolution was at war with all who did not accept it utterly and inwardly, as well as outwardly. Theo believed all this completely, had inspected the whole matter with his cool intellect from the beginning, knew that his passionate conscience, which was concealed by his external worldliness, could only be satisfied by giving himself wholly to this. Wholly and yet secretly. Cause and Party. Conscience and intellect fused. And deliberately disguised, all the time, by an outward *persona* whose cultivation – cultivation of something which anyway came naturally to Theo – was itself a duty, so that he could deceive by appearances and be the better prepared for such work as the Party would, in time to come, require of him.

He said, 'Wieland Breitfall, *SS Sturmführer*. That's the private Nazi élite, the – '

'I understand about the SS. Tell me about Breitfall. Intelligent?'

'Not very. Sincere.'

'I dare say. Attractive?'

There was a tiny pause before Theo said, 'I suppose one could say so.'

Marcus laughed.

'My dear Contor, he attracted you. And you him, I imagine. I know you rather well, you see. Why hesitate? You saw him several times, this nephew of your host, of the so-called liberal writer, Fischer. Several times. The association might be useful one day – after all, within Germany itself there can be no overt connection between the Comrades or anyone close to them and the Nazis. The Nazis have been spending a lot of their time beating our people up and so forth – not without cause or response I'm delighted to say! Hitler has explained, in his charming way, that Marxism is a primarily Jewish phenomenon. He has told his people that the first task of their Party, in power, must be to stamp out Marxism. He's not in power yet, of course. But it will probably come. Brüning, their Chancellor, resigned yesterday, as you know. From our point of view he's no loss. He planned restoration of the monarchy, of all things! This new man, von Papen, will play with the Nazis, thinking he's using them until he finds they're using him.'

'You reckon, seriously reckon, the Nazis will one day be in a position of power?'

'I do. I do indeed. I should maintain contact with your friend Wieland, if I were you. In fact, you are to do so.' There was no change in Marcus's tone. The nature of their relationship had been established long ago.

Theo said, 'Desmond Dillon had a bit of trouble with the Nazis, as it happened. He – '

'By the way, your friend Dillon is writing a book, you told me. What sort of book?'

'A novel. He –'

'How does he earn his living?'

'He's got a certain amount of money of his own. He's recently started to work for a publisher but he doesn't think he's going to like it. He's got ideas about journalism. I was telling you, he had this trouble, he was in a nightclub. They attacked a Pole he was with. The Pole died.'

'Such things were not infrequent in Germany at election time. They had just elected their President.'

'Quite. We – Desmond and I – met this Pole on a train, the

one who died. Among other things he had a remarkable story to tell about collaboration between the German Reichswehr and the – the authorities in the Soviet Union.'

Marcus looked at Theo with a slight frown.

'Well? This has, sometimes, been mentioned in newspapers. Even here.'

'Is it true?'

'It's not my business,' said Marcus. 'Nor yours, Contor. If it were true, why not? The Red Army needed to build itself up after its sufferings. It would have been natural to draw on German advice, I have no doubt.'

'But, Marcus, the *extent* of the thing, if this Pole were to be believed! I know our – the British – Disarmament Commission in Germany was disbanded in 1927, but well before then it appears that the German firm, Junkers, were building – are still building – aircraft, military aircraft, for the Germans at a factory near *Moscow*. That there's a German flying centre at a place called Vitupol where they've trained a whole generation of military aviators – we met one, incidentally. Then there's a tank school at Kazan, on the Volga or somewhere. A tank school! It's all remarkable! I don't know what Hitler would make of it if he came to power, as you expect. And if it's true, the Comrades, surely – '

Marcus said, thinly, 'Did the Pole say all this?'

'No, he hinted at it. But his girlfriend told Desmond Dillon, and he told me. She knows it all. Chapter and verse. She disapproves of it.'

'Does she indeed?' said Marcus. 'This well-instructed, informative young lady. How does she know these things?'

'She's a journalist. She's a mixture of races. Hungarian, Polish, German, the lot. She gets around. She hears things. She told Desmond that this flying man, Langenbach, whom we met on the train has been working in Moscow, at the German office that coordinates all this. It used to be called "ZMO" – I don't know what that stands for. People who work there or who undergo training in Russia are discharged from the Reichswehr. They are civilians. Then, she says, they join up again.'

'She knows a lot, this lady. And talks a lot.'

'It may all be nonsense.'

'Your friend established a close relationship with her?'

'Yes,' said Theo. 'Yes, that certainly.'

And Marcus said, 'Then you know her name. May I have it please?' And as Theo gave it he thought of Desmond, his friend, could see Desmond's eager face, and knew that he, Theo, had crossed one particular frontier in obedience to his faith, and that there would be others.

CHAPTER IV

'Des, why was Mother so keen we were all invited together, you, me and her, the same weekend, to the Marvells? I feel as if I'm being taken out at half-term, you too! Hilda Marvell wrote, "so lovely if you could be here at the same time as Desmond and Patsy, and we could enjoy you all together." Hell, we're middle-aged!' It was June 1932.

Emma Dillon made a mock-scowling face. She was an extremely pretty girl with olive skin, straight, dark hair and a soft voice, almost a whisper at times. It could appear affected but was not. Her eyes, like her brother's, were very brown. They were twins. Desmond chuckled.

'Mother had the idea and prompted her. Hilda's brother-in-law Alan married Mother's cousin – pretty remote, the one who then married old Adrian Winter. Why do those people – Marvells, Winter, Mum – why do they seem as if they came from a different *century* to ours? They're not all that much older – Mum was only nineteen when she had us! Early forties now – but even she just sees things differently. Not nineteen years differently. Utterly differently. And with the men it's impossible to communicate at all.'

'You still haven't explained why Mum wants us to be at Bargate at the same time.'

'I suppose,' said Desmond, 'that she feels she doesn't see enough of us, even though we all live in London. We don't go round often enough.'

'No. We don't.'

Desmond and his twin shared a house on Campden Hill and had been supping there alone together. Their relationship with their mother, beautiful, youthful, exquisitely dressed Mrs Dillon, was wary.

Emma sighed and said, 'Anyway, whatever the reason, they've asked us and we can have a good gossip with Cousin Hilda. Why do we call her Cousin Hilda? She – '

'I've told you – and there's no reason. Her sister-in-law was Mum's cousin Veronica.'

'Pretty remote, as you say.'

'Utterly remote. But Mum likes what she calls the Bargate connection.'

'So do I. I like the house, I like the food, and I like the Marvells. The children may be at school but I like old John and Cousin-Hilda-to-us. Incidentally, I don't think she is in the least keen on Mum, whatever Mum thinks.'

'You may be right. So it makes it all that much more of an imposition. Anyway, they've invited Theo. And I want you to know him better, I'm delighted. Mum liked him when they first met when I was up at Cambridge. In fact they've met often now and they get on astonishingly well. Theo's a bit arrogant intellectually, and I thought he'd regard Mum as – well, rather superficial, shall we say? But they clicked.'

'I'm glad,' said Emma. 'What a relief for you.'

Desmond smiled and said, 'The Marvells have asked him because Adrian Winter is coming over, and Theo is having another approving or disapproving eye run over him – he's desperately hoping to inherit Winter's seat in Parliament when he gives up. Which he wants to.'

'Des, is he a serious person?'

'Theo? Yes – he acts very off-hand, very languid. He's always been like that. But he's clever and ambitious. He'll go a long way.'

'Has he a conscience?'

'Odd question,' said Desmond. 'Haven't we all?'

'You know what I mean.'

'Yes, of course.'

They always knew what each other meant. Their relationship was very close indeed. Each knew, almost infallibly, what the other was thinking. And, even more infallibly, what the other was feeling. They were quiet now, both contemplating Theo Tate. Emma recalled saying good night to Theo after a dance three months ago. He had suddenly put his hands beneath each of her elbows and stared very hard into her face, holding her so powerfully that she couldn't move, her body against his, her eyes held by his. He'd muttered, 'Don't move. I'm looking. I want to remember.'

And his eyes were hypnotic. Then, abruptly, without the slightest gesture of tenderness, attempt to kiss her, word of affection or explanation, he had dropped his hands and moved away. She was a little shaken, recalling the experience. She had never been alone with him before. She had no idea when or whether she would see him again. Now he was to be at Bargate, a friend of Desmond's, a prospective Conservative candidate, the most casual acquaintance of her own.

'Don't move. I want to remember.'

Emma said abruptly, 'This girl in Berlin, Des –'

Her brother understood that they were still discussing the same general subject. People. Possibles. The fluttering of the heart, maybe.

'The girl in Berlin. What about her?'

'You looked after her when her man was killed. Romantic. Did you fall for her?'

'Yes. In a way I did. Which you knew.'

Emma smiled at him and he said very softly, 'Did you have a thing?'

'13th April. I jotted it down. Right?'

Desmond thought and said, 'Right.'

They were silent for a little. Since childhood they had realized, without inner disturbance, taking it for granted, that any strong emotional experience of one was sometimes felt simultaneously by the other, even from afar. It did not always happen, and it was not until Desmond was nineteen that Emma suddenly mentioned it, saying, 'You knew, I realize you knew. Just like I did that other time. I wrote it down. It was like a telephone bell ringing in the mind, is that it?' And Desmond had said, 'That's it, yes, Em.' They had been a little frightened, they had known but never spoken it; and then it had been a curious surreptitious game, never mentioned to others in any circumstances. But Emma, more analytical, tended to write such peculiar sensations in a diary, to check with Desmond afterwards, calling them her 'things'. It was part of life, part of the unique sensation of twinship.

Now Emma said, gently, meditatively, 'Sonja.'

'Sonja, A remarkable girl.'

'Older than you, Des. Right?'

'Right, or probably right. And beautiful. And sharp.'

'Contact still?'

'Contact still. Wonderful letters, Emma, really wonderful. And fascinating about what's happening in Germany. I'm going there again early next year. I'm determined, and I can get away. Maybe for only a few days.'

'And Sonja still thinks a bit of you, does she?'

Desmond smiled. He said, 'I certainly think about her, anyway. And she's clever – deliciously clever as well as just delicious. And well informed, you see. She knows a great deal of what's going on in the world. We live in a sort of cocoon in this dear little island, wrapped in our security and our prejudices. And our comparative comfort.'

'Some of us do,' said Emma, 'some not. Do you know the present unemployment figures?'

Desmond shrugged. Emma would be breaking into a canter soon, on her left-wing hobby horse. Now she told him the unemployment figures. She began describing the conditions of life among some of the people whose habitations her job led her to visit. It was not the first time.

'One woman with a baby – old newspaper, used after the fish and chips had been eaten! That was the nappy, Des! And the dirt! Please don't tell me these things are unavoidable! You talk of comparative comfort in England!'

'You know how uninformed I am about domestic politics. You must preach to Theo.'

But he smiled at her with love. Her heart was as sound as a

bell. There were corrective things to be said on the other side of any debate about unemployment and poverty, he had no doubt. And Theo would say them, given the chance. Desmond hoped that Bargate might provide the chance.

'Emma works for the probation service, you know,' her mother said rather sleepily to anybody listening. 'I think it's marvellous. She drives her car everywhere. Prisons, of course, and very disagreeable places where they go and live, you see. She works terribly hard, poor love.'

Emma smiled without humour, a gentle, patient acknowledge-ment of the sort of thing her mother irritatingly said. They were lunching at Bargate on the Sunday, a delightful English June day with a huge bowl of strawberries being pushed around the table and Hilda Marvell urging people to second helpings. Theo Tate had arrived the evening before. John Marvell, at the end of the table, was being mildly flirtatious with Patsy Dillon. A gentle man with a slight limp, a weather-beaten face and hair which would soon go grey despite his comparative youth – he was forty-two – he was the best of hosts, a quiet, courteous, twinkling man whose personality exuded kindness. He had been brisk and impulsive when young, but most of that, like a good deal else, had been drained off between 1915 and 1918. Only when he thought some basic moral principle was being derided did he now appear, very occasionally, fierce and formidable.

Adrian Winter had driven over to lunch from an hotel where he often stayed when visiting his constituency. He had listened with interest to Desmond and Theo's brief reminiscence of their visit to Leningrad and Berlin. Talk of Germany, where his wife had died tragically in a Munich riot some years ago, could always be painful in its evocations, but Adrian had never dodged a topic in his life. After that frightful experience in Munich he had, indeed, gone out of his way to nourish his few connections with Germany and Germans. And he followed their politics shrewdly.

Adrian, a large, handsome, florid man, now over seventy years old but mightily well preserved, liked Theo Tate, liked what he saw and guessed of the young man's potential. He might do – he might do very well. And he's a deep one, thought Adrian, there is a lot that doesn't show. Adrian had served on and off in the House of Commons for forty-four years – an immense span. He had been a youngster when first elected. He had seen the giants – and how gigantic they seemed compared to today's men, he thought; the young chaps won't agree, they think it's an old man's fantasy about his youth, but I'm right, they *were* of greater stature, the best of them. On both sides.

The constituency was sound, thank Heaven. He'd always taken trouble with its members, made clear his affection for them, much of it sincere by now. They'd been good when his health had first driven him to resign, a long time ago, before 1914, when he was a boy of fifty-two! Then they'd asked him to come back, during the War. The War! How very, very many it had taken – Members, constituents, all. And then, apart from that heart business in 1923, he'd been much better in health and stayed on – and he'd enjoyed it, there was no denying that. One couldn't give up, duck responsibility during the crisis, after all. And there seemed so many crises now. 1926, General Strike – Baldwin had handled that cleverly, it had to be conceded; generously too. 1929, Labour forming its second administration – again, Baldwin (whom Adrian never originally admired) managed the business of Opposition intelligently, courteously. Then came this crash in America, followed by a ripple of disaster throughout Europe – a crippling slump in world economic activity, massive unemployment, falling values of every asset, particularly land. There had to be a national Government, whatever it was to be called, to pull the country towards some sort of consensus. The old King had seen matters very clearly and MacDonald was right to form it, however much some of his own party hated him. To shrug shoulders and resign would have been to run away, Adrian had thought. He himself had not intended to fight another election but the circumstances of 1931 were so extraordinary that a man couldn't quit at such a time. He stood – he'd never had a bigger majority.

But soon it would be time to go. '35 or '36 would see another General Election and before then a man in his seventies must give way to a successor. To a youngster. He'd already talked several times to the chairman of his constituency party, John Bates, and to a few cronies. There was no very obvious local man, and he knew that although they reckoned he was past it they'd still respect his views. A nominee of Adrian Winter's was in with a head start. Would this young Theo Tate do? Exquisite-looking boy – almost too exquisite, with those long eyelashes and delicate skin. But sharp. And witty. And deep.

Yet it might have been inept, Adrian reflected, the Marvells asking him to meet Tate at Bargate. It was, on the face of it, perfectly natural – Veronica, Adrian's beloved second wife Veronica, had been earlier married to Alan Marvell, killed in '17, and the families had always been friendly. Adrian had always been fond of both John and Hilda, known them since they were young things. And there was Patsy Dillon, Veronica's cousin; and Patsy's boy, this agreeable, brown-faced Desmond, with his twin, who were popular at Bargate, it seemed. Adrian reflected as he looked at the young Dillons and then at Hilda. There had been a story about that once, had there not? He put the thought away. The Dillons were a lively couple, they had quality. And Tate was a boon companion of Desmond Dillon. Contrived? Hardly – and what if it were? There was a general interest in finding a talented successor to Adrian, and the Marvells shared it. But the ineptitude, if you could call it that, lay in the fact that Hilda Marvell had a young brother, Stephen Paterson, who was also mad keen on a political career. And Stephen Paterson had also been mentioned to Adrian as a 'possible'; but not by his sister, Adrian thought. She's entertaining his rival, Tate; and she's asked me to meet him! Well, perhaps she knows nothing about it, Hilda's not a political woman. Anyway, why shouldn't she act as she wishes? Stephen Paterson was, someone had told him, by no means a favourite brother of Hilda Marvell.

Tate was talking now about the forthcoming Disarmament Conference, to be held at Geneva.

'The German representatives are bound to have their hands tied, week by week, by the situation at home, one imagines. They've got to show something like success, in getting a measure of French disarmament, or Allied agreement to more, much more, German equality. Anything less than that and the Nazis will sweep the board in Germany. They've hardly got much room for manœuvre, would you say, sir?' He smiled at Adrian, without deference but without bumptiousness.

'I would say exactly that,' said Adrian, 'exactly that, and more. The Germans will not wish to break up this Conference. They still need a great deal of international goodwill. But unless they can show that the Conference is a genuine attempt to revise the provisions of Versailles they will, at some time or other, walk out. And that will be bad.'

'What should be conceded?' asked John Marvell. 'We've hardly got any strength to reduce, as far as I can make out. We've got no money for anything, my Army friends tell me we've got the same weapons we fought the War with, and we've not built a capital ship in years.'

'It is the French,' said Adrian Winter, 'who must make some substantial gesture. It is hard for them – they, too, have a public opinion which is obsessed by the Boche. The Boche occupied French soil for four years! But only France can pre-empt Germany disrupting the Conference.'

'Does it matter?'

'I think it does matter. If Germany walks out at Geneva it will be harder to keep a moderate sort of government in Berlin. Geneva bridles the Germans, it seems to me. They have to behave responsibly to some extent, while there.'

'Why wouldn't they anyway?' said Hilda Marvell. 'Why do we assume they don't want peace, just like everybody else? And, after all, they've got hardly any arms now – no tanks, no aeroplanes – '

'Hilda, you're a military expert!'

'These things are in the paper again, all the time! I must say if I were a German, not allowed a tank or an aeroplane and told to live next door to the French who've got masses of both – and to do so *for ever* – I think I'd get fed up.'

Adrian Winter nodded and said, 'Exactly so, my dear Hilda. But don't underestimate the possibility of irresponsible forces coming to power in Germany. Really irresponsible.' His voice was quiet and even, and everyone who knew the story realized that his mind was with Veronica, his adored Veronica, struck down by accident when involved in the Nazi *putsch* in Munich in 1923. Dead. Adrian had been in Munich. Adrian knew from first-hand experience how violent politics in Germany could become, how fragile was the stability of the young German Republic.

He added, 'Nor, in my view, should one underestimate how fast they might again acquire formidable strength. I'm not a military man, but I have a high regard for German efficiency. I know some of their people, and they are immensely capable. There is a tradition of brilliant organization. And of planned expansion.'

John Marvell found his voice.

'That was all right, Adrian, in the days when you just needed meticulous plans to call up and train masses of men carrying rifles. Or even lances. But now, as Hilda says, we're moving into the age of the tank and the aeroplane. I don't know much about tanks or how they'll do – but aeroplanes are going to dominate the battlefields of the future, if there ever is one, which God forbid. And I can't believe even the Germans could expand fast in the age of the tank and the aeroplane, unless – '

'Unless they had, already, a powerful, numerous core of people trained in tanks and aeroplanes,' remarked Theo very softly, 'and we know they haven't, don't we? Or don't we?'

Adrian Winter also spoke softly. 'People say there have been certain violations of Versailles in that respect. Flying clubs really training Army pilots in Germany, that sort of thing. I believe some people in the FO think we might compile a dossier and face them with it at a critical moment in the Geneva talks. We'd say, "Don't act so downtrodden, we know what you've been up to." I suspect the difficulty lies in assembling worthwhile evidence. That sort of thing has got to be authoritative and convincing. If it were shown to be ill-based or trivial – and I've got a feeling it may be – it would be disastrous. But I expect our people in Germany are working on it.'

Theo was watching Desmond carefully. Now Desmond raised his eyes to Theo's and gently shook his head. The time might come – almost certainly would come – to talk confidentially to someone in authority. It might even be to Adrian Winter. But not yet. And not at the Bargate lunch table. 'There are certain people,' Sonja had said, perched naked on the edge of the bed, gazing at him with a frown, beautiful, 'certain people who would kill me if they heard me talk.' This, thank God, was England, tranquil, leisurely, far from that frenetic atmosphere where people could speak of killing as part of the political dialogue, where people wore uniforms and stamped on each other, where civilized men like Kitzi Fischer reckoned that with a turn of the political wheel they might become an endangered species. This was peaceful England; polished mahogany and gleaming silver, a Sussex dining room in June. But the time to speak of Sonja's confidences was not yet.

Adrian Winter said to him, indicating a change of subject, that he understood Desmond was writing a novel, a historical novel with a German or partly German background. Might he be going back there again some time or was his material complete? No, Desmond said, not complete. And yes, he hoped to go back there again one day. Perhaps next year. To Berlin. Even as he said it, casually, he made up his mind. Of course he would, he must, return to Germany soon. He could suddenly hear Sonja's voice, and he said, 'In fact I think definitely I *will* go. Next spring at the latest.'

During these exchanges, although he tried to avoid it for he found the contact made him uneasy, Theo found his eyes often met those of Patsy Dillon, and in Patsy's eyes was a smile. For the truth was that, in the words of Marcus, Theo knew Patsy a good deal more than slightly.

He had first met her with Desmond, of course; and then at parties – 'Hullo, Mrs Dillon!' – and then by appointment for some innocent-sounding occupation, casually concealed from others. They had discovered shared enthusiasms. She had one day said, after a visit to a picture gallery, 'Come back to South Eaton Place and I'll give you a cocktail. I've a small picture I want you to see, I want your opinion.'

And a little later, knowing now quite certainly what was to come, mastering the very slight disquiet, the sense of conventional inappropriateness that this was a friend's mother, he had found himself standing very close to her, cocktail in hand, and had put the glass down carefully and put his arms tightly around her and known that her murmured, 'Steady, Theo,' and then 'No, really no, my dear boy,' were invitations to continuance, to the busy activity of fingers and lips.

And thus, as if the most natural and exquisite thing in the world, to bed. With Patsy he had first appreciated how young and delicious can be the body of a woman in age past first youth. She had flattered, she had amused, she had ultimately enchanted him.

Marcus knew this. It was Marcus's business to know such things and Theo's duty (still periodically resented) to relate them. Theo, albeit ashamed of the lapse, still enjoyed the guilty knowledge that of one thing Marcus was unaware. Once Patsy had been teasing him in bed. Their affair had been going on for about two months. They had drunk a bottle and a half of champagne and Theo had been sleepy, rather tipsy, and congratulating himself lazily on the possession of this glorious woman with her smooth skin, sensuous nature and long, slender limbs.

Patsy murmured, 'You're a conventional boy, aren't you?'

'That's a bit offensive, Mrs Dillon.'

She had chuckled. 'Out of bed, anyway. Very straight. Very conservative. You'd be shocked silly by some of the left-wing friends my little Emma sometimes introduces to me! Perhaps you ought to widen your horizons, little sweetheart.'

It was the champagne, Theo told himself regretfully later. He had suddenly felt it imperative to shake Patsy's affectionate condescension. He had not – or he thought and hoped not, for the truth was he had no absolutely clear recollection afterwards – told Patsy anything that really mattered. The fact of Marcus (and, anyway, who was Marcus?) was of course concealed. But Theo thought he remembered saying to Patsy, 'I'd like to tell you one or two things about what I'm really like!' And he had then talked, talked ideals, talked as a revolutionary, talked as a

Communist. He thought next day that he also remembered Patsy saying something like, 'It's all talk. What can a boy like you really do?' And himself answering, 'A good deal. One is part of a great, disciplined set-up, a small part, a wonderful set-up. One day you'll see – ' And then, as far as he could recall, there had been an end of seriousness and another mingling of flesh and cries and gratification. Next day it worried him, for Patsy had a disturbingly retentive memory. But Patsy was only interested in the personalities, the minutiae, the unimportant, social periphery of politics, Theo told himself; she'd probably not understood a word he was saying. Never would he confess this single lapse to Marcus. Marcus would take it over-seriously. It could be the end of Theo. And, although he never allowed himself to think about the ultimate dénouement of all this, in certain circumstances, if Theo became important, it could be the end of Patsy.

Since then, however, there had been many joyful encounters and no reversion to 'what I'm really like'. Now Theo knew that Patsy enjoyed catching his eye when she could at the Bargate table – enjoyed it wickedly, conspiratorially. When she did, Theo now found himself embarrassed; but, simultaneously, he could see every line of her body in his mind's eye like some primitive hermit entertaining visions of naked temptresses in his cell.

Emma was in love. At twenty-six, thought absurd or abnormal by what passed for friends, it was the first time. Emma had once, at the age of twenty, imagined that she was deeply enamoured of a friend of her mother, a man of forty-two. Her mother had laughed at her. 'You'd better take care.'

Emma had flushed and fumed and avoided seeing the man whose name was Tom Scarpe. Avoided seeing him in company, that is, and most of all in the presence of her mother, Scarpe's contemporary. But one day Scarpe had kissed her and kissed her, not for the first time, and persuaded her to have dinner with him. And she had been entranced. He was small, brown-faced and neat in all his movements. His wrists were slender, his hands thin and birdlike. He had persuaded her to dine again. And again. Then he had asked her to go to Paris with him.

'Two days, where nobody will know us, nobody stare at us! Emma, I long to show you Paris. You've never been there, it's monstrous.'

She'd agreed. She'd contrived excuses, alibis, terrified. It was impossible to talk to Patsy, her mother, about anything, and certainly not about Paris with Tom Scarpe. The weekend itself had been – well, fair, she admitted to herself, then and later. She supposed Tom Scarpe was good at that sort of thing and she had a gloomy feeling that she was an unpromising partner. The fact was that on return to England she cared for Tom a good deal less than previously, whereas every authority had implied that she'd be his slave by then – man of experience, attentive, energetic, generous . . .

But it hadn't happened like that. And Emma had devoted herself more and more to her work in the probation service. She was, she knew, particularly good at it. She had been regarded as a peculiar eccentric to look for a job at all and such a job in particular; and they'd been unwelcoming, scepticism thinly disguised, when she'd first been interviewed, surprisingly accepted, initially trained. But gradually she had won respect and she valued it hugely. It was often depressing, but nobody else would know the thrill of sometimes, just sometimes, realizing that one had transformed a life, touched with decency and sympathy something previously insensitive, or brutalized, or simply unhappy. Emma cared passionately about justice, and was irritated by the superficiality and selfishness, as she saw it, of a good many of her and Desmond's acquaintances. When she saw indifference in the midst of hardship, or avoidable suffering dismissed with flippancy, it made her fierce. She was regarded by her mother's friends as an awkward little firebrand, who had joined the Labour Party and then left it in disgust as a plodding, bureaucratic and tedious organization. In fact, Emma's temperament was unsuited to political loyalty or system, being essentially anarchic. She was not, however, a prig. By a merciful quirk of character she was rather vain. She knew she was exceptionally pretty and her figure of the kind that drew men's eyes whenever she passed: and she enjoyed clothes. Tom Scarpe faded into a small and undisturbing part of her consciousness, and had no successors. She loved her twin brother, and wondered sometimes whether there was suppressed incestuousness in their feelings for each other, whether her 'things' should not be ironed out by a competent psychiatrist. Of her mother she was wary. They had, she thought, absolutely nothing in common; but Emma felt, at times, a certain pity – Patsy was lonely, no question. Otherwise Emma enjoyed her friends, enjoyed her fierce arguments, laughed a good deal, adored music, and kept her heart and her senses under pretty firm control.

Then Theo Tate had taken her elbows and looked at her and murmured in that extraordinary way; as if he'd been waiting for her, waiting for years. And had then moved away.

And now, in a few disjointed, inconclusive sentences, with exchanges of glances, the merest touch of fingertips as if accidentally; in a succession of small, subtle ways as the weekend at Bargate progressed, she knew that she was in love with Theo.

She knew that his attitudes – if Desmond were to be believed – were the reverse of all she thought she admired. She had heard Desmond refer to Theo as 'a High Tory – but an intelligent one. A cynic. A man of considerable ambition.' She had enjoyed earlier meetings with Theo, dancing, teasing, briefly arguing with Theo. Theo was Desmond's friend. But Theo was not the sort of creature she had taught herself to respect. His looks, too, were almost feminine – Emma had always fancied something more rugged, more robust. Tom Scarpe, unlamented, had been like a piece of well-worn and well-polished teak compared to Theo. But it was Theo, fair hair, fair skin, quiet voice, pale eyes and all, who now filled her heart, Heaven knew why; although she knew it was his voice above all, his voice cool, soft, a secret laugh in it. It was as if this had been planned from the beginning of time by some remote, immensely benevolent authority. She knew perfectly well he felt the same although she told herself this was nonsense, self-deception on her part. Before dinner on Sunday evening – they were all due to drive to London early on Monday

– Emma had found herself for a moment alone in the Bargate inner hall with Theo, a pleasant, dark, panelled and untidy room where they generally congregated before meals. Theo had crossed the room to her, easily, unhurried. Unsmiling. He had said, very softly, 'This is it, I rather believe.' He'd been standing, once again very near her. Like when he'd said, 'I want to remember.'

'What do you mean "it", Theo?' Her voice was shaky. Other people would come in at any moment. Theo's hand was moving along her arm from wrist to elbow, gently. He sighed.

'You know, I think.' Then he had smiled and murmured, 'Tomorrow. In London. I'll telephone in the evening. *Please* be at home.'

Emma had tried to frown, to look puzzled, to shrug her shoulders. Then some others had come into the inner hall. And Emma was in love and knew it.

'Theo, you aren't trying to turn the head of my little girl are you?'

'Your little girl is twenty-six.'

'Do you have to remind me? I was only nineteen when I had her, but – '

'But,' said Theo softly, 'you're in your forties. And your skin is as smooth as it was when you were nineteen. And your body is – well, not as slender, but entirely delicious. And your capacity for enjoyment, darling Patsy, is quite undimmed. Or so I reckon after some time of more than casual acquaintance.'

'I don't feel I'm behaving very well.'

'You are not behaving very well. You never are. Whatever binds me to you?' He caressed the small of her back and stretched himself lazily. It was late afternoon in Patsy's house in South Eaton Place. Time to get dressed, Theo supposed.

'Patsy, did you get far with Adrian Winter?'

'About you?'

'About me.'

'You're obsessed by your little career, aren't you, lover-half-my-age.'

'More than half. Just more. Well, I mind about it. My future. I think I've got something to offer.'

'As well as – this?'

'As well as this.'

'I talked to Adrian about you with enthusiasm.'

But Theo was not so sure. Confident that if Patsy chose she could carry much weight with Adrian Winter, he suspected that she had done a good deal less than her best during the weekend at Bargate. He did not think – he dared not think – that Patsy had been in the least influenced by whatever drunken revelations Theo had once whispered. Patsy's only criterion for judging Theo's suitability as a Parliamentary candidate was if she continued to care for him: or so Theo firmly told himself. But he had, he supposed, somewhat neglected her lately. Desmond had been around, and Patsy was neurotically cautious about her children. And Theo's supposition was perfectly correct. She had not exerted herself. She had not demurred when Adrian Winter had said, 'A nice clever boy, Patsy. I'd like to talk more to you about him some time. But I'm not going to fuss about all that until at least next year. I'm pretty fit, and the Government is unbeatable at the moment.'

Now Patsy smiled lazily at Theo and said, 'You've not answered my question. I asked if you were trying to turn my little girl's head?'

And Theo shook his own head from side to side, smiling down at Patsy's excellent body and then suddenly swooping upon it, pressing his lips to hers, his hands active, so that Patsy stopped talking.

Part II

1933

CHAPTER V

'It is 1933,' wrote Sonja –

'a New Year in Berlin, my sweet Desmond, my distant lover, and I can look forward soon to another visit from you to Germany which you promised, early in the New Year, you said and I believed. That will be good – you say the book is going well: and just now there is much to observe here. And much since my last letter to you, in November.

I told you then how dreadful the street fights were last summer. Really, it was terrifying to visit parts of the city except in a large group and even then one was careful. Battle going on everywhere, fists, boots, sticks, bleeding faces! Politics, they call it! And no government seemed capable of controlling it. There were times when one hated them all without distinction, these private party armies with their shouts and their uniforms – the Red Front, the Nazis, the *Reichsbanner*. But one must distinguish, I suppose. One had to ask what ultimate vision inspired the backers of each of these gangs of violent louts – or did one? Weren't they all equal in the nausea they produced in one, made equal by their dedication to violence? One sometimes felt so – but above all one longed for someone strong enough to *stop it*!

As you know, they – the Reich Government, von Papen – sacked our local Prussian Ministers on grounds of incompetence in July! Sacked them as if they were useless labourers, and they went without a murmur, and von Papen had yet another election at the end of July, and the Nazis were then the largest single party. Old Hindenburg wouldn't have Adolf Hitler as Chancellor, all the same, and Papen carried on, and it all got worse and worse. And there seemed less and less food in the shops all the time, and the unemployment got more and more grim, and everywhere men were standing holding up boards saying "I will do any work, of any kind, at any time and in any place. Without it my children starve tonight."

And just before I last wrote to you there was yet *another* election – every few months in Germany we have had elections and every election brings more shouting and marching and fighting and trouble! What a system! But when I wrote last I was cheerful, and I sent you an article of mine which they had rather bravely published. The Nazi vote had gone down! By about 15% or a bit more! So I felt hopeful, although it was hard to know what I was hopeful about, except that the brown-shirted ones give me the horrors, the especial horrors. Which you will fully understand.

But it still seemed impossible to govern Germany, no party had a majority, and the day after I wrote to you last, the Chancellor, Papen, resigned with his Cabinet. And poor old Hindenburg didn't know what to do and eventually he asked General von Schleicher, the Defence Minister in Papen's cabinet, to be Chancellor. Prussia had been under what they call martial law since August! And very little good it seemed to be doing, although they did break up some of the largest demonstrations and street fights. The police were really rather brave.'

Sonja put down her pen and moved to the window of her flat, on the upper floor of a pleasant old building overlooking the Grünewald. She heard what sounded like raucous cries from further up the street. It was generally a quiet area. She opened the window a little, cautiously; and quickly shut it, as the inrush of icy air took her breath away. January in Berlin! The last day of January, and each day colder than the last.

'Four elections in a year, beloved Desmond! People said "Schleicher is clever, he knows how to divide his opponents, he knows how to persuade, he understands compromise! He'll get support, he'll get a majority in the Reichstag, he's cunning, you'll see!"

It didn't happen. I think Schleicher was *starting* to persuade some of the Nazis to back him. He gave all sorts of promises, people say, and the Berlin Nazis, Gregor Strasser and his friends, were worried about Hitler's ambitions. Or so they say – I didn't write about that, not wanting a visit from an agreeable little bunch of brown patriots to call on me. Anyway, if there ever was a serious split in the Nazis, Hitler smashed it pretty quickly, and they voted in the Reichstag with complete discipline. And Schleicher couldn't get his majority – by now he was loathed by both the Nazis *and* by von Papen. And by me, I may say! I met him once – charming, slippery, unprincipled. But the old President liked him – he was a friend of his son, a general, a nobleman, I suppose that was enough. Anyway, three days ago he resigned.

What would happen next? More meetings, more rumours, more wild suggestions. People said the Reichswehr were going to take over! They haven't! People said the Communists had another revolution ready! It didn't happen! People said that old Hindenburg, the President, had been arrested! He wasn't! And this morning – this very morning – we learned, the whole of Germany learned, that Hindenburg had sent for Adolf Hitler and asked if he would form a government. They say Papen persuaded the President that it was impossible now to govern *against* the Nazis and that they would only support a government headed by their own leader. The old man demurred a good deal, it's said, but Papen assured him that Hitler would be bridled by the "respectable circles" who – persuaded by Papen – would tolerate a Nazi Chancellor on probation, as it were. We will see. They will see. Anyway, as I write to you this evening, Adolf Hitler is Chancellor of Germany. He has assured us all that he will conquer unemployment, that he will be able to preserve order, that he will at last give us peace. And nearly half Germany seems to believe him. Come soon, sweet Desmond.'

Wieland Breitfall felt, in those early days of 1933, as if he were permanently intoxicated. It was incredible, it would all turn out to be a dream, it was impossible for the human heart to contain so much joy and not be broken by it as surely as if by grief. But day succeeded day and Wieland's heart continued to beat, and the impossible started quickly to happen, and the incredible compelled, each hour, the belief of ever more Germans. And Germany, before the eyes of all the world, was re-born.

Wieland knew, and was patient with the fact, that there were those who doubted. His dear Uncle Kitzi was one of them and it grieved him, for Uncle Kitzi had been like a father, and he admired the Fischer intelligence, the Fischer dexterity with language, what he recognized as the Fischer integrity. But – and the thought was inexpr_ibly painful to Wieland – Uncle Kitzi did not fully realize the depth of national shame that needed to be expunged, the national humiliation that could no longer be borne, the light after gloom to which National Socialism beckoned. The shame and the humiliation came from the dreadful enactments of the Treaty of Versailles, by which the victorious enemies had pronounced Germany guilty – uniquely guilty – of all the horrors and sufferings of the War: and had then treated Germany as an outcast, as a people to keep permanently in subjection, permanently disarmed (to all intents and purposes), permanently weak, permanently liable to the bullying pressures of other nations large or small, whether French, Polish, Czech or what had you. And thus Germany had suffered under a succession of so-called democratic governments which could neither unite Germans nor defy their oppressors. For that, one man – and Wieland's pulse always quickened with sheer love as he thought of it; selfless love, protective love – one man, humble in origins, sneered at and derided, isolated and imprisoned, had been chosen by Providence to speak for Germany and to save Germany. Adolf Hitler.

Wieland had met the Führer personally on only one occasion. It had been at a gathering of newly commissioned officers of the SS – a meeting of ordinands as Wieland found himself thinking, not altogether fancifully, marking that quasi-religious dedication which he shared with most (regrettably, not quite all) of those who had, with him, been accepted for this momentous step, this high honour. A meeting, a celebration – and then their local *Gruppenführer*, a man of enormous prestige and seniority himself, had announced it.

'For ten minutes the Führer himself will be amongst us.'

Two years ago, and Hitler, to the world simply one of a number of struggling political leaders among the chaos of political life in the German Republic, the Republic born at Weimar. But to the élite, to those who understood, who had been accepted, who were the men of the future – to these, how much more! How unbelievably much more! They had been lined up and after a little Wieland had felt the electric current stab at him from immediately in front. His heels had snapped together, his arm had shot up before jerking back to his side.

'*Sturmführer Breitfall, mein Führer.*'

Hitler's hand had gone out rather slowly, deliberately, to take his, Wieland's. Hitler's smile had been friendly, almost conspiratorial, as if sharing with Wieland some private understanding not disclosed to all. Hitler's eyes had been enormously kind, trusting – but, Wieland always recalled, with a touch of sadness in them, too. Hitler had said, it seemed carefully considering, 'Breitfall!' And had nodded, as if judiciously. Wieland knew that this was a man – almost more than a man, an incarnation of spirit demanded of Germany by Providence –

97

who would sacrifice himself utterly and without thought, for his people; a man who would be indifferent to suffering and death, a man with only one dominating thought: Germany.

But the eyes, too, expressed powerful intelligence. Wieland knew that this man not only loved but comprehended: and in every formulation of Party doctrine and Party policy this comprehension was evident. Hitler, Wieland appreciated with awe and love, really knew what ought to be done, to relieve the suffering of the German people. For beside shame and humiliation – national phenomena, stifling – there were appalling individual, human and material tragedies which got sometimes a little better but most of the time much worse. In many cities of Germany a man could not work. In many parts a man could not feed his family. A man could not attain human dignity, self-respect.

Unless he were extraordinarily lucky. Or unless he were a Jew.

Hitler felt for every suffering, every shamed German: Wieland knew it. Hitler was determined that all should be changed, and, given *will* – that key to all – would be changed. Already, after only a few weeks at the head of the Government, plans were being made public, plans for new work initiated by the State, plans to encourage enterprises in which nobody had had confidence for years. And there was a new spirit everywhere, Wieland recognized with wonder, a new sense of unity and comradeship among people, whether National Socialist or not. It was as if, overnight, the shouts and screams of one faction of Germans about another, the war-cries of class and Party – all were stilled, all were dissolved into harmony. The Party's slogans, bill-boarded everywhere, emphasized that harmony. 'Support the motorist. He gives you work.' 'Honour the miner. His toil today is our wealth tomorrow.' 'Protect the family. The People is the great family of us all.'

And so on. Simple stuff, Wieland reflected happily; simple but true. And for so long, indeed throughout his adult life and boyhood, these holy simplicities had been obscured by loathsome, alien philosophies, philosophies breeding doubt, hatred between German and German, and decadence and darkness. And now light was breaking.

Uncle Kitzi had said little recently. Normally, Wieland dined with him once a week unless duty made it absolutely impossible, and if that happened he got a real rating from old Günther. Then *Sturmführer* Breitfall in his black uniform with silver lace, silver buttons and insignia, elegant and now at long last respected as it should be – *Sturmführer* Breitfall would be told off by old Günther just as if he were a naughty schoolboy again.

'Master Wieland, you're not doing your duty by Herr Kitzi. You've not got enough proper family feeling, that's your trouble!'

Wieland would grin, enjoying it, and clap Günther on the shoulder. He knew Günther, too, was unsound about the Party and its vision of a new Germany, but he forgave because Günther, good fellow though he was, was uneducated and a touch simple. With Uncle Kitzi however it was a different matter. After he had, on that wonderful occasion, met Adolf Hitler, Uncle Kitzi had said, 'Has he acquired more respect for truth recently? That's what people need to know.'

Wieland had smiled, his patient smile.

'Truth, Uncle? I think Adolf Hitler is the one politician in Germany who speaks truth, speaks to the heart, even when it's disagreeable to hear.'

Kitzi Fischer had smiled ironically, sipped his brandy and said, 'The man tells lies if it suits him. Facts mean nothing to him. I remember – '

Wieland did not want to hear what Uncle Kitzi remembered. Or, rather, he did not want to hear it again since it would inevitably be a recitation of those events Uncle Kitzi had witnessed in Munich in 1923 when the Führer, ahead of his time, had tried to solve the crisis by a masterstroke and had been betrayed. Uncle Kitzi had tales to tell about 'misrepresentations' by Hitler on that occasion, as if fiddling details of accuracy were of the smallest significance compared to the overall illumination Hitler was now bringing to their country and to their lives. In the end, though, Uncle Kitzi would come round. He was intelligent, he would see it all and marvel. And he was generous-hearted and would openly admit his mistake, would acknowledge and touch Wieland's hand and say, 'Well done. We old ones were wrong.' It would be all right in the end, Wieland knew. Tomorrow belonged to the new Germany.

And foreigners, decent foreigners, the ones whose souls were not corroded by prejudice and hatred, would see it too, in the end, and would be happy to see Germany restored, rather than Germany a putrescent and contaminating corpse. Did they themselves not have some of Germany's ills, albeit in milder form? And did they not want a lasting and just peace, which could never stem from Versailles with its inequities and resentments? Theo Tate for instance – and Wieland was unsure why he had kept Theo's last letter, had it in his wallet, in fact – Theo Tate, with his grace and intelligence and charm, would certainly come to admire what was being achieved in Germany.

'You are having an exciting time over there,' Theo's letter had run –

'And I rather envy you and can imagine with what zest you are throwing yourself into the political battle. I suppose if your hero Hitler wins he will build up your armed forces again in spite of treaties and suchlike. I can't say I'd blame him, or you. To be kept in a state of permanent weakness must demoralize a people, one can see that. As a matter of fact it might not take him as long as our newspapers say – to make Germany strong again, I mean. There are stories that your little Army has been up to all sorts of tricks behind our backs – tank schools, aeroplanes, everything soldiers seem to hanker after these days! The *stories* are that you've been getting round the rules for years, helped by the *Russians* of all people! The Bolsheviks, dear Wieland! I expect you know all about this and will tell me it's nonsense, but it's certainly believed by some people in Berlin. You may remember – '

But Uncle Kitzi remained incorrigible. Wieland had only seen him twice since the end of January, now nearly seven weeks ago, and Günther would be a real scold when he went next week, as arranged. But there had been a great deal to do. On successive Tuesday evenings there was a meeting, a briefing, which led him, apologetically, to telephone that he would be unable to have dinner at the Fischer house. Duty.

And duty had been hard, yet without it Germany could not have been saved. When Adolf Hitler had first been appointed Chancellor at the end of January, it was generally recognized that the Communists had been preparing revolution. Even Uncle Kitzi had not dissented from the fact of that danger, although he had – regrettably – muttered 'Very convenient for your Adolf, if you ask me!' Convenient! Thank God, the Chancellor had acted promptly, arms caches were discovered by the police, searching and acting with an energy they wouldn't have dared display a week before, and Communist meetings and demonstrations had been banned. Something like peace returned to the streets.

Then the Chancellor had persuaded Hindenburg that there must be another election.

Yet another election! In his innermost heart Wieland regretted the necessity although it was no conceivable business of his. It was announced to them, to the officers of his group, at a meeting. Wieland appreciated the way trouble was taken to explain what was intended even in the highest Party circles, so that understanding flowed down through the arteries of the SS and that body – utterly disciplined though it was – could react to circumstances, to casual conversations, ultimately to orders, in a way that was intelligent, anticipatory, informed. Some of the matters explained, painstakingly, to such juniors as Wieland were, therefore, highly confidential. He felt awestruck at the privilege, the trust reposed in him, inexperienced as he was. He would never betray it but it was a heavy responsibility.

They had explained about the election. It was necessary to demonstrate that the Party really had the German people behind it, and that – unlike the Communists – it was a mass party, a Workers' Party, not a small collection of cells posing as the people, as everyone recognized the Communists to be: and many of them Jews and aliens as well. The Party had always been frank, open. There must, once again, be elections.

The campaign had started at the end of February and Wieland had attended a briefing on the evening of the 27th – a painstaking affair, every aspect of persuasion, information and electoral tactics fully discussed, with exact orders given. Exemplary. Then, just as they were about to be dismissed, the door had been flung open and a very senior officer indeed, an *Obergruppenführer*, no less, stood in the doorway.

And started shouting. Next moment they were all running from the room, about to execute the orders so suddenly barked at them. Orders which were not wholly unexpected but which, nevertheless, had made Wieland's heart thump when they came.

It had begun! The Communist Revolution had begun! They had attacked the Government offices, it appeared, and set fire to the Reichstag building itself.

The rest of the night still left Wieland exhausted to remember. SA and SS had been told that they were given special emergency powers as auxiliary constables, to help make the enormous numbers of arrests – several thousand it was said – that the situation demanded. The chief conspirators – the Central Committee of the German Communist Party – had been arrested at their homes. Thank God action had been swift – Hermann Goering, Party stalwart, flying hero of the War, since January Prussian Minister of the Interior in place of the Social Democrat buffoon dismissed the previous year – Goering had taken charge and behaved with the promptitude and courage you'd expect from a flying ace. The Communist Revolution had been nipped in the bud. The night had passed in a confusion of shouts, darkness, occasional shots, screams, the sounds of splintering wood and breaking glass as doors were smashed open to round up the long list of suspects, suspects who would, no doubt, have been bursting into patriotic German homes and seizing patriotic Germans if Goering had not acted bravely and fast. The Reichstag itself had been set on fire by a Dutch Communist – a tool undoubtedly, an alien manipulated by dark forces nearer home. Wieland had never before seen at close quarters so much violence and fear as when those arrested were grabbed from beds, firesides, dance halls, lined up, slapped, made to stand leaning against walls, feet apart, hands spreadeagled for the first search.

Not many were armed, of course. They had been caught out, surprised by Goering's splendid vigilance. Wieland remembered, with oddly mixed feelings, a party of very young boys – most of them dark, probably part-Jewish, strikingly good-looking – who'd been listed as dangerous. He had lined them up and an *SS Mann* went down the line feeling for weapons, handling them roughly. One, slightly older, started to say something and the SS man gave him a stunning thump, first on one side of the head, then the other, so that he shut up and they all stiffened, very still, and the search continued. Wieland then saw that one boy managed to inch his left hand along the wall against which it was pressed, outstretched as ordered: inch it along the wall until it touched the right hand of the boy standing next to him. And this tiny, surreptitious touch, Wieland knew, at that moment of pain and fear and isolation, was intended for comfort and surely had that effect. They were taken away soon after, to separate destinations, Wieland recalled.

Thereafter the old President agreed to certain decrees which gave the Chancellor special powers, and annulled certain so-called civil rights. The SA – about whom Wieland harboured many private doubts and some of whose members he held in hearty contempt – were kept embodied as pretty well permanent special policemen. All this showed Germany the dangers through which they all were still living, and the Party had scored 288 seats in the elections soon afterwards – the majority party in a Reichstag of 600 but without, one had to admit, an absolute majority. That would undoubtedly come. The relief on everybody's face in the streets was there for all to see. At last, people seemed to be breathing, we shall have order.

The new order, precarious though it might be, was epitomized by a ceremony attended by the entire Reichstag in the old garrison church at Potsdam – attended by many others, too: the senior officers of the Reichswehr, leaders of the professions, business and society, even – Wieland was secretly glad to note, for there was a traditionalist within his radicalism – the former German Crown Prince. It was a wonderful day, an unforgettable day. It was as if Germans had finally come to their senses, ceremonially resolved to put behind them the terrible factions and quarrelling and uncertainties of the last miserable fourteen years. Wieland had been on duty with an SS Guard of Honour. It was a consummation. It was also a beginning. On the following day the officers of their group were called together for yet another evening meeting and received a message of congratulation from the Führer for their constancy and efficiency throughout what was described as the 'Testing Time', the *Prüfungszeit* of the last few weeks. And they were given, as usual – an indication of the trust reposed in them – confidential information of what would happen in the Reichstag next day. Every head nodded grateful approval, while every heart beat with nervous anticipation that some of those wretched Deputies might try sabotage. For Hitler, they were told, proposed to ask the Reichstag for powers – limited powers, just for four years – to rule by decree. To act, to do what the country really needed, to solve the problems, to bring hope and bread to German houses; lasting peace to German streets. In a word, to govern.

And the Deputies – with the exception of ninety so-called Social Democrats, wretched saboteurs who had prevented every promising development ever since 1919 and had betrayed the country then – had voted, thank God, for the Chancellor. For the Führer. By a majority of over three hundred he had been accorded power to do good and save Germany. It was 23rd March 1933. And Wieland bowed his head with grateful happiness for himself and for his people, and was sure that one day all, even his beloved, recalcitrant uncle, would understand and believe and share his joy.

The editor of the weekly review was fond of Sonja, admired her style, her wit, her appearance. He knew that she and her product always needed handling with care, but within certain limits he had been prepared to take risks. Sonja's articles might sometimes be scandalous but they sold papers. On this occasion of 26th March, however, he saw her personally, shook first her hand and then his own head.

'Impossible! It's a direct attack – in very immoderate terms –'

'Herr Gallwitz, the Chancellor has been voted powers to govern without, or virtually without, reference to the Reichstag at all. It's obvious, therefore, that only a vigilant press can act as an opposition, scrutinize, argue, in a word oppose. That is all my article does.'

'No, Fräulein Vassar, it is not all your article does. Your article is a vicious criticism of the policy, or some of the policy, just announced by our Chancellor.'

'Well, why not?'

'These are not normal times, that's why not. The State has just been delivered from revolution and anarchy, and exceptional restrictions are inevitable, sacrifices demanded. We must all – '

'You believe that?'

Gallwitz sighed. Success, survival even, demand a certain moral suppleness. This exquisite young woman had none, whatever the grace of her body. He eyed her, not without friendliness, and said, 'Of course we shall continue to make constructive comment – '

'And you don't think my article is that!'

'Leave it with me,' Gallwitz said. 'Some alterations, perhaps –' But he had read enough to know that it would take more than cosmetic surgery to make this fiery screed fit for print. 'Leave it with me.'

She had done so. But then, appallingly, he had gone to lunch and left it on his desk. And when he had returned, the article had disappeared. He grabbed his secretary.

'There was a typescript here. Fräulein Vassar left it. Has anybody but you been in?'

'It's possible, *Herr Direktor*.' The girl was frightened. 'I was out for a minute, but –'

Plenty of people would have seen Sonja in the building. She was well known in Berlin, particularly in the journalistic world. So was her reputation. Gallwitz said loudly to his secretary, 'I have not yet read that article. I am seriously displeased. You will give me a list of everyone here who was on the premises during lunchtime and might have removed it – no doubt in some sort of error, presuming I had finished with it. I will then speak to each.'

They looked at each other, he knowing that she knew he was frightened.

On the following evening, just after eight o'clock, Sonja was alone in her flat reading an American novel, a book by Sinclair Lewis recently translated into German. She knew she should improve her English by attacking the original but the book had been excitedly recommended to her and the translation was tempting. She did not feel like writing. She wondered what old Gallwitz would do with her article – funk publishing it, she felt pretty sure. Supper would be sparse and solitary – a woman she knew and liked only moderately had asked her to come round and then telephoned with profuse explanations that it was now impossible. 'Some other time –'

Then she heard the noise of car doors banging in the street below, followed by what sounded like running feet towards the front door of her block of flats.

Many feet. Heavy feet.

Sonja frowned and went to the window. Two cars, black, unfamiliar, their occupants presumably now in the building.

Then she heard tramping up the stairs. Her flat was on the third floor, and she sat still, listening. The flat door opened off the little hall. Sonja opened the sitting-room door which led to the hall so that she could watch the flat door.

Heavy footsteps, stopping at the third. Loud voices, words impossible to make out. Laughter.

A drunken party?

Then the flat doorbell rang. Simultaneously there was a banging of fists on the woodwork of the door, followed by heavy boots applied to the lower panels. It was a light door. Sonja called out angrily, 'What is it?' and threw the door open.

There were six of them. They wore SA uniform, brown shirts, peaked caps, swastika armbands, brown belts and high brown boots. Sonja found herself wondering, incongruously and not for the first time, how the SA kept warm in winter or cool in summer, since the uniform never changed with the weather. They stood now in a half-circle, hands on hips or thumbs tucked into the tops of belts. Grinning. Gazing at her and grinning. She had, she thought, never seen any of them before. Probably they had never seen her. She realized afterwards that it must have been an agreeable shock and titillation to find that she was good to look at.

'Fräulein Vassar?' The tallest and nearest spoke. He looked about thirty, with a brown, pock-marked face.

'I'm Fräulein Vassar. What do you want?'

'We've some friends who want to make your acquaintance, who've some questions to ask you, Fräulein Vassar. Come on.'

'I'll come nowhere. What do you mean –' but by then two of them had moved swiftly forward and grabbed her by the arms, and half lifted, half dragged her down the stairs. She yelled – 'Let me go! I'll walk! Take your hands off me!' but they still held her, and roared with laughter, and bundled her between them into the back seat of one of the two black cars she'd seen from the flat window. Then they pulled a bag of some sort over her head and still holding her arms, they drove into the centre of Berlin. Or so she sensed, for she could see nothing, but she knew Berlin perfectly, and the sounds of traffic, the swing of the car at corners were all pretty familiar. When they stopped at last she reckoned they were somewhere east of the Reichstag building, but not far from it.

Pushed out of the car, the bag pulled off her face, she found herself in a small courtyard, surrounded by a larger group of SA men. One of them started shouting at her. He was a huge man, broad-shouldered, massive. He shouted that she had published treasonable rubbish about the German State and Government.

'When? If I've committed an offence I'll presumably be prose-cuted. Let me go at once.'

She had, the same man yelled, published lies, libels, 'alien-inspired filth'. Furthermore she had spread, for years, scandals by word of mouth.

'What scandals?'

Many scandals, the man roared, many lies, many stories betraying the good name of Germany. She had gone about saying that the German Army had been hand-in-glove with the Bolsheviks, of all things! She had written lies about the policies of the National Socialist Party. She had never written a decent, truthful, patriotic sentence in her life.

And she was a Jewess.

And she had spent all her spare time fornicating with a Pole, a hater of Germany, as his own writings had made clear. He was, mercifully, now dead.

'But you,' another of them shouted at her, 'are alive. You've said you ought to be prosecuted for treason! Quite right! Well, it may come to that, but meanwhile you can take this as a warning, a lesson. And so can others!'

Then one of them held up before her eyes a board on which was a lot of writing, roughly inked on in indelible ink. She read that this was a Jewess, who slept with anybody provided they hated Germany, who spread lies about Germany, who had libelled the Reich Government and people, who had intimate connections with the Bolsheviks, and who sympathized with those who had set fire to the Reichstag. They were grinning as she read the words, two of them still holding her arms to her sides. Sonja found her voice and said, as sternly as she could, 'Why does it say any of this when it isn't true? And how dare anyone say I sympathize with the people – whoever they were – who set fire to the Reichstag?'

'We know it,' the huge man shouted, 'we know it all right. And now this is going to be a lesson to you, to behave yourself in future.'

Before she knew what was happening they pulled off her jacket – she was wearing a short jacket and skirt. Sonja gasped, with fury and fear and cold in the bitter evening air of a Berlin March. It was icy in the dank little yard. There was – she had not noticed it before – a post in the yard, an upright post set in the ground and about four feet high, which might have been used to hitch a waiting cab or dray horse. The board with its vicious lettering had a cord attached and was hooked over Sonja's head, resting on her bosom. One of them grabbed her wrists and tied them together. Then they pulled her towards the post and attached her tied wrists to a ring at the top of it. Next moment Sonja shrieked, 'Stop it! Stop it!' as powerful hands grabbed at her neck and waist. There was laughter and a cheer and then she felt and heard her shirt and vest torn from top to bottom, her back exposed. Another cheer as a hand snapped the strap of her bra.

Then she screamed as the first cut fell across her naked back. She supposed, looking back on it afterwards as she forced herself to do with sickness and loathing, they were using a long cutting-whip, no doubt kept handy for such ceremonies. She never knew how long it went on because, to her subsequent shame, she fainted after a little while, fierce, searing pain down her back, bilious yellow lights flickering before her eyes, and screams – her own but somehow disembodied – blending with the laughter and applause as the warm blood ran down the skin of her back and soaked into the waist of her skirt.

Desmond Dillon sat up in his highbacked wooden chair in Kitzi Fischer's study and found that his heart was beating so violently that it was impossible to control his voice. Nor had he any particular desire to control it. He had arrived in Berlin the previous evening, 10th April. He had telephoned Sonja. No answer.

There had been no letter from Sonja since early March. He had written twice in that month to say that he was coming, would initially stay with Kitzi Fischer, was longing to see her with his whole mind and heart and body. No reply.

Then at the beginning of April he had sent a telegram:

'Arrive Berlin 10th, staying Fischer, will ring that evening. All love Desmond.'

No reaction.

When he had arrived from the station, been driven to the Fischer house in the suburbs (trying to recall where he and Theo had been stopped by an SA cordon on that first evening exactly a year ago), he had decided, with a stupefying feeling of disappointment, that he must get used to the fact that as far as love was concerned this was a fool's errand, that the thing with Sonja was over. There was, quite genuinely, a good deal which Desmond wanted to do in connection with his book; but it was not that which haunted him on train and boat. Now he felt cold and sick. It must be finished, and he was a self-deluding, extravagant fool to have come at all when she'd not written recently.

After all, what could one possibly expect? They'd made love, fierce, unforgettable, in the immediate aftermath of her Polish lover's murder. Then they'd enjoyed each other, insatiably, secretly, for the rest of his first stay in Berlin, and had found minds as well as bodies meet, so that Desmond had felt more alive than ever before, had felt new tides flowing through his head, and over his limbs, had been excited, transported, supremely happy. But Sonja had been adamant that their affair must be protected from the knowledge of others; and Desmond, realizing that she must be embarrassed by having apparently recovered so instantly from her previous lover's murder, scrupulously observed discretion. Theo knew, of course, but promised to tell nobody, not even their host, Kitzi. And love-making – 'Research for my book: local atmosphere' – took place by day. Then he'd gone home to England and Sonja had said, 'Come again. Soon, but not too soon. I've got a bit of life to repair.'

'Of course.'

'I'm not just a promiscuous cosmopolitan with a gift for pleasure and a busy tongue, you know. I feel things.'

'I know that. I'll write. I'll write often and you'll write back. Perhaps you'll come to England.'

'I doubt it. Not yet. Come back here, Desmond.' She pronounced it with more emphasis on the last syllable than it received in English, attractively, without affectation. 'Come back to Berlin. Not too soon. A bit of time to think. It's all been idiotically sudden – impulse, animality, reaction, unreal. You know that and so do I. Dreamlike, really.'

'Yes. But I want to repeat the dream.'

'So do I. Come back. Later in the year if you can.'

'Most certainly by then. Every night away from you will be restless.'

But Sonja's letters had made clear that it would be better to wait for a little – 'I have to think about things' – and whether they implied another lover replacing the dead Rodoski, Desmond felt jealously unsure. Certainly she wrote with love, but he thought at times that she had a lot of love to give, and it was surely incredible that a woman like Sonja could keep her heart and body intact month after month, living the raffish café-society life she did in the city of Berlin. He half expected her letters to cool, then to cease. He tried to tell himself that this was an aberration anyway, to take an enthusiastic interest in some other woman. It didn't work, and the harder he tried the less it worked. Sonja was in his bloodstream and his blood was always warm. Then, towards the end of the year 1932, they began to write about a visit by Desmond in March or April, and Sonja wrote, 'I can look forward to it' and 'Come soon, sweet Desmond.' And Desmond started counting the days.

He'd tried to telephone her from England in March. The operator had told him that Berlin telephone numbers had been changed and no connection seemed possible. And his telegram might or might have not been delivered – for all he knew Sonja had moved flat and her letter explaining it with a new address had gone astray. But now, here in Berlin, he had tried to ring the old number. And Kitzi Fischer had said nonsense, there's been no change in Berlin telephone numbers. Your exchange operator or ours was being foolish.

And there had been no answer.

Then, a little shyly, he had said to Kitzi that he supposed the person he was trying to telephone had gone away but, late as it was, he thought he might take a taxi and go to an address and see if it appeared inhabited. And Kitzi had said, 'Who is it you are trying to contact, may one ask?' And he had answered, 'A lady I met when last staying with you, Kitzi.'

And Kitzi had said softly, 'Fräulein Vassar. The lady friend of the Pole you saw die. Of course.'

111

'Yes, I – I hope to see her while I'm here. We have written to each other.'

'Sit down.'

'I really think –'

'Sit down. I have things to tell you.'

And Desmond perched in the highbacked chair, with a frown on his face. And Kitzi began by saying that Fräulein Vassar was not in Berlin, had left it for a while after a disagreeable occurrence a few weeks ago.

'I have been informed that she is not here – we have a mutual friend,' Kitzi said, not looking at Desmond. Then Kitzi began to describe the 'disagreeable occurrence', which had been reported in guarded terms in newspapers. And Desmond's breath came unevenly and his hands tightened on the arms of Kitzi Fischer's highbacked chair.

'It was disgraceful,' Kitzi Fischer said. 'One of the worst things of this time. They left Fräulein Vassar, after suffering her punishment elsewhere, tied up, exposed and unconscious in a public place, a street. Nobody admitted seeing her brought there. People stared, shook their heads, passed by on the other side.'

Kitzi had been reminded, since Desmond's arrival, of how much he liked this tall, strong-faced young Englishman who was determined to write a novel with a German background but who clearly understood only imperfectly what a German background now comprised. He appreciated Desmond's somewhat romantic good looks, the dark face, the lock of black hair that easily escaped forward over the right eye until tossed back with a movement of that excellent head, the musical laugh, thought Kitzi, unlike some Englishmen who brayed laughter at you mechanically or some Germans who snorted it. Kitzi appreciated, too, the passion he felt in Desmond, the changes of mood but each mood with depth to it. He regretted the pain this young man was now experiencing, for it was clear he felt something, perhaps a great deal, for the girl. Kitzi did not know her but by all accounts she had turned a good many heads, and if they had been bedmates

112

for a week last year she might well have left an after-taste on this young Englishman's palate which, even twelve months later, he mistook for love. Anyway it was a nauseating business, and for Kitzi shame dominated. It didn't matter whether Desmond Dillon was feeling the additional humiliation of a man whose loved one has been maltreated, defiled: he was right to be utterly disgusted. With Germany.

Kitzi got up and poured some more brandy into both their glasses. It was a moment for strong drink. Desmond was muttering 'Why? Why?' and moving his head from side to side as if the collar chafed his neck.

'Why? Well, it was well known that Fräulein Vassar was critical and contemptuous of the Nazis. She had written some strong articles in earlier days.'

'Was that enough?'

'Perhaps, although I doubt it. Perhaps, too, they resented her conversation. It is said that she talked a great deal, indiscreetly. In particular I have heard that she put it around that there had been, in the past, a great deal of secret military collaboration between the Bolsheviks in Russia and our Reichswehr. To evade the provisions of the Treaty of Versailles.'

There was a long silence. Desmond stared down into his brandy without drinking it. Then he said, 'Why should that make the Nazis want to – assault – her?'

'No doubt they – and the Reichswehr is now Hitler's darling, he's made peace with it, don't forget – find that embarrassing. Hitler's writings, the whole Nazi message, proclaim that Bolshevism is the enemy of Europe. It does not accord well with that – if our Reichswehr have been hand-in-glove with them, from the start. I also doubt,' said Kitzi with a sardonic half-smile, 'whether our Communists wish to publicize it, either. To them the Reichswehr is the arm of the class-enemy. It might shake the faithful to learn that it has, for years, been nourished by their masters in Moscow. Both sides in this quarrel of demons might find themselves in agreement that a journalist who broadcast that matter should be taught a lesson!'

'Isn't it common knowledge?'

'No. It is not common knowledge – not at all. Many years ago there were some disclosures – some very partial disclosures I think – to a secret session of the Reichstag and there was a political row, and the matter was thought "stopped" or "running down" – pushed under the carpet, anyway. Since then everything has been done with secrecy. Of course it's fairly well known that there have been attempts to rearm outside the strict provisions of Versailles – that has been treated as something to joke about, be rather proud of, to wink at, you might say. But the extent, and the details, and this Russian business – no, that can only have been known to a very small circle, I think. To tell you the truth I don't know much myself.

'Internationally, of course, it was in breach of treaty and there would have been repercussions. Internally, in the past, it would always have been political dynamite, outraging both left and right, for different reasons. The left do not want a strong army. The right want no contact with Bolshevism. But it is certainly not common knowledge. Yet I think your Fräulein Vassar knew about it. And I believe she talked about it – although I'm sure she never wrote about it. To talk about it would not be popular.'

'Why,' muttered Desmond, 'do *you* think she talked about it? You didn't know her.'

Kitzi sipped his brandy and raised his eyebrows. He seemed to be considering carefully. After a minute Desmond said quietly, 'Of course, I know you see a lot of journalists, people in that world, your world. I suppose it was – I mean Sonja's stories – talked about – so why *her*? Surely lots of people –'

'The business we're speaking about is only one element, Desmond, and perhaps not the main one. As to how much these rumours were attributable to your Sonja – I don't think widely. I had never heard her mentioned in that context as it happened.'

'Yet you say you "believe she talked about it". Why?'

Kitzi looked at him very directly.

'My nephew Wieland told me.'

'Your nephew, Wieland,' Desmond said softly. 'Your Nazi nephew Wieland. So how did he connect Sonja with these stories? I don't suppose he knew her. Or did he?'

'I think not. You can be assured of one thing, and so can I. Wieland would never get involved in disgusting, mob brutalities of this kind. I disagree utterly with what he calls his political beliefs – he is, at heart, a simple, honourable, misguided boy. And I am very fond of him. But however misguided, this is not his – his sort of activity. And this was the SA. Louts, as I've told you and as you've seen for yourself.'

'Are his lot any better?'

'No,' said Kitzi carefully, unsmiling, choosing his words. 'Not better. Maybe worse, potentially. But gang outrages of this kind are not their style.'

Desmond said, 'I couldn't trust myself not to kill if I had the chance, and a weapon. Or these hands, perhaps.' His voice trembled. He said, 'Any of them. Anything wearing one of those uniforms. Accomplices, in what they're doing in the name of your country, Kitzi!'

Kitzi looked into his brandy and said absolutely nothing.

'How have your people simply stood and watched themselves being taken over by forces of evil?'

Kitzi lifted his head and looked at Desmond sternly.

'You will understand nothing, still less should you write a book of any kind, unless you try to observe exactly why. There are good reasons why this has happened. You saw Germany a year ago. You saw anarchy. Didn't you?'

Desmond grunted and Kitzi continued, his voice low and emphatic.

'Go into the streets now. Walk about. For an ordinary citizen, safety. Personal security. That counts a great deal with people who have known what it is to be without it. Would Germany be unique in that? I doubt it. Then there is the food situation. Your people – the majority of them – don't know hunger. Have never known hunger. Here it has been commonplace. And already – *already*, I tell you, after only weeks – that situation has improved. Don't ask me to analyse that, although I could. It may be a fraud – there are elements of fraud, certainly. But a hungry man whose belly is full for the first time in months doesn't bother about economic theory.'

Desmond's mouth was set in a hard line, his eyes on Kitzi. Kitzi's look was still very direct, stern, a man saying uncongenial things, rejecting comfortable simplicities.

'Then there's our unemployment. Six million – you know that. It will take a little time – but plans and forecasts have already, *already*, been published. I've no doubt whatsoever the Government's policy –'

'The Nazi Party's policy –'

'Certainly. Will first reduce and then abolish unemployment. Do not underestimate, ever,' Kitzi said with a thin smile, 'what Germans can do if they are organized, disciplined, and united.'

'And for this, people are to be attacked and tortured if they step out of line.'

'It can happen. Nor do I excuse it or like it.' Kitzi considered. No, the time had not yet come to tell this young stranger, this agreeable young friend that he, Kitzi Fischer, had also decided that the new Germany was no place for him. It was going to be hard and the timing was tricky. There was always a temptation to delay, and meanwhile –

He said, very gently now, 'As I said, I've heard that Fräulein Vassar is away from Berlin, somewhere in the south of Germany, and I can, if you like, try to discover exactly where. I can do so discreetly – we have a mutual friend, a woman who is fond of her and who trusts me. If you wish.'

'I certainly wish.'

'I am sure you realize how a woman in such circumstances, who has suffered that sort of disgusting experience, might easily feel she could not resume contacts, answer letters, even – even if she loved. She might feel the need for solitary recuperation. She could feel – unclean. I expect you realize that.'

Desmond said, almost inaudibly, 'Please discover where she is.'

Desmond then stood up very suddenly and looked at this tall man with the lined, attractive face, sitting very still in his chair, this man who exuded integrity and who cared for his country so deeply that every shame of this kind obviously went to his heart like a dagger. Desmond considered Kitzi. He said, 'We've got to

116

do these people down, Kitzi! It's them or us. And I include you among us.' He spoke softly, and Kitzi thought he had seldom heard more force expressed by human voice. 'Them or us!' Desmond said again, his voice almost hissing the final sibilant. And at that moment Günther, deciding on that particular day and with a foreigner present that he would be facetiously formal rather than familiar, threw open the door and, drawing himself up and to one side in a mock position of military attention, announced in stentorian tones:

'*Herr Sturmführer* Wieland Breitfall!'

CHAPTER VI

Theo Tate moved into the cover of a doorway and glanced at the brass plate on the door. It said: 'Chance, Chance and Letheby' and he guessed they were solicitors. Solicitors whose office fronted on to a City of London street which was, on this April evening of 1933, the scene of a disturbance, a disorderly meeting which looked as if it could get rough.

Theo was going home from his City office, and because the evening was fine and dry had decided to walk for a little towards the river and take the underground from the Tower of London rather than from his habitual Cannon Street station. And here, on the edge of that dignified square mile wherein so much of the capitalist world's financing was centred, near the frontier between bankers and dockers, Chance, Chance and Letheby had their offices. Reached by a stout door and a porch with a substantial stone overhang.

Theo wondered whether it might be prudent to ring the bell, excuse himself, and seek sanctuary. There were lights showing through a window, so some staff at Chance, Chance and Letheby were still at work. The noise from about thirty yards away grew louder, and Theo, straining his ears, heard the familiar words, 'I tell you, Comrades!' It was impossible now to move further up the street, which was jammed with people, jostling and craning. He recognized, in the press of curious and frowning faces near him, a few undoubted Party workers. They were always identifiable if one had the key. Theo, Conservative aspirant, discount broker, Cambridge graduate, had the key. He knew the Party line, he understood the technique, he was advised by Marcus, during their long conversations, of the subtleties and twists of

Party policy. And he had the key, he had been enabled to observe, he knew the cries, he could identify. In the shadows, a man concealed and waiting, he was nevertheless perfectly informed – more so, he guessed, than the roughnecks, the foot soldiers now yelling their orchestrated lines, were informed themselves.

The Party line, at the moment, was to concentrate especial violence and hatred against any Labour Party speaker whose public record did not satisfy certain strict criteria which the Communists had privately established. The time would come – and Marcus had already discussed it with Theo, in one of their remarkably free discussions, which Theo was later to realize were most exceptional within the movement and constituted a privilege – when the line would change: when Communists would be instructed to organize a 'broad front', a 'popular front', ostensibly against the forces of Fascism; and when the word would go out to blur ideological differences, to emphasize the need to combine all 'democratic forces', and to infiltrate, organize and control. This lay in the future, but Marcus had already discussed the contingency with Theo, as a man talking theoretical strategy to another capable of understanding it. And Theo had been gratified, and privately thought such a change promising, for he found the rigid sectarianism of the movement at present self-defeating. The matter would be decided by the Comrades in Moscow. Meanwhile Labour, with specific exceptions, had to be shouted down. Outside the offices of Chance, Chance and Letheby it was now being shouted down. A Labour speaker was trying to make himself heard – local government elections were due in some wards in London and although the City regulated its own business under its ancient constitution the politics of the metropolis sometimes intruded.

They intruded now. A man near Theo nudged his neighbour and yelled at the speaker, ' He's a traitor to the working class! Where were you in '26?'

The speaker, well known in London Labour circles, could be seen standing up in an open lorry whose canopy was rolled back. He held a megaphone which distorted speech – producing a loud noise but little sense. There was a united roar from about twelve men, close packed, all very near Theo standing in his doorway.

'Traitor! Where were you in '26?'

Through the megaphone the crowd heard an angry bellow.

'I was on strike in '26! That's where I was! I tell you, Comrades –'

Theo saw a nod from one of the men nearest him, a nod to the others. The man was young and fair-haired. Theo thought, without certainty, that the face was familiar – from Cambridge perhaps. The next roar from the group was well orchestrated.

'Liar! Liar! Liar!'

Unsure what to think or whom to boo or applaud, the small crowd, poorly dressed and seemingly apathetic, turned heads to and fro.

'Liar! Liar! Liar!'

'He betrayed the working class in '26,' shouted the man whose face Theo suspected he knew. The cry was taken up again – 'Betrayed in '26.' There was an imperative gesture and the same man stilled them. Then he yelled – 'And in '31!'

'That's right! And in '31!' Their discipline was excellent, their harmony effective.

'Betrayed the workers in '31!'

'That he didn't!' A small man with a scarf and a cap suddenly shouted from a few feet away. 'That he didn't! Jack never betrayed no one in '31!'

'Bollocks! He was a '31 traitor!'

'That he never!'

''31 traitor!' But the man in the scarf seemed in a towering rage. Theo guessed he was personally loyal to the struggling speaker, from whose megaphone phrases like 'Let me remind you, Comrades' drifted incomprehensibly into what was now a babel of shouts. The man in cap and scarf elbowed two onlookers out of the way, pushed up to the fair young man, yelled 'That he never!' and punched the other in the face.

Whereupon four of the crowd, on a signal from a dark-faced, older man, moved instantly upon him. Theo heard a shrill cry, some more shouts, and then realized the man with cap and scarf was on the ground, and boots were swinging, once, twice, thrice. Suddenly the fair man and his immediate companions had melted away. The crowd began to drift, the megaphone was silent, the lorry could be heard starting up. The small man with cap and scarf lay on the ground, moaning and clutching his stomach. There was blood running down his face and he had retched all over his scarf. Theo looked cautiously up and down the now uncrowded street and decided to walk back towards the Cannon Street or Monument underground station after all. The incident had lasted about four minutes.

As Theo travelled homeward he reflected on the nasty little scene. These things were inevitable, and Heaven knew there'd be more and much worse before the struggle was won. It was war, after all, and the skirmishes, the casualties on a patrol, the apparently idiot sacrifice in small, indecisive engagements were a necessary part of war – war in the real world as opposed to theoretical war, war-as-it-should-be-fought. Theo recognized all that, recognized that the whole historic period through which the Party moved to ultimate triumph was going to be protracted. And during that whole epoch there would be ebb and flow, apparent contradictions, switches of strategy and tactic, incidental enormities, casual as well as designed brutality. Men shouting 'Traitor'; inaccurate as to narrow, actual fact but correct taking the long view, the historic view, the view of the march towards the Revolutionary millennium, a march wherein there could be no neutrals, only Communists, workers, class-enemies and traitors. Wherein, too, a lot of men in caps and scarves would say 'No, he never,' and be knocked down and kicked. Or worse. Wherein, it was taken as axiomatic, many Comrades would also be sacrificed, as many had been already.

All that was historically inevitable, all that was comprehensible – indeed it could not be otherwise. The only principles to hold on to were that the world had changed for ever in 1917, and henceforth war was declared between Revolution and those who resisted it; that the Revolution would be triumphant in the end; and that the struggle must be absolutely unremitting, whether or not the public line was conciliatory or dogmatic in its language.

Unremitting and disciplined; wars can only be won if troops are disciplined, trained and intelligently led. Theo was now a man under discipline, a man who, in his discussions, his long sessions with Marcus – and Headley before him – and in his reading, had some claim to being called trained. And, Theo thought with gratitude rather than complacency, Theo was intelligent. Qualified, therefore, to play an important part, albeit a secret part, in the struggle. A part which, like all responsibility, also demanded personal sacrifice. All his life, at present, was preparation, so that when he had achieved position and when the hour and the opportunities came he would be ready.

He found himself, incongruously, thinking of Wieland Breitfall. He supposed that Wieland had been in many a rough-house of the kind he'd just witnessed – but incomparably bloodier. And for such an intellectually contemptible cause, too! Theo thought of Wieland with personal affection. Wieland had so much charm, such grace, such almost childlike concentration! He had, though probably only half-conscious of it, so obviously found Theo extremely attractive – in his emotions, Theo thought with an inward smile, Wieland was certainly most ingenuous. But Wieland's letters now expressed enormous, embarrassing enthusiasm for the present tide running in Germany and Theo reflected with impatience how absurd it was for a man like Wieland, a good-hearted, albeit not very intelligent man like Wieland, to fall in love – there was no other word nor state to describe it – with a garish, reactionary, *lumpen* cause like Nazism: primitive emotionalism masquerading as a philosophy: simplistic, xenophobic nationalism dressed up as social and economic progress! Pathetic! Theo felt sad and superior. Then he thought of phrases in Wieland's last letter.

'You will soon not recognize things here! Young and old, rich and poor, recognizing that with the leadership and true care one for another we can achieve all things. The Führer has decreed a great programme of road building which is going to transform the German economy by lowering transport unit costs – and meanwhile hundreds of thousands of unemployed are enrolling to give substance to this dream. People told us you can't do things like that without having a great inflation again, printing money. Nonsense! It can be managed, and the Führer has shown how. He has a very clever man at the Reichsbank . . .'

And so on and so on.

Wieland, a dedicated Nazi, saw everything, of course, through rose-coloured spectacles, but still certain short-term achievements were probably being scored, and temporary happiness created. A pity, thought Theo with a tiny stab of envy, that it was all illusion. This was nothing but one of the last kicks of capitalism in its penultimate stage, and the more apparently successful it was, the more dangerous, because it would delude workers into believing that the road to a decent future lay along some other road than that of revolution.

Theo's revolution.

Dangerous, too, because this new, self-confident Germany, this sham workers' state, with its lip-service to National 'Socialism', could be an external threat to the home of the True Revolution, the only True Socialism: to that country wherein it had been decreed that the first task was to secure the Revolution within its borders, leaving the worldwide Revolution to follow when and only when opportunity offered. Dangerous to the Soviet Union, in fact. Just at the moment, relations between Moscow and the new German régime were correct. In the past they had been not only correct but even cordial – a certain community of state interest, Marcus had said coldly when a surprised Theo had first raised the odd matter of military collaboration. But Hitler made no secret of his preoccupations. Communism was Jew-dominated and a menace to mankind. Given that violence of feeling, and the powerful potential of the German Reich at his command, it could be that Hitler would one day turn out to be the Revolution's most formidable enemy – a role reserved hitherto for England, or what Theo, even inwardly, had learned to call English ruling circles.

And with that sort and level of external danger the time might not be very far off when the Party would need to wear another face, speak words of sweet, liberal reason, contemplate and then seek to dominate alliances with all sorts of bourgeois parties and organizations. For a limited period, as Marcus speculated, easily, interestingly, loyally. Theo had read French literature at school, reluctantly memorizing reams of French classical poetry. A line of Racine came to his head: '*J'embrasse mes rivaux, mais pour les étouffer!*'

Embrace them to strangle them! He forgot the rest. It was, he thought he remembered, Nero speaking. Theo moved, yawning, towards the underground escalator. Easter next weekend. Easter, and an invitation to Bargate from the kind Marvells who seemed to have taken him under their wing, and must prefer him as a prospective Parliamentary candidate to that tedious, noisy, sexually aggressive young man, Stephen Paterson, Hilda Marvell's brother. Brother, but little loved, thought Theo with hope and excitement. The Marvells were not only friendly, protective almost; they were, too, sympathetic in the matter of Emma. And Emma would be there. She had been elusive recently and he had been intensely busy, but now it was Eastertide and Emma would be there.

'You should not have come here. I did not want you to come here.'

Sonja was standing on one of the bridges across the Main in the exquisite old city of Bamberg in Franconia. The cathedral's four steepled towers loomed on the hill rising from the river, along whose bank the decorated house walls curved prettily like a stage set in some expensively produced opera of the rococo period. Sonja knew Bamberg well. A particularly understanding friend lived here, a widow whose husband had built up a business as a music publisher and left it to his wife. Sonja had loved them both. 'You are like a particularly difficult piece of modern music,' Karl Reitz used to say to her affectionately, 'with a lot of discords and shocks to the system!' He would add with a sweet smile,

'But alternating with passages of great harmony and beauty, of course!' Karl Reitz had died in 1931 and for Sonja the Reitz house could always be a refuge. Especially in unspeakable circumstances like these. Edle Reitz had been quiet, consolatory, discreet. Sonja was frightened of getting her into trouble by their association. Was she, Sonja, not a contaminator now?

'Nonsense. I'm well known in Bamberg, for Heaven's sake! I entertain whom I wish!'

But Sonja was not so sure. Anyway – and she found herself reflecting on it with repugnance at the implications – the Reitzes were at least not Jews. While with part of her she, Sonja, was Jew indeed.

'I did not want you to come here.'

'I know that. I understand. But I wasn't prepared to come to Germany without finding you. I love you.'

'Don't be ridiculous! All that was –'

'You wrote. You wrote "my distant lover". I want to be your not-distant lover.'

'One writes!' said Sonja, trembling, 'one writes! But now you should not be here. I hoped you would not find where I had gone.'

'But I did. Sonja, are you really angry that I've found you? Do you really want me to go away?'

'Yes! I want! Go away!'

Desmond smiled and took her arm, very gently, and very confidently. She had at first started away from him when, a few minutes ago, he had tried to put an arm round her. Her body had been rigid. Then she had let him kiss her lips, her own mouth stiff and unyielding. Now, with something like a shudder, she allowed her arm to be linked in his and they began to stroll down from the bridge and along the riverside pavement. They were entirely silent. After a while Desmond thought he sensed the beginning of relaxation. This was a great woman after all, he reflected, and her resilience was likely to be formidable. Given a little time.

'Desmond, do you know –'

'Yes. I know everything. And I think I understand everything.'

She breathed deeply and Desmond said, 'Talk about it, if you can. Torture yourself by bringing the words, the description of pain even, the brutality, the humiliation out into the open. Like an accident that's happened to you. Or like a soldier wounded in battle, I imagine. If you can – and just now you probably can't. But it will be better to do that, when you can. Better than burying it inside you. Better when you can say – "Do you know what some louts did to me? If I'd had a few friends beside me I'd have watched them being knocked about themselves, but they caught me alone, worse luck!" I know I sound heartless but when you can –'

'Not heartless. Sensible.' She smiled at him for the first time and he felt a small squeeze to his upper arm. She murmured, 'But just now –'

'Of course. Just now you need peace, affection. I'm told you're staying with a very nice woman.'

'Certainly – a delightful woman. But how did you learn about Edle Reitz?'

'Never mind. Would she have me to stay too?'

'I'm not sure,' said Sonja after a long pause, 'I'm not sure, my darling.'

'Because I've no room booked in Bamberg. My luggage is at the station. I called at Frau Reitz's house and they said you had gone for a walk and I should aim for the river. I did. I knew perfectly well I should find you.'

Sonja said nothing.

'So I suggest we return to Haus Reitz and you ask her whether I could stay a few days. I understand your Frau Reitz is rather rich, so I won't feel a rotter.'

'Desmond, it might be better that you stay at an hotel.'

'It might be, but I don't think so.'

He had no intention of telling Sonja that he had enjoyed ten minutes' conversation with Frau Reitz. She had stared at him and said, 'You are the young Englishman she has spoken much about. Who was there when Rodoski was murdered.' And Desmond had said, 'Spoken much about? Spoken recently?' And Frau Reitz had said, 'Not recently. Before. You know about it

126

all?' He'd nodded, his breath short again as it always was when he was reminded of what they'd done to Sonja. And Frau Reitz had said, in a quiet, normal sort of voice, 'You should come to spend some days in my house. You will be welcome. It will be right, I know it will be right for her. It will be good. But she must suggest it.'

'I understand.' And he had set out, with perfect confidence that chance would direct his steps towards Sonja in the throng of the busy old city. And it had happened. It was mid-April.

Desmond had sat in absolute silence, a terrible silence, while Wieland Breitfall had occupied a neighbouring chair that evening a week ago in Kitzi Fischer's study. Wieland's visit had been unexpected and even the urbane, confident Kitzi had been embarrassed. Certain though he was that his nephew, however wrongheaded, would never participate in thuggery of the sort for which Desmond Dillon was now in his heart accusing the whole Nazi movement and most of Germany, Kitzi nevertheless had planned to keep his English guest and his Nazi nephew well apart during Desmond's stay in Berlin. And then Wieland had walked in – for a short visit, to apologize for recent neglect of his uncle. And Desmond had shaken his hand, taken by surprise and too stunned to make some gesture; some refusal of his hand perhaps, even shouts and violence. But that was unlikely, Kitzi thought. He has passion but he has control. And breeding, too.

Desmond had resumed his chair, said no word, once inclined his head when Kitzi, a touch desperate, tried to include him in their brief conversation, but uttered nothing. The atmosphere around him was like frost in a Berlin January. And after ten minutes Wieland had left. Kitzi then said, 'As I told you, he –' glanced at Desmond's face and said no more.

Now Sonja was walking at Desmond's side.

'I don't think so,' he said again, smiling down at her frowning face, referring to her suggestion that he find an hotel. She sighed. Then he felt her arm again violently a-tremble and she almost stopped in her walk, checking him too.

Walking towards them, three abreast, came a little knot of brown-shirted SA troopers. They were laughing and chatting, and

Desmond could see the smiles, the courteous, almost obsequious smiles directed at them by passers-by. The SA men radiated confidence and good humour. The Party had been strong from the outset in Franconia and it was clear these young men were moving among friends. Several handshakes were exchanged, and here and there a salute. It was a fine April day, a time for midday sauntering. The great clock on the cathedral hill chimed half past twelve. Desmond murmured to Sonja, 'Come on!'

'I –'

'I said "come on",' he said, quite loudly, roughly. 'If you intend to go on living in Germany you can hardly keep getting the shivers every time you see a member of the SA! The streets are full of them! And nobody knows you here!'

She snorted, almost with temper. Then he felt her resistance fading, she fell more easily into step with him, arm still linked with his. They passed the group of Brown Shirts and Desmond said, '*Grüss Gott!*'

'*S' Gott.*' One of the group answered, and all three nodded to Desmond, with mild curiosity for so obvious a foreigner, and with no attention for Sonja beyond a half-smile that comes to a man's eyes when he spots a pretty woman. Desmond walked steadily on, and after a few minutes said, conversationally, 'Well, shall we go back and see Frau Reitz?' And Sonja said, with another of her small sighs, 'Yes. If that's what you'd like.'

'It is what I'd like. It is exactly what I'd like.'

'How long do you propose to stay in Germany, Desmond?'

'I don't know. How long do you?'

'It's my home.'

'You should consider leaving home for a little. Bandits have occupied it. Until the police eject them you might be best staying with friends abroad.'

'Like where?'

'Like in England.'

'I don't think so,' Sonja muttered, and he was happy to hear a touch of animation in her voice although not consoled by what it said. 'I don't think so. This thing here will pass. There will be a reaction, perhaps quite soon. You know it's said that they're planning to ban – actually to outlaw – all other parties? All other parties!'

Desmond had heard. Kitzi had spoken of it. And in Wieland's eyes, Kitzi said, it was entirely reasonable.

'Well?'

'Well, people won't stand for it. It's going too far. That only one party should be allowed uniforms and so forth – that, maybe. But to *outlaw all other organizations*! Desmond –'

'You say people won't stand for that. I think they will.'

Sonja was silent, and he knew her heart told her that he, the foreigner, not she, the experienced German journalist, was the more perceptive in this case. Together they walked quietly towards Frau Reitz's house, the months of separation already dissolving into insignificance.

Emma yawned. If, as now, England had a really warm April, it knocked one over; the snows of winter only a week or so ago and here, suddenly, the heat of the sun, a drowsy, deliciously enfeebling heat, a heat which conveyed an almost forbidden joy, so premature was it, so incongruous while the branches of trees were still bare. Bargate, and Sussex, and England generally, were looking beautiful. Emma, like all of them, knew that it wouldn't last. 'We'll pay for this before the month's out,' people said, 'We'll probably be drowned by the beginning of May!' John Marvell grumbled that the early warmth together with the continuing night frosts were a danger to some agricultural and horticultural concerns of which Emma was blissfully ignorant. She said, 'Let's enjoy it while it lasts,' and slipped her hand in the crook of Theo's arm.

'Sure you don't want to go to the point-to-point with the others? We could follow on – Hilda said, "Do what you want."' The point-to-point was very local and had led to no administrative complications in the Marvell household. Some people had decided to support the occasion and watch a few of the races, but no pressure had been applied.

Theo laughed. 'Quite sure.'

'Don't you think you ought to be seen around at local oc-casions?' Emma chuckled. Theo's ambitions were a pretty open secret at Bargate, smiled on by most of them.

'No, I'm really quite sure. We'll walk to the end of the garden and go through that small gate and see if the bluebells are out. I was here two years ago in bluebell time. Nice.'

'Nice.'

Emma's heart was beating quite fast. It was the first time during the weekend that she had been alone with Theo. Hilda Marvell had smiled at her, not conspiratorially but with a sort of gentle and understanding goodwill. Emma tried to tell herself that she was uncertain what she felt or wanted. This was false. She knew perfectly well that she felt her whole body pulsing with increased life when it was near Theo's, and that her heart and imagination were full most minutes of most days with pictures of him. What she found wretchedly uncertain was how Theo himself felt. During these last nine months, rather agonizing months although she despised herself for feeling so, he had been attent-ive, taken her out often, given her dinner, danced with her, kissed her – but lightly, lingeringly, and then broken off, held her, looked at her, smiled and said things like 'Soon?' and then they'd part. 'Be at home. I'll telephone,' he'd said when they'd last been together at this enchanted Bargate, and she'd fallen in love, no doubt of it, she irritatedly supposed and sometimes put in words to herself.

Sometimes he seemed moved by perceptible emotion and she thought he was going to make it clear that his feelings exactly mirrored her own, a condition of utter bliss, a contentment barely to be imagined. At other times he seemed restrained, never unmoved by her but almost as if anxious, puzzled. She always tried to keep her voice steady and topics between them as neutral, as general as possible. If Theo loved her, he'd set the pace all right. To try to lead or encourage would be to court humiliation. Nor could it conceivably work. Not with Theo.

Emma said, as they walked, 'Have you seen or heard anything more of Adrian Winter?'

130

'Yes. He asked me to lunch with him in London and then cancelled it. Said he had a heavy cold.'

'You must have been annoyed. You've got lots of hopes in that direction, haven't you, Theo?'

'Of course. He knows that, everybody knows that. It would be a great thing if he backed me to succeed him when he stands down. Your mother –'

Theo hesitated and they strolled on in quiet for a few moments until Emma said, 'Mother sees Adrian quite often. He treats her rather like a pet poodle but, oddly enough, he listens to her. For some reason he thinks she's got feminine intuition or something. Perceptive about people.'

'And isn't she?'

'You've met her often, Theo. You know she's entirely superficial!'

Theo chuckled.

'That can go with intuition. One's antennae may be sharp although one's interests are silly and one's powers of reasoning negligible.'

'You believe so?'

'I do.'

He was thinking of Patsy, and said, 'Anyway, I think and hope she's put in a word for me.'

Emma said nothing to this, and Theo felt it likely that Patsy, in some mood or other, might have uttered something derogatory about Theo in her hearing; Emma probably assumed such might also have been expressed to Winter. Nothing of the sort followed, of course. Theo recalled Patsy's 'Are you trying to turn my little girl's head?' and supposed, without concern, that Patsy, for her own reasons, had tried to put Emma off Theo. A vain effort, he thought complacently, a futile attempt by a mother whose daughter anyway despised her. But what he himself really wanted he was unsure. He glanced down at Emma and thought how pretty she was, how slender and delicate her bones, how graceful the set of her head. She was intelligent, she was stimulating, she would be an enormous help in a political life. And as she fell into step beside him he thought he cared about her a very great deal

– more than for anybody in life so far; which perhaps wasn't saying a lot.

And as they wandered, the small, icy stab which Theo felt at the heart from time to time disturbed and spoiled his contentment. For his reactions to events and people – even to Emma – could never be simple, could never be untouched by deceit. There suddenly came back to him an indiscreet word from Patsy about Emma. Pillow talk, once. He'd mentioned Desmond and his sister, lazily stroking Patsy's flesh.

'They're not very like you! Are they like their father? Your departed Dillon?'

Patsy had smiled, then said very softly, 'Dillon wasn't their father!'

'*Really?*'

'Really?' Theo could see she enjoyed the sensation of confession, like most women. 'Really!' She'd not answered his amused queries. And on some later occasion he'd said to Marcus, also probing about the Dillons, 'They're illegitimate, as it happens.'

'Ah!' Marcus had shrugged. 'That sort of immorality,' he had said, 'is not uncommon in those circles, of course!' It was of no interest, why should it be, but when Marcus said, 'those circles', something in Theo stirred and itched. Patsy, her lovers, Desmond, Emma, even the unregenerate Theo – these were all 'circles', puppets exactly placed by class as defined by the prophet Marx and presumed, indeed compelled, to act and react in an exactly prescribed way. Even in bed. Theo had smiled at Marcus coolly but had, for a moment, wanted to hit what – astonishingly – he found he was describing to himself as his bloody, vulgar little face.

Now the memory came back to him, and the drab, uncomprehending words and image, 'not uncommon in those circles!' Emma looked up at him suddenly and smiled. With his arm round her now, they sauntered on. Bother her parentage, Theo thought, bother everything but her beauty and her sweetness. I know her now. I need her now. But, alas, alas, she can never know me, all of me.

132

The young Marvells, breaking free from their elders, walked quickly towards one of the point-to-point fences. Anthony, nearly seventeen years old, felt important, secretive and a little guilty. He had bet ten shillings on 'Easter Bonnet' to win the next race, and it was more than he could easily afford. Marcia tried to lengthen her stride to match his. She was nearly three years younger, a dark-haired, rather plump but very pretty girl with brilliant eyes, and a perpetual laugh in them. The Easter holidays were always particularly enjoyable, with everything at Bargate emerging from winter, a crackle of frost succeeded by a warm sun on the fortunate days. This holiday Monday was one such. Anthony's tweed cap was set very straight on his rather narrow, handsome head. His mind was fiercely on Easter Bonnet.

'Ant, what do you think of Tate? Theo Tate?'

'I don't like him.'

'Nor do I. Any reason?'

'I don't like the way he watches people, with that little smile. Then, if you speak to him, he widens the smile as if he were pulling a string.'

'Mum and Dad like him. They want him to be our MP when old Mr Winter gives up. Him, not Uncle Stephen.'

'Anything would be better than Uncle Stephen. Hurry up,' he added as Marcia showed signs of flagging. A glance at his watch told Anthony that the race was due in four minutes and their selected fence was still some way off across the rolling parkland in which the point-to-point was set. Still, these races always started late.

'Anything better than Uncle Stephen,' Marcia nodded, turning her head to peer towards the starting point of the race, some five hundred yards behind them now, 'but I hope it's not Mr Tate. He'd always be coming over, or staying or something. I can't think why Mummy likes him.'

'He's very good-looking. Makes himself very agreeable.'

'He's not what I call good-looking. He looks like a girl. Almost.'

'He's dead keen on Emma.'

'Well,' said Marcia judiciously, 'she's keen on him. That's

133

certain. I'm not so sure about him. Do you know another thing?'

They only had a hundred yards to walk now, and the race had not started. Anthony slackened pace, relaxed a little, and said, loftily, 'What other thing?' He imagined he should not encourage Marcia in any improper conjectures.

'What other thing?'

'Just this. Emma's mother –'

'What about her?'

'Remember she was staying here, and Desmond *and* Emma all together. And Tate, last year. House was full.'

'Last summer. Of course I remember. It was school leave.'

'I went into the library on Sunday morning before lunch. I thought everyone was in the garden. The door was open, and immediately I walked in – I was still behind the screen – I knew there was somebody in the room. I stopped for a second behind the screen.' A large screen protected the Bargate library from door draughts.

'What about it? Who was it?'

'Tate. With Patsy Dillon.'

'Why shouldn't they be?'

'I put my eyes to the screen gap, Ant. He'd got her in his arms all right. Kissing her something fierce, he was.' Marcia giggled. At the time she had, as it happened, been somewhat shaken. Theo Tate, although a grown-up, was a young member of that species. Patsy Dillon belonged to their mother's generation. It was upsetting. Anthony frowned. He said in a worldly-wise voice, 'I expect she likes mothering him, and he plays up. He's a friend of Desmond's, and we know how old Winter dotes on her, so Tate butters her up, obviously.'

'I suppose so,' Marcia said, 'and the mothering was being quite fun as far as I could see.'

'You've not talked about it?'

''Course not.'

'Don't. You'd no business to spy. And Mum would be upset and not know what to say.'

'Ant, I didn't spy! I –'

'And now shut up.' Anthony gripped with a feverish thrill a

pair of his father's binoculars as a bell chimed to tell them that nine Adjacent Hunt competitors were setting off towards the first fence.

On the same day that the Marvells enjoyed a Sussex point-to-point and Emma walked with Theo Tate in the Bargate woods, Desmond lay with Sonja in his arms in a bedroom of Frau Reitz's house. Frau Reitz had announced that she was making a day excursion to Nuremberg to where *ein alter Vetter* was unwell, and all through the afternoon Desmond and Sonja had lain on one of Frau Reitz's large beds, making love, talking drowsily, sleeping a little, and making love again. It was the first time in Bamberg – Desmond had arrived three days earlier, and Sonja had smiled, patted his arm dismissively and said good night each evening in a way that showed she meant it; and Desmond for once was determined not to hurry her.

But the previous evening Frau Reitz had announced her plans, and after they had wished her a safe journey and she had reminded Sonja of one or two domestic details, the door had closed and a taxi had been heard starting up to take Frau Reitz to the station. And Desmond had turned, and with a gasp of passion now impossible to stem any longer, seized Sonja and held her close. And within minutes they were upstairs, naked and alone. And the hours passed magically, more magically than any Desmond had ever known. Frau Reitz had been generous and hospitable, saying that Desmond must stay at her house as long as he wished. Desmond was deeply grateful. He suspected that the old cousin's indisposition was not particularly serious. Frau Reitz had been very exact and explicit about when she would be returning home that evening. Seven o'clock. A good woman, Frau Reitz, although sometimes Desmond thought her eyes were uneasy.

Now, in an interval between love-making, Sonja clearly wanted to talk about the Nazi phenomenon – at first no doubt forcing herself to do so, but then speaking with more and more freedom and passion. Desmond was glad. The dark places needed the

135

light of frank description letting into them. There were matters which needed exorcism, and only Sonja could do that. His arm caressed her bare shoulder.

'It is not,' said Sonja, 'just what's happening inside Germany. I am sure that will pass – maybe this year in spite of everything. They are already more than can be borne, these people. But it concerns everyone – the whole world.'

'Certainly it concerns everyone. Behaviour like this –'

'Desmond, when they are really well established in power, if it comes to that, they will throw off their masks, you know. There will be a great drive towards rearmament.' Desmond knew that she had said 'when' they are really well established; adding 'if it comes to that' as a near-despairing rider. Whatever Sonja's brave talk about the Nazi régime being unlikely to last, he knew that she had, inwardly, given up hope of seeing its end. He nodded to what she said about rearmament – it was a matter in which her contacts and her information had always allegedly been outstanding. Had that not led, indeed, to – to the beastliness?

Non-committally he said, 'There's this disarmament conference at Geneva, of course.'

'Of course. But who thinks that Hitler will stay at the table for long? Read his book! For a bit, of course, things will be kept quiet, played in a low key. But later –'

'That won't necessarily alarm everybody as much as you think, as much as perhaps it should,' said Desmond. 'Lots of people in a country like England think Germany has been kept in a pretty ignominious position, you know. There'll be at least a bit of sympathy for some muscle-flexing. And, after all, German armed forces have been kept at such a ridiculously puny level that any really big change is bound to take years and years, I imagine. In these days. I'm not a soldier, but –'

'No. You are not a soldier, but you think it's obvious. My dearest Desmond, have you forgotten those things I once told you, about the secret preparations, their secret understanding with the Soviets? Things that were done long before Hitler, but he's inherited the benefits? Things which *they* told me I'd talked about too much though God knows why they reckoned so or who had told of me? Have you forgotten?' He wished she would forget all that. It had, largely, got her into the horrors of March – Sonja's painful account had corroborated Kitzi's suspicions on that score. All that story, anyway, belonged to the past.

'Of course I've not forgotten.'

'They set up a special office with a branch in Moscow in '23, you know. To organize the design and manufacture of weapons we've been forbidden. *GEFU – Gesellschaft zur Forderung gewerblichen Unternehmungen* – that was its name. "Industrial Undertakings", very harmless! And it started these training schools I told you about – the flying centre near Lipetsk –'

'And the tank centre at Kazan, on the Volga. You told me. But Sonja –'

'When there were some revelations they disbanded the office, but they kept the practice going, I can tell you.' Sonja's voice was remorseless. It was a subject on which she had a certain obsession. She was determined to impress its significance on Desmond. 'This has given the Reichswehr a trained, experienced cadre, you see. They will expand very fast when Hitler gives the word. The Luftwaffe too – there will be a Luftwaffe, of course.'

'Of course. But Sonja, darling, it's still going to take years and years, you know. And it's never been clear to me why, if what you say is true –'

'It is true.'

'Why the Russians have been doing it. What the Bolsheviks have got out of it. After all, Hitler has always described Bolshevism as the greatest enemy, hasn't he? In which,' added Desmond, 'I think I incline to agree with him.' Sonja nodded, as if used to the question.

'There was this Marshal Tukachevsky. Have you heard of him?'

'No.'

'Ex-Czarist officer. Very young, brilliant, joined the Reds. They made him head of the Red Army in about 1925. He arranged most of it. He wanted to pool experience. He wanted

137

Soviet officers to go on our military courses, to attend our *Kriegsakademie* although its name has been changed, to learn our ways. It was natural. After all,' said Sonja, and Desmond was amazed to recognize in her voice, despite her views and background, a note of unquestioning pride, 'our training has always been admired by everybody. It was natural the Russians should wish to learn from us. They always have. So their officers secretly attended our military schools.'

'And still do?'

Sonja said, 'I'm not sure. But, as you say, from what Hitler says about the Soviet Union one can't imagine that sort of thing can go on long. Meanwhile both sides have benefited, you see. And it will make everything go quicker here, very quick indeed when Hitler decides. Then you'll all see why one says it's not just an internal problem here. They have been sowing the dragon's teeth, Desmond – like the warrior-goddess told Cadmus to plant, and then, as he watched, the soil heaved and instead of corn growing he saw spearpoints show, and helmets and finally armed men, rising from the ground, ready to fight. You know the story?' Desmond smiled at her and started to move his hands across her body and search her again with his lips. They had been discussing, he thought, quite a long time. He said, 'I seem to remember they then started fighting each other!'

But Sonja did not smile back and for a moment did not respond to him. Desmond knew that she still needed to talk. So be it. There were still several hours before Frau Reitz's return.

'A strong Germany again,' Desmond said slowly but without any particular stab of concern, for he thought the idea right, however vicious and criminal the régime which seemed set on bringing it about. 'A strong Germany. But it's not for that I want you to leave, my love. It's *Nazi* Germany.' For Desmond, in these hours at Bamberg, had discovered in his heart a real, a profound tenderness for Sonja and had several times reiterated that she should leave the country. As a mistress she was delicious, as an intelligent, quick, perceptive human being she was fascinating. He realized, with a certain self-contempt, that she might not entirely fit into his life in England. Sonja was incurably – 'well,' Desmond thought with self-mockery, 'she's utterly, utterly *foreign*!' But Desmond thought that what he felt for Sonja was very certainly love now. They would not stay together for all life – that was unlikely to be Desmond's way and he was pretty sure it would never be Sonja's way. Yet even in that he might be mistaken, and he loathed the idea of abandoning her in a country which, for her views and her indiscretions and perhaps for her blood as well, regarded her as something of an outcast. And might again savage her as such. Yet when he had earlier said, 'Come to England with me,' she had said, doggedly, 'No. It is impossible. I have good friends here. All this will pass.' He knew she did not believe it and his heart ached wretchedly.

He had murmured, 'Perhaps a visit to London, darling? In the summer?' He thought that something disguised as a temporary visit might provide such a relief from insecurity that she would seek to stay, although God knew how that could be accomplished. Desmond would, he thought, manage it somehow. But Sonja, he knew, had no mind for flight.

'London?' he had said. 'In the summer?'

Sonja was realistic. She was genuinely stirred by Desmond, but she recognized that their affair was an interlude, although it had meant something to her, her letters to Desmond had been sincere, her emotion when he found her in Bamberg a genuine reaction. She had muttered 'Perhaps', and smiled at him. Perhaps indeed. It would certainly be joyful. She had never been to England. But there were devils to exorcize here at home and Sonja could not yet face the fact that her incantations might be inadequate to the task. Meanwhile they were in bed and their bodies were content. It was something.

Emma lay on a raincoat stretched on the grass in a tiny clearing in Bargate woods. Theo's arms were tight around her. They had kissed and kissed. No more. Once Theo murmured, 'Do you think –?'

'Think what?'

He had pressed his mouth to hers again. After a little Emma said, 'What's this all meant to mean, Theo?'

'I'm not sure.' His hand caressed her ear.

'We ought to be getting back.'

'Why? They'll be at their beastly point-to-point for hours yet. Emma, you're interested in politics.'

'In a way. My politics aren't yours. In fact, they're the exact opposite of yours. Hey –' Theo's hand was gently moving up and down beneath her skirt. She discouraged it, smiling at him and he smiled back and said, 'I doubt that. Not really. You care about people.'

'I certainly do.'

'So do I . We simply differ – if we differ at all – about the best way to help them.' True so far, Theo thought. True so far. It was always rather amusing how infrequently one's words had actually to be lies. Interpretation was all.

Emma said stoutly, 'You're a dyed-in-the-wool Tory. You're trying to get a Conservative seat. I don't believe any Tory could feel as I feel –'

'Not any?'

'Not any. And Desmond says you're a real deep-blue sort, Theo.'

She added, 'And you're doing various things you oughtn't to do at the moment.'

'License my roving hand and –'

'I seem to have heard that quotation before. You've got rather a vulpine look about you, even when you smile –'

'Foxy?'

'Perhaps I mean lupine. Wolfish!'

Theo laughed, and put his hands behind his head. Emma felt enormously happy. Theo looked very tenderly into her eyes and said, 'I repeat. I care about people. I want them to have better lives. I want to improve society. I mind about the feeblenesses and the uglinesses and the discordances in our country. You're with me in all that.'

'In aims, yes. In policies, never.'

'How do you know?'

Emma, stronger on grievances than remedies, was unsure and looked at him with a small frown, smugly wishing that they could stay lying on a raincoat in Bargate woods on this astonishingly warm, dry April day for ever.

'Emma, you're terribly good for me. You could help me enormously. Disagreements on things like political measures don't matter a damn. Two people need some sort of argument between them to produce the best of both. A dialogue – that's what a relationship has to be.' His hand was active again. Emma didn't stop him, but thought she'd keep the conversation as political as possible.

'Theo, what about things going on abroad? What about Germany?'

'Well, what about Germany?'

'I mean, the Nazis, and all that.'

'The Nazis and all that? What are you talking about? They're a nasty bunch, but –'

'Darling Theo.' Emma heard herself say that with a thrill of forwardness. Kissed they had. Theo's hands had been active in caressing her and were still at it. But endearments had been few.

'Darling Theo, there's a story that you're rather keen on the Nazis, that you've travelled in Germany, that you've got friends. I rather gather some people – I mean people who might matter to you, people in Adrian Winter's constituency, that sort of thing – don't approve.'

'Good God!' Theo moved his hand from under Emma's skirt, raised himself on an elbow and stared at her.

'Good God, that's utter nonsense! It's a travesty! Who on earth –'

His eyes were angry. Emma thought how beautiful he looked when animated thus. She felt a thrill and smiled at him.

'I expect it amounts to very little. I was in the room once when Hilda Marvell was having tea with Mummy and Adrian. Adrian Winter. I can't remember which of them it was who first said something like – "Theo Tate's a most intelligent man, and I hope he's not taken in by his German friends. One of them is a complete Nazi, and yet Theo thinks the world of him. It can't do him any good!" Something like that.'

'You can't remember which said it?'

'No. It might have been Mummy.'

'Yes,' said Theo savagely, 'it might have been Mummy. And what did anyone else say?'

'Oh, nothing much. Hilda said people didn't really take much interest in foreign affairs. Adrian nodded, and said, "I'm sure Theo will see through the Nazis in due course. Pity. That sort of thing gets distorted in the telling." '

'He said "Pity", did he? Like that?'

'Yes. He did. You see, Adrian's first wife whom he adored, Mummy's cousin, was killed in a riot the Nazis provoked. Adrian obviously feels sick whenever he thinks of them in power. He's awfully fair about Germany as such, as you know. But Hitler and his gang really upset him. Rightly, as I'm sure you really agree.'

Theo was looking at her with his mind working. He said, abruptly, 'Emma, let's go back to the house. I think I need to write a letter.'

'OK. What letter?' Emma felt a sense of anti-climax. An enchanted hour had ended, and ended with tiresome suddenness. It was colder, too.

'A letter to *The Times*.' Then he turned her to him, took her in his arms again and whispered, 'Do you know, I believe I love you?' And Emma walked back, comparatively contented, at his side.

Theo's letter to *The Times* was published on the Wednesday after Easter. It drew several admiring sequels and a number of people telephoned to say that he had put, and put brilliantly, exactly what they and every decent-minded person had been thinking. Theo discussed the Nazi assumption of power – as yet, simply a Nazi Chancellor, with the Nazis the largest single party, rather than an outright attempt to strangle opposition. The letter expressed in concise, thoughtful terms the resentments which

Germans of every political colour had harboured in the aftermath of the War: it reminded, eloquently, of the German people's sufferings from defeat, starvation, revolution, inflation, and then starvation and unemployment once again. Everyone, wrote Theo, sympathized with the just efforts of any German government which determined to attack evils at source and to prevent their recurrence. Nor was the appeal to patriotism one which Englishmen despised, however stridently expressed. But, Theo's letter continued in a tone like that of an anxious friend, certain things reported now from Germany would alienate every well-wisher, would repel exactly those from whom Germany should in other circumstances expect understanding and support. Theo touched upon some of the cruder brutalities that had been publicized at German election time, he wrote sternly of the vicious language by some 'vociferous members of the dominant Party' about Jews and foreigners, he referred with measured gravity to the rumours that the government was planning suppressive action against rival political organizations. His letter ended with a plea to Germans, in or out of government – 'Help your friends here to help you.' It was a masterpiece of balance and of principled, understanding exhortation. It was also comparatively short. Theo, a young man, could have been criticized for presumptuousness in apparently addressing a foreign nation from so exalted a private viewpoint. But in no way could he have ever again been thought gentle towards National Socialism.

Emma was entranced. There was a phrase in it – 'if you make genuine steps towards solving the scourge of unemployment from which we are all bleeding, we will watch, admire and learn. But –'

'It's a wonderful letter.' Theo showed it to her immediately it was drafted. The point-to-point party had not yet returned. Theo put his cheek against hers and murmured, 'Go on helping me.' Then he murmured again, yet more softly, 'For always, perhaps.'

He meant it, he knew she was becoming necessary to him, that calculation and true feeling were beginning to blend, that life without Emma was daily less enticing a prospect. There would be problems, pushed into the shade by the attractions. And Emma put her arms round him and told herself that together they could beat the world.

CHAPTER VII

The chairman of Adrian Winter's constituency Conservative Association, John Bates, was an old friend. Bates spent in each week two days and one morning in the City of London. The morning was always Thursday and often on Thursday afternoon when the House of Commons wasn't sitting (and sometimes when it was) Bates used to drive to Addington golf course and play a round with Adrian Winter. It was an agreeable way to chat about the state of England in general and the constituency in particular: but more often than not they simply enjoyed the golf and the fresh air.

On the last Thursday in July 1933 they were playing their round, the first for some weeks. John Bates had decided that he would, once again, press the matter of a candidate to take over from old Adrian. They had had a constructive talk at the beginning of the year and Adrian had advanced some ideas. Since then he seemed to have shelved the subject. But it needed resolution, Bates thought – this National Government would seek a new electoral mandate some time in the next two years – it was predominantly Conservative in fact if not in name, and a good many people felt the situation should be recognized by an overtly Conservative administration, returned as such by the people, without too much delay. Bates understood that Baldwin was of the same mind, but he would, of course, choose the best tactical moment. Nevertheless Prime Ministers kept their counsel and these things could happen quickly, unexpectedly. It was essential to be ready, and a new man would need time to get his face known in the constituency. Labour had made such a hash of things that there shouldn't be much doubt, but Bates believed in caution and groundwork. He remembered the fiasco of 1906 when Tory seat after Tory seat had fallen to Campbell-Bannerman's Liberal forces, with their idiotic programmes and specious promises. The Tories had been out of office as a party until the twenties in consequence, and the wounds were still raw.

John Bates shook Adrian's hand at the clubhouse and they set out on their round, both silent at first. Bates had seen too many examples in various walks of life of men hanging on to office, believing themselves indispensable, doubting the capacity of any successor, until long after the moment they were useful. Adrian was wonderful – a shrewd, conscientious, popular Member who'd done them proud and carried his years buoyantly; but he'd first come into the House in the 'eighties and everyone knew he should have gone before the '31 election. He'd talked then of 'duty', of 'the crisis', of 'soldiering on'. Of course! People did! And old Adrian had been splendid earlier, coming back again after a spell of ill health had made him resign the seat before the War, serving through the demanding 'twenties, not to speak of the War itself. He cut a lot of ice in the House; everybody said so, despite his age. People listened to him, trusted him, knew he was far beyond personal ambition at seventy-two, not far from being father of the House. In the constituency he was indefatigable, courteous, sensible. It was hard to do these things without a wife, and God knew that Adrian had suffered in that direction, but he never let them down, whatever the occasion. A great Member.

But a great Member who was in danger of outstaying his welcome. He shouldn't face another election, another Parliament. They must find a new man. It never occurred to Bates to say to himself 'or woman'. Not in their particular constituency.

Driving a short, straight ball to a little plateau on the crook of a left-hand dog-leg hole, John Bates said, 'I suppose you've been going on sorting your ideas out about a young chap to take your place, Adrian, when the sad day comes? You had some thoughts when we talked a few months ago, I remember.'

'Oh, I've got ideas I'd like to discuss with you some time, John.' Adrian Winter also hit a short, steady drive, very straight and rather low. The weather and the course were dry and the ball ran a good way. Adrian looked at it with modest satisfaction, smiled at his companion and said, 'No hurry, John. No hurry. God's been good to me lately. I'm pretty fit. And things in Parliament are quiet just now. None of the gruelling stuff we used to go through when I was younger! Night after night – Lord, I don't know how we stuck it! With Asquith tight as often as not, and by no means the only one! Night after night!' He chuckled, reminiscent, and the two caddies, walking respectfully at a little distance, saw the chuckle and grinned back, without having heard or shared the cause of it.

John Bates nodded, smiled sympathetically. He made himself say, 'Still, Adrian, we've got to have a new man in position well before a general election. You've said that yourself.' And suppose you had another heart attack, he thought! You're seventy-two, damn it! We've got to grasp this nettle. Driving down to Addington he had told himself that he would indeed grasp it. Now, taking a number three iron from his caddy, he topped his ball, which nevertheless ran on straight and fast over the hard turf, down the hill, clear of trouble. The two men fell into step again.

'You've said that yourself,' he repeated, 'and after all we're in mid-Parliament, and this National business can't last for ever. You're better informed than I am, Adrian, but it seems to me we've got to have our plans ready.'

Adrian Winter grunted, a sound expressive of reluctant acceptance rather than agreement; a rather querulous sound. He said, 'I think I've talked to you about a young fellow called Theo Tate.'

'You have.'

'He's clever. And keen. Got charm. Handsome boy, articulate. I believe he'd do well in the House, make a name. I doubt if any party would ignore him for long.'

'Well? He's got no county associations, I believe you said?'

'Lots of friends. He'd have supporters all right.'

'Married?'

'Not yet,' said Adrian, 'but I suspect it's not far off.'

'That would help.'

It might have been tactless in view of the tragedies of the other's life but John Bates knew him too well. They had often discussed the matter. He said again, 'That would help.'

They were silent for a while, putting on the fast, beautifully kept green. Adrian made no direct response about the electoral advantage Theo Tate could derive from matrimony. It was the conventional wisdom, but in this case he was far from sure. John Bates said, with careful casualness, 'Hadn't I better meet him?'

'Perfectly easy to arrange,' said Adrian, a little gruffly. 'He's often at Bargate, for instance. John Marvell. And as you know, because we discussed that too, you've got another hopeful there. Stephen Paterson, Hilda Marvell's young brother.'

'Paterson's got stronger connections.'

'But he's less intelligent, John! And, frankly, less likeable. Nothing like the elder Paterson brother.' For Hilda Marvell's elder brother, Cosmo Paterson, had been a unique person, an adventurer, a creature of original mind, dancing eyes and unpredictable charm, killed as the Germans had marched forward on their last supreme attempt in the West, in March 1918. Cosmo had been different.

John Bates said, with a touch of obstinacy, 'Still, of the two, young Paterson's got stronger connections. He's well known and although that's not the same as being well liked, it's a good deal. Adrian, this young fellow, Tate – I ought to tell you that a number of people have spoken to me about him. Not altogether favourably.'

'Really?' Adrian was ready for this. He simulated puzzlement, handed his putter to the caddy and paused on their way to the next tee. He had just won the hole and the course was uncrowded.

'Yes, really, of course it's no secret that he's ambitious, looking for a seat, has been down quite often, knows the Marvells, knows you. But there's a story going around that he's too keen on the Huns. Apparently he goes there quite often – holidays, I imagine – and has some pretty close Hun friends. I don't for a moment suggest it's important, but people are getting a bit restive about Germany. This Hitler practically making himself some sort of dictator and so forth, all parties except the Nazis banned, Germany being obstructive in the Disarmament Conference at Geneva. You know and I know, Adrian, that your average constituent doesn't care a halfpenny damn what's going on in Germany, but if Tate is really as pally with some of them as is said – well, a clever opponent at election time could exploit it, you know. I think the Selection Committee would need to be happy on that point.'

'John,' said Adrian Winter forcibly, 'damn the Selection Committee! It's your job to make sense of them. And now listen to me. You'll agree I know something about Germany?'

John Bates acknowledged it, embarrassed. Everyone knew, could never forget, that awful time when Veronica Winter had been killed. And Adrian had had a heart attack in the same week. Ten years ago.

'Well, I can tell you, Theo Tate talks a great deal of sense about it. They, the Germans, have got a point of view and to understand what's happening it's necessary to see it – not necessarily sympathize with it but see it. Young Tate does. Did you read a letter he wrote to *The Times* at about Easter-time? It was masterly – fair, balanced and morally absolutely unequivocal. I think I know something about the Nazis, John.' His voice was steady, and there was pain as well as strength in it. 'I don't need lessons on that point. But young Tate has got it absolutely right. If my constituents feel like rejecting him because he knows what he's talking about, because he sees more than one side, they're fools. And what do they want? Another war?'

A little later on the same fine July Thursday, another conversation about Theo Tate's prospects was taking place in equally attractive and tranquil surroundings in another district on the frontiers of London. In one of the agreed pick-up places used by Marcus in his communications with Contor a tiny slip of paper had specified Thursday; six o'clock in the evening; Hampstead Heath, by a particular crossing of tracks, exactly described. Theo had a telephone number to ring in case of difficulty, such as not being able to keep an appointment, or urgently desiring one (a facility never yet used). He did not ring it. Hampstead Heath at six would do very well. Theo welcomed the arrangement, for he was experiencing a certain restlessness, unease even. A talk with Marcus would bring security. Talks with Marcus were sometimes astringent but the aftermath was peace, a peace Theo recognized, from intuitive understanding, comparable to absolution. For with Marcus there was always at least a touch of the confessional.

Theo had been brought to his beliefs, and had slithered without complaint into the curious twilight world which Marcus and Contor inhabited, by a mixture of motives. First – and he sometimes needed to remind himself of this in simple terms, for it was often obscured by the deceptions imposed on him to practise – he had felt thoroughly guilty when all about him other people were deprived, hungry, unemployed or undernourished because of the hand life had dealt them. Beneath a manner he kept deliberately flippant and ironic, Theo had felt sharp pain when he perceived others suffering and himself immune. This was the straightforward, sometimes simplistic human sympathy of the natural do-gooder, the champion of the underdog, one of the Emmas of England. Theo was much too complicated a person to accept pity as a sufficient guide to action, but he still told himself from time to time that a person could only come to Communism if, at the start, he resented the inhumanities of the existing system so strongly as to find them intolerable. Theo, therefore, thought he loved Emma not least for her generous sympathies. And although he knew that these were, in essence, liberal rather than doctrinaire (making Emma one of those described contemptuously by Lenin as useful idiots, unreliable because undisciplined, essentially weak), nevertheless Theo sometimes acknowledged, in secret, that he had come to the Party because he had once felt like Emma. That had been the beginning of it all.

Then there had been Theo's intolerance of muddle and sentiment. At Cambridge the Party had been comparatively well organized: Theo had observed it carefully while undergoing his long period of indoctrination and discussion with Headley. Headley had, of course, been insistent that Theo must show no overt sympathy with even mildly left-wing movements or causes, but

Theo had watched and noted. Among the Communists there were many different types. There were people who professed a certain intellectual sympathy with Marxism, with the Soviet experiment, but who were, Theo knew, essentially detached. They would remain objective, would feel free to criticize, would flirt with the Revolution, but could never be relied upon to risk body and soul, to obey without question, to tack and turn if ordered. Sometimes such intellectuals attempted to adopt what they thought was a proletarian manner, habit of mind, voice even. This, Theo observed, drew a good deal of contempt from those whose credentials were more authentic. He shared the contempt – these people made themselves absurd and he was grateful that his own path had been differently mapped. Nevertheless such men and women obviously had their uses, although those uses were limited. The Party demanded secrecy and discipline at the centre, but it could be helped by a well-meaning cloud of rather fuzzy, ephemeral supporters at the fringe.

Next, of course, there were the fanatical, blatant, Party members, raising money, distributing leaflets, organizing meetings, acting as stewards, relishing the jargon, warmed by the sense of belonging, stunned by revelation, utterly loyal. The Adlers of the world. The foot soldiers. Theo watched them, remarking how emotional was their attachment to the Party. If their faith was ever to be shaken, for instance by some really extraordinary contradiction or upheaval of policy which they could not, really could not swallow (and Theo had formed the view they could swallow most things), then the Adlers of the Movement would be utterly lost, wretchedly unhappy, suicidal. All that gave life meaning and colour would have been crushed and they would be wandering in a world without landmarks, lost souls. Theo knew that the Party needed a lot of Adlers. He found their naivety irritating and their lack of humour tedious – he had, of course, debated with them in the guise of an alien, a class-enemy, an unbeliever. Their ignorance, too, provoked contempt: the average Party member or official at the Adler level made it a positive virtue to read nothing published by the 'bourgeois' press, and lived in a world alone, isolated from criticism, blissfully free from contact with awkward facts. But in spite of Theo's personal and fastidious antipathy to this rank and file, as he thought of them, he realized that nothing would be achieved without them.

Then, last, different, discovered only at length, brought to play their intoxicating, sometimes deeply troubling role, there were those such as Theo. Someone who had been instructed to live a life of dissembling. Someone whose function was to gain a position of power, prestige, responsibility in this enemy, capitalist world in order to work more effectively for its collapse. Someone from whom the highest possible degree of discipline and secrecy was demanded. Someone sufficiently dedicated to obey without question, sacrifice personal interests and emotions without demur, turn or move when the Party decreed it. Without argument.

To betray. In order to keep faith with a higher ideal.

Theo liked the sense of conspiracy – it was congenial to him. He liked, too, the awareness that he knew more than the people among whom he moved, possessed secret keys which would have astounded them. Theo had always had a good opinion of himself – The Tapir's, then Headley's preliminary flattery had been shrewdly aimed – and he had often felt a certain twinge of resentment that his contemporaries, although generous to his qualities, did not hold him quite as high as he should be. But now, although they might never know it, he was high indeed. Within an inner circle, an élite they could not possibly comprehend, he was a man who would ultimately tidy them all up and sweep them away. A man of history! There was, he often felt and had felt since he first reflected at all on the state of the world, a sense that Europe was heading for what could be called an almighty crack-up. Contemporaries laughed at the idea but Theo was sure of it. Now the Party told him he was right, explained it, forecast the pattern of things with awful clarity. All this gave Theo serenity. And Marcus reinforced it. But all serenity, perversely, was now at risk, and the risk was Emma.

They were walking slowly, on that Thursday evening, avoiding too much exertion in the July humidity. Marcus was a heavy man and easily puffed. He sweated freely. Marcus was too controlled a human being to have 'moods', but today his responses to Theo were curter than usual, his questions more abrupt. He wanted to know whether Theo had any reasons for further optimism about his likely selection as candidate for Adrian Winter's seat.

It was not unreasonable, Theo thought, that this was what they chiefly talked about. His use to the Party, after all, lay in the future. The Party wanted a man – or, no doubt, another man – in the House of Commons. They also wanted a man they thought likely to be promoted once there, a man with ministerial quality perhaps. They wanted their man thoroughly camouflaged, untainted by the slightest suspicion of sympathy with themselves, indeed carrying the reputation of an intransigent enemy. They took a long view. And since this was Theo's part it was natural that they monitored his progress carefully; and, now and then, with a touch of impatience.

Marcus said, 'We think there will be a British General Election in about two years' time, perhaps less. Your Mr Winter's supporters will wish to have his successor ready to fight before then. I am surprised the matter has not gone further.'

'I think Adrian Winter himself doesn't much care to face retirement. He knows it must come but he dreads the reality, the moment. The House of Commons has been his life. He'll miss it horribly.'

Marcus found it impossible to sympathize in even the smallest degree with a human being governed by such an obsession, but he knew England pretty well by now and he nodded, unsmiling. He also knew that Theo Tate, Contor – although he had never shown signs of deviation or disloyalty – equally found a certain fascination in the curious political game enacted in this capitalist world, so that the part he was scheduled to play would not be unrewarding. Contor would be like an actor playing a king, relishing his technical skill in simulating another's character yet romantically enjoying, too, the voice and air of royalty. Well, why not? The Party could use most characteristics, if suitably directed.

He said, 'Will you be seeing Winter again soon? Will your name be brought again to his attention? What about the lady, the Mrs Dillon who is supposed to have influence with him, you say – have you been able to press her a little?'

'I've not seen Patsy Dillon much recently.'

'Should you not do so? Are you not still lovers?'

Theo disliked this line of conversation. He recognized that it was entirely permissible – Patsy too had a role in the scheme which both he and the Party hoped would unfold, and to Marcus her relationship with Contor rated a significant paragraph in the file, if nothing more. But when Marcus spoke her name Theo saw Emma's face, felt Emma's cheek smooth against his, Emma's caressing hand at the back of his neck, could instantly see Emma's great eyes so full of trust and love.

He said, 'As I say, I've not seen her for some time. I believe she's away.'

'A lover should know, I think. A lover who hopes his mistress will exert herself to help his career should not leave her alone "for some time" as you put it. And it could also be said,' continued Marcus quietly, 'that such a lover, with such ambitions, might be best advised not to pursue the lady's daughter so obviously.'

They walked on in silence. Theo was angry and confused. He had known this moment would come sooner or later. He felt Marcus glancing at him.

'Contor, you even have an idea you might marry the girl?'

'Well,' said Theo, 'I might, as it happens. And would the Party object?' He tried to combine irony with genuine inquiry and it didn't, of course, work. Marcus took the question exactly.

'I believe the Party would object to nothing which helped your – political career. The reverse. But marriage is a very intimate thing – they would, naturally, be concerned whether your discretion could survive such a relationship. You obviously understand that.'

'Yes,' said Theo, 'I understand that. Obviously.'

'I take it there is no question of the young lady becoming one of us.'

'I think not. Sympathetic to ultimate objects –'

'Oh –'

'But not to methods. Organization. And so forth.'

'I see,' said Marcus contemptuously, 'one of those. Well, you must be careful. And you should clearly not antagonize her mother.'

'The constituency will prefer a married candidate.'

'Is that so? You must use your own judgement in this matter, Contor. The Comrades will judge only by results. Of course.'

'Of course.'

'And now tell me, have you been in touch again with your young Nazi friend? Breitfall? We agreed that you would maintain that contact. It can be useful, the Party has been driven underground in Germany, as you know. It is less easy than it was to undertake work there, to get information, contribute ideas and so forth. *Agitprop* there is now a complicated, underground matter –'

'And likely to become more so.'

'Certainly. Of course all this has been expected. But an informal and unsuspected channel of communication like yours with this young man can have its uses. Do you plan another visit to Germany at some time, by the way?'

'It's possible.' Theo had been contemplating an expedition to Bayreuth. Unusually for an Englishman of his generation, he adored Wagner. He said, 'Next year, maybe. Of course it depends on how things go here.'

'I agree. And how things go with the Dillon girl I dare say.'

'It is ironic,' said Theo, not responding to this, 'that I'm supposed to be better disposed towards the Nazis than my Conservative, patriotic, possibly – future – constituents like! Ironic!'

'Much must appear ironic in the short term. That seems to me excellent – I had heard of it. It fits the picture of a devout patriot, sympathizing with Hitler's obsessive hatred of Marxism even though wary of any German ambitions which could threaten the interests of England. Excellent! And you wrote a very good letter to *The Times* by the way.'

'You thought so?'

'I did. So did our Comrades. Beautifully in character. Really,

Contor, it was almost as if you believed in the sentiments of your letter!'

Marcus wore something like a smile and Theo looked at him with a tiny twist of the gut which he recognized as dislike. He said, 'I did believe – anyway in some of them!'

Marcus continued to draw his lips wide, a smile that contained only cynicism. He shrugged his shoulders and said, 'We are at war, Contor! We are at war!'

It was a reminder, a reproof, a stab of icy wind in the hot, slumbrous Hampstead evening.

Ever since their stay at Bargate at the same time as their mother in the preceding year Hilda Marvell had encouraged the young Dillons to look on the place almost as home. She found both brother and sister enormously attractive. The girl had a lot of silly ideas, of course, impractical, a dreamer, out to put the world to rights between tea and dinner, all that. But she had real quality, Hilda thought, and John Marvell agreed; her heart was generous, her mind was quick, she had a lovely spark to her. And pretty – unusually pretty, with that skin, the very dark hair, the huge eyes. The children liked her too – both John and Hilda respected the judgement Anthony and Marcia displayed. Hilda was not sure whether she hoped Emma would marry Theo Tate – on the whole she supposed she did. He was handsome, clever, ambitious. Everyone seemed to think he would be picked to succeed old Adrian Winter, and a connection with Emma and thus with the Marvells seemed entirely suitable. Hilda was not, however, entirely sure.

But Desmond Dillon was fond of him, obviously counted him a great friend, and that, thought Hilda, was a mighty big point in his favour. She loved Desmond. She liked to see young Anthony Marvell's obvious admiration for Desmond. Desmond was a young man who liked to leap before he looked, who was a touch unpredictable, who had a generous share of what Hilda inwardly called divine impatience. No woman would ever know exactly where she was with Desmond – Hilda approved of that.

Desmond was restless, Desmond was a charmer, but underneath the skin of the adventurer, Hilda was confident that a true heart beat. Inwardly, Desmond had integrity. One could be confident of the decency of Desmond's reactions, she was sure of it. Desmond and Emma were staying at Bargate for the weekend, once again. At lunch on the Saturday, John Marvell said, 'You've been over in Germany again, Desmond?'

'Yes, that's right. In April. Working on the book. One can live awfully cheaply there!' Desmond grinned.

Hilda said nothing. There was a story about an entanglement with a German girl. Most unsuitable by all accounts. Poor Desmond – too trusting, no doubt! Vulnerable!

'It looks as if the Nazis have got a real stranglehold. Made themselves the only party and so forth. Banned everyone else. It's pretty worrying. How was the atmosphere? Aren't people rather frightened?'

Desmond took a little time to reply. The question, often put, brought Sonja's face and body so vividly before his eyes, the horror of what they had done to her so instantly to his imagination, that he had to control himself very carefully. He was also determined not to mislead. Eventually, he said, 'I don't think the ordinary German feels frightened, no. Frankly, I think most people are relieved.'

'Relieved? To lose a lot of their civil liberties overnight? To –'

'I think, sir, that one must appreciate how insecure life has been in Germany. People here tend not to realize that throughout last year an average of two people died in Germany *every day* from some sort of politically inspired outrage. There's been so much violence, such lack of order – as well as so much economic chaos – that relief at increased personal security is likely, for most Germans, to outweigh any loss of political rights. Which anyway,' Desmond added, 'are not particularly strongly rooted in Germany.' He spoke with quiet authority, and they were all listening.

'I understand you. And their sense of personal security really has improved, has it?'

'Without doubt. There is order. There is confidence. There are even the beginnings of prosperity.'

'And what about the Secret Police, and so forth? What about the Nazi thugs? Are people simply accepting that as part of life?'

'Largely, yes. I believe people believe – or are trying to believe – that the Nazis will grow quieter, more responsible, now that the street battles have in effect been won. Unless one nails one's colours to the mast as some sort of enemy of the régime, one can live more quietly and more respectably there than for some time.'

'You sound quite friendly towards it all, Desmond.'

'I'm not,' said Desmond, his voice not entirely steady, a note recognizable as anger in it, 'I'm not at all. But I think we must see it clearly. Germany is not seething with discontent. And when one travels there one does not feel any stifling sensation of tyranny.'

'You surprise me a little,' said John Marvell. 'And what about their foreign policy? Are they going to drive a coach and horses through the Versailles Treaty? Rearm?'

'The Versailles Treaty is Hitler's strongest card. All Germans resent it – you know that, sir. Yes, I think in due course that's exactly what Hitler will do. And when he does – begins to rearm in earnest, I mean – it will be hugely popular. Nazi prestige will soar.'

'And we and the French will do nothing, I suppose.'

'And we and the French will do nothing. How could we?' He paused, inviting some reply, some suggestion that the former Allies should take up arms to enforce a treaty most Englishmen by now regarded as unfair and ill-conceived. Nobody spoke. Desmond, reflecting Sonja's judgements, said quietly, 'Hitler won't hurry, I suspect. And they're all still talking disarmament at Geneva.'

'Armament, Disarmament, Rearmament, War,' said young Anthony Marvell. 'What on earth do people want to fight for, anyway? Why shouldn't Germany be treated just like everyone else?'

'I'm not sure,' said his father, smiling at him. 'I'm not sure.

But there may be reasons, I rather think.' And Desmond, whom Anthony so admired, said softly, 'There may indeed.'

'Des, how's the German woman of mystery? Are you still in deep?'

The twins were gossiping in Emma's room before going down to dinner at Bargate the same evening. Desmond had recently moved out of the house on Campden Hill he and Emma had shared for some years – suddenly, without acrimony, both had found the arrangement constraining. Each in an individual way felt that their twinship, their profound love, needed careful handling. They'd lived in the same house for long enough. It was typical of their affinity that each came to the same conclusion at the same time.

A consequence was that they had seen surprisingly little of each other during that summer of 1933. It was now late August.

'Still in deep, Des?'

'We write to each other a good deal.'

'And she's not leaving the beastly country?' Emma had learned from Desmond of Sonja's ordeal and been incredulous and nauseated. Perhaps now that Germany had what looked like a stable government, however, such nightmares would recede.

'Not leaving. I've asked her to find some reason to come here but she says she can't. Not at the moment.'

'At lunch today you sounded very balanced about the Nazis. It must have cost you a good deal, Des, considering what they've done to your girl.'

'It does,' said Desmond, 'cost a good deal. But one must try to remember not to fuss and fume, to save oneself for action one day.'

'Action?'

'Action! I've got a very definite feeling there'll be things to be done. I don't know what, when or how, but I've got the feeling!'

Emma said, quietly, 'I know what you mean. Des, is your book taking all your time?'

'No, I'm restless and I've been longing to tell you. Journalism – do you know I've actually got a sort of newspaper job?'

Desmond had given up his job with a publishing house after a short try and lived on a small private income. He had existed, additionally, on a tiny publisher's advance for his novel: his novel-of-our-times, set in Revolutionary Russia, Revolutionary Germany. His novel which had only, so far, reached chapter seven. He had submitted one or two impressionistic articles on his travels to a weekly review which specialized in foreign affairs and been gratified to have them accepted. Payment was niggardly, he told Emma, but the editor had said, 'Would you be prepared to cover Germany, France, Western Europe in general? I'll pay modest expenses, travel and so forth; not much more – a bit less than the going rate per column-inch I'm afraid, but we can't splash money about, as you know.'

Desmond had no particular reason to know, but he accepted with alacrity. A little more spending money, and some almost free travel would be welcome. It would help rather than hinder the book. And although he knew that he would never make a real newspaper man, never shine as a reporter (being allergic to instant comment as well as to sensational exaggeration), he felt that he had it in him to be a journalist in a more reflective sense. Possibly, he thought, in an investigative sense one day. Desmond was discovering a certain taste for trying to get to the bottom of things, for uncovering faces behind masks. It was regrettable that in Nazi Germany both face and mask tended to be repellent. Although not all the time, he grimly acknowledged. Not all the time.

Emma was delighted. 'Will the articles carry your name?' And when Desmond said they would, she clapped and laughed.

'Theo will be envious!'

'Em,' said Desmond, 'what about Theo?'

'What about him?'

'Are you going to marry him?'

'I might. Would you mind?'

'Of course not.' But his emotions were far from clear. A gong sounded.

'We must go down.' Desmond fidgeted with his black tie and said, 'Does Mother know it's likely?'

Emma did not dispute 'likely'.

'She's got an idea. She and I don't bare our souls to each other.'

'Still –'

'As you say. Still. I'm lunching with her on Monday.'

'Theo's proposed to you?'

'Sort of.' Desmond could see from her secret smile, her dancing eyes, that she was certain, that she was in love, really in love, that she was thinking of nothing but his fair, quizzical, enigmatic friend. And it was, in fact, six weeks later that *The Times* and the *Morning Post* carried an announcement on the last day of September that a marriage had been arranged and would shortly take place between Mr Theodore Tate, son of the late Captain D'Arcy Tate and Mrs D'Arcy Tate of 99 Albion Street, and Miss Emma Dillon, daughter of the late Major Brinsley Dillon and Mrs Dillon of 101 South Eaton Place. Desmond had already telephoned his congratulations to Theo, having spent an hour packed with rather confused emotions in Emma's company a few days before. And by then Kitzi Fischer had suddenly appeared in London.

'Of course I remember you! Don't be absurd, my dear fellow! Just because we haven't seen each other for several years – I'm delighted! You must lunch with me some time, or dinner or something. How long are you over here?'

'That I cannot for certain say.'

Adrian Winter was sitting over breakfast in his very comfortable London dining room in his house in Charles Street. He felt uneasy. He remembered Kitzi Fischer with affection – he and that nice fellow von Premnitz had been great supports when he'd gone through his bad time, lost his wife, been isolated in Munich amidst a violent sea of south German rioting and political uproar in 1923. Fischer had felt grievous responsibility because the Nazi blow which felled Veronica had been apparently aimed at him.

In consequence Kitzi Fischer regarded the late Mrs Winter as some sort of saint and martyr. Not quite in character, Adrian thought with wry affection, she was a stunner my Veronica, but no saint! Nevertheless Fischer was a charming and intelligent man and they'd maintained desultory contact. Tragedy is a strong bond. Now, however, Fischer had appeared in London in the last week in September and was saying he didn't know how long he was staying. There was, too, something doom-laden in the way he said, 'I cannot say.' People ought to know how long they were staying in foreign countries. They could, even the nicest of them could, become nuisances. Adrian said genially, 'Where can I get hold of you?'

Kitzi mentioned an hotel. 'Mr Winter, I very much wish to speak to you seriously, and perhaps rather soon.'

Adrian's heart sank. He had guessed as much.

'I'm afraid I'm very caught up for the next few weeks. What about lunch around the middle of October? You'll still be here?'

'I will.'

'Plenty to talk about.'

'There is.'

Adrian rang him later and suggested Monday, 16th October, in as easy and social a way as he could manage. He heard Kitzi Fischer say '16th October' with a depth of meaning which made lunch at Adrian's club sound like a conspiratorial assignation. He found himself hoping very much that Kitzi had not done anything foolish, or fallen foul of the new German authorities, bloody though they were. People like Kitzi, however honourable, could be most troublesome.

Adrian would have liked to talk over Kitzi's arrival with somebody acquainted with him. There was Desmond Dillon, of course. The boy had been staying in Berlin with Fischer, he remembered, as had Theo Tate. But something held him back from contacting young Dillon. Kitzi must have already done so, he expected; and Adrian thought he'd like, first, to learn from Kitzi himself what brought him to London. There was nobody else to whom a gossip would be welcome, nobody else in London at present who would even understand what he was talking about.

Patsy Dillon had been away for a fortnight now and wasn't expected back until November, well after his lunch appointment. Adrian would have liked a talk, a comfortable, ruminative talk with Patsy, beautiful, entertaining Patsy, about Kitzi Fischer. He would have liked a talk – another talk – about Theo Tate, soon to be her son-in-law. He would have liked to draw on her feminine shrewdness, masquerading as flippancy, as the hunch of a scatter-brained frivolous woman but in reality sharp and quick. But Patsy was away – had gone off to Antibes or somewhere the same day Emma had announced her engagement. Most oddly, Adrian had thought – an engagement surely demanded a mother's supportive presence! But these were curious times, and modern girls were peculiar, with their independence and their contempt for sentiment and appearance – and pretty young Emma Dillon was as peculiar and independent as any, so perhaps Patsy's departure, leaving her daughter to manage the business of engagement single-handed, was of no consequence. It was a bore, however, for him, Adrian Winter, who missed her! Now, as he reflected on a forthcoming luncheon and, no doubt, a deep conversation with Herr Fischer of Berlin, Adrian felt he was denied support he had a right to expect, and turned the pages of *The Times* with a good deal of irritation.

CHAPTER VIII

'Certainly I know,' said Adrian Winter. 'It was headlined in the Sunday papers. Your country has withdrawn from the Disarmament Conference at Geneva.' It was Monday, 16th October, and Adrian's weekend had been mildly disturbed by the news of Germany's defiant behaviour. He had been spending two days in his constituency, a pleasant time of year. Everyone there had pestered him for an opinion on the matter. Adrian was locally regarded as a man of European understanding, a reputation not altogether without foundation, albeit exaggerated. He had said to people, 'We can't tell how much it matters. We certainly need the Germans at the table if we're to get these talks beyond the talking stage, as everyone wants. The Germans are saying that the French won't give an inch, nor will the Poles, nor will the Czechs; so why should they, the Germans, accept the situation indefinitely, without being free to redress the balance? That's their line.'

'They started the War, Mr Winter. And they lost it.'

'Of course they lost it,' said Adrian, who was a fair-minded man and had come to the conclusion that the starting of the slaughter had been a more complex matter than most Englishmen understood. He added, 'Still, time moves on, you know. We've all got to live in the world together. The other fellow's obsessions are facts, even though they may be tiresome facts.' Adrian could talk like this without arousing misgivings, his patriotism undoubted. Privately, German quitting of the conference table at Geneva made him uneasy. There was something – something *brutally over-dramatized*, he said to himself, in Hitler's gesture; already people, Adrian included, were saying 'Hitler' when they

164

meant the German Government. The German Chancellor had certainly adopted a very personal style in international relations.

And at a weekend too!

'We've all got to live in the world together.' He had the same conversation several times, feeling stale and unoriginal. Not that he found people much the wiser back in London. Some said that it was just another negotiating tactic – the Germans would return to the table when they had made their point: the thing was to stay calm, nod the head and do nothing. Others thought France should go through the motions of making some concessions. France, after all, had a huge army, was immensely strong. And Poland, the newly created Poland, had a lot of troops, by all accounts, sitting on Germany's eastern border with no love lost. You had to recognize that the old Hun had a point of view. Besides, the Germans had walked out of the Geneva talks before. They'd be back. Play the hand quietly, without excitement. Quite so, Adrian said, just what I tell people down in Sussex. But he remained worried, less by the development (international conferences were punctuated throughout history by dramatic withdrawals, misunderstandings, returns) than by the – the *style* of it.

Controlled. Brutal. Calculating. And calculating exactly what? He looked rather wearily at his lunchtime guest and said again, 'Headlined in the Sunday papers. Were people in Germany expecting it?'

'I, personally, was expecting it.' Kitzi Fischer looked round the dining room with interest. They were lunching at Adrian's club in Pall Mall. Senior statesmen in black frock coats, long deceased, looked sternly down at them from the walls. Across the room a solitary member was eating lunch reading a propped-up newspaper and wearing his hat, a normal custom in earlier times but now conveying something deliberately anachronistic, something defiantly anti-modern. A wine waiter smiled deferentially at Adrian and showed him a bottle of Aloxe Corton before pouring. It was all, thought Kitzi, calm, dignified, unruffled. And why not? Although such scenes could be mirrored in Berlin there was something here, Kitzi's imagination told him, which was especially far removed from the stridency and unpredictability he had so recently abandoned. For Kitzi, nominally a visitor researching a series of articles on contemporary British literature, had quiet plans whereby he might stay a good deal longer than advertised. Perhaps for ever.

There were stringent exchange control regulations, of course, so that money might have been difficult, but, years before, Kitzi had published a series of much-praised articles in an English review, on the influence of German romantic authors on late Victorian English novelists – and, to his astonishment, publishers had wanted to issue them as a small book. That had been in 1927, he had been delighted, and had kept the modest proceeds on deposit with an English bank. So far, Kitzi could live.

There had been no difficulty about his leaving Germany and he, a severely wounded ex-officer, had as yet experienced no personal harassment; but he knew that 'they' realized what he thought of them, amd were watching him warily. Meanwhile the Berlin house was empty, caretaken by faithful Günther, and Wieland Breitfall permitted to use it as he wished; a permission which must enhance security, however lamentable the reason. Kitzi hoped there would be none of those rough intrusions followed by apologies and smooth murmurs of regret for error which some of his friends had experienced at the hands of the Party. Not that there was anything in the house he minded being seen by prying or hostile eyes – in the matter of papers Kitzi was careful. He looked with liking at his host, sipped his Burgundy with enjoyment and said quietly, 'I was expecting it. They have wished to make the French and Poles seem provocative. To give an excuse.'

'If you ask me, Mr Fischer, the French – and the Poles, and the Czechs for that matter – *have* been a bit provocative in these disarmament negotiations. They've hardly given an inch. If Hitler was determined all along to break it up they've made it easy for him.'

'Mr Winter, what I mean is that whatever the French or anybody else do, the German Government are determined to rearm. And greatly to expand our armed forces. Furthermore, in this they will have the overwhelming support of the German people.'

'Understandable,' Adrian observed slowly. 'Understandable, you might say.'

'Yes, you might. And I am sure you and everyone here realizes that in doing this the Nazis will be guaranteeing for themselves the support of the Reichswehr. Of the generals, the officers, the sergeants, all. And Hitler has need of that support.'

'It will take a long time, I imagine. This rearmament.'

'Less than is supposed. All the plans have been prepared for years. They will make them public very soon, before the end of this year. I believe they intend something like sixty army divisions, half of them what are called "first echelon", already embodied –'

'*Sixty divisions!*' Adrian was not a military man, but in the War the entire newspaper-reading public had become versed in the nomenclature and scale of such things. 'Sixty divisions! It'll take years!'

'Not once conscription is ordered.'

'In defiance of Versailles!'

'Naturally, in defiance of Versailles. Adolf Hitler has become German Chancellor specifically to defy the Versailles Treaty. I am sure you understand that.'

Adrian tucked into an excellent steak and kidney pie and said, 'And what about weapons? Modern weapons? Aeroplanes? And don't forget that's what the English are most bothered about – air warfare. They've been filled up with stuff about the next war seeing air-raids on an unimaginable scale, the English Channel no longer relevant, all that sort of thing! What about –'

Kitzi interrupted him and said that of course these things would not be done overnight but that impressive groundwork had been prepared. 'You are no doubt aware, Mr Winter, that our small Reichswehr have to some extent organized the development of weapons of war forbidden to us Germans, and have also trained cadres in such weapons. Tanks. Aeroplanes. All that was done in Russia. And, of course, firms like Krupp have bought control of certain foreign factories and companies, in countries such as

Sweden: and have been manufacturing experimental arms in such places. That's quite well known in certain circles in Germany. Perhaps here, too.'

'Perhaps,' said Adrian. He doubted it.

He stared at Kitzi. There had been periodic scare stories but in common with most Englishmen he'd discounted them, not altogether unsympathetically.

Kitzi said, to Adrian's surprise, 'Your young friend Desmond Dillon knows rather a lot about that. He discovered it from a lady – a lady in Berlin he is strongly attached to. She is very well informed, a journalist with contacts in other East European countries. Desmond Dillon learned a good deal: I know that. I also know that the young lady was brutally assaulted by Nazi thugs, to teach her a lesson. She had written anti-Nazi articles, but also, I think, they made it clear they thought she knew too much about this business – these secret military developments, with Bolshevik help.'

'How did they know? Did she talk freely, in Berlin?'

'Perhaps. But she certainly talked to young Dillon. And I believe the word got back.'

'Poor girl,' said Adrian. 'What did they do to her?' Kitzi told him. He said, his face very stern, 'I have a nephew of whom I am very fond. He is causing me great pain. He is a Nazi – a dedicated Nazi. He is an SS officer. You know of the SS?'

'Certainly. Does Desmond Dillon know your nephew?'

'He does. And I think – I have not asked my nephew directly, he would lie to me and he is a bad liar, it would embarrass us both – I think that my nephew, Wieland, was aware that this young woman spoke of these things to Desmond Dillon. And that Wieland reported the matter. He would never have had a hand in the sort of brutality I've described, but I remember his reactions at the time – it was early this year, a bad time – and I know he had learned of this girl's indiscretions and assume he reported the matter. With unfortunate consequences. I could see his embarrassment.'

'How did he learn? Surely Desmond didn't tell him?'

'No,' said Kitzi. 'Not that. Certainly not that.'

'Desmond must have been deeply upset.'

'He was indeed. Mr Winter, as I have said, Desmond Dillon is well informed on this business. Do you not think he might be persuaded to write an article or series of articles? For publication?'

'He's got some sort of journalistic job already.'

'So I believe. Mr Winter, could you not persuade him? I have already talked to him on the telephone but he is away from London for a few days. He was at first somewhat reluctant. I am sure he would listen to you. And perhaps you could assist in the matter of publication?'

Adrian knew, as presumably Kitzi did not, that the British Government had been actively considering giving some publicity to flagrant German breaches of the disarmament provisions of the Versailles Treaty. He didn't know how that matter stood. He'd better talk to someone, he thought. Furthermore, Kitzi's conversation had given a new dimension to what 'flagrant breaches' might mean. An informative, even a sensational, article by a well-informed Desmond Dillon might alert people, might show the Germans their game was perfectly well known, might bring them back to the negotiating table, rather fewer cards in their hand, in clear breach of treaty and so forth.

Or it could do the exact reverse. Yes, he'd better talk to someone. It might be useful to the Government to know that Desmond's pen could be available. Indirect stimulation of an independent journalist was a time-honoured device of government. Adrian said, 'I gather young Dillon didn't like the idea of writing something, when you talked. That right?'

'That is right. He fears causing more trouble for the young lady.'

'Well – might it?'

'I doubt it. She is being silent, writing nothing, has – in Nazi eyes – perhaps learned her lesson. And he could write with care.'

'I don't suppose,' said Adrian reflectively, 'if what you say is true, that the Nazis – or the Reichswehr, the Army chaps – are too keen on it being widely known how chummy they've been with the Soviets. They may be as sensitive about that as about cocking snooks at the Allies for breaching Versailles – they don't care a damn, now, who knows the latter.' Kitzi nodded, smiled thinly, and said, 'Nor, I presume, are the Communists anxious that their Comrades should be aware how much they have helped the cause of detested German militarism! But these things have happened, and they will greatly affect the speed with which Germany will now be able to rearm. I believe this matter needs exposure, if some sort of European balance is to be maintained, if peace is to be preserved. I believe people should be alerted – early. Now. I think our young friend Dillon should write his article.'

'It's unlikely to be read with much enjoyment here,' Adrian said drily. 'The British favour a quiet life. We've got a by-election going on in London, a place called Fulham. I'm told the mood is very pacifist, all for disarmament, and so forth. People don't want to be disturbed, you know.'

But Kitzi said obstinately, 'I think Dillon should write his article,' and for a moment looked round the room as if at inhabitants of a different world.

'Mr Desmond Dillon?'

'Speaking.'

'Mr Dillon, my name is Langenbach. Kurt Langenbach. We met once in rather peculiar circumstances.'

'I don't think I –'

'It was on a train. A train between Stettin and Berlin. We were introduced by a Mr Rodoski, a Polish gentleman who had an unfortunate accident in Berlin soon afterwards.'

Desmond's heart missed a beat. Rodoski! Rodoski, bibulous, quarrelsome, affectionate, then lying dead in the foyer of a nightclub with the scornful, sneering faces of young SA men in plain clothes around him. Rodoski, lover of Sonja. Sonja, walking naked into the room, with the shock of Rodoski's death still in the air between them. Sonja needing and giving a great deal that night. And now Langenbach. A particularly gifted aviator. A man only half-remembered, with a strong, clever, rather cynical face.

'Yes, Herr Langenbach. I remember.'

'Perhaps we could meet some time, Mr Dillon. It would be nice to see you again. You see I am attached to the German Embassy in London for a short while, maybe a few months only.'

'Really, Herr Langenbach? I didn't realize you were in the German Foreign Service.'

'Not Foreign Service. I am attached to the office of the Military Attaché. Temporarily.'

Sniffing round British Air Force developments, I suppose, Desmond thought. Langenbach gave what sounded like a friendly chuckle down the line and said, 'I read your article about Germany, Mr Dillon. Very interesting.' Desmond's article had been published on 7th November. Five days before.

'Thank you.'

'As a matter of fact there are one or two things not quite right. I thought you might be interested to talk about them. Would you perhaps lunch with me one day?'

Desmond afterwards remembered that lunch with a certain grimness. He had not been enthusiastic about accepting, but Langenbach was courteously pressing and Desmond reflected that if he were determined now to be an investigative journalist of the European scene he must not let any fastidiousness impede his contacts. Langenbach, on the face of it, was agreeable enough. It was essential to hang on to the truth that there were Germans like Kitzi Fischer, like Frau Reitz, like old Günther. They outnumbered the sort of brutes he couldn't think of without his knuckles itching; and perhaps Langenbach was one of these, skilful flying man though he might be. They agreed a day for lunch, one week hence; and they lunched well.

Desmond happened to be dining with Theo that evening, whose wedding to Emma was now to be in the spring. Emma was away for a few days. He told Theo all about lunch.

'You remember Langenbach, Theo? He came bursting into our compartment on the Stettin train. Then we – or I – found

171

out later that he is one of their best flying men. Undercover instructor, and so forth.'

Theo listened without pleasure to this recital. He was in a bad mood, and Desmond's conversation was not improving it. He crumbled a piece of bread irritably. He had been summoned the week before, at short notice, to an unscheduled meeting with Marcus. Marcus was annoyed. Marcus had reproached Contor as if he, Theo Tate, had himself been guiding Desmond Dillon's pen.

'I have made it clear,' Marcus had said, 'that the Comrades do not in the least welcome publicity for these exchanges with the German reactionaries, made for purely tactical reasons in the long-term interests of the Revolution. I told you that when you first brought the matter up yourself.'

'You did, Marcus.'

'Your friend has gone out of his way to write up the story. With a lot of detail. That is a pity.'

'I didn't know what he planned.'

'Why did you not know? He is to be your brother-in-law. Why were you not informed?'

'Marcus,' said Theo gently, 'it will take more than marrying his sister to get Desmond Dillon submitting all his journalism to me. He's a very independent man.'

Marcus did not smile. He said, disagreeably, 'He got a great deal of information from that woman in Berlin. The Polish whore.'

'Not exactly a whore, I think,' said Theo equably. 'And only part-Polish.'

'The woman certainly surrendered to your friend very quickly, whore or no whore.'

'So it appears. Marcus, there is nothing I can do about all this.'

Marcus had said, grimly, that he hoped Theo would at least make clear to Desmond Dillon that his articles were unhelpful and inaccurate. Theo asked 'unhelpful to whom?' with an attempt at injecting some humour, but Marcus abruptly ended the meeting.

Theo told Desmond that he remembered Kurt Langenbach

172

perfectly – had, furthermore, met him on no less than two occasions in London. An elegant, cultivated man with quite a wide circle of acquaintances, it seemed. Desmond nodded. 'So I've since discovered. He's obviously over here finding out what he can, using his beady, expert little eyes on whatever shows of the RAF. Insofar as it exists.'

'I suppose he was embarrassed by your article.'

'He talked about it quite genially. He said that I had exaggerated some things, got some details wrong – all very calm and civilized. His point was that it was only to be expected that Germany had resorted to subterfuge, since the provisions of the Treaty of Versailles were so unjust. "You would have done the same," he said. That's always unanswerable.'

'What was the object of lunch?'

'I think,' said Desmond carefully, 'that he wanted to find out if I planned more articles. If I knew more.'

'What's the answer?'

'Yes. And yes. He was pretty frank that he hoped any future efforts of mine would be produced "in the light of this conversation, which you may have found helpful in explaining certain things, Mr Dillon". He didn't quite have the cheek to suggest giving me a hand with composition, but almost. He obviously couldn't make up his mind whether I was an irreconcilable enemy or just uncomprehending. He also threw some flies over where I got my information.'

They were dining in a small, dark, panelled chophouse on an upper floor just off the Strand. Theo helped himself to some vegetables and remarked how watery English cooking of greens insisted on being. 'We have much to learn. From almost everyone. Desmond, I'm bound to say I think your article was a mistake. Can't you cancel the next one? They really aren't very clever.'

Desmond stared at his friend, irritated and astonished.

'Why on earth do you say that?'

'I think the whole business is just dirt-raking. Associating the German military with the Bolsheviks, spinning a sensational story about secret arms deals, manufactures, training – it can't possibly help produce an atmosphere in which sensible negotiations about disarmament can take place.'

'Why not? If these things happened, why shouldn't people –'

'You only have some pretty obscure sources for all this, Desmond.'

'My sources,' said Desmond softly, 'entirely satisfy me. Why should we go out of our way to avoid embarrassing Berlin? Or Moscow, for that matter? I believe that negotiations based on false premises are a mistake, and it's a false premise that Germany couldn't become strong very quickly. It's another false premise that the Soviets are a bunch of innocents in the matter.'

Theo grunted. He had other reasons for irritation. Emma was away from London, had been away for two days. She had been summoned by a girlfriend who lived in the north of Scotland and whose recent marriage was suddenly threatened with disaster for obscure reasons. Emma had a small number of very intimate girlfriends towards whom she felt huge responsibility. Theo knew them all and disliked them all, although he pretended otherwise. The probation service could apparently survive a short time without Emma being in London and she had taken a night train to Inverness. Theo felt abandoned. He saw Emma most days now, he was greatly looking forward to marriage in the spring, and he was not far from the condition he supposed people meant by being in love. Certainly Theo could see Emma whenever he closed his eyes. Certainly he felt a lift of the heart, discovered a curious and unwonted inarticulacy when she entered a room, when she came towards him, arms outstretched, eyes shining. Certainly he enjoyed, above all things, talking over his future, their future, with Emma. So loving. So perceptive. So wise. She had promised only to be away a week. Until 24th November, she said. 'I might even get back sooner!'

She had gone north by the night train two days ago, and Theo had seen her off from Euston station. He had then taken a taxi to his club, infrequently used. To his annoyance he had found scaffolding up outside the building and a hall porter in shirt sleeves rather than his customary Oxford blue, brass-buttoned tailcoat.

'Club's closed, sir.'

'Closed? Why? It's not summer!'

'This repair work, sir. All members should have had the letter. Committee's apologies, special three weeks' closing in November.'

Theo thought he remembered something. The man told him which clubs had agreed to receive members of Theo's as guests during this period of inconvenience. Theo reckoned he'd try the nearest, once visited by him and remembered without enthusiasm. He began to walk without buoyancy along Piccadilly, missing Emma.

'Theo, darling!'

'Patsy!' said Theo with his slow smile, eyebrows raised, heart quickening. He was uncertain how this encounter should go.

Patsy had been abroad, in the South of France, for some time. Theo's engagement to Emma had hurt her and she found difficulty in sorting out her emotions, squeezed as they were between what she supposed must be the conventional attitude to a future son-in-law and a daughter's happiness (and in some ways Patsy was entirely conventional), squeezed between these expected and respectable attitudes and her feelings for Theo. For the truth was that Patsy, at the age of forty-seven, was hungrily in love with twenty-eight-year-old Theodore Tate. It had always, she told herself, been idiotic, undignified, certain to bring ever more unhappiness – how would they look when he was forty-one and she was sixty, for God's sake? She told him, often, that he must be sensible and find a nice girl and marry her. Then she had seized him with fierce, near-despairing tenderness and prayed to whatever deity listened to Patsy's guilty supplications that it wouldn't happen. Patsy adored Theo's coolness, his looks, his rather sardonic sensuality, his enthusiastic appetites, his lightness of touch. She knew she possessed nothing of his inner self and the knowledge made her all the more avid for his company. Their affair, sporadic and with long intervals between meetings, had now gone on for nearly two years. It was a well-kept secret – unusually for Patsy, who was not reckoned a discreet woman. She had however been adamant. No friends, above all no family

– and, supremely, not Desmond, not Emma – must ever suspect. She could never, she told herself and frankly told Theo, bear the ridicule, the 'old enough to be his mother thing', she whispered to him. And Theo chuckled, and stroked her smooth flesh, girl-like at forty-seven, and promised. And kept his promise faithfully; for, as in most of the business of his life, concealment of his intimate concerns suited him very well.

Theo's own feelings were straightforward. He found Patsy enormously attractive. She was the most enjoyable and memorable sexual partner he had so far experienced, and he thought about her physical presence, about how she looked, smelt, felt, a good deal when they were apart. Desmond had first introduced them, of course, in Cambridge days: but there had been a long gap and suddenly one day they'd met, on neutral ground, and she was no longer his university friend's mother but a beautiful and entrancing woman who wanted him. And, as the most natural thing in the world, they'd met again; and met alone; and become passionate if occasional lovers. And Patsy took a warm interest, a mistress's interest, in his causes. Theo had no intention of complicating life by allowing this relationship to become unduly binding but, for now, it was delightful. He realized that sooner or later there would be pain (for Patsy), and for himself the mild discomfort of causing it. But meanwhile, and until something happened –

Then Emma had happened.

Theo recognized, with annoyance, that Marcus had reasonable grounds for his scepticism about Emma. Emma complicated things. Emma was sincere, single-minded, idealistic and incorruptible. She would go her own way, be immune to any but the most exalted influences. Emma, of all the girls Contor might fall for, was the one most likely to produce difficulties in that devious and important life which was Contor's. The first difficulty, clearly, was Patsy.

Patsy, predictably, had taken Theo's news badly. To start with, Emma had insisted on telling her mother before Theo had the chance to get in his word. Patsy, of course, had been alert for some time. 'Are you trying to turn my little girl's head?' she had asked, anxiety behind the smile. But it had come as a shock. Emma had telephoned Theo to say that she didn't know 'whether Mummy's pleased or not. But frankly, I don't think she feels much unless it touches her own life directly – Des and I don't mean a great deal, let's face it!' Emma said, too, that Patsy had announced she was going abroad, a sudden decision, extraordinary.

Theo had managed to have a few secret moments with Patsy nevertheless. She had tried to appear indifferent.

'If it's what you want, dear boy! Try to be nice to her!'

'Patsy –'

Then she'd been in his arms, crying. Patsy cried a great deal less than most women and Theo had only once seen her in tears before. He had done his best, murmured that of course it was difficult but that she would always, always be immensely important to him, always, always. Then she'd pulled away sharply, tried to smile, said 'Go now – son-in-law!' and called out that she promised to behave enormously well at the wedding. Theo had gone down the stairs at South Eaton Place, cursing. And Patsy had left England so that it had not been necessary to think about her for a while.

Then, suddenly, with Emma travelling to Scotland on the night train, there had been that unexpected cry, that smile beneath a street lamp, that instant confusion of memories and emotions; embarrassment, surprise, and many more.

'Theo, darling!'

'Patsy!'

They'd chatted, tried to be conventional, distant, 'social', as people hurried by. The November evening was threatening to be raw. Patsy said unimportant things about where she'd been, how delightfully warm the Midi still was, how she thought she'd go back there after a few weeks in London, the English autumn depressed her, she didn't know why she'd come home before the spring, how she'd not yet seen Emma or Desmond, talked on the telephone of course but they were all rushing all over the place, weren't they. She was looking to left and right, not looking at Theo. Then she'd put a hand lightly on his sleeve.

'Well – I suppose the three of us have to talk about my little Emma's wedding plans some time, now I'm back –'

Then he'd realized she simply couldn't speak, was choking back tears, misery, something. He heard himself saying, 'Patsy, I'll come and see you. Please,' and saw Patsy nod, try to smile. He heard her whisper, 'Yes, we'd better say goodbye, hadn't we!'

'Yes – a proper goodbye, Patsy darling!'

He knew trouble now threatened. Patsy sighed and said, 'Telephone. I'm in tomorrow evening.'

Theo nodded that he would. And did. All that had been two days ago.

Now, therefore, as Theo heard Desmond Dillon talking about Langenbach, about German rearmament, as he listened to Desmond defending his published article with passion, he felt the sour sickness of persecution. He, Theo Tate, was hemmed in by these people. He had wanted freedom and power, and on the road been content to enjoy conspiracy and intrigue. Now they – Marcus, Patsy, future brother-in-law Desmond, even beloved, valued, Emma herself – they seemed to be hitting him to and fro like a tennis ball across a net. Suddenly, Desmond seemed to think the conversation should be switched to more congenial, family concerns. He smiled affectionately at Theo and asked how long Emma was going to be in the north.

'A week. Back about the end of next week. Said she might try to get down sooner, but I doubt it. She'd have let me know. No news is bad news.'

Desmond was privately happy that old Theo was obviously out of sorts over Emma's short absence from London. He'd always regarded his friend as so essentially cool and detached that he'd had difficulty believing Theo could love as Emma deserved to be loved – with ardour and demonstration. It was good that her man so clearly missed her presence, was a touch upset. Desmond, of course, was jealous. But any man who sought to marry Emma would earn his jealousy and at least Theo was a worthy object of it, a creature of quality.

It was six o'clock in the evening three days later, Wednesday, 22nd November, and Adrian Winter decided to walk back from Sloane Square to Charles Street in Mayfair where he lived by himself in a pleasant red-brick house, too large for him but familiar now. He had no home in the constituency since he'd sold Faberdown, his Sussex property for which he'd lost all taste with no wife, no heir. A rich, generous man, he was content although lonely with his London life. He enjoyed the House of Commons and secretly always looked forward to the ending of recess. He entertained a certain amount, giving small dinner parties at Charles Street. He found now that unless the House was sitting late he preferred to go to bed early. He used his club – one of his clubs for he belonged to several – for luncheon, and played bridge in the most congenial of them now and then. He walked a good deal in London, knowing that it was important for his health and anyway enjoying the sense of independence, almost of anonymity. Adrian kept a car, and a chauffeur who lived in the mews behind his Charles Street house and whose wife was Adrian's cook. A parlourmaid and a housemaid, both in their fifties and both jealously devoted to Adrian, lived in attic rooms and preserved for him a background, a routine. It was comfortable, it was privileged. But it was lonely. Adrian had a great many female acquaintances, people he was glad to chat to, sometimes entertained, whose houses in the country he would occasionally visit. He had, however, few women to whom he found he could really talk, in whom he could confide as he had once confided to his wives. Especially to Veronica.

But there *was* Patsy Dillon. And although Adrian, no fool, knew that Patsy Dillon was a shallow creature in many ways, she nevertheless had the quality of sympathy, those instant perceptions, that way of going to the heart of the matter without it being clear how she got there, which was what warmed him in a woman. He enjoyed Patsy's company. Patsy was a hugely attractive lady. He'd once wondered whether Patsy might not make an excellent third Mrs Winter, but then had shied off, fatigued by the prospect of so much effort, so much ever-present intimacy.

Better not be an old fool. Better, at this stage in life, take Patsy as he found her, in small but frequent and agreeable doses. When she was away from London he missed her a good deal.

It had been good to hear from a mutual acquaintance that Patsy had recently returned from the place near Antibes which she'd apparently so fallen for, which she often told Adrian he should visit – without success, for Adrian, smiling, explained that he particularly loathed the Mediterranean coast of France. Now it appeared that Patsy was back in London. The telephone in South Eaton Place tended not to be answered but Adrian had often called at the house unbidden and welcome. He was on good terms with the one maid who looked after Patsy completely, assisted by a woman who came in on weekdays. Adrian imagined, with sympathy, that Patsy must be hard up, although South Eaton Place was a good address and the lease of the house (not a long one, he remembered Patsy had once confided to him) must have a certain value. But Patsy was unlikely to be flush with money and when in London no doubt needed to live pretty quietly. Perhaps these excursions to the South of France had some sort of peculiar economy to justify them – he knew she'd several times let her London house for the season, and even for odd fortnights.

Now, as he swung along Eaton Square towards St Peter's Church, slow but erect, a black Homburg hat slightly raked, a black overcoat with fur collar covering his broad shoulders, a gold-banded umbrella acting as a walking stick, tapping the pavement, he saw a very slender, graceful figure moving towards him on the same side of the road. Furthermore, the figure wore a broad, happy smile and showed every sign of halting in front of him.

'Hullo!' said Adrian, also halting, lifting his hat, smiling with great warmth, 'hullo, young lady! Are you on duty, looking up one of your old lags in Belgravia, may I ask?'

Emma laughed. Eaton Square was well lit. The sun was almost down, but Adrian could see she looked radiant. She's a stunner, he thought, those bones, those eyes! Emma wore a small fur hat, perched at an angle. Adrian thought Theo Tate was a very lucky fellow. He hoped that if, *if* that business came off, that business about which he was particularly anxious to talk to Patsy, the collaboration he'd need to have with young Theo would lead to at least a little time spent in the company of his wife. An exquisite creature!

'No lags around here, Mr Winter! Nothing so amusing!'

Adrian smiled at her, not wanting to bring their exchange to an end, warm in his coat.

'I suppose not. I suppose not.' He asked her whether she'd seen her brother lately.

'Not for a bit. I've been in Scotland for the last few days. Got down this morning as a matter of fact. I'm just going round to see Mummy.'

'Ah,' said Adrian, 'well I don't think she's at home. I've just been there.'

'Is Maggers there?' Maggers was the nickname for Patsy's maid, used by all who knew Patsy well. Adrian shook his head and said that nobody had answered the bell.

'I called on spec. Haven't seen your mother for a bit. Understand she's just back from the South of France.'

'That's it, she is,' said Emma. 'We've only talked on the telephone so I want to see how she is, have a good gossip.' This was rather overdone. A good gossip was the last thing this mother and daughter ever enjoyed. Emma added – 'Also she's got a book in the house I particularly want to borrow. About Greece.'

'Why do you suddenly want a book about Greece?'

'Because Theo and I might go there for our honeymoon and I remembered reading this book about life in a particular village, and how magical it sounded. Mummy's got the book unless she's lost it. I can't remember the name! Or the author!' She described it briefly, laughing delightedly. Adrian shook his head. 'Not my sort of book from the sound of it. When's the wedding, Emma?'

'April. Date not quite fixed but it'll be in London and you'll propose our health, we've discussed *that*. It's quite the most important thing, so there must be no question of your going off somewhere!'

'April,' said Adrian. 'Ah, well, that ought to be all right. And you want me to propose the toast, eh?'

'Theo's determined on it. Just as I am.' Adrian nodded. He could imagine.

'Well, Emma, I'd best be walking on. Looks as if you've had a fool's errand. I'm sorry.'

'Not a bit,' said Emma. 'I've got a latchkey of Mummy's house! Maggers is deaf and doesn't hear, often as not, even when she's in. Why don't you come there with me! I'll look for the book and you can relax in one of Mummy's armchairs. She'll probably come back while we're there and get a nice surprise.'

Adrian could hear in her voice the indifference to Patsy. Emma had come for a book, and if it could be taken without a tedious talk with her mother, so be it. Even when engaged, even after not seeing her parent since the end of September. Adrian understood, or thought he understood, the unsatisfactory nature of Patsy's relationship with her children. She spoke of it from time to time. It troubled her – but not much, he thought. Bending forward he kissed Emma's cheek.

'Off you go. And if your mother's back at the house, tell her you saw me and I'll be getting in touch with her. Might telephone this evening or tomorrow. Want a talk.'

'I will!'

Emma danced off towards South Eaton Place.

Emma had come down from Scotland two days earlier than planned, and had found a difficult and disturbing backlog of work. She had gone straight to her desk from Euston that morning, had slaved at files all day, composed – or re-composed – a difficult forward diary of visits, and sadly only managed to telephone Theo at his office at quarter past five. Time had flown and Theo had already left.

'Damn!' He would probably go to a club. Emma had yawned. She felt tired, having slept little in the train. Then she brightened, thinking of the future, the spring, a honeymoon in Greece. Then, on impulse, she decided to go to see her mother and borrow the book which had suddenly come into her mind when in Scotland.

After all, she tried to tell herself, I really must see Mummy anyway. She doesn't get much of a welcome on return here from abroad, and I don't expect Desmond's done a thing about her. And the book, she was sure, was about exactly the place she and Theo should visit.

Together. In April. She thought the book had been called something like *The Hill above Vanakos*. The more she recalled it the more she wanted to look at it again, now, this very evening. There was no answer from her mother's telephone and she set out, taking the tube to Hyde Park Corner and walking through Belgrave Square. And met Adrian Winter.

As she strode on towards South Eaton Place, Emma wondered whether she should have taken advantage of that chance encounter to press Theo's cause. Casually. Adrian had seemed so extraordinarily friendly, even affectionate. He'd looked pleased when she'd said that both Theo and she were determined he should propose their health at the wedding. He was greatly attached to Emma's mother. He'd obviously taken to Theo on the occasions when they'd met. Might she not have said –

Said what? Emma chuckled to herself. As like as not she'd have put her little foot squarely in it! 'We *do* hope, Mr Winter, that you'll back Theo to stand in your place in your constituency. And soon!' Something like that! People, Emma reflected, do not always enjoy discussing their replacement, whatever their age or rumoured intentions.

As she turned the corner into South Eaton Place Emma found herself feeling guilty because she was not in the least looking forward to seeing her mother, although she knew Patsy was lonely and vulnerable. South Eaton Place had never conveyed the atmosphere of a home, even when Desmond and she had been adolescents there. It seemed alien, someone else's house in which they were welcome, had shelter as of right, gave as their address. But not home. Emma would normally have decided that this was because of their mother's essentially unmaternal personality, but now she wondered. She felt such happiness now, such a glow of loving and being loved that there should, she told herself, be something to spare for her mother. Had she – and Desmond, but especially Emma – not been hard, in thought, on Patsy? Widowed, fairly impecunious, extravagant in foolish ways but without a partner to counsel, guide, restrain; had Patsy not had rather a difficult life? It wasn't, Emma thought with a touch of generous contrition, exactly her fault that she was, mentally and morally, so out of sympathy with both her children. Desmond and Emma often speculated together that they must both more closely resemble their father – 'Dear, dead Dillon' as Desmond sometimes called him, a puzzled, wry note in the voice. None of this was Patsy's fault. In future, Emma resolved (not for the first time) she would be nicer to Patsy, more devoted, more demonstrative. She felt noble at the resolution, but heard herself give a small sigh. There were no lights showing from the first-floor drawing-room windows, nor from the fanlight over the front door. Patsy could not have returned.

Emma let herself into the house, which felt still and empty. A landing light was on, and Emma knew, with a familiar, unacknowledged tickle of irritation, that in winter Patsy seldom turned it off, for the stairs were dark. She went quietly up to the drawing room in search of *The Hill above Vanakos*. But it did not seem to be there.

Having got so far Emma wondered whether the book might be in another room, perhaps in a bedroom. Conceivably Patsy herself might have taken it up – Emma remembered that her mother had read it and liked it in a detached sort of way. She might, she just might, have returned to it. It was highly unlikely that she would have taken it to Antibes. South Eaton Place was not a house full of books but there was one good bookcase in the drawing room and another on the landing, with *The Hill above Vanakos* in neither.

Emma climbed the stairs, and opened the door of her mother's room. The curtains were undrawn. London's uneven light from distant street lamps and the failing November day came through the large bay window, a window which gave on to the side of the house facing away from South Eaton Place. Emma switched on the light. Books would be on the table beside the bed. From the pillows of the bed, however, blinking and astonished, looked up at her the faces of Patsy and Theo, fresh roused from brief slumber, a sheet half-covering their naked forms.

CHAPTER IX

Desmond knew that the winter of 1933 was the worst season of his life so far. There might be later anxieties and failures: but for sustained unhappiness and the sense of repeated, remorseless hammer blows of adverse fortune the period which started in that last week of November took some beating. And, as often happens, a sunlit time had only just and suddenly vanished. In the autumn Desmond had done his best to feel happy at Emma's happiness – generally with a good deal of success, success only occasionally diminished by the feeling that in spite of long friendship he knew Theo Tate less well than he had always supposed. In the autumn he had discovered that his instinct for journalism had a sound core: he had a job, modest but intoxicating in the trust it implied, and so far everything he submitted went well. They talked of a brief assignment in Paris in the spring. In the autumn, too, he had had a letter from Sonja, the first for some time but heart-warming. She was, she said, thinking very seriously about a visit to England, perhaps early in the New Year.

'Or would I be an embarrassment, *Hirschchen*?' She pretended to think that Desmond looked like a stag, and giggled at his difficulties in following her pronunciation of the diminutive. As he read the words he could hear her voice, see the movement whereby she followed laughter with a swift pace towards him and into his arms. Her letter took him back to a bedroom in Frau Reitz's Bamberg house. The months had gone by but it was as it had been, and her curious writing on an envelope still made his heart race. My God, Desmond muttered to himself, how I want that girl! Sonja told him, rather obscurely, not to reply – she would write again soon with more definite plans. She sounded composed. She wrote from a Berlin address – not that of her previous flat. She had presumably found some traveller to carry the letter for her since it had been posted in London. Quicker, Desmond thought, although it did not seem so, for Sonja's letter was dated six days before the postmark. Thought, erroneously, to be quicker.

Or more secure.

Anyway, Sonja's letter had made clear that he could expect another very soon. That had been in the middle of November and life seemed good. Then, within a week, he had, out of the blue, found in his letter-box at breakfast time an envelope in Emma's handwriting and a long period of nightmare began.

At first he stared at the envelope without recognition. They never wrote to each other. There was the telephone if she was back in London. Or even if she wasn't. Desmond ripped the envelope open, frowning. For a minute he simply failed to take in its contents, a note on two sides of unheaded blue paper. A note written on 25th November.

'Des,

I've gone back to Scotland, to Alison Chisholm. Please do two things.

First *don't* try to get in touch, and *don't* tell people where I am. I'll probably only be with Alison for a few days anyway, but I'll be away from London and out of touch. I've written giving in my notice at my job.

Second, send the enclosed to the newspapers.

Sorry. Look after yourself, darling Des,

E'

'The enclosed' was a separate piece of paper saying that the marriage arranged between Mr Theodore Tate and Miss Emma Dillon would not now take place.

Desmond telephoned Theo at once.

'Theo, what on earth's going on?'

Theo sounded very odd. He talked in a peculiar, sing-song voice and said something about sudden realizations, if timely, being merciful. Albeit painful.

'Theo, what the hell are you talking about? Emma's broken off your engagement. All right – that's your and her business. But you might give me an idea why.'

Theo, still in a curious voice, not his own and somewhat slurred, said some more about timely revelations of true feelings, sad mistakes avoided.

'I can't understand what you're talking about,' said Desmond, exasperated. 'She was mad about you, as far as I could see. Have *you* gone cold on the idea?' He felt angry and with little inclination towards tact or gentleness. There was a lot of pain in all this. Theo was saying 'I? I?' in a sort of mock-Shakespearian way. Desmond realized, with shock, that Theo was extremely drunk. It was a quarter-past eight in the morning. He slammed down the telephone, jigged it, and asked the operator for his mother's number.

It rang interminably. After what seemed an age he heard a quavering voice say 'Sloane 5599'.

'Is that you, Maggers?'

'Sloane 5599. Whom did you want?'

'MAGGERS!'

'Sloane –'

'Maggers, it's MR DESMOND!'

There was a pause and Maggers said, perfectly normally, 'Good morning, Mr Desmond. Did you want Madam?'

'Yes I did.'

'She's gone abroad.'

'Maggers,' said Desmond as patiently as he could, 'I know she's been abroad, but she's back now, isn't she? I heard she got back at the beginning of last week. Is she awake? I want to talk to her.'

'She went off again yesterday.'

'You mean,' said Desmond, head spinning, 'that my mother returned to England from the South of France, spent exactly twelve days here, and has now *gone abroad again*?'

'I packed the same cases,' said Maggers with resentment. 'I'd not had time to sort everything out, wash, iron, mend, not from the last time. She's gone with everything in a terrible state, I was ashamed.'

'Where?'

'Yesterday morning, Mr Desmond. She was on the telephone to that Miss Grant in the travel agency, then the car came at –'

'WHERE?'

Maggers said, irritably, that she didn't know where but presumably Madam had put it in her letter to Desmond. All Maggers knew was that she was to put all mail into large envelopes, weekly, and send it to Desmond, presumably for onward transmission.

'She left money for the stamps,' Maggers said grudgingly, 'and you'll know what to do with the mail, Mr Desmond. Like she says in her letter, I presume.'

'Maggers, I've not had a letter!'

There was a long, long silence at this and after a bit Desmond shouted, 'Maggers?' into the speaker.

'Yes, Mr Desmond. Well, it's a funny thing, but I put it out to post to you. I expect it explains where Madam is and so on, then bless my soul if the man didn't come with the laundry, and half of it what I wanted to pack for Madam! It was too late by then, of course, and what with that and one thing and another –'

'Maggers,' said Desmond, clearly, firmly, kindly, 'You still have the letter to me there, unposted. Is that right?'

'Well, Mr Desmond –'

'Keep it,' said Desmond, 'I'm coming round.'

Patsy's letter was brief. It said that she had decided on the spur of the moment to go back to Antibes. London in November had got her down. She'd wired for her room, Miss Grant at the agency had been angelic, she was wretched not to have seen Desmond but knew he'd understand. Just for a few weeks probably. She'd had an absolute neurosis about it and could stand England not one day longer. There was no hint of reproach in the letter that Desmond, although knowing of his mother's return, had made no hasty effort to see her himself.

'Mrs Chisholm?'

It was several hours later. Throughout the middle of the day there had been no reply.

'Who is it, please?' The voice was high, precise, nervy. Desmond could picture a slight, rather taut woman, perhaps with prettiness marred by anxious eyes, lack of confidence betrayed in occasional clumsiness. There was no alcohol in the voice, however. Desmond knew that Alison Chisholm, complete with fragile marriage, was one of Emma's lame ducks. He had never met her.

'Mrs Chisholm, it's Desmond Dillon. Emma's brother. Is my sister staying with you?'

Silence.

'Mrs Chisholm?'

'Yes, hullo. Well, she has been but she – she's gone away.'

'I see. Can you tell me where she's gone, please?'

'I – I don't really know.'

'Mrs Chisholm,' said Desmond gently, 'I'm afraid I don't believe you.'

'I'm sorry, I –'

'I'm sure you can tell me where Emma is. I know she doesn't want me or anyone else to contact her but it really is *very – very* – important that I do so. I promise you that. I don't want to pester her but I must talk to her. So please, Mrs Chisholm –'

Desmond looked at the black earpiece, spoke a little more, and replaced it, sighing, on its hook. Mrs Chisholm had hung up. He telephoned Theo again and tried to speak casually.

'Theo, do you happen to know how I can contact Emma?' He knew that Theo was unlikely, in the circumstances, to be able or willing to help. Emma, presumably, was fleeing Theo above all people. But it was, surely, reasonable to discover *something* about the circumstances, the terms of this break, Emma's mood. Desmond wondered again whether Theo himself had decided to break the engagement, leave Emma to swim by herself through the dark waters of humiliation. Last time he'd not responded to that query. But last time he'd been drunk.

Theo now at least sounded sober. Strained but sober. He said he had no idea where Emma was. He didn't know she was in Scotland until Desmond told him. Desmond tried to keep his voice calm, gripping the instrument like a man who hated it.

'Theo, I'm naturally worried. I'm not prying, but Emma seems to have disappeared. I presume you two had some major disagreement – that's your business, but naturally I'm concerned that Emma may be alone and unhappy. Can you tell me nothing to help me find her? I'm not taking sides, I just want to find her.'

'I think you told me,' said Theo, 'that you had had a letter from her.' Desmond realized that Theo's drunken memory of their first conversation was hazy.

'Of course. Telling me it was all off between you. Sending me an announcement to that effect to put in the papers.'

'Which you haven't yet done.'

'Which I haven't yet done. I want to talk to Emma first, for God's sake. I want to *understand* what's happened. I can get no sense out of anybody. I've telephoned several friends of Emma and nobody's seen her. She's walked out on her job. My mother, believe it or not, has gone abroad after less than two weeks in this country – gone abroad *again*! Very helpful! Nobody knows a thing and the idiot neurotic Emma's been staying with in Scotland pretends she knows nothing either. Theo, I don't want notices in *The Times* saying it's all off if it's really a tiff, a misunderstanding, a parcel of nonsense. And if I can't talk to Emma I must talk to you. When can I see you?'

'Desmond,' said Theo, still in his strained, stilted voice, very quiet, 'Desmond, I think you had better send that notice to the papers.'

'Then you can explain to me why.'

'Let us say that I am sure Emma is serious in what she has asked you to do. And is unlikely to change her mind.'

'Then it's possible. Unlikely but possible.'

'No,' said Theo, and he sounded immensely tired. 'No, it is not possible.'

'Theo, *why*?'

There was a long silence.

'Theo?'

'Yes, I am here.'

'You sound odd.'

'I am odd. I hate talking about intimate matters on the telephone.'

'Then come round here.' Desmond was speaking from his flat. It was four o'clock in the afternoon and Theo was in his office. Desmond, more often than not, worked at home.

'I can't come round there. Not today.'

'Tomorrow then. Meanwhile I refuse to send any damned notices to bloody newspapers.'

'Refuse all you wish,' Theo said, tonelessly. 'It will have to be done some time, by somebody. I will come and see you tomorrow evening. I am taking a week's holiday, starting next weekend as it happens. I will come round tomorrow at six o'clock.'

But next morning, by the first post, Desmond received a second letter. A letter, this time, with a German postmark.

The letter was written in careful, exact English, a dictionary probably at hand, usage only occasionally puzzling as to meaning. Flicking to the second page Desmond read 'Yours with respect, Edle Reitz.' There were one and a half small, closely written pages, the handwriting large and generous with words tending to spill and lap over the lines above and below.

'Dear Mr Dillon,
You understand that our friend you visited is not staying here any more but returned to Berlin after you left away. I write to you because I think you will not have letters from her any more. There is trouble and she has been taken away somewhere. I do not know. I think it good you don't write letters and you will not have letters from her. I am your good friend and I send you my greetings from a whole heart. I hope I have your house right on the envelope.'

No mention of Sonja's name. Obscure – but, no doubt imprudently, not very obscure. 'There is trouble and she has been taken away somewhere.' What on earth had happened? There were stories, no doubt grossly exaggerated stories, Desmond had thought, of the arbitrariness with which law was now being enforced in Germany. There had been illegal brutality during the chaotic times which the Nazis, whatever their own criminality, had succeeded in bringing to an end; and Sonja had suffered from that illegal brutality in a way which would always make Desmond sweat to think about. But now –

'There is trouble and she has been taken away somewhere.'

It was imperative to discover more. It was probably essential to talk to Frau Reitz, as a known and trusted friend of Sonja. The telephone – and he had no number for the Reitz house – was certainly not the answer, even if he could make initial contact. There must be a visit, urgently. Sonja must have many friends in Germany of course – in the world of journalism and writers she knew everybody. There would, obviously, be agitation going on if, as Frau Reitz's words could only mean, she had been taken in for questioning under some gross travesty of justice –

'She has been taken away somewhere.'

Cryptic. No mention of police. No mention – might there not have been mention? – of a lawyer active on Sonja's behalf. Desmond sat, fingering the letter, his imagination unbridled. Why had Frau Reitz not written, 'she has a clever lawyer, Dr Schmidt, his address is –' or something of the kind? As an intimate friend of Sonja's, she must know such things. Then there was the unmistakable prohibition:

'I think it good you don't write letters.'

Who, Desmond wondered distractedly, would *know* anything? One might have to start with Frau Reitz. One would have to move from Frau Reitz to some appropriate level in Berlin. One would –

Another thought would not go away. One must not get Frau Reitz into trouble. 'There is trouble –' She had, Desmond suspected grimly, found the right English word. Or so he supposed.

There was only one person who could give authoritative advice about these things and he, inconveniently, was not in Berlin where he was needed, but in England. Desmond had seen Kitzi

Fischer several times during the last two months, had discussed with him the article he, Desmond, had written about German clandestine rearmament, had enjoyed, as ever, Kitzi's shrewdness, his humour, his warmth in friendship. But Desmond had observed, with understanding sadness, that Kitzi was edgy, lonely, uncertain what to do. Was he already a refugee? He did not know. He had not decided. Ostensibly he was on a prolonged visit to England, indulging in academic research of a kind. Actually, he was talking to as many people as he could get to listen about the trends he perceived in Nazi Germany. His time was spent – Desmond was ashamed that the phrase automatically formed itself in his mind – in pestering people. Pestering people who, on the whole, did not wish to hear. It was miserable to see Kitzi, the attractive, the irresistible Kitzi, in the role of a bore. Kitzi had been staying in lodgings in South Kensington, and seemed to have enough money, although Desmond supposed that even for a comparatively wealthy German, foreign currency was not easy to obtain. Desmond did not know of Kitzi's nest egg in sterling from his previous authorship, and Kitzi, it was generally supposed, was far from wealthy. Still, he seemed to manage.

Desmond telephoned Kitzi's lodgings and a woman, presumably the landlady, answered. She was well informed on Kitzi's movements – Desmond supposed Kitzi, no doubt forever expecting a call from some influential and sympathetic acquaintance, ensured he could at all times be contacted.

'Mr Fischer's away. He'll be coming back to his room in two weeks from now. I've told him that will be all right.'

'Can you tell me where I could find him?'

A hesitation. Kitzi had probably briefed her carefully and she was being faithful.

'I'm Mrs Hodgson. Could you tell me who it is speaking, please?'

'My name is Desmond Dillon.'

'That's right,' said the woman, sounding relieved, 'that's right, he said Mr Dillon might ring. That's you.'

'That's certainly me. He's a close friend. I've seen him several times since he came to London.'

'He's gone to Oxford.'

'To Oxford? Have you an address? A telephone number?' Kitzi had a number of acquaintances in the academic world and was probably staying with one of them.

'I've an address I can give you,' said Mrs Hodgson, and did so. She added, 'I've no telephone number. He didn't know it. He said he'd tell me when he found it out but so far he hasn't. He only went yesterday, you see.'

'Thank you. You don't, I suppose, know the name of the people he's staying with?' It was an address which Desmond, from a slight acquaintance with the university, suspected was in North Oxford. He guessed that Kitzi had embarked on some tentative crusade to mobilize Oxford opinion about the dangers from today's Germany. Mrs Hodgson didn't know the name of Kitzi's host, if he had one, and Desmond asked her to let him know if Kitzi made contact with a telephone number. He sat down to write a letter to Kitzi, and get it into as early a post as could be managed. Kitzi should then undoubtedly read it tomorrow, or, at the latest, the day after, on Thursday, 30th November.

Theo settled into one of Desmond's chairs and accepted a whisky and water. He looked at his friend, unsmiling, his face almost appearing unfamiliar, so empty was it of the usual quizzical curl of the lip, raise of the eyebrows, mockingly wrinkled forehead. Since arriving, he had said no word beyond 'Hullo'. It was for Desmond, his silence implied, to make the running. And Desmond, his mind now full of Sonja as well as Emma, found it hard to do so. He thought he loved two women in the world and they both seemed to be in a lot of trouble. And both lost as well. Desmond sipped his own whisky, and noticed that Theo's glass was already half empty.

Desmond felt stiff and pompous. His usual rather happy-go-lucky, buccaneering temperament had been quite incapable of shrugging off this misery which he suspected had invaded his beloved twin. He heard himself saying that he had no intention of butting in, Emma's and Theo's lives were their own, obviously if people decided it was a mistake to go ahead with a marriage it was only right – and honest, and brave – to be frank about it and call it off. Painful, but absolutely right. Nevertheless –

He floundered. Theo looked at the whisky in his glass and gave him no help at all.

'Nevertheless,' Desmond said, 'I'm very fond of Emma, as you know, and I expect the business has upset her, and it worries me I can't contact her. It seems to me a time when a brother owes some support. Or may.'

Theo said, 'When the family should close ranks, eh?' There was something like a smile, faint and entirely humourless, on his face now.

'I don't think of it in the least like that. It's not a matter of closing ranks or taking sides. And it's me, a twin brother, not the family. We're hardly a family, anyway, as you know. And my mother's gone abroad. That's one thing I've simply got to discover from Emma – whether she's told Mummy. I can't have Mummy suddenly reading of the end of her daughter's engagement in a stale copy of *The Times* sitting in a café at Antibes!' He tried to smile and said, 'Perhaps you know – what Emma's told Mummy, I mean.'

Theo was silent. Then he raised his empty glass and his eyebrows simultaneously.

'May I?'

'Of course.' Desmond moved across the room to the decanter. Old Theo was certainly putting it back. Theo watched Desmond pour a rather small measure of whisky into his glass, and said, 'No.'

'No what?'

'No, I don't know what Emma has told your mother. But I think I can say that I doubt very much whether news of – of Emma's intentions – will come as a shock to her.'

'To Mummy, you mean?'

Theo nodded.

'Theo, how *is* Emma? I mean, did you have a ghastly row?'

'I don't know how she is. No, no row.'

'Just suddenly decided it wasn't a good idea?'

'Something like that, I suppose,' said Theo. 'Something like that. But I really don't want to talk about it. And I've no idea at all where Emma is. As I've told you. And in spite of the woman in Scotland you described as an idiot neurotic pretending she knows nothing, I have no doubt she has a forwarding address. At the least. I expect a letter will find Emma if you choose to write.'

'I don't want to write. I want to talk to her.'

'And she, it appears, doesn't want to talk to you. To be frank, neither do I.'

'Well, I can't make you discuss it. It's your business. And Emma's.'

'Quite.'

'But I'm worried, as I said. I think that natural.'

'I'm sorry you're worried,' said Theo, with the old irony in his voice, 'very sorry. But of course, other aspects of the matter cause me concern as well. Even, perhaps, more concern.' His voice was not quite steady and Desmond, looking at him, felt contrite for failing to consider that Theo was probably suffering a good deal himself. If Emma had thrown him over, with Theo beseeching her to remain true to their engagement, he was probably going through hell. Desmond, caring passionately about Emma, had been unfeeling, he realized. He got up and rather awkwardly put his hand on Theo's shoulder.

'Anyway, old Theo, I'm terribly sorry about it. I'm not asking anything. Just saying I'm damnably sorry. A thing like that must be an awful knock. I'm sorry for both of you.'

'Thank you. Desmond?'

'Yes?'

'I wonder if I could have another drink?'

'Of course you can.' Knowing that he was doing it badly but that it had to be done, Desmond said, with a sympathetic smile, 'I expect you're doing a good deal of this!'

'Whisky? Yes, a good deal.'

'Don't overdo it, old boy.'

Theo smiled, taking back his glass. Looking into it he said, 'Tell me, Desmond, have you anything else worrying you? Besides your sister?'

Desmond stared at him. 'Why do you ask?'

'Because I know you rather well.'

Desmond nodded. It was a relief, and why not? He told him about Frau Reitz's letter. Theo listened carefully. 'I suppose you've discussed it with our friend Fischer?'

Theo, always less enthusiastic than Desmond about Kitzi, their original host in Berlin, had nevertheless dined once with him and Desmond since Kitzi's arrival in London. He knew how the land lay.

'He's out of London, Theo. I've written to him. He'll get it tomorrow or Thursday, anyway. I've asked him to telephone. I've a good mind to go down to Oxford, talk to him.'

'Of course. You appear a free agent. No office stool.'

'Well, I *have* a sort of office stool; I'm working quite hard for my paper, but I can largely fix my own hours, I do most of it at home.'

'You presumably now plan to go to Germany? In pursuit of the facts?'

'I must,' Desmond said grimly, 'I must. But it's difficult. You see I've got a series to do for my paper, and if I want to keep this job it's got to be done. They're understanding people but they're tough and this Sonja affair is purely private business. I couldn't get away for at least a month. Not without giving the job up – but I may *have* to give it up, I can't live with this uncertainty. But first I need to talk to Kitzi Fischer. I know his view will be worth having.'

'You couldn't discover a need to cover a story in Germany rather urgently?'

'No. I'm not that sort of journalist, sadly. And anyway, they want me to go to France in the spring and I've promised I will, I'm working it up. They can't run to too many foreign assignments.'

'Desmond,' said Theo, a new and stronger note in his voice, 'I told you I'm starting a week's holiday, this weekend.'

'So you said. It's an odd time for it.'

'Emma originally explained that even after return from Scotland she was going to be particularly busy. Freddie Malone is going with several friends to a place he's been lent in the French Jura. Even in December I'm told it's lovely. Emma says – said – she can't get away. Freddie got up a party, and I said I'd go for the first week.'

Freddie Malone, a rich, cheerful extrovert with a boisterous sense of humour, was not a natural intimate of Theo Tate, Desmond thought. But Malone had a wide acquaintance and was as generous as he was loyal to his friends.

'It would have been pretty dull without Emma, but she wanted me to – she said we'll be together our whole lives, let's give it a spice by a bit of separation now. She said that,' said Theo, trying to keep his voice steady, 'she said exactly that. Of course we would have had a few days together after she came south, before I left. And it's only for a week. But now –'

'Well?'

Theo sighed.

'Now, believe it or not, Freddie himself has got bronchitis. He telephoned this afternoon. The party would be nothing without Freddie, although he's talking nonsense about the house being there, everyone can go. I've cancelled. I'm at a loose end for a week. I need a change but I'm not going to the Jura in a party I wouldn't enjoy. I was probably going to drop out anyway. I don't feel like social life.'

Desmond nodded, watching him.

'I could go to Germany for you,' said Theo. 'I could go on Friday.' It was Tuesday. 'I could try to find out what I can. I'd telephone you from there if you like. Anyway, I'd be home in a few days. I've got to be back in the office on Monday week.'

'Theo, it's an incredible offer –'

'Not at all. As you can imagine, I need a change, and to concentrate on someone else's troubles might help dilute unhealthy absorption in one's own. Let's take it that I'll go, shall we? Now, I'd better have some details. I suppose I start with your ungrammatical Frau Reitz –'

'I have had your letter,' said Kitzi's voice on the line. 'I am very distressed for you.'

'I need to talk to you. Ask your advice.'

'Of course.'

'I hate the telephone. Could I come to Oxford to see you?' Kitzi had rung immediately he had received Desmond's letter, first post on Thursday. It was still only nine o'clock. Desmond said, 'I expect you're very busy, but I could get a train as soon as possible and be with you by lunchtime.'

'Today, that will be all right,' said Kitzi carefully. Desmond knew that Kitzi liked to appear very fully occupied, a small and understandable tot of self-deception about the success of his self-appointed mission. In reality, Desmond suspected that whether in London or Oxford time often hung heavily on Kitzi's hands. They fixed a meeting place and Desmond telephoned Theo. Theo sounded brighter than the day before. He said, 'I've got my ticket.'

'Theo, you're still serious?'

'Of course I'm serious. I leave by the boat train tomorrow morning.'

'I'll ring this evening,' said Desmond, his heart already a little lighter at the prospect of activity. 'I'll ring after I've talked to Kitzi Fischer. He's bound to have some good advice, some contacts.'

'Don't ring this evening. I'm busy.'

'When then?'

'I'll ring you,' said Theo, 'before I leave.'

'Don't forget, Theo. It may be important.'

'I won't forget.'

'Theo, I think, obviously, I must contribute –'

For the first time since the start of the business Desmond heard Theo give a short laugh, and say, 'Not at all. I do intend to enjoy my little holiday as well, you know.' And also for the first time Desmond realized that for a good many hours he had given no thought to Emma.

Three and a half hours later Desmond was sitting opposite Kitzi Fischer in the Randolph Hotel in Oxford. The dining room was tall-ceilinged and dark. They sat at a table by the large plate-glass window, the austere façade of the Ashmolean offering little inspiration or comfort. Desmond had already explained by letter and on the telephone the little he knew about Sonja, and Kitzi was not a man to whom things needed saying twice. His face was very serious. Desmond had opened their luncheon with one or two smiling trivialities, an inquiry about Kitzi's health, about what he was doing in Oxford. Kitzi cut into this with impatience. He was fond of the English but disliked their hedging about of grave matters with artificial flippancy.

'The Reitz name is well known. She was not very discreet to write even as much as she did.'

'You think letters are opened?'

'Of course letters are opened. Still, not all letters can be opened all the time. Not yet, anyway. Have you the Reitz letter?'

Desmond gave it to him and Kitzi grunted.

'"Taken away somewhere." There are already quite a number of people who have been taken away somewhere, I have already told you that. I have told many people that. I think they don't all believe me.'

'You mean, arrested and not brought to trial? Not openly accused?'

'I mean arrested and not brought to trial and not openly accused. Our Government has taken special emergency powers. You know that. Your papers have printed it. I have been saying it to everybody who will listen since I got here. Special emergency powers, so that people who are thought dangerous to the State can be locked up. Without trial.'

'And you suppose Frau Reitz means that has happened to Sonja.'

'I am quite sure Frau Reitz means that has happened to Sonja.'

'Who can help?'

'That,' said Kitzi Fischer, 'is a different and difficult question. For that you need someone who is sufficiently influential in the Party.'

'I suppose one starts with a lawyer –'

'That is likely to be useless. This is not a question of law.

201

There is unlikely to be a trial. This is an administrative matter.'

'I imagine the best thing first of all is to visit Frau Reitz.'

'I suspect it would not be the best thing at all. Frau Reitz may have taken risks already, in writing to you. I do not advise additionally inflicting on her a visit from a foreigner.'

'Kitzi, what do you suggest?'

'I have three names I could give you. I would not wish it to be known it was I who had provided them. Any one of the three might be well placed to discover what has happened and why. That, after all, is the first step. It would have to be personal contact, of course. No writing. No telephoning. Of course there is also my nephew Wieland but –' Kitzi shrugged his shoulders. He did not wish Desmond to meet Wieland. He could still see Wieland's embarrassed face when he heard of Sonja's whipping. Something would show, and there would be trouble of one sort or another.

'I'm immensely grateful to you.'

'When do you leave? For Germany?'

'I can't go myself, at least not quite yet. But I've been wonderfully lucky. You remember – of course you remember, we were both your guests, you know him well – Theo Tate?'

'Yes,' said Kitzi slowly, 'certainly I know Theo Tate. Of course. And I have seen him here, in England. We dined together. You too. You must remember.'

Desmond nodded apology for an idiotic question.

'He's got a week off. He's going to Germany on my behalf. You may know he was engaged to marry my sister –'

'*Was* engaged?'

'Yes. I'm afraid it looks as if it's all off. Very sad.'

'Ah! Your sister is unhappy?'

'I suppose so,' said Desmond, feeling hopeless about the whole of life. 'She's out of touch with me. She's gone to the Highlands of Scotland and cut herself off from me and from everyone. I can't contact her.'

'It is bad, that. Another anxiety.'

'Yes. Anyway, Theo's offered to go to Germany and find out what he can about Sonja. He offered at once – he's a very close friend, of course, and I won't let the business of him and my sister spoil that. So Theo's going – he leaves tomorrow.'

'I see.'

'And he'll telephone me before leaving. I'll give him the three names you're going to tell me.'

Kitzi poured wine into their glasses, his eyes on Desmond. Then he said quietly, 'No. You will not give Theo Tate the three names I was going to tell you.'

'Desmond, I'm just off. Taxi at door, one minute.'

'Good luck, Theo.'

'Did you get anything from Kitzi Fischer I should know?'

'Yes. He suggested you contact his nephew, Wieland Breitfall. You can convey Kitzi's greetings to him. He – Kitzi – is here quite legitimately, you see. No embarrassment to his nephew.'

'And he thought Wieland might help, did he?'

'I doubt it. But he couldn't think of anything else.'

'I see,' said Theo. He sounded contented, calm. 'I'll do that,' he said. 'I planned to get in touch with Wieland anyway. He's in the bloody SS, after all, so he must be able to find out something. I'll bet he squirms with embarrassment but I'll get something out of him. I'll ring directly I get back, Desmond. Don't fuss more than you can help.'

Desmond had looked an astonished question across the Randolph luncheon table at his host, when Kitzi had said, quietly and firmly, 'You will not give Theo Tate the three names.' He had sipped his wine, brow knitted, watching Kitzi. Kitzi had looked very seriously into his own glass.

'I say that because I do not trust your friend Tate's discretion.'

'Why not?'

Foreigners, thought Desmond, always like making mysteries. No straight answers to straight questions, even when there was trust – and he was confident there was trust between him and Kitzi.

'Why not, Kitzi?'

'I think he spoke to my nephew about your Sonja's – shall we

203

say revelations? I told you in Berlin that Wieland heard of your Sonja having talked, talked freely, in a way he would have been instructed to think was damaging to Germany. He would certainly have thought it his duty to report this. I can imagine no way of Wieland learning except from your friend, Tate. He certainly did not learn it from you.'

'He certainly did not!'

'All this is conjecture. But I know my nephew very well. I could see he was very, very embarrassed, personally embarrassed by the – incident. You probably find it impossible to imagine that emotion in a *Sturmführer SS* but he is a sensitive, idealistic young man. To me it was clear that he felt a certain responsibility. If Wieland were informed and had reported, then he could not avoid feeling guilty about –'

Kitzi paused and shrugged his shoulders. Desmond had supplied – 'About what happened!' and Kitzi had nodded. Then he had said very quietly, 'Tate and my nephew liked each other. A good deal, I think. It will be interesting to discover what Wieland says to him. Perhaps not much. And perhaps he – Tate – will not report it to you exactly.'

'Why shouldn't he?' Desmond had spoken strongly. 'He's my closest friend.'

Kitzi remained looking at him very directly, and had then said, simply and courteously, 'But I do not give you the names of my friends. Not for Theo Tate.'

Desmond had known that there would be no change on that score. His temper had risen – he had already persuaded himself that in Kitzi's 'three names' might lie the key to Sonja's freedom, and he was angry that Theo could not be given that key. But as he thought of Kitzi's suspicions about Theo's indiscretion he acknowledged that they were not unreasonable. He had, no question, talked freely to Theo about Sonja, and Theo might – just might – have been idiotic enough to mention the conversation to Wieland Breitfall, in a bantering sort of way, rallying Breitfall on German association with the Bolsheviks in spite of Hitler's denunciation of them as the enemies of mankind – that sort of thing, thought Desmond without conviction. But, right or wrong,

Kitzi had felt sufficiently convinced to hold back his trust from Theo; and Desmond wondered whether, now, it was worth Theo going to Germany at all. Probably yes, he felt miserably, at least he'd talk to Breitfall, damn his SS soul. He, Desmond, certainly could not trust himself to do so. Anyway, he couldn't possibly find a reason to stop Theo, in his generosity, now making the journey. He surely couldn't make matters worse.

Kitzi had then changed the subject, and, surprisingly, had said, 'I think it is probable I, myself, will have to return for a visit to Germany quite soon. Perhaps in February or March.'

'Kitzi, that would be wonderful! I'm sure with your contacts –'

'But not quite yet. I have some people here I must still see. Also an important man is due here from America next month, and I have an introduction to him. But shortly after that I may return to Berlin. Perhaps only for a short while, I do not know.'

'Why, Kitzi?'

Kitzi said, 'You remember my servant, Günther?'

'Of course. Strong, silent man.'

'I may have mentioned that Günther had once quarrelled with local Brown Shirts. That he hated them and they him.'

'You did.'

'They have been making trouble for him. In small things, but he is upset.'

'Can't your nephew –'

'Wieland, I think, cannot help. He is fond of Günther but the SS and SA – there is jealousy between them. It would be represented as an SS officer trying to interfere in some legitimate province of the SA. It would be said the SA were investigating some minor infractions, disloyalties, and that *Sturmführer* Breitfall, acting out of personal motives, tried to impede etc., etc., I can imagine it all.'

'How petty!'

'Of course. And I don't expect it amounts to much. But Günther is unhappy, and I may have to return. For a while at least. To do what I can.'

'How do you know about this, Kitzi?'

'He writes,' said Kitzi. 'With difficulty, he writes, Günther.'

He fished a piece of paper from his coat pocket, ran his eye over it and started translating aloud, smiling now and then:

'"– they call me to come into their place and ask questions. They say it's my duty as a good German to answer. I tell them I know my duty and was doing it for the Fatherland when most of them were in short pants. They ask me about you, Herr Kitzi. I tell them what to do with their questions, and they get angry and ask if I know there's a new Germany now. I don't understand them. Then they say, go now, and behave better in future. To me! Herr Kitzi, will you be coming home soon? I don't understand things any more, Herr Kitzi. You will find everything absolutely in order, I promise –"'

Kitzi smiled, mouth twisted. Desmond said, 'Poor Günther.'

'Yes, poor Günther. I think I will still be able to make such people ashamed of themselves. They are an ignorant lot, most of them. And Günther, like me, is an old soldier.'

Their lunch at the Randolph was over, and, feeling a great misery which induced something like nausea most of the time, Desmond had returned to London, to send Theo Tate on his journey to Germany, his own feelings by now ambivalent. It was harder than it had been yesterday to determine exactly what old Theo was up to. There wasn't time, however, to have it out with him, to say, 'Theo, did you open your mouth about Sonja to Wieland Breitfall, by any chance?' In the event there simply wasn't time, and anyway that episode was over, the tears shed, the milk spilled.

As to whether his own article about German rearmarment could have somehow been attributed to Sonja's fault, Kitzi had been reassuring and Desmond had nodded gratitude. But he knew he would never be sure.

CHAPTER X

The burn ran into the sea loch, its last cascade over a rocky lip on the steep hill face about two hundred yards from the loch's edge. The loch itself was stormy and cruel-looking when the wind blew, particularly the west wind. When the weather was still the surface of the water was smooth and reflective. The open sea was seven miles away, round a headland jutting into the loch from the north bank: the sound of the sea was present always, sometimes remote, sometimes close and threatening, again depending on the weather. The sea, thought Emma, sounded like the traffic in London if one were hearing it through a window in some tall building, the noise pressing or distant depending on the time of day and on whether the window was open. Or was it that in the sound of traffic one could, if one listened with the ears of imagination, hear the rhythm and music of the waves? She had once been told of a Skye girl who had emigrated to London and who would sit for hours at a window, homesick, listening to the noises of the city and somehow hearing within them the clamour of the sea.

But the music of the burn, rushing down the hillside over stones, splashing over the rocks from small pool to small pool, was never remote, never dependent on conditions, was the perpetual accompaniment of the hours. The burn water was peat-brown and sky-silver, and now, in December, was particularly beautiful because there was already ice in the pools, there had been exceptionally early snow, and water only ran with difficulty and sparkled its reflections of sun and snow as it slipped downwards, resisting the pressure to freeze. On a hillside opposite, a sister burn was now unmoving, a column of ice: a sight not generally seen until January;

but that slope had little sun, while Emma's burn spent many hours in the sunlight. For this December, astonishingly, was a month of brilliant blue sky, snow on the hills down to the water's edge, and bright, bright sun. At night it was cruelly cold but by day the place had a brilliance which the West Highlands of Scotland only displayed intermittently in the mists and rains of summer when most visitors saw them. 'They keep the road clear,' Alison Chisholm had said in her jerky way. 'They're very good about that. The snow's been early and deep and it's been freezing harder than usual since the last week in November, it's been more like January or February. But a dry spell's been forecast, very cold but you might get sun. And I'm lucky in that the track to the croft is only twenty yards. That's what makes it possible to go there in winter. People think one's mad, of course.'

'Of course.'

The croft was in a remote part of the west coast, on a long arm of the sea surrounded by mountains, great, grey rock faces showing themselves starkly above and below the snow line. Snow lay on the deer grass and bracken, covered the foreshore now, with the loch waters lapping over it. A post van and one bus passed on a daily journey along the twisting, climbing road, a road one vehicle wide with regular passing places scalloped into the hill. Otherwise the sound of traffic was rare in winter. The only noise came from the call of seabirds, wheeling and dancing above the water: and from the tumbling of the unfrozen burn; and the distant sea.

Alison Chisholm had acquired the croft, a stone, white-harled dwelling place about to fall down, unwanted, the last of what had once been a viable crofting township, as these remote settlements were called. Alison Chisholm, loving the west coast and its wild places, hankering after refuge from now one, now another distressing aspect of a life for which she felt inadequate, had shown energy and efficiency – qualities she surprisingly possessed and could display when will was present – in restoring the place, making it weatherproof, even giving it such rudimentary services as the locality could sometimes offer. There she had created a sanctuary, a comfortless lair in the middle of beauty and desolation. The nearest inhabited house was five miles away. And Alison, confusingly finding herself for once in the role of Emma's comforter rather than the other way round, had said, 'You can go to Camuseaigh!' It was twenty-two miles from the Chisholm house.

Immediately she had known this might be very unwise. Emma said she needed total solitude, but was this right? Emma had told her little – a breach, a break-up with Theo whom Alison didn't know. Restlessness, suppressed hysteria, impatience with Alison herself, a lunatic intention to 'go off somewhere and walk for a few days'. On the hill! In December! At least Camuseaigh had lamps, a stove, a large number of tins and, Alison reflected guiltily, a good many bottles of whisky. She could hardly remove them, under Emma's eyes. Not that Emma had ever shown the slightest propensity to drink, but under stress anybody could do anything.

'You can go to Camuseaigh! You won't be bothered there.' Alison's errant husband was due back next morning off the night train from London. Emma and he did not like each other. Emma had been with her for three days. Later that day Desmond would telephone. Life was tricky.

Alison had driven her over beneath a brilliant sky, the mountains etched against it like miniature Alps, the islands on the western horizon now and then visible as their road breasted a rise. The sea was a dark, dark blue.

'I'll forward letters. Postie comes by you once a day.'

'There won't be any. Desmond may try to bully you, but he's unlikely to write.'

'Well, if he does I'll send it on. I'll come over on Friday, Em. I think three days ought to be enough for anybody to get the first sorting-out process over, oughn't it?'

'Doubt it. But come.'

'If you get desperate hitch a lift with Postie. There's a telephone at Ardveaich and we'll come to the rescue.'

Emma nodded. The prospect of complete isolation was already bringing a certain peace. Or numbness, perhaps, she thought. There can't be peace.

Emma had brought a supply of books from Alison's, and the latter, too, had pressed on her a writing pad and pencils. 'Write down everything you feel, everything that comes into your mind,' Alison said. 'It's very therapeutic.'

Emma tried it, with moderate success, and read while the light lasted. When Alison arrived on Friday, Emma said, 'I'm all right, and I love it, and I'd like another week!'

She did her best to look happy and robust. It was a brave effort. And on the Tuesday morning when she had been seven days at Camuseaigh a letter was brought by Postie, a letter which must have just missed Alison's Friday visit. Alison had redirected it and Emma took it, smiling, glanced at the writing on the envelope, agreed with Postie that it was good to be alive on a glorious day like this, and went behind the croft as he drove away in the little red van with a gleaming gold 'GR' on its side. Hidden by the croft wall, Emma was violently sick on the snow. Then, feeling very tired, she trudged back into the croft's downstairs room. It had bare boards on the floor, a grate in which she kept a peat fire going, and rough stone walls. There were several kitchen chairs and one comfortable and broken-down old sofa with the stuffing coming out of it. Emma sat on one of the kitchen chairs and dragged it up to the plain deal table. She looked again at the envelope and then forced herself to open it.

'I don't know where you are but Desmond has given me Mrs Chisholm's address and if you aren't there I expect she knows the somewhere where you are. It can't be Hell because I'm there and we'd have met.

I suppose all I mind about, the last drop of comfort I could hope for – but with little hope I'm afraid – is that I can persuade you that all I said to you, at all times, was true. I said I loved you. I spoke truth. I told you that you were infinitely precious, that your sheer quality makes every other woman one has ever known appear insipid and valueless. That was exact and remains so. I said that my deepest emotions had been uninvolved with

210

any other human being until I met you. That, too, is the simple truth.

These assertions, I imagine, must now disgust you. To be loved by someone who (you must, and rightly, tell yourself) can betray you by sleeping with your own mother is perfectly foul, like being desired by some singularly unattractive animal. Of course, there is no merit in me whatsoever. To tell you, as I do, that my 'thing' with your mother was of not the slightest importance, a physical weakness between an older woman and a young man, not without precedent – to say this is merely to insult both you and her. And to explain, as I also do, that 'a last brief encounter' appeared a kindness, shameful perhaps but entirely without significance, is to excuse nothing. And, indeed, I can excuse nothing. That everything, miserably and finally, ended between us in one instant is obvious. As I wrote at the start of this letter, however, I have, just, that one small hope – that one day, with whatever difficulty, you will be able to believe that about my feelings for you I have neither lied nor exaggerated. Ever.'

The letter had no date, it had neither beginning nor end, neither signature nor endearment. How could it? Emma turned it over in her hands, and a whisper gentle like a child's sigh caught her ear. For the first time in seven days a wind was getting up.

'And how is my uncle?' asked Wieland Breitfall. 'You have seen him?' They were dining in a dark, pleasant, rather old-fashioned restaurant in a small street leading off the Kurfürstendamm.

Theo said Kitzi Fischer seemed well, working at something or other, had visited Oxford as well as London. He didn't want to spend the evening talking about Kitzi. Wieland had taken Theo's hand with great warmth when they met, had looked into his eyes intently, had smiled winningly. Wieland's *Gruppenführer*, no less, had said to him, 'This Herr Tate can be persuaded to look

211

at matters from our point of view, it is said. He may become quite an influential young man in England. He has been critical of Germany but is open to reason. That has come from the Embassy, where he is known.'

'Good, *Herr Gruppenführer*.' Such confidences were flattering. Privately, Wieland doubted Theo's significance but the Embassy must have got some sort of information if they had actually communicated a view about young Theo Tate, aspiring British Parliamentary candidate. They were thorough, no doubt, a thoroughness which made Wieland feel proud and secure.

'He is coming to Germany for a particular reason?' Theo had sent a cable to Wieland, proposing dinner.

'I cannot say, *Herr Gruppenführer*.'

Now Theo looked at Wieland, and Wieland thought his companion's pale, smooth complexion and narrowed, rather mocking eyes were still very beguiling. And his – his *atmosphere*, Wieland said to himself, the impression Theo conveyed, was still curiously attractive. Somewhat enigmatic, humorous more often than not, and attractive. Wieland smiled at him. The evening was, as anticipated, being pleasant. Wieland's emotions were seldom examined by himself. He responded to people spontaneously, enjoying charm and good looks in others, his sexuality clouded by a rather immature and only half-comprehended romanticism. Overlaying this, yet another skin of feeling beneath which his deeper instincts muddled their way around, was his dedicated sense of duty, his passionate correctitude. And, paradoxically infusing all, there was a genuine and often troubling kindness of heart.

Theo opened a new subject.

'I want to ask whether you can help me, Wieland, help me to get some information. You remember my friend, Desmond Dillon. He met that girl here, Sonja – the girl of that Pole who was killed in a row in a nightclub when we were here together. Desmond fell for her.'

Wieland nodded, raising his eyebrows rather censoriously. He certainly remembered, with some embarrassment.

'She talked pretty wildly, I think I mentioned something about that when I wrote to you –'

You did, thought Wieland, you did. He said, 'She had not a good reputation.'

'Maybe. She certainly got Desmond into her bed pretty quickly, old Rodoski the Pole not yet cold! The point, Wieland, is this. The girl's in some sort of trouble, it appears.'

Wieland said nothing to this. It was the preliminary to a good many conversations, these days. Somebody was in some sort of trouble. With the authorities. Occasionally one could do something helpful, there had been excessive enthusiasm, a careful inquiry from even a junior SS officer could lead to reconsideration at least. More often the person in question had been foolish or worse, undeserving of the solicitude of others. In this case he was already briefed.

'Desmond believes, Wieland, that she has been arrested. On what charge, of course, he has no idea.'

'That may be. We have certain emergency regulations, you understand. But the young woman you speak about has been acting and speaking very unwisely, very disloyally. As you know. Writing, also.'

Theo did not take up the obvious imputation, that he, himself, had previously provided at least part of the case against Sonja. He nodded, as if resigned, and asked whether it would be possible to discover Sonja's whereabouts and when the case against her might be heard. It would, he said, be helpful to let Desmond know something, just something, if that could be done.

'My friend,' he lied, 'obviously appreciates that the girl may be a fool and have nobody but herself to blame. But –'

He kept all censure from his voice. 'Do not,' Marcus had observed, 'get too involved in this matter.' Theo, for the first time, had sought an urgent meeting with him after making to Desmond his spontaneous offer to go to Germany.

Marcus had looked sceptical, asked the purpose.

'If I'm to keep my reputation as a man who is thoroughly critical of Nazi practices, but prepared to see their point of view, talk to them, this is the sort of thing I ought to do. There was an opportunity and I took it.'

'The opportunity,' said Marcus, 'should not lead you to involvement. Complications. This young woman whom the Nazis have picked up and presumably interned is not one whom you should particularly wish to help. She is well known.'

'She is very anti-Nazi. She has published strong articles.'

'She is very anti-Nazi, Contor. She is also very hostile to our Comrades, and well known to the Party in Germany which is itself having a hard time as you are aware. This Sonja is a bourgeois idealist, a sentimentalist it appears. We do not in the least wish to encourage a non-Communist opposition to the Nazis in Germany, Contor. The Nazis will beggar Germany with their programme, and the working class must be taught to look only to us to pick up the pieces, as you say here.'

Theo had observed, rather maliciously (for he enjoyed occasionally twitting Marcus, gaining a sense of illusory independence therefrom), that he had heard a large number of the working-class Comrades had actually joined the National Socialist Party. He also commented that Marcus had sometimes forecast a time when it would be Party policy to make common cause with left-wing bourgeois parties, with 'bourgeois idealists', for 'popular fronts'. Marcus, however, had been obdurate. That did not apply to Germany. In Germany 'bourgeois opposition' – especially Social Democrat opposition – to Hitler was to be discredited. The sort of approach which, it was understood, Sonja had represented in her writings was to receive no sort of support. And nor was she. So firm was he that Theo supposed he had the Party line quite recently established or confirmed; and by what he referred to as 'the highest level'. Marcus had also said, 'Of course, you are rather disturbed emotionally, Contor. This engagement, this young woman here –' but Theo had broken in, more savagely than he had ever spoken to Marcus, and said he wished to discuss the business of Emma not at all. And Marcus, surprised, had given him a searching look, and said no more.

So that now Theo nodded lazily to Wieland and said, without concern, 'Nobody but herself to blame. But you might be able to discover something which I could tell her friend, my friend, Desmond Dillon. You understand these things, Wieland. It's important that people in England who might be friendly to you should not get the wrong impression. If people disappear, without publicity, without trial, it can give the wrong impression.'

Wieland repeated that Germany had needed to contend with a real internal emergency. There had been plots, revolutionary plots. It was by no means certain they were all uncovered and rooted out. The most unlikely people had cooperated in treasonable manœuvres. The phrases slid from Wieland's lips, his well-formed lips, his expressive, graceful mouth, thought Theo, watching him without pleasure, nodding, comprehending.

It had been necessary, undoubtedly, to intern certain individuals, Wieland said. The German people themselves demanded it. They had suffered a long time from violence and the threat of violence. They had turned with enormous gratitude to the Party as representing decency, firmness, true German values.

'And to Adolf Hitler, who has had the clarity of mind to see what has to be done and the firmness of purpose to do it. On the unemployment and economic front, also –'

Theo interrupted. He had been drinking fairly heavily during this rhapsody but he had heard on a previous occasion Wieland's wide-eyed praise of the Führer's economic achievements and he reckoned they had better conclude the subject of Sonja. He must, after all, have something to take home to Desmond Dillon. Don't get involved, Marcus had said, don't seem to be over-concerned with this unimportant little bourgeoise, don't antagonize. Your relationship with this Fascist might be quite useful here and there, Marcus had said; while the internment of the girl is a matter of total indifference. In fact, it may even be better so. Well, Theo said to himself, a little fuddled for the wine was scented and strong and the atmosphere of the Berlin restaurant extremely warm, well, I'm not involved. But I must take *something* home. To preserve my credibility, as they say.

'Wieland, perhaps you could discover *something* – something I could say. About this girl.'

Wieland, spruce in his black uniform with silver buttons and swastika armband, smiled agreeably at Theo and said that if Theo could join him for another 'nice dinner' at the end of the week, he would tell him anything that he could. Wieland looked at

Theo with affection and told him that it would not be helpful to the 'young woman' if foreigners appeared to be agitating on her behalf. Lawyers? Theo wondered. Nor lawyers, Wieland agreed, pressing Theo's hand as he said good night; lawyers were likely to be quite inappropriate. Already aware of the facts in Sonja's case, Wieland nevertheless reckoned he should explain to his superiors Theo's persuasive points about English reactions, English opinions. This, after all, was a young man they themselves had said might be of significance one day.

Emma had been seven days and nights in the croft and was beginning to feel again. At first she had only desired flight – flight from Theo, Desmond, from anybody who knew her, flight above all from the smallest possibility of encountering her mother. Flight from London. Alison Chisholm, fragile, vulnerable, five hundred miles away in the Highlands, represented illusory refuge. Alison herself was so much in awe of Emma, her own tower of strength hitherto, that her very feebleness was helpful – here was no prying intruder, no aspiring comforter. Emma wished confidences with no one. She needed solitude and a chance to recover the ability to feel. She was numbed, dead. She had, at Alison's first visit, told her that she was 'loving it', but the truth was she could not imagine herself with sympathy, sensation, emotion: ever again.

But she knew this was nonsense, and she told herself that enforced physical activity, an absence of people, and the willpower to face facts and put words to them would provide the beginning of a cure. The croft, adequately warmed but needing personal effort in order to keep alive and the place habitable, made Emma exert herself, which she knew was a great deal better than being cosseted. She was alone, and although some would have thought that unhealthy, she believed it was good. As to the mental and moral effort needed to look at her situation – Emma said, aloud, as she trudged through the snow round the croft, that her mother was a woman without principle, had always been thus, and her daughter had known it. Little love and certainly no respect existed between them. But Theo –

And there, in her solitude, Emma found it difficult to force words out. She had truly believed that Theo loved her, really loved her. She had completely given her heart to him. He had intrigued her, conquered her, she wanted nothing else and nobody else. And all the time Theo must have been creeping into her mother's bed because he enjoyed Patsy's body, had formed that secret habit and did not fancy breaking it. Nothing peculiar, Emma said aloud, listening to the sounds with loathing, nothing unusual in a man enjoying at least two women simultaneously, professing – even sincerely professing – love for one and being unable to suppress an itch for the other. Plenty of precedents. Wasn't that life, to take with a shrug and a sad laugh, and make the best of? He said he loved her still. Perhaps he did. Patsy would be guilty and frightened. She'd bolt. So might it not be possible –

No. It wouldn't. She banged the snow off her gumboots and shut the croft door against the rising wind. It wouldn't. A chapter had ended suddenly and violently, but it was important to send self-pity packing and start to live again.

And on the eighth day Emma thought that feeling was returning. Although she was ashamed of the fact, Theo's letter had touched something in her. She had made up her mind never to believe a word of excuse if he ever proffered one, but she could not help herself, and the discovered vulnerability was at least a sign of life. She decided to take more notice of her surroundings, to explore a little more ambitiously. She had been pleased to find that the snow on the hillside, although almost completely covering it, was not yet deep. It was possible, even agreeable, to crunch upward on the whitened deer grass, snow helping movement over the buried rocks and carpeted bracken. She thought a short climb, parallel to the tumbling burn, would give her a superb view down the loch. The day was brilliant again, a sky, sea, and landscape of blue and brown and white and gold.

Emma began to scramble upwards, soon feeling tired on unpractised muscles but, at the same time, extremely well. She had set her eyes on a ledge beside the burn, which looked to be about two hundred feet above loch level. It was necessary to have a goal, but as she heaved herself upward the two hundred feet began to appear an underestimate. Keep on, she said to herself, pausing more and more frequently to recover her breath, keep on, it's nothing. She determined now not to look round until she reached her objective – a glance had shown her that she was going to be rewarded by a tremendous vista. Every yard climbed, she was sure, would bring more beauty to the eyes.

At last she brought one aching leg up to the other, straightened and sighed; and turned. She had reached the ledge. In the clear morning the sight was incredible. The loch seemed now to lie far beneath her – many more than two hundred feet, she said aloud in self-congratulation. To the south the hills rose steeply, their sunfree faces dark and bitter, the skyline serrated and dramatic, deep blue sky a background to the jagged peaks. North of Emma her own hill climbed up and up, to a summit she knew was likely to be beyond her or anybody else's powers before the spring. She would, she thought, revisit in the spring. This was magic, this was Heaven.

To the westward she could see clear over the headland which masked Alison Chisholm's croft from the open sea; and Emma now looked along the great sweep of the loch to the Sound which separated the mainland from Skye. The Sound, appearing so close she felt she could almost leap into it, seemed not only near but narrow. Beyond it lay the Isle of Skye, low brown hills in the foreground and behind them, just north of west she reckoned, the terrifying mass of the black Cuillins, clear in the morning light, enormous, menacing. Emma gazed at them, fascinated. After several minutes she realized that for at least an hour she had given no thought to Theo, Patsy, or her own emotions.

She stayed a little longer on the ledge and then decided, reluctantly, to start the descent. It would not be as simple as the climb. The rocks, ice-covered, could be seen and avoided in the ascent, but a misplaced boot on the way down, with a body's weight above it, could mean a twisted ankle or some uncomfortable bruises at best.

Emma felt hungry and began her journey. But after a few minutes' slithering and scrambling she swore aloud. 'Damn! Damn! Damn!'

She had taken what seemed the easier path. Unfortunately it led not down the hill the direct way she had climbed, but to the course of the burn. The sides of the burn were particularly steep, a bad way to attempt the descent. It looked, Emma realized with irritation, as if she would have to struggle back the way she had just come, to choose a better line. She stood for a moment considering.

There was an alternative. If she could cross the burn, the far side looked as if it offered a gentler slope down to a point on the loch some hundreds of yards west of Alison's croft. From there she could walk through level snow along the water's edge to the track which ran from the tarmac road to the building. The only problem was to cross the burn, cascading noisily down at this point. The pools were frozen and a thin patina of ice covered the rocks which studded the watercourse. The nearest pool, however, was not wide and two flattish stones stood out of the ice, with only a narrow, unfrozen channel between them. Below the pool was the burn's next fall, about twenty foot down to the next, broader pool. Then came another long fall.

Emma put her left gumboot firmly on the first rock. This way down looked much preferable to a laborious climb back to find the way she'd come up by. Steadying herself she put her right boot on the next stone. A longish stride with her left leg would now take her to some shingle, clear of snow, beneath the burn's farther bank. Emma put her weight on her right foot and took her stride. As she did so she felt her right boot slip on the ice, and next moment knew that her whole body, utterly helpless, was sliding, gathering pace down the sloped ice to the lip of the ledge over which the burn was rushing to the next pool. And the next. And the next.

'Herr Tate,' said the smart pageboy. 'Telephone. This way, please.'

Theo had spent a good many hours exploring Berlin. His last visit, when Desmond and he had stayed with Kitzi Fischer, when he had met this really rather endearing Wieland, had been too brief. He wanted the chance to do what in better times he enjoyed – walk, alone, the streets of a foreign city, use his eyes, receive impressions and digest them. Theo was still profoundly disturbed. He had written to Emma with a good deal of sincerity. He had stumbled into a perfectly beastly situation and there was no way he was going to stumble out of it. He minded not in the least about this idiotic Sonja, shared without difficulty Marcus's indifference in that direction. He had volunteered to help Desmond because – as he told Marcus – it was consistent with the image of himself he was projecting; because (by now in only a very small way) he was fond of Desmond: but primarily because he needed a change, wanted to get away. He felt sickened by life, miserable. Emma had fled. Patsy, according to Desmond, had also fled – as she would, Theo reflected bitterly and unreasonably, as she would. And Theo, too, needed temporary flight. Even to Berlin. A different city, different sights, different faces. Even Nazi sights, Nazi faces.

Theo acknowledged to himself, as he explored, that this last violent kick of bourgeois capitalism in its tawdry, borrowed revolutionary garments, was not unimpressive in a flashy sort of way. There was no doubt that people looked happier, more secure, more prosperous than when Desmond and he paid that earlier visit. Of hunger, destitution, resentment, there were no signs at all. The place was peaceful. There were large political banners and slogans everywhere, but –

But, a small voice inside Theo, instantly suppressed, murmured, there are plenty of them in Leningrad too! No, Berlin in Marxist terms was an enemy capital, held by the imperialists sitting on the bowed shoulders of the working class: or something. But it had its effect. Theo found, as he wandered, that he was almost enjoying himself in those moments when he succeeded in forgetting he had lost Emma. The hotel, too, wasn't bad. He followed the page and entered a capacious, padded box. The boy closed the door, indicating the telephone, and shut him in. Theo perched on a stool. Wieland, probably.

'Hullo? Theo Tate.'

Theo heard one or two obtrusive clicks. Then an operator's

voice said, 'Herr Tate? *Moment, bitte*,' and next he heard Desmond's voice, clear, unmistakable.

'Theo?'

'Desmond, where are you?'

'In London. Theo, I thought I'd just ring to see how you're getting on.'

'All right. I've seen Wieland.'

'Well?'

'I'm seeing him again on Saturday.' It was Wednesday now. 'He knew a bit about it. He hopes to find out more.'

'Theo, all this is good of you, but I think I'd better come over. To hell with this damned job.'

'No, Desmond, you should *not* come over. It could make matters worse. Wieland trusts me. Much best leave it with me. I will discover all I can. I promise.'

'It's not only discovery that's needed. It will probably be action.'

'Yes – well, that may be harder. But I'm quite sure, Desmond, your arrival would not help at all.'

Desmond said, 'Perhaps you're right,' resentfully. They chatted for a little. It was, Theo thought, a surprisingly good line. The call must be costing Desmond a good deal of money. There seemed little point in it. He knew that if there was anything Desmond could say about Emma he would have done so. He was fussing about this Sonja woman – understandably but uselessly. How uselessly would need to be revealed gently and slowly. Meanwhile –

'Des, we'd better ring off.'

There was a silence, so that Theo at first supposed Desmond had done exactly that.

'Desmond?'

'I'm here.'

'We'd better ring off. This call will have cost you a good deal.'

'Theo –'

'Yes?'

'Theo – something curious has just happened.'

'What do you mean?'

'I don't know. I don't know what I mean. I – when you were talking just then I felt – I felt as if my heart was stopping. Does one have spasms, attacks, at my age?'

'No. Imagination. Do you feel ill now?'

'I feel most odd.' But Desmond, unlike Theo, believed he could recognize the feeling, and the thought terrified him.

'Have a stiff whisky. Goodbye, Des. I'll ring when I get back.'

On the second occasion, on the Saturday, Theo had insisted Wieland dine with him at his hotel. Wieland had demurred.

'You are a visitor to Berlin. I will show you somewhere –'

'I want you to be my guest. The hotel is a nice place.'

Settled opposite Theo, smiling at him like the old friend he felt he had become, thinking how delightful, how amusing this influential young Englishman was, reflecting how creditable it would be – and there were surely signs of it – if he could be brought to understand more of the National Socialist viewpoint, Wieland raised his glass, looking at Theo over the rim.

'To our friendship!'

Theo thought with irritation that this sort of tomfoolery had to be endured. It was the price of dining with Wieland, in itself not disagreeable. He, too, smiled over the rim of his glass. Then, putting it down, he looked carefully at his fingernails and then up at Wieland, a serious expression on his face.

'The Sonja girl, Wieland. You kindly said you would find out what you could.'

'Ah, that,' said Wieland, without enthusiasm. 'Yes, it is true that the girl has been detained. It appears she has been involved in some very suspicious business, very dangerous, very disloyal.'

'Is she to be charged with anything?'

'Perhaps. But now she is being detained.'

'Can you tell me where?'

'No,' said Wieland, 'I cannot tell you where.' There was an unusually hard edge to his voice. It was not the business of foreigners, however agreeable and even influential, to think they could interfere in these matters. He had been sharply reminded of that when he had reported his last dinner conversation with Theo. Furthermore –

'I cannot tell you where. And it would be bad if her friend, your friend, Herr Dillon, tried to make contact or came here. It is not allowed. The regulations are that she must be kept securely, not visited. Please tell him that. It is as I said before.'

'I don't suppose,' said Theo gently, 'that he thinks it would be useful to come to Germany. Not for a moment.' Wieland said nothing to that. He knew better. He reckoned it was time they changed the subject. He had done as promised – confirmed the facts about Sonja, or most of them. She was in one of the new camps, no doubt being subjected to a certain amount of healthy re-education. Theo showed signs of harping on the subject.

'I suppose it hasn't helped her that she's mostly of foreign extraction, Polish and so forth. And was the girlfriend of that Pole, Rodoski.'

Wieland looked blank, rather too blank. Relations between Germany and Poland, he said, were excellent. A ten-year pact had been signed only last month between the two countries.

'I remember,' Theo observed, 'Rodoski talking about the Germans and the Russian Bolsheviks regarding Poland as the enemy of both, as a symbol of the Versailles Treaty. Germans and Russians had a common interest in the destruction of Poland. Something like that.'

'That is not our Government's view. You are quoting,' said Wieland, 'some of the old German Imperialists, perhaps. The Old Guard. All is changed now. The Führer has cultivated friendship with the Poles.'

'I see,' said Theo. 'I see. Well, at least I can tell Desmond that Sonja's Polish connections aren't counting against her.'

'All that will count against her is if she, herself, has worked to undermine the State.' And Theo said again, 'I see.'

Sufficient duty towards Desmond had now been done. And Marcus would not be dissatisfied. He finished his glass of wine and saw that their bottle was three-quarters empty. An observant waiter hastened away for a replacement. Wieland had drunk little

223

and Theo, finding the scented Main wine much to his liking, was already feeling more expansive.

'What first attracted you to National Socialism, Wieland?'

Wieland sighed, a sigh of relief at having, he hoped, disposed of the tedious matter of the girl (part-Jewish too, as it happened, although he had not found it necessary to introduce that factor into their conversation): but a sigh of pleasure, too, at so sympathetic an inquiry on the subject nearest to his heart. He began to talk, to talk in terms already familiar to Theo but with an urgency and sincerity whose force Theo recognized. Wieland, he reflected with a certain inner sadness, was a believer, all right.

'When I was young it seemed to me that the people all around me cared nothing about others. I was born in 1906. The same year as you,' he added, smiling self-congratulation at his knowledge or memory of Theo's *curriculum vitae*, 'and when I was twelve years old we were told Germany had lost the War. And then, for some years, everybody was hungry, and everybody was in despair. And every month there were new parties and new slogans; and every month things got worse. But the people around me didn't much care. You see, we were living in the country, we didn't do too badly, we – my family, our immediate friends – were all right. And they seemed to be indifferent to the misery in which most Germans were living, and indifferent to our shame – we were told, all the time, that it was all our fault, Germany's fault. We knew that couldn't be true, but we had to bow our heads and accept it, accept the guilt. Then we saw ourselves being robbed.'

'Robbed?'

'Robbed. The French occupied our industrial Ruhr, they took what they wanted, saying we owed it and they hadn't been paid. In the east of the country the Poles took our lands, they drove out our people, they raped our women, German women, when they felt like it and their authorities just shrugged – well, what did it matter, it was only a German! Then, all over the east of Germany, and here in Berlin, there were Jews. Jews from Poland, Jews from Russia. They bolted from Poland, they bolted from Russia. And they began to acquire businesses and shops and so forth from Germans who had been ruined by the War, and by the inflation which followed the War – followed because our currency was inflated to pay the war debts the Allies imposed on us.'

'How?' asked Theo. 'How did these Jews manage this?' Wieland had spoken with emotion. He obviously believed all this, it wasn't simply acquired rhetoric.

'How? Well – there were many ways.' Wieland was hurrying on, wanting to get to the heart of the matter, the moment when the first flicker of dawn appeared.

'In all this suffering, it seemed to me people didn't *care*. They grumbled, but they didn't *burn* like I burned. Then, one day, I heard him! I heard the Führer! I was twenty-two years old. He'd been imprisoned in a fortress after a patriotic attempt in Munich.'

'I remember.'

'I went to a meeting. The Party was still quite small. He was superb. He spoke to our hearts – there were only about fifty of us. He *understood*. He *cared*. You could see that every suffering German, every hungry German, every German without work, every German deprived of pride in his country – you could see that Adolf Hitler felt for each one of them as if it were himself. And you could believe that however few were his supporters, in those days, the forces they represented must triumph in the end. He explained how the race, if true to itself, could vanquish all. And had often done so in the past.'

'"To vanquish all" – that's a tall order, Wieland! For any race!' Theo quoted an overworked phrase: '"Politics is the art of the possible, you know!"'

'No,' said Wieland proudly. 'Politics is the art of making possible tomorrow what appears impossible today. Have you ever felt like this, felt that you've at last met someone who cares as you care, who's repelled by what repels you, who can show you a better way?'

Theo was watching him coolly. He nodded and said, 'I understand you perfectly.' He had been replenishing his glass freely during Wieland's harangue and was finding, without surprise, that the absurd superficiality of Wieland's account of Germany's recent past – a superficiality he would have liked to illumine by the Marxist analysis he was competent to expound – was, nevertheless, rather touching. There was no doubt Wieland had passion. And he, Theo, had also once discovered a revelation, a better way, an escape from the shallow and mindless materialism of contemporaries, a faith in the future, a solution. The difference was that his, Theo's, revelation was rooted in practical historical and economic reality; whereas Wieland's was based on grotesque romances about race and destiny and suchlike curiosities. He filled his glass again, trying to pour some into Wieland's. Wieland shook his head and then raised it, looking interrogatively over Theo's shoulder. Theo turned, to see a pageboy approach.

'Herr Tate?' The boy carried a salver on which was a white envelope with lines across it. A telegram, unfamiliar in appearance but unquestionably a telegram.

'Excuse me, Wieland.'

A little later Wieland said politely, 'It is not, I hope, bad news?'

'Yes. It's bad news.' Theo instinctively reached out for his glass and drank the wine down. A waiter was hovering.

'*Zwei Cognac!*'

The man bowed and hastened away.

'I regret,' Wieland said conversationally. 'Perhaps you wish to telephone or send a telegram, maybe? Perhaps I can help?'

'I want to try to make a telephone call to England.'

'They will get the number for you,' said Wieland expertly. With authority he raised his hand and another pageboy came scuttling. Wieland spoke in peremptory tones.

'The number?'

'It's a Herr Dillon,' said Theo, aware of Wieland's eyes on him and caring nothing, 'in London. Here's the number. Please tell me when you have got him to the telephone. Whenever it is.'

Wieland said something Theo didn't catch to the boy who hastened off. To Theo he said, 'It will be quick, I am sure of it. I have told him to mention an – an authority which will make it quick, I hope.'

'Thank you.'

They drank brandy and a difficult silence lay between them,

226

previous conversation hard to resume. Astonishingly soon, Wieland said, 'Here he is' and the boy came back. He addressed Wieland, who looked stern but nodded dismissal. Theo had not caught the page's words.

'He says they have spoken to someone at Herr Dillon's house. He is not there. He is expected back from somewhere – Scotland?'

'Probably.'

'Expected back tomorrow morning. Is there anything else we can do?'

'Nothing else. Nothing at all.'

Theo found his mind blank. He could make excuses, break this dinner up, go to bed. Better not. Better any relief, any society. Even this conversation, by now tedious.

Theo finished the rest of his brandy in three gulps and stuffed the telegram into his pocket. He looked at Wieland, breathing rather heavily. Suddenly he felt overwhelming distaste for Wieland, a desire to knock some sense into the handsome head of this helpful, courteous, simpleton sitting the other side of the table. He leant forward.

'Let's go on talking about your National Socialism, Wieland.'

Wieland shrugged his shoulders and said, 'Perhaps I did not make it clear. Perhaps it is hard for you to understand.'

'I understand perfectly. You minded about the state of your country – minded passionately. You wanted to follow someone who could do something about it. You heard Adolf Hitler speak and thought you had found that someone.'

'I did.'

'The trouble is that your analysis of the problem was entirely wrong. And it follows, of course, that your view of the remedy is wrong also.'

Wieland frowned and said, '*Bitte?*' Theo turned and caught the waiter's eye.

'*Noch zwei Cognac!*'

'Thank you,' said Wieland, 'no more.'

'Well, I will.'

Theo had closed his eyes for a second, seeing the scene called up from darkness by the telegram in his pocket. The room seemed to be spinning and his heart leapt unnervingly, the wine and brandy knocking him off balance. The waiter, bowing, set another full glass before him. He focused with a little difficulty on Wieland.

'Wrong!' he said. 'Wrong analysis, Wieland. You've seen the whole problem in superficial, mechanistic terms. Let me explain.'

But although he knew he talked for a while, he never remembered afterwards how much he did, actually, manage to explain; and had only a dim recollection of Wieland standing at some time, bowing, saying words of thanks for dinner, then apparently helping him to his feet and towards the hotel lift. Theo woke at six in the morning, Sunday morning, feeling vile. He reached out his hand for the telegram which he had, he saw, pulled out of his pocket and put on the table by his bed. He read it once again. It was signed 'Desmond'.

> 'Regret Emma had fatal accident in Scotland last Wednesday. Mountain fall. Died instantly. Funeral London Monday.'

'Desmond,' said Theo, 'it's me. I've been trying to ring you for a long time. Naturally.'

Desmond's voice was flat and tired. 'I've been to Scotland. Fixing things. Just back.'

'Of course.'

'When do you get home?'

'I'm crossing from the Hook of Holland tonight. Desmond –'

'It's all right. It's in the afternoon.' Desmond gave him the funeral's details. It had not been possible to tell Theo earlier, he said. They had not found Emma until Friday afternoon.

'The telegram,' said Theo, 'must have taken some time. Desmond, it said "Died instantly!"'

'She broke her neck.'

'There's nothing to say, Desmond. Not by either of us. Your mother –'

'My mother,' Desmond's voice said, crackling unnaturally down the line, 'is in the South of France, as you know. She is

228

apparently ill. Or, anyway, too ill to travel to England and attend the funeral. That is what she says.'

Desmond, in London, hung up the telephone earpiece. Nineteen hundred and thirty-three. The year had started with Sonja's letter about Hitler's advent to power. It had not improved with the passing of the days.

Part III

1934

CHAPTER XI

Kitzi Fischer's letter to *The Times* appeared in that newspaper in April 1934. Before posting it to the editor he had shown the text, with modest pride, to Desmond Dillon. Kitzi, back in the same lodgings in London, had booked his passage to Berlin in June. He told people that he had business there, and would decide whether he would stay or leave when he had looked around. Meanwhile his old servant was finding life difficult.

'I left him with a lot of responsibility. He is an excellent fellow but it wasn't entirely fair. I must go and see what's happening.' In fact Günther had written one rather reassuring letter, to the effect that he'd been left alone recently. Nevertheless Kitzi felt a prick of conscience. He had been in England 'engaged on literary research' for over six months. And, to tell a truth he wished to confess to nobody, he was by now running out of money.

Kitzi also explained to anybody who happened to be listening that 'a good many people' in Germany were getting sick of the régime. The old President, with all his faults, was said to have been several times on the point of sending his Chancellor packing. Desmond, loving Kitzi and deeply respecting his knowledge of his own country, nevertheless heard these speculations with incredulity. Furthermore he regarded Kitzi's plan to return to Berlin with the deepest misgiving. They were dining together at the end of March.

'They'll arrest you. From what you've told me –'

'No, they will not arrest me. I am quite well known, I have many acquaintances in various parties. I did not respect him but I knew Schleicher well, for instance, before he became

Chancellor. I have several times dined with Papen, with *Franzchen*. These men have played a most unwise game but they are not evil, they –'

'Kitzi, they're not in power. The Nazis are in power.'

'Of course the Nazis are in power, and they naturally loathe me. I would be ashamed of myself if it were otherwise. But I know a number of them, too. Furthermore, the Nazis have not yet got it all their own way. Papen is Vice-Chancellor, after all. There are some decent men about. In spite of the appalling sentiments of the top Nazis, my dear Desmond, Germany is not yet Bolshevik Russia! Certain proprieties are still observed.'

'You say that! When you yourself told me that what has happened to Sonja is not unprecedented, that you have heard of other cases!'

Desmond had been living for four months in a grey light between night and day. There had been no word of Sonja. To everyone he knew who might have knowledge or influence he spoke of Sonja, and people were helpful, noted details, promised to speak to 'well-informed Germans with no illusions about the régime'. It produced nothing. Desmond spoke to a well-placed friend in the British Foreign Office, to a much-esteemed journalist with contacts throughout Europe, to Adrian Winter. It yielded no results. People were kind, solicitous, felt for him: but they could not help. The esteemed journalist had been brutally frank, and by that very brutality kind.

'I knew her, Dillon. Admired her greatly. I'm afraid she was courting danger. She wrote too well and too bravely. There were old scores to pay off and they've been paying them off. And wasn't she Jewish?'

'Jewish blood. She was a German citizen.'

'By ordinary standards, yes. By theirs, today, she probably rates as a human being with virtually no ordinary civic rights. I'm sorry to have to say these things, but it's no good fooling oneself – people are disappearing over there, you know.'

And so, day and night, Desmond lived with the grim misery of loving a woman who was helpless and in the absolute power of an unprincipled authority which hated her. He told himself that this couldn't go on for ever – the worm would turn in Germany, a great civilized nation after all, a nation that respected order and legitimacy. But there was no word of Sonja as the early weeks of 1934 passed. The esteemed journalist gave one word of advice that Desmond found particularly hard to accept.

'Don't go over there and start to interfere yourself! It's bound to make matters worse. Make your inquiries, follow it up, through third persons.'

'Why? I need to *do* something.'

'You mean, you need to feel you're doing something! I sympathize. But the truth is that to start thrashing about in Germany will, at the best, achieve nothing, and at the worst prejudice your girl's case. Your name's known there, after all. Your friend Theo Tate talked about you in the context of the girl, you've said so.'

'You mean I'm a marked man in Germany!' Desmond didn't smile, absurdly self-important as the description sounded about a twenty-eight-year-old writer without influence or connections.

'Not necessarily. I don't mean you'd be arrested or anything like that, a British passport is still honoured if one keeps the law. I only mean that if you went there and started visiting lawyers, seeking out Sonja's friends, all that, you'd be more likely to do harm than good. Do them harm, I mean, and probably her too.' It was the same message that Theo had brought back after his brief and fruitless visit.

'You'll do no good, old boy,' Theo had said. 'No point in tramping round the Fatherland upsetting everybody.'

'I don't care a damn how many I upset.' But he had known, wretchedly, that the advice was probably right. He would go to Germany if and when there was somebody to see, good to be done. Kitzi was of the same mind. Kitzi had listened and nodded and said, 'Stay here. At present.'

'Kitzi, you once said you knew some contacts who might help. I know you weren't prepared to give them to Theo, but now I can go myself and to hell with my job! Will you –'

Kitzi said, sadly, that there had been developments in Germany which made it certain no acquaintance of his could help in the matter. They had the same conversation many times, including the day at the end of March when Desmond expressed his foreboding about Kitzi's own plans. Desmond told him grimly that his views were inconsistent. On the one hand, Kitzi had said 'certain proprieties are still observed': that he, Kitzi Fischer, would not be arrested simply because he was known as a critic of the régime and a man of integrity with a bold pen. On the other hand he now admitted that he knew nobody of influence in Nazi Germany to whom he could introduce Desmond with a chance of eliciting information about or help for Sonja.

Kitzi sighed. To tell the truth he believed little of what he reassuringly told Desmond, but he knew that if only for old Günther's sake he must at some time travel to Berlin. He found he could not yet face the possibility of permanent exile. And even Kitzi, a fearless facer of truth, could often not bear to contemplate what he suspected was happening in Germany, and happening with frightful speed: the extinction of civil liberties, with the broad mass of people happily assenting. As to foreign affairs, Hitler had withdrawn from the Disarmament Conference and set Germany on the road of rapid and overt rearmament; and had submitted his policy to a plebiscite of the German people which had approved it by a majority of over ninety per cent a few months back. All this was true and painful, and during his stay in England Kitzi felt he had managed all too inadequately to explain, to convince, to warn. His English friends had been most understanding, but they clearly assumed that winds would change and blow Hitler away. Meanwhile Kitzi found that he was terribly missing his country, the sound of its language, the sharp, stimulating air of Berlin. He was adamant that he should and could with safety return there – 'perhaps for a short while only'. He made it a matter of political calculation, but the truth was that his heart was sick for home. He would, he decided, go in June.

But Desmond's months of darkness were not only because of Sonja. Since Emma's death he had felt only half-alive. No blame attached to Theo – poor Emma had not killed herself for love, it had been a slip, an accident, no question. And Theo was obviously cut to pieces by it. In spite of the breach between him and Emma (not known to all: Desmond had never sent Emma's notice to the newspapers, determined to talk to her first and failing to do so), Desmond regarded Theo as the person closest to him when he thought of Emma. Theo had loved her.

But Theo seemed almost to be avoiding him. For that awful Christmas, Desmond had stayed at Bargate where the Marvells, as usual, were quietly understanding. Hilda Marvell in particular had taken him into her arms in a way remarkable for so distant a family connection – he heard Emma's voice describing it, mocking their mother for her inaccurate claims to Marvell cousinship. Hilda had held Desmond close.

'Dearest Desmond. How has Theo taken it?' The Marvells knew nothing of a rupture between Theo and Emma.

'Hard, I think. I've hardly seen him. He seems to want it that way.'

'I wrote, of course. Poor man – although I have to tell you the truth, Desmond, he's not my favourite person. As you know I've done a bit to help him, put him in the way of old Adrian Winter and so forth. Emma and him – it seemed enormously suitable, both clever, both so handsome. But about Theo – well, I hate saying it now, but there's something –'

She sighed.

Desmond, loyal, told her that Theo was an outstanding human being.

'Let's hope he becomes the Parliamentary candidate. They couldn't do better.' He found he cared little, one way or the other.

Hilda said little to this. It appeared that she had invited Theo, too, to stay immediately after Christmas. He had declined.

'And you, dear Desmond – what about your own life? Still working for that paper?'

'Of course. I'm off to France in the summer. I've got to do a series on French reactions to what's going on in Germany. I can mug up most of it here in the spring but I've got them to agree a short spell actually over there, before we go to press. Rather challenging! I shall be writing other articles in the meantime of course.'

'They don't – your employers don't – seem in a hurry for the series, the French series!'

'They seem to think,' said Desmond, 'that this year will get more, rather than less, interesting. In Germany.'

'Are you qualified?'

'Certainly not! But I've got a lot of contacts, I think I'll soon know where to begin.' Desmond was, indeed, finding his only solace in work and investigation. He had a keen nose for both facts and opinions, had discovered in himself a shrewd ability to draw a companion on by half-questions, tentative observations – draw a person somewhat further than intended. And in the case of this particular assignment the situation in Germany exercised such a beastly fascination over his mind that to work on it, in this case to work on it by investigating French attitudes to it, would provide a certain relief, an illusion that he was not far from Sonja, the scratching of a sore. And work kept Emma from the mind, did something to compensate for that feeling of being only partly in this world.

Hilda Marvell had said, 'I suppose you won't have time, when in France, to get down to see your mother. Is she better? Poor Patsy, it's all been terrible for her.' Her voice was uninterested.

'I've not heard recently. I'll be in Paris, I think all the time. But, as I say, it won't be until May or June.'

Kitzi had been sceptical about Desmond's mission to France. Desmond reminded him, when they met in March and talked about Kitzi's letter to *The Times*, of how he, Desmond, would be in France at the same time that Kitzi would be back in Berlin, if he persisted in that venture. Kitzi grunted. Of the French, he was surprisingly dismissive.

'They kick us only when we are down! When people like the Nazis flex their muscles the French will look for ways to excuse doing nothing.'

'I doubt if that's fair, Kitzi.' But Desmond recognized, with an inward smile, that behind Kitzi's fervent hostility to the Nazis was a devoted German patriot whose feelings towards France remained, at best, ambivalent. Kitzi loathed Hitler: but he had been wounded in '16, in Champagne.

Kitzi's letter to *The Times* was a plea to its readership to rest their attitudes in foreign affairs on moral principles. The letter rehearsed, in familiar terms, the argument that many provisions of the Versailles settlement had defied those principles, and had imposed, solely by right of victory, grossly unjust settlements upon many of the races in Europe, not only the Germans. President Wilson's idealistic fourteen points, accepted by Germany, had been largely frustrated by greed or by the passion for revenge. There could be no lasting peace on this basis. All this had been said often. The sting in Kitzi's letter was in its tail.

> 'Nevertheless it would be not restitution but a second betrayal if a determination to right the wrongs of Versailles became confused in the mind of Europe with an apology for inexcusable acts by the Government of Germany. Germany needs the understanding of her neighbours if justice, long deferred, is to be done to her. That understanding can only be withheld if, in its domestic policies, the German Government shows itself isolated from the mainstream of liberal European tradition. All who love Germany and believe in Europe will, therefore, pray and work to see that no such accusations shall apply.'

Desmond pursed his lips.

'You criticize my letter, Desmond? Not good?'

'It will be regarded by your countrymen as attacking your own country in the foreign press.'

'Not at all! I only say –' he read again and aloud the last section.

'"Understanding – withheld *if*", *if*, Desmond, "the German Government shows itself isolated!" I am stating a consequence that can be avoided. Friendly counsel, Desmond! That is the logic of it.'

'Nonsense,' said Desmond robustly. 'Everyone in Germany knows what you think. You're warning people here not to let their sense of guilt over Versailles blind them to the character of Nazism. That's what you're doing, and it's perfectly obvious.'

'Yes, but Desmond, I make clear that the German Government, in its own interests, can avoid condemnation by –'

'Of course it can avoid condemnation. By being entirely false to all that it openly and shamelessly stands for. Kitzi, don't post that letter. It will tell nobody anything they don't know already and it will do you yet more harm. But if you *do* post it and *The Times* publishes it, stay in England. Don't go back to Germany.'

But Kitzi said that he must at least pay a visit to his home, to Berlin.

'May and June are pleasant months in Berlin,' he said absurdly, rather pathetically, seeking to obtrude a note of normality into a situation which Desmond felt to be crowded with menace. 'And since I shall not return for several weeks, there will be time to observe the reactions, if there are any,' he added, not meeting Desmond's eye. Desmond felt that his friend's clear sight had sadly deserted him. And Kitzi posted his letter, although he delayed a week or so. It was published on 14th April.

It was in early June, a few days before his Uncle Kitzi's announced return, that Wieland Breitfall attended a lecture for selected SS officers which he found particularly interesting. The occasion was agreeable – there was a short reception beforehand, toasts were drunk, gossip exchanged. Wieland found himself talking to an older colleague, generally well informed. He found that they were speaking in low voices, he was at first unsure why. Then he appreciated that his companion's sentiments were of a kind to be treated as 'confidential'. The older man murmured, 'You've heard the latest about Röhm?'

'What latest?'

'Stormed at the Führer himself! Told him the Reichswehr is unreliable, disloyal to the Movement, packed with reactionaries, should be virtually abolished! Told him, once again, to build a new army based on his SA!'

'Incredible! When the Führer has managed to unite everyone, the generals, the business people –'

'Röhm doesn't see it like that. If you ask me he's drunk with ambition. The Führer's patience is extraordinary, but he's got a terrible task. I'm told that the Reichswehr High Command is pretty sore at Röhm's antics –'

Wieland knew that Röhm, the SA Chief of Staff, had had an interview with the Führer on 4th June, but it was believed to have been confidential. This sort of stuff was rumour, and the incessant criticism of the hugely expanded SA now prevalent within the SS made him uneasy. Louts many of the SA might be, but Germany could surely gain nothing from bitter enmity between the wings of the Party itself. Yet Röhm, for his part, was said to have stridently abused the SS – to Himmler himself – in March, to have called them 'protectors of reaction'! Röhm had talked wildly in his speeches about the Revolution being 'incomplete until the SA State existed' – whatever that meant! Röhm, pudgy, gross, face criss-crossed with duelling scars, blatantly homosexual, surrounding himself with a coterie of pretty young aides – ironically, most of them with aristocratic names – Röhm had actually summoned a personal press conference in April, at which he had shouted that theirs was a National *Socialist* Revolution, and those who forgot that emphasis were reactionaries – bourgeois conformists or worse: shouted it in a way which implied that the SA, alone, were competent to manage events. 'The SA,' Röhm had declaimed, 'is the will of the German Revolution!' And from the start of that year, there had been a series of incidents between the SA and Reichswehr. All this Wieland knew.

It was also whispered, incredibly, that after the Führer had made a clear, authoritative pronouncement in February, firmly defining the separate duties of the Reichswehr (to defend Germany) and the SA (to work internally and in the political field), Röhm had spoken to his cronies about Hitler in outrageous terms, saying that 'the Corporal should be sent on leave'! For Röhm wished the German Army to absorb the SA, to give military rank to its leaders, to become a National, a Revolutionary Army – under his, Röhm's command.

You couldn't expect the Reichswehr to tolerate such a thing for one instant, and the Führer – rightly, Wieland said loyally to himself – had no intention of causing outrage to the Reichswehr. So Röhm had been infuriated at the pronouncement, at what people reckoned was the Führer's statesmanlike way of cutting the SA down to size. No doubt there were a good many reactionaries about, with too much surviving influence – but one had to *trust the Führer*, Wieland knew. They had vowed obedience, faith, utterly unquestioning loyalty. These current trends within the SA were a negation of the National Socialist ideal which they, the SA themselves, had done so much to promote. It was vile, it was divisive. As Wieland had said to his colleague, the Führer had done so much, so wisely, so tactfully, to unite old and new, to heal wounds. Only four weeks earlier it had, for instance, been agreed that the Reichswehr would wear the swastika on their uniforms – it would have been incredible even a few months ago.

Still, these rumours were probably grossly exaggerated.

Then they had trooped into another room for the lecture, and the lecture was fascinating. Furthermore, by concentrating upon a real enemy, it provided Wieland with some relief from contemplation of internal Party feuds and disloyalty.

The lecture was given by an ex-Communist. A lively lecturer, he explained his original motives, his enlistment in the Communist Party, his indoctrination, the language used. He made them chuckle with his description of exactly how a Communist could argue that white was black because the Party had declared it to be so. 'Or red, brown perhaps!' Wieland's neighbour whispered. Wieland frowned. The joke was in poor taste. The lecturer was now a respected member of the National Socialist Party, had seen the criminal folly of his earlier ways and was much in demand.

But certain phrases used by the lecturer, phrases current in Communist jargon, caught Wieland's ear. That night he sat down in his small flat and tried to reconstruct a conversation in an hotel restaurant one cold December night a few months ago: Theo Tate's flushed, exquisite face a few feet from his own, speech increasingly blurred, but expressions memorable as he explained to Wieland the absurdity of his, Wieland's philosophy. And

Wieland, for the first time, had heard a touch of passion, of genuine heartfelt emotion in his English companion's voice as Theo had talked more and more glibly and had got more and more drunk. They had talked mostly in English that night but Wieland's English was good. He translated to himself now the lecturer's jargon phrases into Theo's tongue.

Next morning Wieland asked for an interview with his immediate superior, and spoke at length, standing stiffly to attention. The other looked at him speculatively. It was a good thing that Breitfall was showing some alertness and intelligence in doctrinal matters, whether or not there was anything in this particular suspicion of his. Breitfall's uncle, that pestilential Fischer, was expected back in Berlin. Fischer had a good many respectable friends but was disloyal to the core and it could only be a matter of time before accounts were settled with him. Meanwhile *Sturmführer* Breitfall –

'You have done right to report this, naturally. It can be checked out. It may take a little time. Keep your normal contacts with this Tate.'

'No contacts. An occasional letter, perhaps.'

'Since he was here?'

'No. Not since he was here.'

'Our people regard him, if I remember correctly, as a promising young English Conservative politician. One who, despite certain misunderstandings, has shown himself not wholly unfriendly to the Reich?'

'That is so, Herr *Sturmbannführer*. That is Herr Tate's reputation. In London.'

'And now you think –'

'As I listened to yesterday's lecture these phrases in argument were suddenly familiar to me. When I spoke, for instance, of the atrocities of the Bolsheviks, he spoke of my having been seduced by purely mechanistic accounts. The inner reality was different. Words like that.'

'Inner reality!' said SS *Sturmbannführer* Krumper. 'An English Conservative! Well, well! Thank you, Breitfall. The Party has got some pretty useful Communists, KPD members deliberately not pulled in, kept for just this sort of checking, as you know. We'll see what we can find out.'

Wieland saluted and withdrew. He had not enjoyed making his report. When he thought of Theo it was still with a certain admiration and affection – there was something magnetic there. Admiration had dwindled that night at dinner as he had watched Theo get steadily more intoxicated and incoherent; and affection had all but disappeared under Theo's aggressive, sneering on-slaughts on his, Wieland's, beliefs. Nevertheless there had been, for a little, a small flame that touched them both, the warmth of a light, recognized, mutual attraction. It was a pity that this should have been extinguished by suspicion – but it had been a duty, without question, to report that suspicion. Theo and his inward beliefs were not important and were certainly not matters for the German authorities; but in small things as in great, Wieland recognized, truth is worth discovering and recording.

Two days later Kitzi Fischer arrived back in his house in Berlin.

In these early months of 1934, Theo found, without surprise, that his chief and perhaps only source of personal comfort was the Party. He had for the first time used the emergency procedure to arrange a meeting, before his December visit to Germany, and had encountered a sceptical, somewhat disapproving Marcus. Since then he had invoked the system three times. He recognized, and Marcus recognized, that there was no direct reason for this. Theo's circumstances had not changed. He had no reason to suppose that he did not still stand an excellent chance of becoming a candidate for Parliament in Adrian Winter's safe seat. The Central Office knew of his hopes and were discreetly encouraging, he had done all that a sensible aspirant should do, he had – he hoped decisively – dispelled the absurd rumour that he was over-friendly towards Germany: while giving no breath of sus-picion that he was other than loyally Conservative.

Theo did not need Party guidance on any particular aspect of life. He had nothing of consequence to report. Still, he needed to see Marcus. And he realized that this was because Marcus, alone, knew almost all about Contor and could thus be talked to, confided in, with that absolute lack of constraint which brings relief. Marcus, and through Marcus the Party, represented peace, comfort, home. There was no other refuge, there were no other reassuring arms.

In the matter of Emma, Marcus, originally sardonic about what he called 'the little idealist', had on the whole been wonderfully understanding. Theo had stumbled a little over his account of Patsy, Theo's relationship, Emma's discovery, Emma's flight, Emma's death. He had repelled Marcus's initial remarks with something like savagery. Finally, Marcus had been patient, comprehending, kind. With part of his mind Theo recognized that his own efficacy, in Party terms, was not enhanced by the recital. The Party did not like emotional crises; they made men and women unreliable. Emotions were bourgeois luxuries, largely redundant when the Revolution eliminated false values and pretences between the sexes, between people. But meanwhile Marcus was a tower of strength, clear-headed, generous, of course unshockable. Marcus, as he himself often said, and sometimes with a hint of menace, a whiff of the bully, knew Contor very well. Just now, that knowledge was comforting indeed. With Marcus, and only with Marcus, could Theo feel free.

Desmond, once to be his brother-in-law, old friend, long-term companion, induced in Theo now feelings of particular disquiet, and he avoided him. It had, of course, always been true that Desmond knew nothing of the inward Theo, the politically conscious Theo, the secret, contriving, Marcus-directed Theo: thus there could never be other than superficial relations with Desmond. Nevertheless, Desmond represented to Theo youth, shared laughter, Cambridge, the lighter side of life; and more recently he had been associated in the mind's instant images with Emma. Theo had always enjoyed Desmond's spontaneity, his buccaneering quality, the sense that Desmond might on the spur of the moment defy any conventions and get away with it. This was very different from Theo and he relished it. They had, after all, shared a lot of fun over the years – and, Theo sometimes said to himself a touch sardonically, one can't be a Communist twenty-four hours a day. But he never shared that heresy with Marcus.

Now, however, Theo felt repelled by the thought of Desmond and the compulsory falseness which Desmond's presence demanded from him, Theo. It was not only Theo's conspiratorial, political life which now separated them – it was the guilty, the terrible circumstances which had driven Emma to Scotland, it was the deception, it was betrayal, it was Patsy. For comfort in these days, Theo needed frankness. And only with Marcus was frankness possible.

Marcus observed Contor very shrewdly. He knew that if this long-term investment was to flourish, the human being needed nourishment. Marcus would never have put in the same terms Theo's own heresy about the impossibility of being a Communist twenty-four hours a day but something of the kind was not far from his mind when he said, not for the first time, 'Your political career here – you will derive some ordinary human enjoyment from it. Quite apart from its ultimate aim – our ultimate aim.'

'Certainly.' Theo was grateful for this sort of recognition, so different from the humourless Communist archetype of legend. 'Certainly,' he said, 'the political game stimulates me. I know I shall enjoy the House of Commons, if I get there.'

'That has moved, that matter?'

It was summer, a pleasant June day on Hampstead Heath.

'A little.' Adrian Winter, sad for Theo, grieving for Emma, touched to the heart by what he supposed must be his admired Patsy's sorrow for a lost daughter, had written a charming letter in December.

'A little. I heard from Winter, as you know. Sympathy and all that. Of course he didn't know that – that there had been any difficulty between Emma and me. But now I gather that the constituency Selection Committee is likely to meet early next year. It seems an age away, but it's only nine months. It shows he's definitely told them he's prepared to stand down. I've not seen him in recent months, I don't want to seem pushing. I think we're going to be staying at the same place in Scotland, in August.'

'Ah,' said Marcus, 'I am glad to hear that, Contor. That is good.' He smiled at Theo and they both knew, and did not need to express to each other, that Theo's status as tragically bereaved fiancé could only improve his political chances; and Theo now seemed within something like sight of success.

'*Combien?*'

Desmond had been lucky to get the taxi. Early June in Paris should be delightful, a time of song and sunshine, girls in elegant hats smiling over Pernods at café tables in the morning light. Instead rain had started to fall heavily at midday and every taxi in Paris seemed suddenly occupied. Desmond had needed to go some distance to lunch, an important lunch with an important contact, a veteran Paris reporter of the political scene, sceptical though friendly about this young English pseudo-journalist and his investigations: but accepting him because the introduction was from an old friend and the veteran reporter was prepared to help. Desmond, from the slender allowance his employers could afford, would be paying for the lunch. The veteran reporter had suggested a restaurant which Desmond suspected would be expensive and had established was some way from his hotel. He had passed a useful morning paying calls, taking up his introductions, explaining his own objects, giving a good deal in return for what he hoped to obtain, giving from the store of his own brief and bitter experience of Nazi Germany. Desmond, in the first half of 1934, had been reading hard and talking a good deal, asking a lot of questions, picking a lot of brains and laying the foundation for what he and the editor of the review for which he worked both hoped would be a distinguished sequence on the whole Franco-German question, particularly as seen from France. The sequence was to run from a mid-July number, and Desmond's visit to Paris was intended to set the whole series of articles in an authoritative frame. Meanwhile, he had been writing other pieces for them; and his own book was near completion.

It had been a good morning: then the rain came. But almost

the last taxi in Paris stopped in the rue St Honoré and here he now was outside a large plate-glass window with a rain-soaked awning above it. And, his watch showed, with five unexpected minutes in hand.

'*Combien, s'il vous plaît?*'

The driver turned, and Desmond felt a sense of shock. It was Kitzi Fischer! A small moustache, unlike Kitzi, but otherwise Kitzi! The same neatness, the same tall elegance, the same humorous twist to the mouth, the same brown, lined face. The same intelligence in the eyes.

The taxi driver said, in perfect and educated English with a slight drawl, that the fare was twenty-two francs. Desmond stared at him.

'You guessed I was English!'

'Of course!' The man smiled agreeably. He looked about Kitzi's age, too, late forties.

'You speak English very well. Do you know England?'

'Not really. But I had an English governess, and I used to shoot in Scotland almost every year before the War.'

'You're not French!' said Desmond. The man took the fare courteously, raising his eyebrows in a gesture of gratitude at the two-franc tip. He said, 'No, Monsieur, I'm not French, I'm Russian.'

'I hear that a great many of today's Parisian taxi drivers are Russians like you.'

'There are a lot of us.' He obviously enjoyed talking English again. 'It's not a bad way of living, and we keep each other company. Most of us were officers of the Emperor. A lot of us are relations and so forth.'

'Tell me one thing,' said Desmond. 'You people must talk a lot about politics. European politics.'

'Little else.'

'And what do you and your friends think of how things are going in Germany?'

'A large question,' said the tall taxi driver, 'and I think there is more than one opinion. But –'

At that moment an umbrella lunged into Desmond, and a fat

248

man with spectacles, arriving at the restaurant on foot and swearing at the weather, seized his hand.

'*M. Dillon! J'en suis sûr!*' He dived through the swing door.

'Thank you, Monsieur,' said the Russian, lifting two fingers to his cap and moving towards the driver's door. He and Desmond had been standing in the rain, oblivious. Desmond said quickly, 'I'd like to talk again. Would you be able to drive me out to dinner tonight?' He gave the name of his hotel. Privately, he was determined to give the Russian dinner, taxi driver or no, and make it worth his while to lose two hours' worth of fares. Hesitating slightly the man said he could be at the hotel – when? Seven thirty? asked Desmond. Yes, said the Russian, that would be all right. His working stint finished at eight today. Excellent, Desmond said, and took his hand.

'May I know your name? Mine is Dillon.'

'André, Monsieur,' said the Russian. It seemed improbable. Desmond smiled at him and said, 'A *nom de guerre* perhaps?' but the Russian, very seriously, said that he was a French citizen. 'Papers in order,' he added, with the hint of a smile, 'name of André.' With a wave Desmond ran out of the rain to join the bespectacled veteran reporter.

That evening Leonid André collected Desmond from his hotel and listened calmly as Desmond explained that he hoped André would take him to a restaurant and dine there with him. Without the least discourtesy André said, 'Why? If I may ask.'

'I want to continue with you the conversation I started when you drove me this morning. About Germany.'

André bowed to the invitation gracefully. On arrival at the restaurant he accepted his fare, disappeared with the taxi, and came into the restaurant seven minutes later looking the best bred man in the room. The resemblance to Kitzi was not so striking – Desmond supposed he had got used to it. It was more a matter of atmosphere and style than exact physical characteristics. Desmond bought aperitifs.

'You reminded me very much of a friend of mine, it struck

me immediately I saw you. A German writer called Christoph Fischer.'

André looked politely uninterested. The name meant nothing to him. He said, 'You are a writer yourself, Mr Dillon?'

'I try to write. I'm at work on a book, a novel, chiefly set in Germany. And I'm working on a series of articles about aspects of today's Europe for an English weekly review. I'm in Paris because the theme of the articles is to be how the French regard present developments in Germany. They're the people principally concerned, after all.'

'Are they?'

'Surely they are? If – and I know it seems far-fetched at present after their ruin, their present weakness – if the Germans ever again became militarily strong, presumably France would again feel vulnerable. To keep Germany weak has been, I suppose, the major French preoccupation since 1918. So they must be watching developments across the Rhine pretty sharply. After all Hitler has made no secret of his intention to rearm. And it may not take as long as people think. Not nearly so long.'

André said, 'Why do you say that?'

Desmond looked at him thoughtfully. It was generally said that this émigré Russian community was riddled with Intelligence agents of every description, recruited by every nation and organization. The French used them, the Germans used them, even the hated Bolsheviks had penetrated their circles from the start. So it was said. Periodically, sensational articles were published on the subject, and fiction abounded. André probably – or possibly, anyway – moved in this shadowy world of which Desmond knew nothing. Did it matter? Almost certainly not, and his reactions might be interesting, if one could break the ice. Desmond therefore told him a little of his understanding of German–Soviet cooperation since the 1920s, of Sonja's revelations (making no mention of Sonja or any other source) of the tank training school on the Volga, the flying establishment near Moscow, the Junkers factories.

André showed interest rather than surprise. He may know

250

more than I about all this, thought Desmond. Or perhaps it touches a nerve, gives him a nostalgic sensation just to find we are speaking of places in Russia, Russian names. They were enjoying a good, unelaborate dinner.

'So you see why I say the Germans may – just may – surprise us by the speed of their rearmament once they get going.' Using the phrase he recalled from another conversation, he said, 'Von Seeckt, like Cadmus, sowed dragon's teeth. They can one day spring from the ground as armed men.' Since André was still silent Desmond added, 'And I imagine your own friends and compatriots discuss these things a good deal.'

André sipped his wine. He ate and drank slowly and sparingly. He looked at Desmond and again reminded him strongly of Kitzi Fischer. Desmond decided it was the combination of intelligence, reserve and – and what? Experience, perhaps, Desmond thought. André had a face that had seen much, much of it terrible, no doubt.

Now he said, 'Of course we Russians talk endlessly, as you know. As to Germany – well, we haven't much love for Germans, we were fighting against them pretty hard until our Revolutionary friends decided to stop it. But since then, if you ask me what I and probably most of my compatriots here think, I would say that the test, the touchstone of everything, would be whether or not a development could help or hinder the end of the Bolshevism in Russia. That is the basis on which we tend to judge everything.'

'You think that likely?'

'Likely? Frankly, no. Not for a long time. But inevitable one day.'

'Why?'

'Because it is so evil, so unsuccessful and so unpopular. To survive indefinitely at least one of those facets must change. And which? To become less evil the régime would need to change its moral philosophy, which is dedicated to atheism, governed by force, and is starkly opposed to what we think of as European cultural liberalism, evolving over the last –'

'And was not the Czar's autocracy?' Desmond interrupted, 'and were not many traditional aspects of Russia also opposed to what you call European cultural liberalism? Is it not a Western phenomenon, and the Russians an Eastern people?'

'If by that you mean Oriental, the answer is No. Russia contains many races but for centuries, at least since Peter the Great, it has been within the main European tradition.'

Desmond was unconvinced. He said, 'Your second reason for the régime's ultimate demise is that it is unsuccessful.'

'Hopelessly so, economically. And must remain so while it is directed according to ruthless economic dogmas, applied regardless of human nature.'

André then talked, and talked in a way which Desmond found convincing, of conditions in Russia. These émigrés, people often said, they're embittered, they're prejudiced, they could never see the Soviet Union straight. Desmond found himself persuaded that André saw Russia very straight indeed. He spoke of the forced collectivization of agriculture, the deportation and murder of whole farming communities.

'The world may never know,' said André, 'how many human beings this régime has already killed. And I expect more will come. They feel insecure and the only answer to that, in their calculation, is to find and butcher more and more "class-enemies", "saboteurs", and so on. The only object of policy in the Soviet Union is the strengthening of control over every aspect of life by the Communist Party. Everything and everybody has to be sacrificed to that.'

Desmond demurred.

'Certain British – and American visitors have been impressed by the Soviet Economic Plans.'

'Those same visitors have not seen the millions deported and dying. They have seen and reported only what the Bolsheviks wished. They have been very great fools. Dupes.'

Privately, Desmond had come to a rather similar conclusion. He said, 'Thirdly, you said "so unpopular". Will that really be decisive? Have not Russian rulers often survived great unpopularity – ruthlessly retaining the instruments of power, caring nothing for the feelings of the people?'

André showed no signs of taking offence at this. He nodded

agreement, and said, 'It depends upon what one means by unpopularity. A tyrant may be hated for his cruelty but if, for instance, he is a strong and successful leader in war the Russians will support him. He is then a father – maybe a brutal father, but still a father. The unpopularity of the Bolsheviks comes from the fact that their cruelty – which has been greater than most of you people here yet understand – has been combined with ineffectiveness in foreign policy, feebleness. If there were war –'

'Well,' said Desmond, 'if there were war?'

'They would only redeem their credit if they showed themselves effective national leaders. Then, maybe, their crimes would be drowned in a wave of patriotic support. But I don't think it likely.'

'And where does that leave the German question?'

'Hitler,' said André, 'has said Bolshevism is a foul disease, an enemy of civilization. I agree with him. You have quoted earlier Germans, Conservatives, von Seeckt for instance, saying that Germany and Russia have a common interest in abolishing Poland. I agree with him, too.'

'Hitler has just concluded a ten-year pact with the Poles.'

'Quite so. And if I were a Pole,' said André, smiling, 'that would make me very wary. I do not think that Adolf Hitler is the most reliable man in Europe. But on your main question, I repeat – my friends and I are likely to judge this new Germany on how it affects the future of Bolshevism in Russia. And for that, it is early to decide.'

They talked of André's earlier life. He had been an officer in a Guards regiment – 'But now I am a French taximan, M. André!' He chuckled, and produced his French identity papers, passport and photograph with a flourish. Desmond realized that for some reason André had no intention, at any rate yet, of disclosing his true, his Russian name. In the general chaos of winter 1918 he had escaped into Turkey. His adventures had been remarkable – once about to be shot by the Bolsheviks, once (as a spy) by the Turks before internment. Later he had actually gone back into Communist Russia, hiding, lying up in refuges provided at personal risk by a few old members of his regiment, travelling in disguise. His object had been to find and bring out a young cousin, a girl with whom it was clear he had been wildly in love. He had ultimately discovered not her but her fate. She was no longer alive.

'She had been a nurse. Then she found herself nursing at the start of the Civil War. The Reds caught her. I met a woman who was there, who got away.'

André did not elaborate beyond a few terse sentences conveying rape, mutilation, murder. Then, surprisingly, he muttered, 'We did the same to them! We – the Whites. It was a bad time. My poor people. Only God knows what they have suffered.'

When Desmond had paid the bill, André thanked him with grace. Slightly embarrassed he said, 'I must not take you home in the taxi. It has been put to bed! Near here, you see.'

'Of course. I'll find another. I've greatly enjoyed our evening. I hope we meet again.'

They shook hands. After walking a few yards up the street, Desmond suddenly heard a call.

'Mr Dillon!'

He turned, and under a street lamp saw André coming back towards him.

'Mr Dillon, I have really been absurdly rude. Of course I must take you home in the taxi! It is the least I can do!'

'No, no! You explained –'

'It is nothing, it can be varied, it is only a short walk. Really, I insist! It is parked in what would be called a mews in London. There are six garages rented by the people who own my cab. Very near.'

'But you explained it's meant to be put to bed!'

'No, no! These rules can be varied. Please follow me. I will walk a little faster and get the car out and return along this street, on this side. It is a long way to your hotel and there are not many taxis. And –'

Desmond had seen some rough-looking characters in the area when they arrived. The lower end of Paris night life, he had decided – but the food had been good, and remarkably cheap. He had left the matter of where to go to André, who had certainly felt it a matter of good manners to spare his host expense. Grateful and touched, he saw André walk rapidly towards a street corner. Then Desmond yelled 'André!' and started to run as fast as he could.

He had been looking the right way. He had seen two figures move from a doorway as André passed, move behind him and then merge with André's figure in a grotesque mass of weaving arms and legs. As he raced towards them Desmond saw that all three were on the ground. André had been attacked, and as Desmond tore towards the struggling group he found himself desperately hoping knives weren't involved. Parisian Apaches were knifemen, everyone knew that! Desmond Dillon with his bare fists and light shoes was unlikely to make much impact, and stood a fair chance of reaching the Paris morgue at the same time as André. Desmond was unlikely, he knew, to be able to bring superior force to bear, and he had already jettisoned surprise.

'André! André! *Au secours!*'

Noise, Desmond thought, as he pounded towards them, noise, disturbance, police perhaps, rumpus! That's the hope! The street appeared completely deserted. Oddly, Desmond was also conscious of a strong desire to hit anybody who hurt André, and hit them very hard. He had taken a liking to André.

'André! *Au secours!*'

André was on the ground, very much alive and struggling fiercely. It looked as if one man had grabbed him round the neck and tripped him from behind. In a split second Desmond saw a wallet lying on the pavement where it had presumably fallen from André's pocket. The second man was swearing and bending over, nursing his left knee; and this second man turned to meet Desmond. He made, however, a foolish mistake. He had presumably only just seen André's wallet, and some instinct made him stoop quickly to scoop it up before facing Desmond. It was an error which gave Desmond a fractional advantage. At the same moment Desmond saw that the man had no knife. These two were not in serious business.

Desmond, yelling something which he afterwards forgot,

launched himself at the second man's throat with his very long arm reaching out. He had studied the arts of personal combat from Cambridge days onwards. Simultaneously, while focusing on the man's eyes, he kicked as hard as he could with the right foot, aiming for that knee he had seen being nursed, that knee which André must have also damaged, a knee in pain. Desmond put everything he had behind his kick, as the man ducked back to avoid the lunge of Desmond's arms. Then he screamed. Desmond felt a mighty throb of exultation as he knew his toe had found its target. At the same moment he heard a second scream.

André, from his position on the ground, had nevertheless brought his own knee with great force into the groin of the man who was throttling him. It was enough to loosen the man's grip. Desmond's own victim had reeled away, his eyes full of agony and hatred. In that second Desmond brought the edge of his right hand in a chopping movement, with all his strength, down on the back of the neck of the man who had been trying to choke André. He knew, as he did it, that the blow was luckily imperfect. It should and could kill, but this victim had a scarf and an upturned collar and the spinal nerve must have been protected. The man went down heavily, but he writhed and moaned, alive. At that moment several whistles blew, and Desmond was aware of uniforms and black capes and peaked caps and shouting. Their private battle was over.

And then there were explanations, reports, suspicion, indignation, some very rough handling by gendarmes of two snarling and rather skinny-looking malefactors suddenly deprived of all power to harm or alarm. Ultimately Desmond and his companion were alone again, and agreed that a drink before parting had now been earned. Desmond insisted that they take a taxi, not André's. But a police car, obligingly, set them down at their request in the Boulevard des Capucines.

'I owe you a great deal of thanks, Mr Dillon.' André was remarkably composed. He seemed to imply that to be attacked for his taxi takings by two thugs was a frequent occurrence. Perhaps it was, Desmond thought – the more, as André observed with disdain, 'Young amateurs! They were nothing. I am deeply ashamed that you were involved.'

'I enjoyed it,' Desmond said truthfully.

'How long are you in Paris, Mr Dillon?'

'Would it be very offensive to you,' said Desmond, 'to call me by my first name, which is Desmond? I shall be here for several weeks, I think, living cheaply as my paper demands, finding out what I can, forming a view, writing. This evening has been part of that process!'

André bowed and thanked him again. In response to Desmond's request but with some hesitation he produced an address, and a telephone number, 'at which I can be contacted', an address in an obscure suburb of Paris. For some reason he had himself suggested they go to the Capucines for their drink – Desmond feared that it was taking André away from home, which surely lay more in the direction of his taxi garage, of where they had dined? That would make sense, but the Russian had brushed it aside.

'Let us get into the centre of Paris, the *grands boulevards*, light and noise!' He had sounded positively lively. But when they parted his guard was up. Desmond knew, and understood, that this charming and cultivated man lived in a world where no intrusion, however well meaning, was permitted.

Gerhardt von Premnitz had lived in Berlin for the last six years. A Saxon, a General Staff officer, severely wounded and taken prisoner by the British in 1917, he had adopted a commercial career in Berlin after repatriation, had been ruined in the general economic collapse which ravaged Germany after the War, and had moved to Munich to work for a newspaper. The *Kaiserreich* had died, the Kingdom of Saxony was no more, the old Imperial Army was disbanded, his family fortune had disappeared, Major Gerhardt Brendthase of the Saxon Guards was a creature of the past. In search of a new life and a new identity he had changed his name to that of his mother, von Premnitz. He had then earned his living, without enthusiasm, in the Bavaria of the nineteen-twenties, and had witnessed the attempted Nazi *putsch* of 1923 in Munich. Shortly afterwards he had returned to Berlin.

He was a tall, sardonic man who kept his own counsel and had seen much. He was close – amiably but discreetly close – to the highest circles of the Reichswehr: his heart was with the conservative monarchists-under-the-skin who still dominated it, sometimes with only a tenuous grasp of political realities. He hoped to see Germany once more strong and proud: but he also hoped for a day when traditional morality would again govern public life. Intelligent, reserved, austere, he had regarded the thuggish antics of the political private armies with distaste and contempt. That the near-monopoly of power recently assumed by the Nazis had instantly quelled disorder and street fighting was good: that the means of this was the dominance of the brown-shirted SA was bad. Von Premnitz respected order and loathed political passion, however patriotic. He knew England well and Adrian Winter slightly. Kitzi Fischer was an old friend and they had worked together in Munich: von Premnitz loved Kitzi, although he sometimes disagreed with him, and thought him imprudent. He had known Kitzi's favourite nephew since Wieland Breitfall was a schoolboy.

On this Tuesday, 28th June, Gerhardt von Premnitz was walking, for exercise and pleasure, in the Tiergarten. He was particularly looking forward to the month of July for which he had arranged a visit to England, a country he had not seen for several years, a country in which he had been a prisoner but which he remembered without animosity. The trip, he thought, would make an admirable break from the somewhat feverish atmosphere of Berlin, and he had been carefully getting funds together and making arrangements. Foreign travel and foreign currency were not entirely straightforward matters these days but Gerhardt had some useful friends. He had confirmed his train and ship reservations that very morning and his heart was the lighter for it.

It was five o'clock in the afternoon and the weather was exceptionally hot. Some heavy black clouds, however, had moved up from the southern horizon during his walk and he quickened his pace. He lived in the eastern suburbs and a taxi might be necessary – and hard to get when the downpour started.

Gerhardt von Premnitz got clear of the Tiergarten and walked fast towards the main avenue which ran for many miles on an east–west axis through Berlin. Unter-den-Linden, Charlottenburger Chaussee, it was broad, magnificent and immensely long. At the Reichskanzler Platz there would be taxis, but the Reichskanzler Platz would take thirty minutes to reach, walking fast. Someone had told him it was planned soon to re-name it the 'Adolf Hitler Platz'! Incredible! Von Premnitz lengthened his stride, and looked hopefully at the sky. It was possible these damned great clouds would miss central Berlin: possible, but unlikely. Then he noticed a slim figure, wearing a soft hat and with raincoat over arm, hastening along the same pavement as himself, thirty paces ahead. The afternoon was very humid now.

'Breitfall!'

The figure slowed and turned. Wieland Breitfall, looking slightly embarrassed, raised his hat.

'Herr von Premnitz!'

'Well, we'd best hurry or we'll both get wet! Surprised to see you – and in civilian clothes, too! Someone told me you SS fellows are having to stand by all the time in case one of these disturbances occurs!' It was true that rumours had been running round Berlin like electricity for several weeks. The Conservative Vice-Chancellor, Franz von Papen, had made a speech at Marburg University ten days before in which he had spoken in not very veiled terms against Nazi excesses, condemning those like Dr Goebbels who seemed to wish for revolution after revolution. Von Papen was a witty, somewhat frivolous man whom Gerhardt did not esteem as a politician, regarding his judgement as facile and his character shallow, but on this occasion he seemed, perhaps for the first and last time, to have spoken for the true Germany, the Germany which was sick of legalized brutality. It had, by all accounts, been a brave speech. Everyone knew von Papen was chiefly referring to the SA, and its leader Röhm – with whom it was said, the ex-Chancellor, General von Schleicher, was intriguing, with a view to cutting Adolf Hitler down to size. And people whispered that the Reichswehr had been blunt with the Chancellor. The new Commander-in-Chief, General von Fritsch, had apparently told Hitler that von Papen's speech was something of a catalyst, that it reflected the views of most Germans and of virtually every German officer. Röhm, the notorious homosexual Röhm, his entourage and his SA, were making Germany impossible; and his arrogant boasting that the SA could and should replace the Reichswehr with a true revolutionary People's Army was intolerable. Something was in the wind, although exactly what and precisely when was harder to tell.

Gerhardt von Premnitz looked at Wieland shrewdly. A young SS officer out of uniform at a time when the whole SS were rumoured to be confined to barracks! A young SS officer walking in the Tiergarten by himself!

They fell into step, hurrying. Von Premnitz sensed his company was not particularly welcome and cared little.

'After a taxi, like me?'

'No, I've – I've got my car. Parked – only about three hundred metres.'

'Well done!' said von Premnitz, 'well done!' The first heavy drops began to fall. Wieland Breitfall knew that some things were unavoidable. There was no hiding his reluctance.

'Herr von Premnitz – I would be glad to help you – I've not got much time, but of course –'

'Which way are you going, my boy?' Wieland told him, speaking vaguely but not so vaguely that a small, a very small suspicion did not begin to form in the other's mind. Von Premnitz said that the direction would suit him admirably. Two minutes later, already wet, they reached Wieland's car.

'I can tell you one thing,' said Gerhardt von Premnitz. Wieland had parked, without explanation, in a side street in the eastern suburbs of Berlin. 'I can tell you one thing you may not know,' Gerhardt said, looking thoughtfully at the handsome profile of the young man sitting at the wheel of the car, 'Blomberg has written an article for the Party paper, the *Volkischer*. Your paper, my boy! It's going to be published tomorrow. And it will say that the Army is one hundred per cent behind the Chancellor. Very properly.' Gerhardt smiled thinly. General von Blomberg was Reich Defence Minister. Gerhardt von Premnitz was close to many of Blomberg's associates. He knew about the newspaper article, and he knew that it indicated very clearly that if Hitler at last decided to settle accounts with the radical wing of his Party he would have the Army's support. But not otherwise. A power game is being played out in these days here in Germany, thought Gerhardt, but this absurdly idealistic Nazi boy beside me probably only sees things in terms of 'loyalty to the Führer', the 'ideals of National Socialism' and so forth. The truth, and it was not hard for a mature spectator of events to discern it, was that Hitler had been deliberating with some agony whether he should stamp on the SA and keep the support of the Reichswehr – but perhaps simultaneously destroying any counterpoise to the latter: or keep faith with the Party old guard and fatally antagonize those who held ultimate armed power in the State – the Reichswehr. Gerhardt had little doubt which road the Führer would choose. Meanwhile there were stories current that the SA themselves were preparing a coup. Gerhardt didn't believe a word of them. He said, 'Is this your destination? I can walk from here.'

The rain was stopping. They had talked in a desultory way about 'the crisis', Wieland speaking little, saying briefly that he had arranged a few hours off, the first for a week. That he 'might be leaving Berlin' the next day. Temporarily. Gerhardt had tried to draw him without much success, and then had volunteered his piece of gossip about the forthcoming Blomberg newspaper article. Wieland nodded without much appearance of interest.

'Thanks for the lift, Wieland,' Gerhardt slipped easily into the intimate first name habit. He'd known the young *Sturmführer* since childhood, damn it! 'You've saved me a wetting!' He opened the car door. The storm was almost over. Wieland's voice cut in, very quiet.

'Herr von Premnitz, please don't go for a moment.' Gerhardt closed the door.

'Herr von Premnitz, I am on my way to visit my Uncle Kitzi, your friend.'

'Yes,' said Gerhardt softly, 'I rather thought you might be. Have you seen him much recently?'

'I saw him last one week ago.'

Wieland started talking in short, jerky sentences. Sometimes he left out a word, left it to imagination. It didn't take long. Then there was a silence, heavy between them.

'Wieland, you must go back to your duty, to wherever you came from. At once.'

'I –'

'No, you need say nothing more. I understand. You can trust me. In every way. But you, yourself, should go back, leaving this quarter as quickly as possible. Return by a detour, I suggest.'

Sturmführer Breitfall looked at Gerhardt von Premnitz, pain in his eyes, uncertainty. God help us, Gerhardt thought, he looks as if he's going to be sick! He got out of the car smartly, turned round and said again, 'You can trust me. Completely. Now go away.'

The storm was over although more black clouds could be seen drifting towards the city.

CHAPTER XII

Wieland's orders were unexpected. He knew that he was to be ready to leave Berlin 'for an important and confidential duty' at short notice, but he was surprised and rather excited when he learned that this involved flying, with a number of others, to Munich in a special aircraft during 29th June. A Friday. In Munich he was to report to Party Headquarters, and would be attached until further orders to a very distinguished officer indeed, *SS Gruppenführer* Dietrich. *Gruppenführer* Dietrich, a hard man, had once been the Führer's driver. He was likely to be in Munich for some mission of the utmost importance – the details of which were no business of Wieland's.

Together with a number of other SS officers, older than him and all rather silent, Wieland flew to Munich that afternoon. He had the impression, slightly disagreeable, that they all knew rather more than he did about what was going on. Wieland was aware, however, that he was likely to be attending more than a conference with *Gruppenführer* Dietrich. Two companies of SS men from the *SS Leibstandart*, the Führer's personal bodyguard, had also been ordered to Munich from Berlin.

On arrival Wieland reported to Dietrich's personal adjutant, whom he knew slightly. Surprisingly, the *Gruppenführer* himself was not in evidence. Alone, unattended, Dietrich had flown from Berlin to Bad Godesberg in the Rhineland, where it appeared that the Führer himself had turned up unexpectedly after a short tour of the Ruhr.

'The Führer was in Essen this afternoon. The *Gruppenführer* had an urgent message – report, alone, to the Hotel Dressen, at Godesberg.'

'Is that a usual resort of the Führer's?'

'No, I don't think so. It's a smart hotel on the west bank of the Rhine, he's decided to spend the night there, it seems. And he's sent for the *Gruppenführer*.'

Wieland said, without giving the improper impression of wanting to know his superiors' business, 'Presumably *Gruppenführer* Dietrich will be receiving some sort of special instructions.'

The other looked at him carefully. He knew Breitfall was a very dedicated officer, a real enthusiast. Dietrich had snapped, 'I want another personal aide during this business – a right and a left hand! They're sending me a fellow called Breitfall from Berlin,' and his adjutant, *Sturmführer* von Hochstein, had nodded acknowledgement. A nice fellow, Breitfall, but whether he was up to this sort of thing von Hochstein doubted. It was all, of course, shrouded in mystery but Hochstein had a pretty good idea of what the next hours might bring. He decided it was desirable to give at least a hint to his new and temporary assistant. He did so. Wieland felt a glow of pride at the trust reposed in him, and a certain sickness he could not entirely suppress. He had known in Berlin, of course, that 'action was intended'. He had seen lists. He knew there would be arrests. But von Hochstein's sardonic expression implied more, a good deal more. And perhaps in Berlin, too –

The sickness began to overwhelm the glow of pride. Hochstein was watching him.

'No sleep tonight! I've had word the *Gruppenführer* is on his way to Bonn airport. It's a two-hour flight. I'll meet him at the airfield here, at Oberwiesenfeld. You stay here.' 'Here' was Reichswehr barracks at Kaufering, on the outskirts of Munich, placed at the disposal of the SS. Von Hochstein had an office and a telephone. In other barrack blocks men of the *Leibstandart* were getting some rest, unaware of their likely duties, but ordered to be ready to turn out at an instant's notice. It was half past nine in the evening and Wieland had been drinking a bottle of wine with von Hochstein – sparingly. Von Hochstein looked at his watch.

'He ought to be in at about midnight or just after. I'll ring you from the airfield.'

They had now had a sufficiently explicit talk.

'Right.'

Wieland dozed uneasily in his chair.

He woke to the buzz of the telephone and he looked at his watch. Quarter past one in the morning! He snatched the telephone.

'Breitfall here.'

It was von Hochstein. He sounded tense.

'Breitfall, listen carefully. I'm at the airfield. The *Gruppenführer* has just been speaking from here to Bad Godesberg. The Führer has decided to come in person to Munich. By air. Now. Arriving at about four this morning.'

'*Jawohl!*' Wieland felt a participant in great events.

'He will be met by the *Gruppenführer* and will then drive to the city.'

'You want me to –'

'You are to do what I warned. Time of readiness five thirty. Clear?'

'Clear.'

Von Hochstein rang off. Wieland knew that certain detachments of the *Leibstandart* were, by this message, to parade, armed and in trucks ready to move, at five thirty. Just over four hours from now. Plenty of time. The subsequent route was perfectly straightforward, too, and there'd be no traffic or impediment. He, Wieland, would be in the leading vehicle if it happened, von Hochstein had said. After arrival at their destination he would at all times remain as close as possible to the *Gruppenführer* – they both would. If it happened. Well, now it was going to happen. The distance from Munich to Bad Wiessee was sixty kilometres, a decent road, a beautiful road. One started on the main Salzburg highway and then one branched right towards the mountains, to the Tegernsee.

It was, in fact, six o'clock by the time the little column moved off from the appointed rendezvous outside the Bavarian Ministry of the Interior. It was a lovely morning, clear, fresh and sunlit, and Munich was still at peace before the usual pleasant Saturday comings and goings. The great ones had arrived punctually from the airfield. Wieland had reported to *Gruppenführer* Dietrich unostentatiously, simply conveying by his smartness and deportment that he was alert and utterly dependable. Dietrich had nodded and shaken his hand. Then he had vanished into the Ministry building where there seemed a lot of activity despite the early hour. A few minutes later everybody, officers and NCOs standing by vehicles, black-uniformed, immaculate; a few civilians of indeterminate status: *Sturmführer* Hochstein; Wieland himself – everybody stiffened to attention. Quietly, without fuss, every right arm shot up at an angle of forty-five degrees.

'*Heil Hitler!*'

Adolf Hitler moved rapidly down the front steps of the Ministry building, his face paler than Wieland had ever seen it. He was unshaven and his eyes appeared to focus on nobody. In response to the salute he flapped his right hand and dived into the waiting car, one of three. Hitler, despite the warmth of the June morning, was wearing a light raincoat and tall black boots. He was hatless. Wieland raced to the leading vehicle, a small police car, leapt in and snapped an order. The column moved off, as fast as was consistent with keeping the vehicles together, towards the outskirts of the city. The streets were still largely empty and it took only a short time to reach the main Salzburg road.

Wieland glanced at the driver.

'You say you know the place?'

'Yes, Herr *Sturmführer*. I know Bad Wiessee. And I know the Gasthof Hanselbauer. It's right on the Tegernsee. A nice spot.'

It had the name of a very nice spot indeed. It was the agreeable resort selected by the SA Chief, Röhm, for a meeting of the higher echelons of the SA before the entire organization was dismissed for summer leave throughout July. Röhm had, at Hitler's request, summoned the SA senior men from throughout the Reich. Hitler himself had suggested he meet them there during the weekend – and it was no secret that Röhm hoped a good deal from this meeting. There had been violent things said, both by and about the SA, in recent months and it was no doubt time to clear the air between the Führer and his oldest, most loyal comrades. The SA chiefs were all due to arrive during the morning at Munich, and fleets of cars had been arranged by the local SA to take them out to Bad Wiessee.

But not Röhm, Wieland knew, as they cleared the last Munich suburbs and the driver, glancing at his mirror, touched the accelerator: not Röhm. Röhm was already at the Gastof Hanselbauer, relaxing before the conference, relaxing with two of the beautiful young aides who constituted his only passion in life beyond that National Revolution which seemed recently to have run into the sand. Röhm, Wieland knew, was relaxing already in the Gasthof Hanselbauer, no doubt after an uproarious evening of drinking and swimming and much else besides. And not only Röhm was already there. Quite a number of the other SA leaders, mostly with similar tastes to Röhm, had been bidden to arrive a few days early, to join the Chief at what was described with grins in the SA as his 'cure'. There were plenty of them there already, Hochstein had explained to Wieland in his quiet voice, eyeing Breitfall thoughtfully. Lucky for him he's not in the SA, Hochstein thought with an inward chuckle. With his pretty looks, Röhm would have conscripted him for his personal staff in no time at all!

Wieland's driver spoke briefly. They would reach Bad Wiessee in four minutes.

At exactly twenty minutes to seven on that morning of 30th June 1934 Wieland Breitfall, revolver in hand, heart pounding, found himself running through the door of the Gasthof Hanselbauer at Bad Wiessee, moving immediately behind SS *Gruppenführer* Dietrich and followed by a noisy and energetic party of the *Leibstandart*. At their head, leader of this violent incursion, shouting as many of them were shouting, was no other than the Reich Chancellor, the Chief Minister of Germany, Adolf Hitler himself. Still raincoated, hatless and booted. A revolver, too, in his hand.

The Gasthof was as previously described to Wieland – wooden

walls, wooden stairs, a long row of bedroom doors on the first floor. To every door there now rushed a member of the *Leibstandart* who kicked it open and went in, pistol or machine-pistol at the ready. Everywhere rang out yells, roars of astonishment and expostulation, the sound of smashing glass, a squeal of pain here and there. Soon a stumbling queue of stupefied SA bosses, men who had until that moment terrified fellow citizens with their power, men who had been virtually unopposed for nearly two years (and been used to lord it, locally, for much longer), now a wretched huddle, bemused, frightened and undignified, rushing down the stairs, pulling on garments, hustled by strong hands towards the waiting trucks. No shot had been fired.

Wieland, however, shadowing *Gruppenführer* Dietrich, had moved immediately behind Hitler himself. Hitler appeared to be in a towering rage. Wieland, enormously confused in his own emotions but hanging on grimly to his devotion to the Führer, nevertheless had the unbidden impression that Hitler had, somehow, needed to work up this rage, that it was not spontaneous. At the second open door they passed, already burst open by an SS man, Hitler stopped, peered and let out a screech of savagery and disgust.

'Heines!'

Wieland, also able to see into the room, observed that Edmund Heines, SA *Polizeipräsident* of Breslau and a particular crony of Röhm, was struggling out of a bed in which a young SA man, naked, was sitting up, gawping in terror at the apparition in the doorway of his Führer, gun in hand. One minute later Wieland was aware of another stout, bandy-legged figure in shirt and breeches being rushed down the corridor by two huge SS men. He recognized the savagely contorted, red, scarred face of Röhm. From the room in which he had seen Heines came cries and the sound of a body crashing to the floor.

It was half past five that afternoon. Wieland had conveyed from *Gruppenführer* Dietrich orders, orders, orders as the events of the day crowded on each other's heels, bewildering, stupefying.

At each snap of the Führer, or of Reichminister Josef Goebbels who had accompanied him throughout, Dietrich in turn gave a quiet command and Wieland or von Hochstein would attend to it, moving fast, seeing that the wishes of Adolf Hitler were instantly obeyed. At one moment Dietrich had muttered to von Hochstein, 'Breitfall all right?'

'Perfectly efficient, Herr *Gruppenführer*. He's known for his idealism and enthusiasm throughout the SS. But –'

'But?'

'Not a hard enough man, perhaps.'

Von Hochstein had served his master long enough for such opinions to be permissible, known to be objective, free of spite. Dietrich had grunted.

When the convoy – SS, prisoners, Ministers and Reich Chancellor – had driven back to Munich in what was still early morning, they had found the first party of SA chiefs heading in Party cars, all unknowing, from Munich towards the keenly anticipated conference at Bad Wiessee. The SA bosses had been ordered to turn round and join the column. Perplexed, astounded to recognize the Führer himself, they had driven behind him into Munich at about eight o'clock in the morning. Wieland had turned many of the cars round himself, voice adequately peremptory, inwardly uncertain whether he was a young officer explaining a request to these Party grandees. Or –

Or an incipient gaoler! For on arrival in the city every SA car with its occupants was escorted by SS men to Stadelheim prison. By nine o'clock the cells were full of the *Alte Kämpfer*, the old campaigners of the Nazi movement. These also included many who had arrived at Munich's main railway station, to hear a loudspeaker announcement that SA leaders should report to Station Office No. 1, had done so, presuming transport, refreshment and a warm welcome awaited them: and were then, in their turn, promptly bundled off to Stadelheim.

Then Wieland had received his next order.

'*Jawohl, Herr Gruppenführer! Heil Hitler!*'

Munich, and the 'Brown House', the Party Headquarters, was packed with junior as well as senior ranks of the SA. The Führer intended to address them personally. All were to be instantly assembled in one of the larger conference halls. And there Wieland, having quickly organized the assembly, listened transfixed as the Führer harangued the faithful. The SA, he shouted at them, had been betrayed by its leaders. While the loyal ranks of the simple *Stürmer* had been faithful, devoted, honest, some of the chiefs – and he raised his voice and yelled, terrifyingly, that some of them were already in Stadelheim prison but others were standing before him in that very room – these chiefs, corrupt, lazy, thieves of Party funds, guilty of every filthy sexual practice, unworthy to bear the name of German, let alone the title National Socialist, these chiefs, seducers, plotters, traitors, had conspired against him, their Führer, against National Socialism, against the Reich – it went on and on, Hitler's voice ever higher, ever louder as he roared at them that they were, every one of them, under arrest! Some might be innocent – a rigorous inquiry would establish it. Others could expect no mercy! And Wieland saw the sweat and the terror on the faces of those hard, confident, swaggering men, heard the tremor in their voices as Hitler finished and as they cried, each vying with his neighbour in enthusiasm, 'HEIL HITLER! HEIL HITLER! HEIL HITLER!' And behind them, very quiet, stood a row of black-uniformed SS, armed, watchful, faces without expression.

Then, later in the day, most of them were assembled again, sombre, fearing all things. And this time Hitler told them, more quietly, that he had established the guilt of a number, all of whom were now at Stadelheim. For the rest, he wished only to be merciful, understanding. His SA had been misled, betrayed.

'Are you with me?' he cried, 'or with those who have conspired to betray Germany?' The response was deafening, and they burst into the Party song, the *Horst Wessel Lied*. Hitler stood, grim and still amid the singing, the deafening roars of 'HEIL HITLER!' Then he told them they were free. They should go home. They should take off their uniforms until further orders, following reorganization. There would be a new chief for the SA. Dismiss.

And now it was half past five. Dietrich's voice was sharp.

'Breitfall! Stadelheim!'

Wieland had been near enough a few minutes earlier to hear the Führer, face contorted as if in pain, speak sharply to Dietrich. He guessed and dreaded what was to come. He ran down the front steps of the Brown House and summoned Dietrich's car with a sharp flick of the fingers. Von Hochstein, already outside, came up to him.

'Six are in the next truck. NCOs. Good men, all.'

'Right.'

At Stadelheim Dietrich, moving fast, as he always did, so that Wieland could hardly keep up with him, marched to the office of the prison governor. Then Wieland heard the quiet words, '*Nicht in Ordnung. Keine Unterschrift.*'

Without a word, as if unafraid of what Hitler might do or say, acknowledging only correctitude, Dietrich nodded, turned on his heel and raced down to his car again. They returned to the Brown House. Ten minutes later they were back at Stadelheim. This time Dietrich held in his gloved hand a piece of paper. Signed.

Wieland stood immediately behind *Gruppenführer* Dietrich as he entered each cell. He heard the words used, identical in each case.

'You have been condemned to death by the Führer for high treason. *Heil Hitler!*' And then, in each case, Wieland followed Dietrich, Dietrich's face expressionless, to a small courtyard in the centre of the prison, with high walls relieved by no windows. Facing one of these walls, and at about ten paces from it, were drawn up in single rank the six SS non-commissioned officers who had accompanied them to Stadelheim, good men all, Hochstein had said, good men all. And, steered by strong hands towards the wall, facing that single rank of SS men, came first one, then another of the once mighty chiefs of the SA, pioneers of the National Socialist Revolution, heroes of the new Germany: now unkempt, shuffling, dazed, still unbelieving of their fate. Several stiffened and shouted '*Heil Hitler!*' And then, each time, again and again and again, there was a sharp command.

'*Achtung! Feuer!*'

And then blood, and sometimes a terrible, inhuman scream as a human spirit refused to quit its body instantaneously, and quiet orders, and figures running forward to drag the untidy, stained bundle away, and the metallic sound of weapons being reloaded.

And then, what seemed hours later, they had driven back to the Brown House. Wieland, feeling numb with shock and ashamed of his nausea, and ashamed of feeling ashamed, heard Dietrich say very softly, as if to himself, 'The Führer has pardoned Röhm!'

And, as dark as any of these images would become in his mind, there was another recollection, stemming from ten o'clock that morning, in the Brown House. Von Hochstein, rushing past him, back to Dietrich's side, as Wieland set off to make some new 'arrangement', execute some order, von Hochstein muttering, '*Colibri* has been ordered. I've sent the word.'

'*Colibri?*'

'Ach, I didn't tell you! No matter. *Colibri* means they're now to start in Berlin.'

The kick at the front door of Kitzi Fischer's house echoed through it, causing plates to jump on the racks where they were always placed in Günther's kitchen. Kick, kick, kick! The door bell rang at the same time, of course, but the kicks seemed to be aimed by someone – by two, or perhaps three, thought Günther listening – who had already decided that no bell was likely to be answered: but that the brutal emphasis conveyed by the kicking might elicit some response. After that, after trying that kicking no doubt for a very short while, they would attack the door itself. But it was a stout door. Herr Kitzi's orders had been clear and sternly delivered. 'Be correct', he had said. 'Be polite, Günther. Tell the exact truth. Don't be in a hurry about it, but tell the exact truth.'

Kick, kick, kick! Shouts, words impossible to make out but unimportant because significance perfectly clear. Open up, damn you, or we'll break down your bloody door! It was 30th June,

1934, eleven o'clock on the Saturday morning; Günther was alone in the house and not prepared to be hurried.

Kick, yell, kick, yell. Then a pause, a silence. Here it comes, thought Günther. At the first splintering crash he'd bestir himself. It would take a good deal to smash their front door, Herr Kitzi's front door. It was a heavy, a splendid door. It could withstand all but a battering ram. They might, of course, shoot the locks and bolts off, thought Günther, but I doubt it. Not at first. The house was so constructed that no ground-floor windows were easily accessible from the street: a solid villa built in 1865, something like a miniature fortress. A dedicated patriot and Pan-German enthusiast, the first owner had indulged in mediaeval fantasies wherein the crusading Teutonic Knights, himself armoured and in their company, had eternally defended German strongholds against Pagan and Slav. His house in the suburbs of Berlin had mirrored these fantasies. Günther knew nothing of this but was glad that the house would always be a hard nut for an intruder to crack. He did not, however, like this silence, and he moved through the hall now, roaring, 'Who's there, who's making all that noise?' in tones with which *Obergefreiter* Günther had once scared the wits out of many a raw Silesian recruit. He slid back the heavy bolts and turned a huge key.

There were three of them. Not SA. No brown shirts. These three were wearing civilian clothes and raincoats – there'd been several heavy showers already that day, although it was June. Above their raincoats were three faces, rather similar. They wore soft, rather broad-brimmed hats. Young – maybe twenty-nine or thirty, Günther decided, although one looked younger still. Cleanshaven. Eyes of all three watchful. One was a big, heavy-jowled fellow but the other two might have been brothers, with narrow, brown faces. There was, Günther noted without expressing anything to himself, nothing of the bluster, the often rather inebriated swagger he associated with the *Sturmabteilung*.

Günther said, 'What in hell do you want, kicking at our door?' Then he remembered that Herr Kitzi had said 'be polite'. There was a black car waiting in the road and he could see another man

273

sitting at the wheel. Grudgingly, loyal to Herr Kitzi's injunction, Günther said, 'Took me time, I was doing a job. What do you want?'

'Herr Christoph Fischer?'

'Herr Fischer's away.'

'We do not believe you,' said the smallest of the three men calmly. He was the smallest but, Günther noted, unquestionably the leader. When he spoke the others turned their own eyes to him, and there was deference in them.

'I tell you, he's away.'

'You are his servant?'

'I work for Herr Fischer. I always have. We were together in the Army.'

With a sharp gesture the leader waved Günther to one side and marched into the hall. He looked about him.

'Show us the whole house.'

'I –'

'The whole house. Quickly.'

They tramped all over it. It wasn't a big place; it was solid and beautifully furnished but the rooms were not extensive. The men opened every cupboard, every drawer. Günther tried to expostulate, to say, 'Who the hell are you?' and they flashed some sort of cards at him. They couldn't be police, why should they be police? But they were totally self-assured. Nobody would call them to account, they implied, for this intrusion. Methodically, roughly, they burst everything open, ran their hands through everything. They went through the large cellars with equal thoroughness. Günther felt particularly sensitive.

'It's Herr Fischer's wine! He has the key!' The wine was in an inner cellar with a separate locked door, a modern lock.

'Is there a second key?'

Günther hesitated. Of course he had a duplicate key of the wine cellar and of course they knew it.

'Open!'

He pretended to look for the key, find it, open up. The swine would pinch some of Herr Kitzi's best brandy, that was certain, but he, Günther, would report that and get them into trouble for it if it was the last thing he did.

They didn't touch a bottle. A cursory look around, then upstairs again. And into Herr Kitzi's study. To Herr Kitzi's desk.

And that desk was turned out as nothing else had been turned out. Every paper was pulled out and thrown to the floor, and on the floor one of them sifted the papers, throwing most to one side, making a pile of others, a small pile. God knew and Günther certainly didn't what was in Herr Kitzi's desk. Günther had shambled round the house with them, outraged, grumbling furiously. Now he could stand no more. He threw himself at the one sifting the pile of Herr Kitzi's papers. 'Be correct,' Herr Kitzi had said, but this was too much. Günther found his voice. 'Hey!'

He felt a blow like a bullet to the back of the skull and collapsed to the floor, just conscious. He was aware of one of the others tucking a pistol back into his raincoat. So the bastard had tapped Günther's head with his pistol butt, God rot him! Günther managed to sit up, groaning. They took no further notice of him and calmly went on going through the contents of the desk. And Günther watched them, his head throbbing, his mind blank. What should he have done that he had omitted? And what in the name of all-seeing God could he do now?

Eventually they murmured to each other, still ignoring Günther. Then the one he thought of as the leader came and stood over him. At the same time, and unseen by Günther, another of the three, the largest one, launched a terrific kick at him and caught him in the kidney –

'Ah-h-h-h!'

There was a pause. Another kick. Günther rolled on the floor, retching.

'Now,' said the leader pleasantly, 'it is time to apologize. I said we did not believe you when you told us Fischer was not at home. My regrets. He is not at home.'

Günther retched again. Both his head and his gut hurt him a lot.

'So, where is he, please?'

'I don't know.'

'When did he leave?'

'Thursday. I think it was Thursday.'

'And you say you don't know where he is?'

'That's right. No idea.'

'Fischer leaves home without any address, any instructions of any kind. You would not know how to contact him if his nearest relative had an accident?'

'He's got no nearest relative.'

'Has he not? Are you sure? As sure as you are that you don't know where he is?'

'I tell you, I don't know where he is.'

And this was so. Faithful to orders, Günther was telling the exact truth. It was hard, bitter hard that even so they nodded to each other: then the leader said a soft word to the largest of the trio, the one who had kicked Günther in the kidney. Then they all three stepped towards the door and paused for a moment and turned. The largest of the trio raised a pistol and emptied one, two, three shots into Günther's chest and they could see, with indifference, that he died quickly.

Gerhardt von Premnitz said, 'You will obey instructions absolutely and at all times. You are a wilful man, Kitzi, and you care little about your skin, but this time it is other skins that are at risk and one of them is mine.'

Kitzi Fischer smiled at him, his smile which was both trusting and intelligent, both innocent and touched with guile. It was a smile which had won Gerhardt's heart long ago, and because of that smile and that winning Kitzi Fischer was now in the attic room of a small farmhouse in Westphalia and Gerhardt von Premnitz was chancing his neck. He knew, of course, that Kitzi had difficulty believing that this really was a matter of life and death. People in like circumstances, thought Gerhardt, always refused to believe in the deadly nature of the times, until it was too late. Things are deplorable, they said and supposed, things are disgraceful, but it's not quite as bad as you make out. It can't be. Not now. Not here.

And not for me.

Gerhardt told Kitzi he would be safe if he obeyed completely, and if, in Gerhardt's absence, he followed the instructions of the farmer. Gerhardt did not elaborate on why he knew the farmer was to be trusted – as so often, it was a relationship of confidence, reinforced by money, whose roots lay in a part of Gerhardt's own life, in the War and before it. It sufficed, Gerhardt made clear, that the man would never betray: that the farm was sufficiently isolated for warning to be received of any visit: that the hole into which Kitzi would then disappear was entirely secure: and that the farmer, Milch by name, had never in any way caused the authorities of either State or Party to suspect his integrity. Milch had joined the Party late, when most other farmers had decided to do so, and he was an unenthusiastic but unquestioning member. He was universally regarded as a good fellow, who kept himself to himself. His wife had died two years before and Milch was looked after by the wife of his cowman, a decent, rather simple creature. Milch's needs were straightforward. He was entirely capable of seeng that no eyes, not even the eyes of the simple wife of the cowman, could detect that another human being was sleeping, eating, hiding in the roof of the farm.

'They would have arrested me, I suppose I expected it,' Kitzi said for the tenth time. They had arrived at the farm in the early morning two days before, 29th June. Kitzi said, also for the tenth time, 'I have been courting it, I realize that. But I always thought there would be preliminaries, warnings. And thanks to you, dear Gerhardt, there *were* warnings, although not preliminaries! So here I am in this attic, instead of in one of their filthy camps about which people whisper.'

'I do not think they would have arrested you. I doubt whether that was the intention.'

'But Wieland –'

'Spoke of lists. Not of the intended fate of those listed. Kitzi, there is news this evening from Berlin, and not only from Berlin. There have been announcements, too, the usual official language about conspiracies against the Reich, conspiracies just detected in time. Armed revolution just prevented. Good citizens can sleep in their beds soundly once again. That sort of thing.'

Kitzi stared at him. Gerhardt was speaking in his usual quiet, unemphatic voice.

'It's becoming pretty clear. They've shot large numbers of people. I have no doubt it was intended that you should be one of them. They – the SS have done the job, it's been supervised by Hitler, by the German Chancellor in person, Kitzi! Hitler, sitting where Bismarck once sat, has been acting as an executioner, with a gang of armed roughs supporting him.'

'In Berlin?'

'Certainly, in Berlin. Goering and Himmler have been running the massacre in Berlin – one can't call it anything else. It's said there were shots from the Lichterfeld barracks every twenty minutes or so, hour after hour. Hitler himself has been in Bavaria with Goebbels.'

'Gerhardt,' said Kitzi, 'who – simply their critics, their political enemies? Surely –'

'Not at all. They've taken the opportunity to deal with some enemies – or those they now class as enemies, certainly. They arrested von Papen, our Vice-Chancellor! Charming! A very dignified way for the German Reich to be seen conducting its affairs – and ironical, too, when one thinks how that old fox helped bring Hitler forward in the first place! But he's been released, it seems. They shot two of his assistants at the Vice-Chancellery – murdered them. They've murdered Schleicher.'

'*Schleicher?*'

'Schleicher. And his wife. Someone was talking to him on the telephone and heard him say, "Hold on, there's someone at the door." Then the caller distinctly heard "Yes, I'm General von Schleicher." Then shots. Their young daughter found them when she came home for lunch. I've had that at second hand, from a close friend. And there are plenty of others, although a lot of it is still rumour. People like General von Bredow, Schleicher's friend. It's said in Munich that they've even shot poor old von Kahr, who thought he'd use Hitler in 1923, and manage to get an independent Bavaria. I was there! Poor old booby!'

'But – I asked – presumably their critics, their opponents, how –'

'That's been incidental – the seizing of a chance to profit by what could no doubt be called a revolutionary situation! Incidental. Your own shooting would have been incidental. No, the main object was to deal with the SA. Hitler obviously decided he had to sacrifice the SA if he was to keep the loyalty of the Army. Anyway, people within the Party as well as everyone else have been getting increasingly fed up with Röhm and his ambitions. Now they've dealt with considerable numbers of them, it appears. Including Röhm himself. It seems that Hitler couldn't face shooting Röhm at first, but he brought himself to it eventually and they did him in in Munich yesterday. And his crony Heines, from Breslau, who was in bed with a boy! And shot there – with the boy! Germany is in a very proud state, isn't it?'

'The SA!' said Kitzi. 'Yes – it's logical. They helped him to power, they conquered the streets, and now they're dispensable! They're too pleased with themselves, and our Chancellor needs more respectable friends. Well, they deserved it, Gerhardt. One can say that!'

'One cannot say that – not about all of them.' Gerhardt von Premnitz fixed his friend with a stern eye. He said, 'You know as well as I do that there were decent young idealists, even in the SA; even some who spoke out about the excesses of the Party and so forth, who retained consciences. My information and my guess is that it is they, for certain, who've been murdered. As well as the leaders of course. It's been an internal Party power battle, Kitzi, and a paying off of scores. And it has been an appalling disgrace to our country, a disgrace which will echo round the world. And the Reichswehr, prepared to see the SA put in its place, have stood aside and permitted it. I've not the slightest doubt, in fact, that our generals not only permitted it but knew it would happen and approved. And I am ashamed. I guessed the sort of thing that was in the wind but this – this slaughter, this gangsterism! I am ashamed!'

'Not Schleicher! Not Bredow! The Reichswehr wouldn't –'

'Of course not. But when you let a tiger out of its cage to

spring at your enemies, you can't be surprised if it turns on a few of your friends as well. Kitzi, this – not only this so-called crisis but the whole German situation – is not going to blow over.'

'No, Gerhardt,' said Kitzi Fischer firmly. 'It is not going to blow over.' He had known for some time, but had persuaded himself that one could look for light behind the clouds. He had returned to Germany from England, to give support to old Günther; and had half-pretended to friends, even sometimes to himself, that it might be possible to remain. Germany was home, the country he loved. No man chooses exile unless under some terrible compulsion.

And now they might bully old Günther again because of him, although Günther had said grimly that he could look after himself, and Kitzi had half-believed him. No doubt Gerhardt could find out about that in time.

'I must get away, Gerhardt, leave the country. England. Then America maybe. There will be plenty like me. Wise Jews, perhaps, among others. The Nazis abuse them, rouse the rabble. They may soon turn their prejudices into law. It's known some Jews have already found it insufferable and are quietly getting out, poor devils. There will be plenty, like me, who will leave the country, seek safety abroad.'

'Maybe. Kitzi, during this commotion and probably for some time, the frontier posts will all have strict instructions, railway stations will be heavily policed, all that. There's been an anti-State revolution, you see, nipped in the bud! Dangerous men are still at large! You're one of them, Kitzi! It won't be easy for you to leave Germany.'

'You are going to England yourself, you said –'

'In the second week in July. I will have no problems. I am not a political man.'

CHAPTER XIII

'Is that Desmond Dillon? Adrian Winter here.'

'Hullo, Mr Winter.' It was 20th July and Desmond had returned from Paris to London for a few days. Adrian was lucky to find him at home before his final ten days due to be spent in France. The first of the article sequence was due to appear this week and Desmond felt happier than for some time. This was achievement of a kind; and the series would run for ten weeks.

'Desmond, there's a curious thing happened. Does the name von Premnitz, a German, mean anything to you?'

'I don't think so.'

'He's a friend of Fischer. You know Fischer of course – you've seen a lot of him, I know. Before he returned to Berlin.'

'I have indeed.'

'Von Premnitz and Fischer were both friends of my wife, your mother's cousin. Fischer reckons she saved his life in those Nazi riots in Munich in '23.'

'I remember the story well, sir.'

'Von Premnitz is over here. He's got some odd stories to tell. They – the decent ones – are terribly ashamed about the recent murders and upheavals and horrors, of course.'

'Has he news of Kitzi Fischer? I've not heard anything for some time.'

There was a pause and then Adrian Winter said, 'I'd like you to meet von Premnitz. I'm going to Scotland next week until the end of August but I've told him to get hold of you. He had your name and he intended to anyway, but he decided to contact me first and I'm glad he did. We're quite old friends, one way and another.'

And five days later Gerhardt von Premnitz sat opposite Desmond at lunch in the Grill Room of the Ritz Hotel. Gerhardt had insisted.

'You must lunch with me, Herr Dillon. I have messages for you from a mutual friend.'

Desmond's heart had been in his mouth for a moment. Could it mean Sonja? But he knew from his talk with Adrian Winter that von Premnitz was referring to Kitzi Fischer.

Gerhardt knew London only slightly now, but he had been to the Ritz and appreciated that its Grill Room was a perfectly appropriate and not inordinately expensive place to take a young man to lunch. Desmond, whose comparatively frugal habits seldom covered any floor of the Ritz, assented happily. He wanted to hear how matters went with Kitzi. The newspaper accounts of the period around 30th June had been sensational; it was hard to tell exactly what had happened; but it was clear that Kitzi was safe or Adrian Winter would have told him.

Desmond liked the look of Gerhardt von Premnitz. He saw a tall, slender man with a strong frame, hair which was almost white, perhaps prematurely white, and a face which appeared ageless: Desmond could not imagine that face other than mature, lined, glance penetrating, lips thin, expression sceptical. But although the man was stiff and rather formidable, Desmond knew that he liked him. The eyes were intelligent but they were not of Kitzi's impulsiveness, his periodic emotional excess, his moral absolutism, his defiant, uncompromising assertions. This man would never say more than he needed. But, Desmond suspected, his heart, like Kitzi's, was unequivocally sound. He spoke English perfectly.

Gerhardt got straight down to business, when they had ordered lunch. Desmond noted his quick, automatic look round neighbouring tables. A conspiratorial attitude seemed absurd in the Ritz Grill, safe here in London, in the summer of 1934, but you couldn't blame him, thought Desmond. Kitzi was apt to glance round in the same way, lean forward, lower the voice slightly. That, today, was the effect of Germany.

'Herr Dillon, your friend Kitzi Fischer has talked to me about you. I know all about that dreadful business of the persecution of the young lady you know, the journalist Fräulein Vassar. I must tell you I have no news for you about that.'

Desmond inclined his head. He had not allowed himself to hope.

'I shall continue to listen, ask, watch. If I can discover anything in that matter I will always get word to you. Always.'

'Thank you. That is very, very good of you.'

'I want to speak of Kitzi Fischer. It is important that he leaves Germany. He is lucky to be alive. At present he is in hiding, absolutely safe for a short while. As soon as can be arranged, it is best that he comes to England. Mr Winter believes it will be perfectly possible for him either to stay here or go to the USA. He has many friends.'

'I'm sure of it. I thought he was mad to go back. He felt he had to see his old servant, Günther. I told him Günther would get on all right without him.'

'You were right. What Günther failed to do was to survive with him. The Nazis murdered Günther on 30th June. The day your papers, inaccurately, have christened the Night of the Long Knives. Most murders, including Günther's, were committed in the daylight.'

'*Günther*!' Desmond called out, so loud that people at adjoining tables looked up, 'Günther! But he had no political interest, he was just a loyal, simple –'

'Soul. Exactly. Anyway they came looking for our friend Kitzi and he had disappeared. That must have annoyed them. And they shot his man.'

Desmond stared at Gerhardt, his mouth grim. Gerhardt's eyes never left his. Gerhardt's voice continued, even.

'They will continue hunting for all those they listed for death or arrest – mostly death. They will continue hunting for Kitzi whom they would certainly have shot. They will not find him.'

'Where is he?'

Gerhardt ignored this. He said, 'There are strict checks on anybody leaving Germany. All places of exit will be watched at all times with lists and photographs and police. It will be routine. From now on.'

'So how do we get Kitzi out?'

'That is what I wish to discuss with you,' said Gerhardt, liking Desmond's use of 'we'. 'That is what our friend Mr Winter, without saying much, implied it might be sensible to discuss with you. To ask for your views, your advice, perhaps your cooperation. Of course it is understood that these things take time.' They talked for a long while, and the luncheon tables in the Grill Room were gradually cleared. Then they moved to the long corridor, half-hall, half-lounge, which ran down the spine of the Ritz, and sat on a small, upright sofa, where they continued talking very quietly. Around them couples drifted in for tea.

It was Saturday, 18th August, when Theo Tate arrived to stay with the Fordhams in Perthshire, and Adrian Winter had already been there three days paying a round of Scottish visits. The Fordhams rented Strathdoe, a medium-class grouse moor and a medium-sized lodge, for two weeks in August, and had done for many years. Adrian Winter no longer shot but enjoyed the company, the Highland air, the picnics, the bustle, the sense of occasion. He liked peering forward from some grouse butt where he had placed himself as companion to one of the guns, observing the distant line of beaters, the white flags, then, with luck, the small cloud of dark objects, swinging over the heather towards the butts, the whirring of wings, the moment swiftly over, the marking of fallen birds, the congratulations on success, the tactful silences after failure. Roger Fordham was an old Parliamentary colleague who had retired from the House over ten years ago – retired too young, Adrian thought irritably, we need men like him. Like me. Fordham had professed himself too busy with other concerns. Once – almost unpardonably – he had said, 'Good thing to make way for a few of the young 'uns.' He was two years younger than Adrian Winter.

The truth was that Fordham, a good fellow, a rich, hospitable, genial, shrewd, good fellow, was not really interested in politics, not interested heart and soul. Adrian was sure Fordham had never missed the House after leaving it. But Adrian was fond of them both. They had no children, just as he had no children, and they entertained the younger generation generously in a way Adrian appreciated and understood. Strathdoe was a lovely place. This year Elizabeth Fordham said, 'There's a young man you know coming for the weekend. He doesn't shoot but he's been staying in Edinburgh and he's arriving for a night on Saturday. Theo Tate.'

'Of course I know Theo Tate. Poor young chap, he –'

'I know. A terrible business. Poor girl, poor Theo. Roger's met him quite a lot recently, sees him when he goes to the City. He's got political ambitions, hasn't he?'

'He has,' said Adrian, 'he has.'

And he decided he was glad to see Theo, poor young Theo. He greeted him warmly on arrival. There was something attractive and yet curiously disconcerting, Adrian felt without putting words to it, in the way Theo walked, in his movements. He was unusually *economic* in his gestures. Adrian watched Theo's entry into the room at Strathdoe that Saturday evening. He looked about him, very still, eyes searching for host and hostess, face expressionless yet alert. Then he moved towards Elizabeth Fordham, every step neat, graceful, almost as if he relished the grace of his own body, cat-like. And yet, thought Adrian, there was nothing pansy about him, he didn't give one that feeling at all. When he came up to Adrian to shake hands Adrian thought, as he always did, what fine eyes the young fellow had, intelligent, clear and compelling.

They found themselves together after breakfast on Sunday. It was raining heavily and in the Sabbath absence of sport, a certain aimlessness pervaded Strathdoe. Breakfast had been late and leisurely. People disappeared into corners with Saturday's newspapers and Roger Fordham explained several times that Sunday's would arrive at about teatime, and that it looked as if it might clear up after lunch. Adrian settled himself in a window-seat with Theo. On the other side of streaming windows water sheeted down impartially on conifers, dark heather and rough moorland grass. Adrian started the conversation.

'Saw Dillon the other day.'

Theo nodded. There had been little contact with Desmond for some time. Adrian lowered his voice, although the nearest fellow guest was in another corner of the room.

'Splendid chap, Desmond Dillon. Bit of an adventurer, a country needs a few like that, not too many. Possibly he might be just the man for a rather tricky business in Germany.' Adrian looked carefully at Theo. He had considered Theo himself when Gerhardt von Premnitz had first unfolded the situation, asked advice on how the thing might be done and by whom. Young Tate, Adrian had been tempted to say. He's a good man. Knows Germany. Cool head, good heart, brains. He'll work something out, and he wants to please me, wants it very much. And, anyway, he'd want to do the right thing and he knows Fischer. But he had swung away, swung to Desmond Dillon. Theo Tate had experienced tragedy recently, had had a bad time. He might be suffering a period of unluckiness – Adrian was a great believer in luck. The same might be said of Dillon, of course, but somehow Adrian didn't think so. He had therefore said, 'Young Dillon. Desmond Dillon. He's your man.'

Now he said to Theo, 'Of course you and he stayed together in Berlin with Christoph Fischer, didn't you?'

'We did,' said Theo. 'A very charming man. He was over here but then returned to Germany. I hope he's all right.'

'Between ourselves he's far from all right. He got away when they wanted to shoot him. On 30th June. Tipped off by his nephew, it appears, who's some sort of Nazi.'

'Some sort of Nazi.' Wieland's charming, sincere face came before Theo's eyes. He nodded understanding. It was comprehensible, but it was news to him. He had wondered. Adrian was talking on, voice low, a bit obscure at times.

'Hoping to get him out between you and me. Young Desmond's the right sort of chap for that kind of thing. Officially, of course, nobody knows anything. Mustn't do.'

'Naturally.'

'Don't want to know anything myself. But let's hope for the best. Hope's hard to hang on to in anything which concerns Germany now. Old Hindenburg's death three weeks ago, and Hitler making himself President as well as Chancellor. Oh dear, oh dear!'

'Terrible, sir. Terrible!'

'I've got faith in what I've always seen of young Desmond. I'm sure he'll keep out of trouble.'

Theo nodded.

Adrian, on impulse, said, 'I happen to know you went to Germany yourself. To try to do something for him in the matter of that young woman I've heard about. In the winter. Hard time for both of you. Damned decent of you!'

He took Theo's hand, squeezed it, stood up and moved off, humming a little tune. Then he turned and said, more loudly, 'I expect we'll see a good deal more of each other, come next year!'

With part of himself Theo felt warmth and reassurance. Adrian was not one to drop such hints without sincere purpose. But increasingly these days he found such signs of comfort hollow or illusory. He sometimes felt like a man pursuing a mirage in the desert, the mirage of an oasis; a man who sometimes doubted even his own thirst.

Theo was driven to Perth to catch the night train to London that evening. On Monday morning, in a London humid and deserted, he received a telephone call, acknowledged it curtly, and travelled on the stuffy underground train without enthusiasm to Epping that evening. Marcus, using coded language for urgency, desired a meeting.

'Contor,' Marcus said, in the green cool of Epping Forest, a place used by them only twice before, 'there is a curious circumstance on which I need your opinion. Perhaps your explanation. Word has come from the Comrades in Germany that the Gestapo have your name. They are making inquiries. They have your name as a suspected Comrade, you understand.'

'No,' said Theo, 'I don't understand. Not at all. I have never, as you know, had the slightest contact –'

'Of course not. But they suspect – enough, anyway, to start checking. They have deliberately left some of the Comrades free – of course, to give them occasional lines, as they imagine, into the Movement, the Party. It suits us well, they deceive themselves.'

'And they've asked about me.'

'They've asked about you, which, of course, has been reported. It is unimportant, in that few of the Comrades in Germany know anything about you.'

'Quite so. And there's nothing to know.'

'Nothing. Nothing except that you are a dedicated Party member, receiving instructions from myself, and playing the part of an aspiring Conservative would-be-candidate for the British Parliament! Nothing at all! And some of this, as it happens, is not entirely unknown to some of our Comrades in Germany at another level. A very senior level.'

Theo looked at Marcus with a disagreeable feeling in his stomach. Marcus's voice had been unpleasant. Now Marcus said, 'Why have these inquiries been made? That is what matters. Who has originated them?'

'In Berlin –'

'I know exactly what you did and whom you saw in Berlin. The only conceivable link in the chain is the beautiful young SS officer, Breitfall.'

'Wieland doesn't suspect me of being a Communist!'

'Ah! "Wieland" does not suspect you! Really? Are you sure? Recall your conversations with him.'

'I've told you how they went.'

'You were under some emotional stress, I know. Recall them again. As exactly as you can.' At one point Marcus interrupted and asked how much Theo had drunk that night. It was an inconclusive, a disagreeable talk. At the end of it Marcus said, 'He must be discredited, this Breitfall. That will be best. If he becomes a poisoned source his suspicions will be discounted – or, at least, less important. That is desirable. I wonder how?'

Theo found at first that no words came. Oddly, for so controlled a person, he several times opened his mouth and uttered nothing, nothing at all. He knew Marcus was looking at him intently. Eventually, softly, throat constricted, aware and simultaneously ashamed of his own unhappiness, he said he thought he knew a way how. He explained it at some length, ashamed of the intense dislike he felt for himself the while. Later Marcus asked about Desmond Dillon.

'I wonder if he knows a little too much about you, this Desmond Dillon?'

'I don't for a moment think so.'

'I wonder,' said Marcus, 'I wonder.' Marcus's eyes were on him and Theo heard himself again describing his conversation in Scotland with Adrian Winter. Marcus listened carefully and thought for some time. Eventually he made one or two remarks in a decisive tone and said, 'Anyway, this seems a good idea, Contor. From every point of view. And I agree that it will be best to have a word with the man Langenbach as well, since you already know him.'

Kurt Langenbach had agreed at once to Theo Tate's suggestion that they lunch together but invited him instead to a small party which was being given at the Embassy in honour of a departing diplomat.

'No, no, I insist. That will be delightful. To tell the truth so many people are still away from London I have not arranged for our colleague quite the gathering I had hoped. You will be doing me a favour by coming. He is a charming man.'

The lunch was for ten people at a round table. Theo found it easy to be agreeable at such occasions; masculine, reasonably intelligent exchanges on the affairs of the day, a touch of light-hearted scandal here and there, an assumption that sophisticated values were shared by all. Conversation was in English and was general, toasts were drunk, short speeches made. Theo enjoyed occasionally putting in a phrase in German to show his ease, his cosmopolitan assurance. After they had had coffee Kurt Langenbach drew his chair close to Theo's.

'You have been to our country lately?'

Theo talked easily about his last visit to Berlin.

'Ah – some time ago. We have had a difficult time, I can tell you! Some very bad people were ready for anything, it seems. It would have been violent, serious, a sort of civil war even. One must really be thankful the Führer acted as promptly and courageously as he did.'

'I see. As a matter of fact at one time I heard all sorts of rumours, touching many people. I even heard that our friend Kitzi Fischer was in some sort of trouble. I think you know him.'

'I know of Herr Fischer. He is a friend of yours?'

'We stayed with him in Berlin. I saw his nephew, Wieland Breitfall, when I was last there. A charming man. I gather Wieland managed to warn his uncle there was trouble on the way. It was all rather confused, one gathers, that June day, I mean.'

'Rather confused, yes.'

'Wieland's very fond of Kitzi Fischer.'

'I suppose so. I suppose so.'

They talked of other things and Theo said he imagined Langenbach was hoping to return to flying soon. 'Presumably,' he said, 'that will come, Germany will take its proper place in aviation as in all else.' Langenbach smiled at him but made no reply beyond saying that he did not expect to remain attached to the Embassy in London very much longer.

'Herr Dillon?' The man in the blue uniform of the German Customs and Passport Control looked at Desmond's passport, looked at the photograph, looked up at Desmond again, spoke politely, decisively.

'Herr Dillon, come this way, please.' He retained Desmond's passport. They had been asked to show passports at the Aachen railway station. It had been explained that holders of foreign passports could get the exit stamp marked straight away and could then join particular carriages of the train and would not be disturbed again. When they crossed the Dutch frontier they would be left in peace, it had been agreed with the Dutch authorities, it was routine. Dutch customs would not wish to look at luggage until they reached Maastricht. There was no halt, no pause between the frontier and Maastricht.

Desmond found himself in a small room with one table and two chairs. The door was shut and nothing happened, nobody appeared. Ten minutes passed. The train was now due to leave in seven minutes. Desmond went to the door and tried it. Locked. He banged on it and went on banging.

After several minutes of this two men appeared. Not in uniform. Grey, rather ill-fitting suits. Large men. They stood just inside the door and looked at him.

Desmond said, 'What is the meaning of this! I have to catch this train. My passport is in order, I am a British citizen.'

One of the men was holding Desmond's passport, flicking over the leaves. He said, quietly, perfectly politely, 'Herr Dillon, you entered Germany five days ago, I see. On 4th September. Travelling from Paris.'

'Well?'

'A short stay, Herr Dillon.'

'Why not?'

'Have you any objection to explaining where you have been during your stay in Germany?'

'Yes,' said Desmond. 'Every objection. Will you explain to me why you are preventing me catching my train? My luggage is on that train.'

'No, Herr Dillon, your luggage has been taken off that train. You need not bother about your luggage. But there are certain questions we wish to ask. Whom have you seen in Germany? Where, exactly – exactly, please – have you been? And what have you been doing? What has been your object?'

'My object,' said Desmond, staring at the man angrily, 'has been to check on certain details for a book I am writing.' His chin was jutting and, unconsciously, he took a number of small paces towards his questioner who regarded him curiously. Desmond went on, his voice hard, 'I have been to several places in these four or five days. I have seen and talked to people in hotels, on trains. I have stayed at hotels in –'

'In Düsseldorf and Lippstadt,' said the same man, still coolly and courteously. 'Yes, we know that. But I ask where, exactly – exactly, I repeat – you have been, when out of your hotel. In these places.'

'I'm surprised you don't know! You are behaving as if I am a criminal. What do you suspect me of?'

The other man now spoke, and said, much more loudly, 'Herr Dillon, you have a German friend. Christoph Fischer.'

A train, a less luxurious train than Desmond's, a train whose third-class carriages had hard wooden benches and one lavatory serving a considerable number of passengers. A train, nevertheless, which was classified as an international express, a small train connecting France and Germany, a train crossing the Rhine, a train running from Freiburg to Strasbourg: a train which, on the day before Desmond's encounter at Aachen, stopped at that point on the German frontier where, by Franco-German agreement, the formalities were observed. On this occasion, 8th September, a Saturday, the formalities appeared to be thorough. A trio, a German policeman, accompanied by one official of the Customs Service in uniform and one man in civilian clothes, were moving through the train. There were five coaches and the proceedings were clearly going to take some time, time allowed for in the schedules of running times, revised and republished.

At each passenger the trio halted, saluted casually and asked to see 'papers'. The train, on a Saturday, was used by a number of people moving in one direction or the other to visit relations or friends the far side of the frontier. Alsatians, although it didn't always do to recognize it, felt themselves as much German as French and often more so. The three officials halted by a tall man in shabby clothes, long body, long legs curled uncomfortably under the wooden bench, stubble of a greying moustache on the upper lip. A distinguished face. The policeman waved his hand towards his cap in something like a salute. He took the proffered documents, speaking before examining:

'*Zösisch?*'

'*S'il vous plaît?*' said the tall man. The policeman looked through the papers carefully, and eyed the photograph.

'*Citoyen français?*'

'*Ja!*' said the tall man, pleased to display at least one phrase of German, '*Ja! Ich bin –*' he struggled. The German, however, was proud of his own mastery of French.

'*Vous êtes français!* I see, M. André,' the policeman continued, 'that you came over a week ago. Last Saturday.' His accent was precise, correct, somewhat exaggerating the consonants. M. André nodded and smiled. 'It's been poor weather! But a beautiful part of your country.'

'You have had a pleasant stay?' The policeman was still fingering André's papers.

'Very pleasant. Very pleasant indeed. But spoiled by catching this damned cough!' It was true that André was wheezing and spluttering a certain amount, a much-used handkerchief held in front of his mouth. He held out his hand for his papers.

'Excuse me, M. André,' said the policeman, 'I will bring these back shortly.' André raised his eyebrows and made a gesture indicating outrage. '*Mais qu'est-ce-que vous –*' But by that time the policeman and his companions had disappeared, leaving André gasping behind his handkerchief.

'Lippstadt,' said the taller man in a grey suit to Desmond. 'Now why Lippstadt, Herr Dillon?'

'I have already told you that I am researching for a book. Acquiring certain domestic and geographic details about Germany.'

'Your book is about Lippstadt?'

'It may be. I have not decided.' Desmond kept his eyes firmly on the taller man, who had spoken most, and he knew he was being successful in maintaining in his eyes an expression of formidable anger.

He had taken a bus from Lippstadt to a place called Erwitte. There, as he had been informed, it was possible to take another bus to a small village called Ostereiden. He had climbed off the bus at Erwitte at the last moment, and had mounted the second bus, bound for Ostereiden, also at the last moment. He had been pleased with himself, tolerably sure that nobody on the second bus had been on the first. At Ostereiden there was a surprisingly large Bierstube, and he sat in it, drinking beer and looking at the local newspaper. Several men were sitting at other tables. They stared at him and he muttered a good day, to which they nodded and continued to stare. After a little they resumed conversation, calling to each other between tables. They all seemed to know each other.

A heavily built man settled at Desmond's own table and looked at him with what appeared more than a little suspicion. Desmond finished his beer and glanced at his watch. Then he looked round the Bierstube. He leant forward and addressed the man, not loud.

'Have they got a "*Herren*" in this place, can you tell me?' To his relief the man nodded and jerked with his finger.

'*Draussen!* across the yard.'

'Thanks.'

'*Ich auch!*' called the man, grinning. Desmond was on his way to the door into the Bierstube yard, and as he reached the evil-smelling urinal he heard the door bang, indicating his companion had emerged on the same errand. Half an hour later Desmond was returning by a series of bus journeys towards Lippstadt where he spent time inspecting the town. Peter Milch was simultaneously driving himself northward towards Delbruck, the papers of André, French citizen, sometime officer of His Imperial Majesty Nicholas, Emperor of All the Russias, in his pocket.

'And where did you go, Herr Dillon,' inquired the man in the ill-fitting suit, 'in the neighbourhood of Lippstadt?' And Desmond, frowning, still indignant, said that he had been to a number of villages by bus, absorbing the atmosphere of the countryside of Lippe; and that it had been helpful to the descriptive passages of the book he intended to write. And Düsseldorf, they wanted to know, could Herr Dillon please account for his movements in Düsseldorf?

He had told them very bluntly, on their first inquiry, that he most certainly knew Herr Christoph Fischer but that he had not visited him, had not seen him, had no idea of his whereabouts, and would be delighted to be informed since Herr Fischer was a particular friend, and if the gentlemen in grey suits – but they had interrupted, frowning, and it was clear to Desmond that they did not believe him. He said no more at that time, and smiled inwardly, for he had spoken at all times the precise truth albeit with omissions. Düsseldorf, they said, the evening in Düsseldorf? And Desmond began, cautiously, secretly, to feel that he had won.

'Have you finished with my papers? What's all this about?'

'Almost finished, M. André. Formalities. You say you entered Germany one week ago.'

'That's correct. 1st September.'

'By this route.'

'By this route, yes. I've been visiting friends.' He had the names of friends. He much hoped, however, not to give them. To his relief the policeman nodded and said, 'I'm stamping your passport, the exit stamp, you see. The curious thing is that the paper's been defaced, or so it seems.'

'What do you mean, defaced?'

'As if there's been an exit stamp removed, just where mine is going now.'

'I can't understand that. I just handed it over, like I did to you. For the entry stamp. Perhaps the fellow put on another beside it by mistake, and then tried to scratch it out, seeing his error. Is that possible?'

'No,' said the policeman, unsmiling, 'that is not possible. One moment please.'

'I can only just hear you!' said Desmond Dillon into the telephone mouthpiece, speaking slowly, loudly and clearly. 'It's a bad line!'

But although André's voice was distorted it was certainly he. Desmond could envisage that tall frame and quizzical look, eyebrows raised, expression thoughtful.

'Where are you, Mr Dillon?' André did not take easily to Desmond's request to use his first name.

'Maastricht. It took longer than I expected for various reasons. I'm catching a train to Brussels in one hour and then coming on to Paris on a slow night train, arriving tomorrow morning as agreed.'

'It went well?'

'Tolerably well. Has our friend made contact?'

'Not yet.'

Desmond's stomach heaved. Contact should have been made on the previous day. André was talking, calmly.

'Of course, I'm looking forward to the meeting very much. You know how a Frenchman feels without – without certain essentials of life! Certain –'

'Yes, yes, of course! I'm very, very grateful for all this. You know that. I'll see you tomorrow. I expect you'll get a call this evening, and it'll be clear by the time I arrive.'

André replaced the receiver on its hook, also hoping very earnestly that he would get a call that evening. But Desmond's train rumbled through the darkness to Brussels; and then, from another station, towards the French frontier; and to André, in Paris, no call came.

'M. André,' said the policeman, 'these gentlemen wish to speak to you.' He indicated two men in civilian clothes, indicated them with deference. They looked at the tall figure with its shaven bristles of a moustache, looked at the papers, looked again at M. André, *citoyen français*, making terrible noises into his handkerchief, apparently breathing with difficulty. Then one of the two spoke sharply to the policeman and turned on his heel. 'M. André,' said the policeman. 'It will be necessary for you to leave the train. These gentlemen wish to speak to you elsewhere. Follow me, please.'

CHAPTER XIV

Adrian Winter had moved fast. The telephone line from London to Paris had been adequate and Adrian had understood Desmond clearly. With a small part of his mind Desmond found himself admiring the old boy. It wasn't difficult to understand how reluctant he was to give up the House of Commons, which he had first entered in the 'eighties of the last century, and where he certainly reckoned he would be hard to follow. By now Desmond had come to regard old Adrian, with affection, as an ancient buffer who needed things explaining with care and not too fast, an old gentleman whose long Parliamentary experience no doubt gave him a valuable 'feel' for the House, but who was well past the age for coping with emergencies.

Not so. Adrian had understood perfectly. He had, indeed, cut Desmond short and gone straight to the heart of the matter, a matter of which Desmond had so far been scrupulous not to disclose too much. Adrian had a position, must not be embarrassed. There was no hint of that now.

'Mr Winter, I can only suppose there has been some sort of hold-up at the frontier. Our friend, our German acquaintance –'

'V.P.'

'Hullo? I said, Mr Winter, that our German acquaintance –'

'I heard you. V.P. Go on.'

'Yes – yes, exactly. Well, I've spoken to him in a pre-arranged way, no question of compromising him. The man we're talking about was on the train all right.'

'As a Frenchman.'

'Yes. As a Frenchman.'

'And now no word,' said Adrian Winter, 'or not as far as you know. But you wouldn't know, would you! You wouldn't know if the Boche authorities were detaining a Frenchman, had even, perfectly correctly, informed the French authorities of the fact. You wouldn't know. And you don't know how to ask.'

'I can find out, I'm sure.' Desmond had faith in the resourcefulness of the deeply troubled although uncomplaining André. Adrian knew nothing of André.

'Are you there, Dillon? Hullo, Hullo.'

'Yes, I'm here, Mr Winter.'

'This is what I will do. Best to go in at the top on these occasions.' He gave Desmond a few brief and unambiguous instructions.

'Delac is a good chap. We made friends on an inter-Parliamentary get-together during the War and we've kept up with each other. Lot younger than I am, and now, as I say, a Minister. If anyone can help, Delac will. Go and see him. As soon as you can.'

'*M. le Ministre*, I'm most grateful that you have received me –'

Michel Delac inclined his head. Adrian Winter had in fact spoken to his private secretary since he, Delac, had been having a particularly difficult interview with the Foreign Minister throughout the morning. Adrian Winter had, however, always been helpful to him from the earliest days when, a young Deputy, he had been making his way. Winter knew everybody in England, it seemed, and Delac had made it his business to cultivate a knowledge of England. He was always ready to do Winter a service. This now took the form of giving a few minutes of his time to a young Englishman with a bold eye and a rather impetuous manner, whose business Winter had not chosen to disclose.

Desmond disclosed it. Or part of it. He said that he had been befriended by a Russian émigré, a taxi driver in Paris. They had agreed to meet again, and Desmond knew that M. André – 'a French citizen' – had taken a week's holiday to visit friends in

Germany. A mutual acquaintance had, it was known, seen him on the train to Strasbourg. From Freiburg. From Strasbourg M. André had planned to take a train home to Paris, to meet Desmond.

He had not arrived. Would it be possible to discover whether anything had happened to him en route? The situation in Germany now –

Delac observed that this was, in the first instance, a matter for the police. They were speaking in English, Delac's fluency in which he enjoyed showing off. Why did Desmond think André was not in Paris? He had probably taken a different train. It was, he reflected privately, an odd business for Mr Adrian Winter to be concerned with. So odd, in fact, that he said, abruptly, 'You say this man is of Russian origin?'

'Certainly. He was an officer in the Imperial Army. A charming man.'

'No doubt. And certainly not a Jew?'

'Certainly not a Jew.'

'With friends in Germany. Have you the address of these friends, with whom he was staying?'

'Not exactly.'

'What does that mean?'

'I do not know,' said Desmond, 'anyone I could ask about his time in Germany, except the mutual friend I spoke about already, *M. le Ministre*, who assured me André was on the Strasbourg train. Last Saturday.'

'Perhaps your M. André met someone on the train and decided to stay a day or two in Strasbourg! Some charming encounter, maybe!'

'I think not, *M. le Ministre*. He would definitely have come as quickly as possible to Paris, once in France.'

'Once in France again, M. Dillon.'

'Once in France again, *M. le Ministre*.'

The Minister looked at his hands, fingers outstretched, palms on the polished surface of his desk. Then he looked up at Desmond and smiled.

'When are you leaving Paris, M. Dillon?'

'I intended only a short stay this time. But of course I was meeting my friend André, and now –'

'Now your plans are uncertain. Of course. Where did you come here from? And when?'

Desmond said that he had come by train from Brussels. He conveyed, very politely, that this might not have a great deal to do with his request to the Minister. The Minister was still smiling at him agreeably. He understood perfectly what was going on behind Desmond's eyes.

'And where, M. Dillon, had you been before reaching Brussels? Had you spent some time in Belgium, travelled there from England, perhaps?'

'Not exactly. A short stay in Brussels. I –'

'Had come from Germany, I dare say.'

Desmond wished Delac would stop smiling. There was a long silence between them. Delac seemed to be considering. He looked at his watch. Then he looked up at Desmond, very sharply. No smile.

'M. Dillon, M. Adrian Winter is a good friend of mine. I would always wish to help him or any friend of his. Including, of course, yourself.'

'Thank you very much, *M. le Ministre*.'

'I will cause inquiries to be made, at the level of officials, whether our German friends have any knowledge of a French M. André, said to have been last seen travelling by train from Freiburg to Strasbourg last Saturday.'

'Thank you, most sincerely. May I ask how long such inquiries are likely to take?'

'I cannot say. I am afraid I do not think I can promise you great urgency.'

'I see.'

'Nor, perhaps, would it be appropriate to imply to the German authorities that the matter is particularly significant.'

'No,' said Desmond, 'perhaps not.'

'I will do all that. And now, M. Dillon, may I offer a word of advice to yourself?'

'Of course, *M. le Ministre*.'

'I suggest you return to England. Leave your address and English telephone number with my secretary. If we hear anything I will arrange to inform you in England.'

'Thank you. I must explain I have been coming to Paris quite often, *M. le Ministre*. I am engaged on a series of articles for a London paper. I –'

'No doubt. But you periodically return to England.'

'Of course. I was due to go on Thursday. But –'

'I suggest you do so, M. Dillon. For a while.'

The Minister arose, hand extended, smile gracious. Desmond thanked him again. He realized that it would be better to leave it there and he was given little choice. Delac bowed him from his splendid office, smile still charming. A minute later he touched the bell on his desk and his secretary, a dark-haired, suave young man, reappeared. Delac gave him a brief instruction.

'Tell them not to waste time. I am personally interested.'

'Of course.'

'This young man is trying to run political dissidents out of Germany. There's plenty of that, as you and I know well. There must be no connection. If this "André" turns out to be of particular interest to the German authorities we want nothing to do with it.'

'In that case,' said the secretary, lifting his shoulders respectfully but emphatically, 'he is unlikely to be a French citizen, one would suppose!'

'Precisely so, Malibon. Precisely so.'

Somebody had told Delac that his charming young secretary was particularly friendly with a pretty girl at the German Embassy, and he had said to himself that it would need watching. At the moment, however, he doubted whether it was significant. Malibon had his way to make.

Desmond was due to stay with the Marvells at Bargate that weekend. As more often than not, Adrian Winter would be there; and Desmond had looked forward to reporting to him, thanking him for giving him, Desmond, the chance to be useful;

saying that, as Adrian knew, all had gone well, although Desmond didn't want to go into detail. Now, as he sat in the Paris to Calais express on Thursday, bumping over the rails running across northern France, he reflected that it was likely instead to be a grim weekend. There would be anxious talk between Adrian and himself, talk in corners, the hospitable Marvells excluded. There would be an account of failure – unless something changed, something turned up. And he, Desmond, had let André down very badly indeed. Normally resilient, Desmond felt as guilty about that as about anything. When he had first answered Adrian's request he had seen the way clear. André was exactly the right sort of man for that kind of favour. And André had been instantly cooperative, a wonderful man, his heart in the venture, damn the risks, no thought of self.

'You saved me from those French bastards! Of course I'll help. But, Mr Dillon, they're pretty important to me, papers. If I have to go to the police and explain I've dropped them into the Seine by mistake life gets difficult!'

'Of course.'

They'd talked it over, quickly. André would travel into Germany on 1st September by train and return two days later. He would thus get his passport stamped with the obligatory entry and exit marks and dates. They would then carefully obliterate the exit stamp. Desmond would thus convey to Kitzi papers showing entry to Germany on 1st September – in proper form to receive a new exit stamp when he crossed the frontier. Once in Paris Kitzi would go to the small hotel André had recommended. They'd all meet, with luck! Kitzi's own papers were perfectly adequate for subsequent entry to England.

And now Kitzi had not arrived. And André was without papers, a taxi driver vulnerable at any moment to the official bark of the gendarme, the demand almost more peremptory than in any other language – '*Vos papiers?*'

And there was nothing, absolutely nothing, Desmond could do about it. His instinct had been to stay in Paris, but Delac had clearly preferred him out of the way and Delac, Desmond knew, guessed more than could be acknowledged. André himself had nodded when the interview with the Minister was described.

'Right, Mr Dillon. He wants you out of France. Why not? He knows what you're up to. He doesn't want involvement. He'll make official inquiries, that's all. It'll probably meet a blank wall – the Germans won't know, they'll regret, that'll be that. If they've caught your friend.'

'Grim, André.'

'Grim, Mr Dillon. Desmond.'

'And what about you?'

André had said that after a few days he would report loss of papers, that they might have been stolen. That way, if the Germans politely returned them one day to the French customs or police, explaining they'd turned up inexplicably in Germany somewhere, André would be covered by some sort of a story.

'Nothing else to do, Desmond.'

'I'm terribly sorry.' Desmond told André that the Germans must have somehow been suspicious of the Dillon name.

'They questioned me about everything. Why?'

'I expect they knew you were a friend of this M. Fischer.'

'All the same – I'm not an old friend and he's got hundreds of friends. And imagine all the other people who the Nazis are after, if the papers are to be believed, and no doubt all with hundreds of friends and ordinary names! It doesn't make sense! They dropped on me, they grilled me. They had something. But if that something came from the German end, from the people hiding Kitzi – M. Fischer – then I think I'd have got some inkling when I spoke to his friend, to M. von Premnitz. I can't add it up – still, they can't have been on to me because of any connection with *you*, that's certain. It was *my* name that caught their attention.'

André said that one could never tell when dealing with police in a place like that. Nazi Germany. Bolshevik Russia. Gestapo. Cheka. One could never tell who had talked or to what effect. Desmond said again, 'I'm terribly sorry.'

'It's not your fault. It was a good idea. I made a run, got the papers stamped, rubbed out the exit mark – a good idea. Believe me, I had early experience at getting people out of places. Russia! That was really something! Cheer up, Desmond, we'll have some more to drink – and you go back to England.' Desmond agreed, hoping desperately that before he left there'd be a tap at the door, a tall, limping, grinning Kitzi Fischer clutching the papers of a French taxi driver, one-time officer in the Army of His Imperial Majesty, Nicholas. But it didn't happen. All he had been able to do was to leave money with André to cover the expenses of contacting England if Kitzi turned up or any other news broke. Even then André refused to accept much. With every hour that passed without Kitzi's appearance Desmond felt sicker.

It was a smooth crossing, and Desmond reached London at five o'clock, feeling as if he had been away for a year. At first it had been extraordinarily stimulating, and although it had now all gone wrong he had felt strung up, fully alive, glad that the attempt was being made. The days in Germany had been good – very good: the sense of risk (and, he acknowledged, there probably hadn't been much), the anonymity, the thrill of the clandestine. Then Paris, after his return there, with its disappointments and its anxieties, turned into a place of bloodiness. Bargate would be as near Hell as so agreeable a place could be, Hell because of old Adrian Winter's kind, disappointed eyes, the sense of anti-climax, the sense of failure. Desmond let himself into his flat. He was due to have a talk to his editor next morning, Friday, and go to Bargate in the evening. He picked up the pile of letters on the floor of his tiny hall and moved into the sitting room, settling himself on a sofa, mail beside him, feeling flat and tired. Glancing through the envelopes he found, without pleasure, one addressed in his mother's hand. Patsy was still in the South of France, Patsy had spent the summer being 'still very low and out of sorts, darling', Patsy had been unable to return, because of severe illness (she said) to Emma's funeral, her own Emma's funeral. Patsy was an irregular correspondent. It had not been a year in which mother and son had been close. He decided to open Patsy's letter last, and did not look forward to it with any eagerness. When he ultimately started to read it he read fast, frowning, astonished. Then he went back to the beginning and read it a second, and then a third time.

'Adrian Winter's telephoned,' said Hilda Marvell. 'He's going to be later than he thought. Very odd of dear Adrian – he always arrives in good time on a Friday, whether the House is sitting or not. But he's sent a message not to wait dinner for him. Most peculiar. And he also asked, Desmond my dear, what time *you* were coming! He knows you're staying because I told him, and he was very pressing about it – "Desmond Dillon really is arriving at Bargate this evening, Hilda, you're sure?" that sort of thing. Very strange! I didn't know dear old Adrian and you were such cronies!'

They were walking in the garden at Bargate, the long yew hedges recently clipped and pleasing to the eye, with their well sculpted silhouettes and neatly shaped recesses.

Desmond smiled at her, his mind still confused. He said, 'I'm sorry, Cousin Hilda, I didn't quite –'

'Didn't quite what?'

'Catch what you said.'

Hilda Marvell looked at him intently. He was young, handsome, a favourite of hers and not in the least deaf.

'Desmond, you weren't listening!'

'Well –'

She smiled.

'I just said that Adrian Winter is going to be late for dinner and all he seemed to be interested in was whether you'd be here for certain. That's all. But something's on his mind.'

Desmond nodded. It was only too explicable.

'And something's on yours, Desmond. You're not here at all! Trouble?' She was a woman whose affectionate directness could not give offence to anybody she really cared about, and Desmond had always been one of those. He suddenly felt it intolerable to keep everything locked within himself. Was it to be for ever? And Emma was gone.

'Cousin Hilda,' he said, his mind involuntarily going to his mother and to the way he and Emma had mocked what they thought of as Patsy's pretensions in getting them to call her 'Cousin Hilda'. 'Cousin Hilda, I want to say something very difficult to you.'

'About some business you're undertaking for Adrian Winter? That's what his voice implied.'

'No. Not that. There is something in that, and something awful, too. But this is different. I've just had a letter from my mother.'

'Ah!' said Hilda, eyes watchful.

'In this letter – I got it last night, I'd just got back from France, it was waiting for me – my mother says that Emma and I –'

Again the silence, as if, whatever his will for disclosure, nothing would come. Hilda took his hand and he left it in hers. He was shaking. Hilda said, in an ordinary voice, 'You really want to share this with me?' And Desmond nodded. For the third time he said, 'Emma and I –'

Hilda patted his hand. She knew, she was sure she knew, what was coming, though God knew why that hopeless woman Patsy Dillon couldn't keep it to herself as she had done all these years. Hilda imagined that Desmond, feeling utterly confused, was about to tell her that the twins, he and Emma, were the children of her brother Cosmo Paterson, the brave and beloved Cosmo Paterson, killed in 1918. And that Patsy had just disclosed the fact. And the shock must be unbelievable.

Hilda had adored Cosmo. Cosmo had been erratic, unconventional, splendidly unscrupulous when pursuing an object in which he believed. He had wandered over the world when still a very young man, getting into trouble and getting out again, forming impossible loyalties, falling for impossible women, but utterly staunch when someone he loved was in trouble. Cosmo, a hero from an era which now seemed as remote and improbable as the Middle Ages: Cosmo, with his quick, alert movements, his thin, brown face, his agility, his laughter, his gift for languages: Cosmo, whom she had loved unlike any other, and thanked God her husband, John Marvell, had known and loved as well: Cosmo, found at last by a German shell, when the world seemed to be crashing about them during the last great enemy offensive of the war, March '18, when Haig had spoken of backs being to the wall; Cosmo the unique. And Cosmo had been in love with Patsy Dillon.

He had never confided that in Hilda, and Hilda had never liked her. Patsy and Cosmo had been very young – their love, and what Hilda was convinced had been their love affair, had followed Patsy's early and very obviously unhappy marriage to a handsome, dull, conventional man, Dillon. Hilda's own mother had said, soon afterwards, in the gentle, euphemistic manner of the times, 'I hope Cosmo isn't seeing too much of young Mrs Dillon.'

There had been murmurs here and there, the Paterson parents frowning, saying little: Cosmo elusive, then going off on one of his obscure journeys and adventures. Two babies, twins, born in 1906. Cosmo, still only twenty-one years old, somewhere in the remoter provinces of the Ottoman Empire. The Dillons had seemed more or less 'settled', the matter was unpursued. No scandal.

Hilda looked back at it, the killing time, the dance of death which these first decades of the century had witnessed. And all so young, she thought, so young and unformed. She still missed her elder brother every day, and cared little for the younger, Stephen, with his noise, his opinionated talk, his political ambitions. She loved her children. She loved her husband and home. She had loved Cosmo.

And, from the first, she had been quietly sure that these delightful children, Emma and Desmond, were Cosmo's. With the perception of an adoring sister she had known, without words, all about Cosmo's passion. She had always been able to see Cosmo in Desmond's eyes, sometimes a little in his movements, his darting liveliness. Emma had been more tranquil, less obviously a creature of Cosmo's blood. And now, surprisingly and no doubt improperly, Hilda found she was happy. She knew what a shock this must be to Desmond, but she resolved, in the seconds that followed Desmond's stumbling 'Emma and I –' to tell him that his mother was wonderful, nobody had the right to blame who did not understand, and – although it would be necessary not unfairly to discredit poor dull, dead Dillon – that he had had a unique, a wonderful father. And their secret relationship gave Hilda joy. All these things flashed through her mind, and she resolved, above all, to be loyal to Patsy whom she detested, and who had chosen so inept a moment for her disclosures, with the poor boy trying to recover from his loved sister's death.

Hilda said softly, 'Darling Desmond, I think I can guess.'

He muttered, 'Can you? Was it obvious to other people?'

'Not entirely. But I – well, I was –' She had started to say 'devoted to my eldest brother', but checked it. Best discover at least how Patsy had put it. After all, Hilda herself had only guessed at Cosmo and Patsy's relationship. There had been whispers, smiles and pursed lips but nothing more. Perhaps even Dillon had known nothing. Hilda hoped so. She said, 'Can you tell me something of what your mother said? If you want to, dear Desmond.'

'She wrote,' Desmond said, almost inaudibly, his mouth set, 'that Emma and I must have hated her, she has no way of making me understand, but that since I will have heard only Theo's side of the matter she must simply say that Theo Tate was the sort of aberration a foolish, lonely, middle-aged woman can only too easily suffer. An aberration deeply regretted. She asks for a word of forgiveness, when I find it possible.'

Hilda sat like a statue of stone in one of the yew-lined niches of her own garden. Desmond managed another sentence.

'She says "Emma and I" – so she knew that Emma knew. Somehow. She reckoned, I suppose, that Theo told her, God knows why.'

Still Hilda said nothing, and Desmond whispered, 'So Emma died, with that –'

'I understand, my dear. I understand.'

'And my mother presumed I knew. From Emma. Or Theo. But I didn't.'

'I understand. Don't think cruel thoughts about your mother, Desmond, whatever you do. We're all flesh and blood, frail, fallible human beings.' Hilda, as shocked as she ever remembered, nevertheless knew that Desmond would loathe himself

308

one day if he surrendered to easy condemnation. She said sharply, 'I expect you've been a fallible human being yourself at times, my dear! Don't allow yourself to abuse your mother in your mind for not living up to higher standards than yourself.'

It was a shrewd blow, not unjust. Desmond muttered something, and then smiled, and Hilda thanked God for it. It was Cosmo's smile. She took his arm and steered him towards the house. Damn Patsy!

Desmond said, 'I'd no right to tell you. None.'

'None. But never mind. It's best to share these things with someone. Nobody else need ever know of our talk.'

'No reason to burden you, Cousin Hilda – or blurt out my mother's secrets to you! Or my feelings! It's not even as if we're really relations. I'm sorry. I'm in such a muddle, I can't do anything right.' But Hilda, pressing his arm again, said, 'I think it's a good thing you did. It's put some poison into you and the wound needed lancing.'

There had been other hints in the letter, strange hints, things which Desmond needed time to arrange in his mind. Desmond smiled at her gratefully, and they walked back towards the house with a few whispers of peace audible now and then through the turbulence.

They had dinner, John and Hilda Marvell, Desmond, and the two young Marvells making the most of the last week of the summer holidays. They were an attractive pair: Anthony just eighteen, colt-like, rather exaggerated in his movements; Marcia, fifteen now, with eyes that could give a lot of trouble one day, Desmond thought. They were fond of Desmond and in the agreeable atmosphere this family invariably generated he started to feel a certain return of normality, a tiny stirring of relief from what had recently become a many-sided nightmare. But Adrian Winter was arriving later, and the business of Kitzi, the agonizing business of Kitzi, was yet to be discussed. Theo he put resolutely from his thoughts. With luck he could avoid seeing Theo, he thought with distaste, precursors from Oedipus to Hamlet prowling unbidden round his mind when he gave them half a chance.

John Marvell said, 'Did you know this fellow Prost at Cambridge, Desmond? Fellow the *Sunday Mail* ran that long article about?'

'Prost? Gustav Prost? Yes, I knew him. There were very few Germans, but I met Prost – he was very popular. On some sort of exchange scholarship, Cambridge's answer to the Rhodes scholars! What about him?'

'What sort of chap?'

'Very amusing, very good-looking. Rather outstanding as far as I remember. Cultivated by all the smartest and brightest, that sort of thing. I didn't know him at all well. Why?'

'Extraordinary article about him. Apparently he's been writing some sort of reminiscences of Cambridge for a German paper, and the *Sunday Mail* has been reporting it, giving excerpts.'

It didn't sound very interesting. Desmond looked politely attentive. Anthony chimed in. He had read the article in question and at eighteen he felt very competent to contribute.

'Prost is a Bolshevik, Desmond. A Communist.'

'*Was* a Communist,' his father interjected. 'The point of the article was that he's seen the light, the new German Nazi light, and they've got him to explain to their German newspaper readership what he was up to at Cambridge!'

'German propaganda, presumably.'

'No doubt. Still, it's pretty slanderous stuff. I've no doubt our people here are looking at it carefully – even if sceptically! Prost writes that he was recruited as a Communist at Cambridge.'

'There were plenty of Communists at Cambridge,' Desmond said, 'no secret about that. I certainly don't remember Prost was one of them. It sounds most unlikely.'

'Point is he writes that he was told not to join the Party or be open about it. He was to become an undercover man. Work underground for the Communist International or whatever they call it. For Soviet Russia in reality, of course. Outwardly Prost would be an anti-Communist – or non-political. He was to make his way in Germany as a lawyer. Secretly he'd be an agent for them, for the Communists.'

Desmond was not greatly interested, although it was surprising in the case of Prost, who had been fashionable, sought after by Cambridge society, sophisticated. He said, 'The *Sunday Mail* would like that, it sees Bolsheviks everywhere, doesn't it!'

'Quite. I'm bound to say the excerpts are rather convincing – but, as I said, slanderous. I'm surprised the *Mail* printed them, although there was a lot of stuff explaining that this was what the Germans were being told and British readers ought to know, Cambridge a great British institution, that sort of thing. But the *Mail* named no names, although it's clear the German papers were explicit. Prost claims he was recruited for the Communist undercover boys by a well-known Englishman in London. That he was passed to this man by a Cambridge don. He describes the fellow, indicates the part of London he lives in.'

'I must look at the *Mail*, Cousin John. It sounds rather amusing.'

Anthony had been trying to interrupt his father several times and managed now to get in his word.

'Daddy!'

'Well, Anthony?'

'You know Barney Blackstone, whose father is a Cambridge professor? I saw him at tennis at the Constables on Wednesday. Blackstone's father knows all about this Prost business. He knows exactly who Prost was writing about, the Communist who recruited him in London.'

'Does he indeed,' said John Marvell, repressively. 'Well, I hope he keeps a guard on his tongue or libel lawyers will be after him.'

Anthony was undeterred.

'Blackstone's father said it was obvious from Prost's description he was talking about a man called Headley. Everyone knew him, apparently.'

'Everyone knew him!' said John Marvell ironically. 'It doesn't sound very discreet! One has always imagined Communist secret agents to be masters of conspiracy! What do you think, Desmond? Name Headley mean anything to you?'

Desmond was silent for a moment or two, putting some recollections together. He said, 'I think Headley is, or was, a perfectly open left-winger. Perhaps too obvious to play the sort of games Prost suggests, if Prost really was referring to Headley. Several people I know, more or less open and convinced left-wing people, idealists, people I respect, all knew Headley. One heard his name quite often.'

Anthony was bubbling, enjoying his informed participation in this very adult conversation.

'Yes, but Desmond, don't you see, that was Headley's disguise! He was obvious, open, so that nobody would suspect he'd also a secret part to play! Mr Blackstone was really interesting about it. He'd worked it out like a puzzle and talked as if it was all fact, all true.'

'Instead of which,' said John Marvell, 'it is Mr Blackstone's interested surmise, based on what he thinks a German means, who has written in another language, in the papers of another country, and who has obviously been employed to spread scandal about Cambridge and England by someone like this Dr Goebbels! I don't think I'd base my verdict on Mr Blackstone's evidence, would you, Desmond?' He smiled. Desmond was silent, neither assenting nor disagreeing, lost in thought. And at that moment the Bargate butler came in and told John Marvell that Mr Winter had just arrived.

Adrian Winter took his place almost as one of the family. Since his own home, Faberdown, had been sold it was at Bargate that he felt most at home. He kissed Hilda and Marcia, shook their hands, explained his lateness, thanked Hilda for accommodating it, sipped a glass of claret with enjoyment, ate sparingly but rather fast. It was not until after dinner, as he, John Marvell and Desmond sat over a decanter of port that he addressed a word to the latter. Anthony had been given permission by his father to leave the table and join his mother and Marcia. Forbidden port by one of his indulgent father's few prohibitions 'until you leave school, at least', he had abandoned them with alacrity. He and Marcia were engaged in a particularly exciting game of backgammon, interrupted at a critical stage by dinner.

Adrian said to Desmond, quietly, 'Let's have a word afterwards.' He turned back to John Marvell, on his other side. But John had got up from the table, with a murmur of apology, to look for a cigar for Adrian. Himself a non-smoker, he had, untypically, neglected to provide.

Desmond muttered, 'Bad news still, I'm afraid. No sign.'

Adrian looked at him, expressionless. John returned to the table. There was a silence.

'Before you were here, Adrian, we were talking about that odd article by the young German who was at Cambridge. Desmond, here, knew the fellow.'

Adrian nodded. It was, thought Desmond, unlikely that he had seen the paper in question or was in the least interested.

'Young Anthony was full of gossip about it,' said John, smiling. 'Told us a lot of scandal, young scamp! He'll have to watch his tongue!'

Adrian said nothing and considered his cigar. Shortly afterwards they left the dining room and Desmond saw Adrian say something to their host before drawing him apart.

'This way!'

Adrian led Desmond, with confident step, to John Marvell's own study, a companionable, cluttered room with a huge desk and two comfortable chairs. He settled himself, looked again at the tip of his cigar and then looked very straight at Desmond.

'I've had two telephone calls this evening. That's why I've not got down before. First was from my friend Delac. Seemed to think I'd be interested in a Frenchman called André, in trouble with the Germans over his papers, somewhere on the frontier.'

Desmond sat very still.

'Fairly low-level, but Germans weren't satisfied. French contacted them. To cut a long story short it appeared that a certain,' Adrian paused and puffed, 'a certain financial inducement might cause the German functionary to be amenable. Delac indicated that the French could manage this. If the money was forthcoming. He said he thought I'd wish to know.'

Adrian drew on his cigar.

'Had to make a decision. Some days gone by now, it appeared, and André still held, protesting. French were prepared to handle the financial inducement. Not prepared to make a formal *démarche* and so forth. Delac put it very tactfully to me.'

Desmond said, 'How much, sir?'

'In our money, a thousand more or less.' Desmond gasped. It was a year's salary for a moderately successful man. Adrian's face was impassive.

'Second call was because I asked him to give me fifteen minutes to think and then ring again. He did so. I told him to count on me. It's all arranged.'

'I don't know what to say, sir. I feel I failed, that it should have been better managed.'

'Don't think so. Take it I've got it right?'

'Entirely right. And I know that when he can manage it Kitzi – well, you know him, he'll work his hands to the bone until he repays.'

'Bother that.' Adrian Winter was a rich man. 'Bother that,' he said, 'but anyway I've left word – via Delac's office – that I want this M. André to telephone here immediately he gets to Paris. And since my call telling them to go ahead was a good many hours ago I expect we'll hear something tonight or tomorrow.'

It was half past nine the following morning that Adrian was called from breakfast table to telephone.

'A call from Paris, I think the operator said, Mr Winter.'

The telephone at Bargate was in a back passage. Adrian got heavily to his feet. They were all in the dining room. Breakfast on Saturday at Bargate was generally a leisurely affair unless some sporting occasion beckoned. He nodded to Desmond.

'Come along.'

Desmond stood by as Adrian gripped the earpiece and put his mouth to the speaker.

'Hullo? Hullo?'

Then –

'Delighted to hear you. Yes, of course I expected it. We

314

look forward to seeing you over here soon. What? Tomorrow? Splendid.'

Then there was a pause and a crackle of voice from the other end. Adrian frowned.

'Didn't get all that, I'm afraid. You say you're with who? No, don't fully understand, but Dillon's here, he'll explain.'

More crackling. Adrian looked puzzled. He said, 'I see. I think I see. Very odd. Well, the great thing is you're well. Look after yourself. Here's Dillon.'

Desmond grabbed the telephone.

'Hullo, Kitzi!'

'Desmond,' came Kitzi's voice, very faint. 'I am with your friend André. He has told me of your own experiences.'

'They were nothing, Kitzi. Nothing.'

'They were far from nothing. As I have just said to Mr Winter it is clear from them, from the fact of the questioning of yourself, as well as from the line taken with me – it is clear our friends the other side of the Rhine were watching. For you. And associating you with me.'

'Hard to understand.'

'Perhaps. Nevertheless they were uncertain, Desmond, they did not know, right to the last, that I was not genuinely André. If they had broken me no negotiation and no money would have rescued me. I would not be here, my friend. I would not be alive.'

Kitzi paused and the line crackled. Desmond heard him say, obviously with an urge to talk, to flaunt the possibilities of imprudence once safe in France, and shortly to be safe in England, 'The money did the trick because they were able to tell themselves André was a man of some mystery with friends in high places in France! Once it was on that basis, as opposed to a suspected German traitor, they could, with good conscience, accept a certain sum to repay them for their trouble! Your French friends did it wonderfully – I can guess it all now.'

'Not my friends, Kitzi. Adrian Winter's.'

'Now I ring off,' came Kitzi's voice. 'My heart is full. You – and Mr Winter – have –'

315

'Oh, nonsense, Kitzi!' Desmond, spontaneous and unconventional in much, had the orthodox English horror of being on the receiving end of gratitude. 'See you very soon, Kitzi!' he called, and rang off. Adrian was waiting.

'Told you, did he, that from what he's learned from this French chum of yours about your own travels – of which I know nothing at all yet, young Desmond, nothing at all – as well as from his own experiences, Fischer reckons the Germans were warned about your attempt? But not in detail, presumably, so it succeeded.'

Desmond nodded gravely, 'I suspect that's so.'

'And that he reckoned, amazingly, that they were uncertain of his identity – uncertain enough to accept a French bribe, shrug shoulders, look the other way.'

'Wonderful.'

'Hope von Premnitz is all right.'

'I hope so too.'

'Warned, were they?' Adrian was walking back slowly towards the inner hall at Bargate, Desmond at his side. The family had abandoned the dining room now, and were talking loudly among a welter of morning papers in the inner hall.

'Warned!' Adrian said thoughtfully. 'And about you. Now, I wonder how, Desmond. I wonder how.'

Desmond saw Kitzi Fischer in London a few days later, and thought that Kitzi looked ten years older. His face, lined yet ageless with its expression of gentle goodness sometimes touched by irony, was now the face of an old man. A few months in Germany and the stress of events since 30th June had marked him so. He took Desmond's hands without a word and there were tears in his eyes. 'You did bravely, dear Desmond.'

'Kitzi – I'm so glad.'

Kitzi shook his head. 'Of course I rejoice to be free, to be alive. But because I am alive others, much worthier than I, are dead or worse. We had better get this over. It eats me all the time and at least you will understand. You heard about my man, Günther. Premnitz told you.'

'He did. I'm very, very sorry.'

'He died because I went back to Germany, unnecessarily. He died because, like a complacent fool, I thought they would only persecute me in a small way and I would deal with them, send them scuttling. I was a fool, an arrogant fool. I acted against my own judgement. Finally, of course, Günther died because I allowed myself to be persuaded to run away.'

Desmond said nothing, and Kitzi resumed, his voice still carrying all the grief in the world.

'And then there is my nephew, Wieland. They will not let him go unpunished. They are bound to associate my escape with him, sooner or later. Sooner or later. Perhaps already. Premnitz will get word to me if he hears and if he can, but I have not seen Premnitz since the end of August. Since he made the last arrangements with me. With me and yourself.'

He sighed. Desmond knew that whatever his nephew's politics Kitzi loved Wieland Breitfall, exempted him from his general revulsion from all things National Socialist. Kitzi sat silent, thinking about Wieland and the fate his own escape had probably brought upon Wieland. They were in Desmond's small flat in London, a touch of autumn in the air.

'I will tell you something more about Wieland. You know there seemed to be a certain affection between him and your friend, Theo Tate. They corresponded. They met, as you know, when Tate came to Germany last winter, hoping to discover something about your poor friend, the Vassar girl.'

Desmond nodded. He did not wish to discuss Theo Tate. He thought he knew anything Kitzi could tell him. Theo, he was morally sure, had originally betrayed Sonja's indiscretions. First to Wieland. And by the medium of Wieland to the Nazi Party, thus bringing her to the beastly treatment which Desmond hated to express in words. He had thought about it a long time. He knew. He cared nothing for Wieland Breitfall's fate, although he cared for Kitzi's sadness. About Theo he wished to hear no more from Kitzi. He had guessed a good deal and did not need Kitzi's confirmation.

In this he was mistaken. Surprisingly, Kitzi said, 'I refused, once, to tell you names of some who might help your girl, because

I did not wish them disclosed to Theo Tate. At that time I distrusted his discretion, because I thought he sympathized too much with the Nazis, influenced by my nephew.

'I was right to distrust, but mistaken as to the reason. Oddly enough, Wieland himself suspected something in your friend some time ago, and told me of his suspicions. I believe they may have substance. I think Theo, and Theo's politics, are a fraud.' He expanded on this in brief, astonishing phrases.

There was a painful, silent pause.

Then Kitzi pressed his case. 'Is it impossible?'

Desmond sat very still for a long time. He tried to arrange certain recollections in his mind. He tried one hypothesis and then another. Kitzi talked again, speculatively, resignedly, watching Desmond. At length he said again, 'Is it impossible?'

And Desmond said, 'No. It is not impossible.'

For long winter months Desmond immersed himself in his writing, now and then talking and reminiscing with Cambridge friends, thinking, thinking. Once or twice, with distaste, he read again Patsy's September letter to him, read it carefully. He saw Theo Tate now and then, not by arrangement, and thought he looked very ill. They talked little on those occasions and others were always present. Desmond wrote to his mother that nobody should condemn another and certainly no son a mother. His letter was stilted, pompous and insincere but try as he might he could not improve upon it. He felt hesitant, often apathetic. Somehow the winter passed. 1935, people said, would almost certainly witness a British General Election. Events abroad seemed quieter once again.

Part IV

1935

CHAPTER XV

The proclamation in Berlin was made on 16th March, 1935. Service in the armed forces would henceforth be compulsory. Faithful to Article 22 of the National Socialist published programme, there would be 'abolition of a mercenary Army, formation of a National Army'. In peacetime the Army would consist of twelve Army corps and thirty-six divisions. The last traces of Versailles were obliterated. As conscripts reached the Reserves, the number of divisions on mobilization, based on those Reserves and based on the commissioned and non-commissioned officers trained by the *Hundert-tausend Mannheer* and at last enabled to play a part commensurate with their abilities, would be doubled and doubled again.

British newspapers carried the story, a story whose impact still seemed remote to the majority of their readers. It was, presumably, a matter of tardy justice, comprehensible national dignity restored – and several commentators pointed out that, anyway, France had just extended the period of service of every French conscript. Hitler, it was implied, had reacted understandably.

Two days later, 18th March, further reports from correspondents in Germany described Hitler's appearance at ceremonies to honour German heroes of the past on the annual Remembrance Day. The Führer – the offices of President and Chancellor, Head of State and Head of Government, now merged in his person – was flanked by the aged Field Marshal von Mackensen and by the German Crown Prince, eldest son of the last Kaiser. The old order was seen to be buttressing the new. The Minister for the Armed Forces, General von Blomberg, proclaimed that

321

the Army had laid foundations 'upon which a God-sent architect could build'. 'Then this man came –' the General intoned impressively. The God-sent architect looked grimly at the assembled dignitaries. Squeamishness of the old guard had been mastered: at least for a while. One day, inherently unreliable, inherently hostile to the National Socialist Revolution except where it coincided with their primitive and reactionary beliefs, one day they would give trouble again, no doubt. Nevertheless they had done something, though not enough, the old guard. The dragon's teeth had at least been sown.

Gerhardt von Premnitz was one who read von Blomberg's speech with particular scepticism. 'A God-sent architect,' he said to himself, 'a murderer and liar as well! How long will my old friends have to play with him?' Gerhardt knew that the shadows over Germany affected most of the country very little and his old colleagues in the Reichswehr hardly at all. Shadows like the internment camps with, it was rumoured, their particularly harsh régimes for 'subversive elements'; that horrible business last year when there had been wholesale murder carried out in the name of security; the racial laws which virtually deprived Jews of the ordinary rights of citizenship; the increasing strength and autonomy of the SS, in spite of Hitler's assurance that the Army alone should bear arms in the new Germany – these things had little general impact. The uniform of a German officer did not – as it had done in the Kaiser's day – protect its wearer from the ordinary proceedings of civil and criminal courts, but it certainly meant that the Gestapo and the more zealous prosecutors of Nazi ideology kept themselves at a respectful distance. There were, indeed, motives now for some Reserve officers to apply to return to full-time service, motives beyond pride in uniform and status. Such a change of direction in a man's life sometimes meant economic sacrifice, but it also ensured a certain immunity from harassment. These were peculiar times, thought Gerhardt, peculiar times, but they might settle down, when the first excitement of Nazi achievement had worn off. Managing the German economy during a period of massive rearmament was going to need remarkable skill, and once that rearmament was complete – well, thought Gerhardt, the French and British and Poles will recognize they're talking to equals once again. That's what everybody, even Hitler, wants, after all! The man's a blusterer, a bully, but at heart he's insecure, he longs for recognition, acceptance – and in his case that means acceptance of the new, strong Germany he reckons he's largely created. No doubt European stability will come at the end of it, despite all the thuggery and theatricals, whose first act I saw in the Bürgerbräu-keller in Munich twelve years ago! Gerhardt smiled at the memory; an uneasy smile, for he was unsure of all things now.

He took up his pen to resume the letter he was writing to Desmond Dillon. It pained him to write, for he liked and admired Dillon, but he had promised he would pass on anything he learned; and he now had learned. He had arranged a secure method for the letter's transmission, too: he had been introduced to a young Englishman at a reception at the Austrian Embassy in Berlin two days ago, and they had discovered they would meet again with mutual friends three days later.

'I might wish to send a letter to an English friend – the posts are slow –'

'I'm off on Friday. I understand perfectly.'

'Thank you.' The young man looked sensible and reliable. Gerhardt wrote in a firm, regular hand. He was writing in English, and now and then had to search for a word or expression: but not often.

> '. . . this acquaintance of mine was recently released from internment. It is better not to name him. These releases, like some of the arrests, have appeared to be arbitrary, without great logic. I have seen my friend since release. He's lying low, as you say. One has still to be careful but things are getting better.
>
> While in internment he met your friend, Fräulein Vassar. Now I have to tell you something hard, and I am very sorry. Fräulein Vassar has not been treated well. Because

she is partly Jewish she has been in a separated part of the camp. He found Fräulein Vassar is a patient in the hospital. She had been ill, very ill, but she had not received proper attention – it is, I think, what we may call a feminine disease. Her condition had deteriorated. My friend was working in the dispensary. He did what he could but when he was released – suddenly, and without warning so he said no farewells – it was clear that Fräulein Vassar would not leave the hospital alive. She will not leave that camp alive, and she may be already dead. Whether more timely treatment could have saved her life I do not know, my friend does not know, and you cannot know. I do not like to write this, but I must. I know very well the pain it will cause you and I send my expressions of sympathy, but it is better to put the matter clearly and plainly.

I do not like, either, to write my friend's last words on the subject. When he told me he supposed Fräulein Vassar will soon be dead, may already be dead, he said, simply, "I hope so." I will make no more comment on that but express, once again, my grief . . .'

Yes, thought Gerhardt, finishing his letter with sadness and shame, recalling his English friend with affection, simultaneously contemplating with definite if reluctant satisfaction the prospect of a Reich strong, united, and at peace – yes, these are peculiar times and there are sacrifices being made, and causes for much disquiet. He added a discreet postscript sending his affection to Kitzi Fischer. 'He knows now,' the postscript added, 'that his misguided young nephew is also in trouble. I am afraid it was inevitable sooner or later.' He felt reckless as he sealed the envelope. If the letter were discovered he, Gerhardt, would be finished anyway. And, of course, Wieland might talk.

Desmond Dillon received the letter on 22nd March. He felt no surprise. He had known within himself for a long time that he would never see Sonja again. Now he, too, prayed that she no longer lived, that she was at peace. Desmond had just heard that in Sussex a successor to Adrian Winter as Parliamentary candidate was about to be selected. The von Premnitz letter supplied the tiny additional spur to action needed. He telephoned Theo Tate at his office and asked him to come round to his flat next evening. They had not talked to each other for months, but there was something unsurprised in Theo's voice when he said that yes, of course, that would be all right, he would come.

For many months Theo had been going downhill and knew it.

The moment when he had first looked into himself and loathed what he found was that morning in the previous September when he heard that Desmond Dillon was safely back in England, shortly to be followed by Kitzi Fischer. Theo inspected his feelings and knew that although he wished neither ill the fact was that they could do him harm. Their safe return had not been anticipated, not been planned. They – through contacts, circumstances – could and one day, perhaps after years, would, deduce things about him, Theo, which were intended to remain for ever unknown. Until the final triumph, in which Theo found it these days harder and harder to believe, when all things could be known.

Meanwhile Theo knew that the escape of those two from the Nazis was bad news. And, simultaneously, he realized that he was hating himself for that knowledge. 'What sort of human being have I become?' he said aloud to himself as he looked at his face when shaving. "I sent a friend, I sent Emma's brother – I sent Desmond to the Gestapo, arch-enemies doing our work for us, all unwitting. I sent a friend to the Gestapo in order to help protect – what? The secret that I am not what the people among whom I live think me to be!' Theo found he was saying this sort of thing to himself rather often during those winter months of 1934. And he drank a good deal, sometimes by himself. Mostly by himself.

Sometimes he thought about Wieland Breitfall. No pity need

be felt for Wieland Breitfall, Fascist, SS officer, enemy of the Party, enemy of the true Revolution, enemy by definition of Theo. But he remembered Wieland's face, his voice, his enthusiasm, the affection in his eyes when watching Theo; and he knew, with a small part of himself, that to have personally played the lead role in sending Wieland to whatever fate he was now suffering – if he is alive, thought Theo, which is perhaps improbable – this had been duty, admirable and just; and was, nevertheless, vile. Why so? Theo asked his face angrily, speaking aloud and slurred. Because, the face answered, Wieland's undoing was a decent act, the warning and deliverance of his uncle. It is for that you managed to betray him.

And damnably often he thought of Emma. He thought of Emma's smashed body on some God-forsaken Highland hill, lying in the snow for the days until they found her. He thought of Emma's eyes when she had found Patsy and himself in bed, her round, terrified eyes as if the horror of what she saw, so incomprehensible, was beyond the bearing. He thought of the little moan Emma had given before she had fled on that ghastly evening. He thought of Marcus, advising persistence in the liaison with Patsy, interested in Patsy exerting her influence for Theo's political career, mistrustful of the relationship with Emma. 'My heart was really stirred,' Theo said, aloud again, 'they can't stand that. Makes one unreliable!' And thoughts of Emma would be followed by the heaviest drinking sessions of all. Heavy and solitary.

He was jumpy about everything now. A man he hardly knew started talking politics at his club.

'Do you know Stephen Paterson? He's mad keen to get a seat, to find something before the next election.'

'Yes, I know him.'

'Apparently he's lined up for old Adrian Winter's seat in Sussex! Winter must be a hundred!' The man knew nothing of Theo's own ambitions. He nodded and said 'Ah!' Afterwards, he asked himself how much he minded – if it were true. Marcus would mind. And Theo, for the first time, found himself saying aloud in the privacy of his bedroom that he wasn't sure he cared whether Marcus minded or not. And now Desmond had asked him to come round.

Desmond had decided some time ago that no complex scheme of revenge was practicable or would give him satisfaction. As he contemplated what he believed to be Theo Tate's record and character, with revulsion and the shock of a friend betrayed, he knew that he would like to make Theo suffer terribly, writhe with pain. But he also appreciated that he could not possibly contrive this, lay traps for Theo, intrigue to bring Theo down, betray Theo as Theo had betrayed. Such melodrama might be neat but it was implausible, and in the circumstances probably impracticable. With unaccustomed gravity he also recognized that such a retribution could turn to ashes in the mouth of the man who exacted it. All revenge, thought Desmond, is probably futile. In the end.

But he had determined, as an act not of revenge but of justice, to tell Theo exactly what he knew and what he suspected. Desmond had telephoned not only Theo but the House of Commons to ask and secure an appointment to see Mr Adrian Winter MP, that very evening. Adrian's reactions to that conversation, Kitzi's words in well-remembered phrases, Prost's curiously compelling articles, and other straws in the wind that had once blown over the Cambridge fens had coalesced to make sense to Desmond. These things he would say to Theo. And although he knew that he could not induce shame, or remorse, or anger even, at least he would have the grim satisfaction of explaining to Theo that as far as concealment from the world was concerned, the game was over. And he knew, with a peculiar and perhaps irrational confidence, that Theo would not be able and probably would not try to brazen it out. Then he could be given the letter, the small, perhaps unworthy, morsel of vindictiveness Desmond had reserved to himself; and he patted Adrian Winter's letter in his pocket as he sat in the window of his small flat on that March evening and waited for Theo to arrive.

Theo knew immediately that trouble was in the air; tension was crackling in the small room. Desmond gestured him to a chair, did not offer him a drink, said, 'It's time we had a talk,' and then started to speak in a low, conversational voice, holding up his hand on the few occasions Theo attempted to interrupt. It was not quite a monologue, but it was clear Desmond was determined not to be drawn into argument or debate; and very soon Theo recognized that the only thing he himself felt was immense exhaustion.

Desmond began by saying, 'I know it all started at Cambridge. Cambridge was the key. I thought I knew you well, but I never realized that side of you, the Communist side of you. I suppose it was The Tapir who made the first contacts for you – you never went near the university Communists, or Socialists for that matter. You laughed at them. You were the elegant sophisticate, the young Tory who stood out as intelligent in a party of boors, the well-informed mocker of the simplicities of others.' Theo knew that Desmond had thought about all this a lot, had formed phrases in his mind before Theo's arrival. Desmond was not using his customary rather impulsive, rather violent language. All this was careful! Planned!

'I remember you told me about your meeting an odd chap, Headley, rather distinguished, all the wrong ideas of course, but good company. I remember it cropped up that you had met him quite often. I suppose I wondered why, but idly. He's had a lot of publicity lately. People say he's gone abroad. Probably one day he'll come back, respectable, saying he was victimized by scaremongers and so forth. We shall see. I think he recruited you, Theo. And that you know what I mean!' Theo gazed at him, completely expressionless. All he could think of were the enjoyable, the amusing moments they had once shared together: Cambridge, London, Leningrad, Berlin. And they had been going to share family, to share Emma.

'My mother mentioned you to me once in a letter. She used an odd phrase. She wrote, "Theo, so obsessed with his secret life, his dreams of Revolution. In the end that would have made Emma unhappy. It didn't matter to me, of course." I know now what she meant. When I first read the letter it puzzled me, but it doesn't puzzle me now. Curious that you betrayed yourself to my mother. I didn't think Communists permitted themselves pillow talk. But you're a curious man, not quite impermeable perhaps.' Theo drew in his breath sharply at that. This was the first intimation he had had that Desmond knew of the affair with Patsy. So, his mind whispered, he could expect no mercy. Desmond's voice went remorselessly on.

'I imagine that your function was to remain covert, at all times; to become a Member of Parliament, ultimately useful because unsuspected, a man of influence, respected in our society: but with a life dedicated to betraying that society. No –' for this was one of the occasions when Theo opened his mouth to speak, 'let me go on. I know you wouldn't think of it as betrayal. I've no doubt you've managed to persuade yourself of the rightness of what you've been trying to do. But it's betrayal by my lights. You're not a spy, Theo. You haven't tried to ferret out secrets. You've *done* nothing disloyal to the country – in fact you've done nothing at all. That's not been your job. Your job has been to become and to wait. Become an important man. Wait for further orders. But in doing that you've twisted and turned, and although you would say you've not betrayed your country, you've certainly betrayed your friends. You've dedicated yourself to another cause than the one you've been born to and shammed loyalty to, but you've concealed it and pretended, pretended. I'm not going to argue about that cause, your cause, and the crimes it's stood for and justified. This isn't a political debate, Theo, it's a personal accusation. You've lived a lie. And you've contributed to a number of things I don't like at all. I'm going to describe them to you.'

'*Sturmführer* Breitfall,' said the presiding *Gruppenführer*, 'have you got anything else to say? Beyond what is already recorded here?' He touched a pile of papers, a transcript of the Inquiry's disciplinary proceedings. Wieland shook his head, standing very erect, his hands to the sides of his breeches, thumbs to the front, palms flat. He had been under arrest since 31st August. It was now 23rd March. For once they had been in no hurry.

'Your conduct,' said the President of the SS court, 'has been referred to *Reichsführer* Himmler personally. Every circumstance has been taken into account – your early dedication to the Party, your zeal, your previous good conduct, the talents which led to your promotion to your present rank. Taken into account, also, has been your scrupulous performance of special duty when attached to *Gruppenführer* Dietrich during a period of crisis for the Reich in June and July last year. Taken into account has been your vigilance in reporting an English undercover Communist whom you suspected, whether accurately or not I do not know and is unimportant. None of this can be allowed to offset one overwhelming truth. You have been chosen for the supreme honour of serving as an officer, a man of responsibility in the SS, one selected to set at all times a shining example of loyalty, unselfishness and honour. You have betrayed that responsibility. For selfish personal reasons, directed by a misplaced sense of family affection, you betrayed to your uncle, Fischer, that it was the Führer's intention that he should be dealt with. His words, writings, actions and beliefs were completely incompatible with loyalty to the new Germany. He had been a deplorable influence. Your relationship to this man had been overlooked in view of your own apparent devotion to Führer and Reich. That indulgence, it is clear, was a mistake. The *Reichsführer* acknowledges it as a mistake. You have disgraced your uniform.

'You will wear it no longer. The sentence of this properly constituted disciplinary court has been confirmed by the *Reichsführer* and is as follows: First, you are hereby deprived of the rank of *Sturmführer SS* and demoted to the grade of *SS Mann*. Second, you are immediately thereafter to be expelled from the community of the SS. Third, you will be confined, until a sufficient period has elapsed for the *Reichsführer* to be convinced of your rehabilitation, in a strict-régime camp. Dismiss.' He did not look up as Wieland stiffened, clicked his heels, raised his right arm to an angle of forty-five degrees, barked '*Heil Hitler*', turned around and marched from the room. The other members of the court, at a signal, rose, saluted in similar fashion and took their leave.

The presiding *Gruppenführer* was left alone with the papers and his confidential adjutant and secretary. The proceedings had taken place in the *Gruppenführer's* office. He put his fingertips together and examined them.

'A sad case, Roth. A bad case.'

'A disgraceful case, Herr *Gruppenführer*. The operation in question was a matter of the greatest delicacy and confidentiality, orders verbal, absolute trust essential. As was said, this was betrayal. Breitfall could, with his proven lack of principle, still cause endless trouble.'

'No,' said the *Gruppenführer*, 'no, that won't happen. You are right in saying that his knowledge of certain events could be exploited to harm Germany, but it will not happen. His stay in the camp will not be a long one. Nor will he leave it. Administrative instructions have been given.' He nodded to Roth who saluted, gathered the typescripts and withdrew, feeling warmly satisfied. He had never liked Wieland Breitfall.

'You passed to the Nazis,' Desmond said, 'talk about my girl, Sonja Vassar, which you knew would get her into trouble. The intention, indeed, was to get her into trouble. Your Communist masters, I presume, disliked Sonja's knowledge and frank exposure of the degree of military cooperation between them, the Communist régime in Russia, and the German Reichswehr. It would shake the faithful, who were instructed to distrust the German military, it would upset the ranks of the Party if too widely talked about, it would be a mild embarrassment. Not more – a mild embarrassment. So, to prevent further development of that mild embarrassment, you passed the word of Sonja's revelations, you betrayed her and my confidence. You told your pretty friend Breitfall about her, he passed it on, and you got a brave, beautiful girl bullied, assaulted, flogged and ultimately sent to a concentration camp. I know, because Breitfall told Kitzi Fischer, that you passed on this information. Once I thought it was simply indiscretion on your part. Now, I believe you did it because it was considered expedient by your masters.

'Did you know what would be the consequence? Probably. But you never cared. You must have simply been told that it

331

would suit the Party if she were shut up. So, by feeding the Nazis with gossip, you got them to do the Communists' work for them. True, Theo?'

Theo inclined his head. The gesture was eloquent, explicit. He had already determined how he would react. He knew, and knew that Desmond knew, it was the end of the road. They had been close once.

'Then you betrayed Kitzi Fischer. That is one of your most recent achievements. You learned from Adrian Winter that I was going to try to get Kitzi Fischer out of Germany, that he'd been tipped off and escaped murder when the Nazi killer squads were on the rampage last June. You got word to the Germans – I don't know how, you couldn't use Breitfall this time, he'd been responsible for Kitzi's escape in the first place; at least he's done one decent thing – you got word to the Germans that I was going to make the attempt, so that they could watch me and I could lead them to Kitzi. They did watch, but I had a lucky break. Beginner's luck. I didn't lead them to Kitzi. As you know. But it was no thanks to you. True, Theo?'

Again, very gravely, Theo bowed his head and Desmond continued: 'I never told Adrian Winter the details of what I intended to do, so you never knew them – he might have told you, because he trusted you at that time. Because of that it's obvious the Germans were never certain they'd caught Kitzi – they held him, you see, but they never cracked his identity although they were suspicious. In the end, a bribe persuaded a German official to drop the case and agree to believe in the false French identity Kitzi had assumed.

'So you failed there – but God knows why your Communist friends wanted to betray Kitzi to the Nazis and why you did. Because it must have been you, Theo. You or a certain man in Germany whom I know. It wasn't him, he's honest, he's at liberty and he never betrayed anybody. No, Theo, it was you. Thanks to you I might be interned in Germany by now. And Kitzi Fischer would have been shot. Why?'

Theo spoke now for the first time, almost inaudibly. He seemed anxious to help, to clarify.

'We wanted to discredit Breitfall. He suspected me – that is one reason, no doubt, why you are talking in this way now. He suspected me and he told his uncle, who has discussed it with you. We wanted to discredit Breitfall. We passed word by – by certain means we have, likely to be convincing to the Nazis, that Breitfall had tipped Fischer off, helped him escape last June. To make it convincing we also passed word that an attempt was due to smuggle him out of Germany, and that you were likely to be active in the matter. I knew no details of course, so we gave none. And, as you say, that didn't work and Fischer escaped. Believe me, I was delighted when I heard that you were safe and he was safe – I thought it quite unnecessary to tip the Nazis off about that side, it would have been enough simply to tell them it was known Breitfall had warned Fischer. But the Comrades have devious minds, they wanted to show Breitfall up as completely unreliable – and thus talking nonsense about me; and they reckoned the message would be more persuasive if it was passed with a tip-off about Fischer's impending escape. I'm so glad the bloody Nazis slipped up over that, I really am.'

Desmond stared at him, digesting and believing. It filled a gap in his comprehension, and was none the less disgusting for that. He took from his pocket a letter.

Theo had never before seen Marcus look nervous. On every occasion Marcus was assured, sometimes abrupt and formidable, but master of the situation. Now, on 24th March, 1935, he looked uneasy; he was even sweating, although they were not walking fast, overcoated and hatted, round the Serpentine in Hyde Park. A central rendezvous, a curious meeting.

Marcus said, 'We are unlikely to meet again.' It was the first thing he said. Theo, who had his own announcement to make in due course, looked at him with dull surprise.

'Why?'

'I am unlikely to remain here much longer.'

'Ah!' thought Theo, 'recall!' And, as he looked at small beads of sweat running down Marcus's pale, intelligent face, he guessed at the inner terror of his companion, his comrade, his long-time guide, instructor, master. In their recent conversations over the last three months, in what was left unsaid as well as obliquely hinted, Theo had discerned that ripple of panic which was spreading throughout the Party, which had started in December.

On 1st December, 1934, Serge Kirov, an important member of the Politburo and virtually head of the Party in northern Russia, had been assassinated, shot at point-blank range by a student in the Smolny Institute in Leningrad. The assassin was a young Communist. In the weeks that followed there was talk, there were statements, there were even reports, uncontradicted, by the Foreign Press Corps in Moscow, that the assassination had been the work of a corrupt, counter-revolutionary group within the Party itself. There were whispers of mass arrests. There were reports of confessions; then more arrests and more confessions.

And stories of executions; and yet more executions. It appeared that 'counter-revolutionary elements' had penetrated every corner of the Party! Whether at home in the Socialist Fatherland, or in the Party abroad, there had in consequence to be vigilance, and stringent examinations. Theo had remarked to Marcus, echoing a worldly cynicism which he knew perfectly well Marcus shared, that it would no doubt be a good opportunity to deal with unreliable or difficult elements within the Party, to consolidate the leadership of the Revolution, on which so much depended. Marcus had made no answer. And the reports and rumours increased.

That had been three months ago. Now Marcus had been recalled. And sweat ran down his face.

Theo's own emotions, unbeknown as yet to Marcus, were too strong at that moment for him to feel much for another, but as he glanced at Marcus he knew that he pitied him. He, Theo, had depended greatly on this man, had relied utterly on the link between them. He now had difficult things to say to Marcus but he could not be indifferent to him. And Marcus had been recalled. Strange, although never until now have I felt it so, thought Theo, that I do not know his name. And probably never will.

Marcus was talking, hurriedly and without seeming to mind much what he was saying, of the new Party line. It sounded like a mechanical recitation.

'It is necessary to support popular fronts, coalitions of anti-Fascist forces. This is not a time for the Party to be isolated. We are to appear in the vanguard of popular forces, while, of course, retaining our own integrity. It will be necessary for Comrades to join other parties, to become members of all manner of bourgeois institutions.'

'That has always been the way of my life, Marcus.'

'In your case,' said Marcus, 'the object and the duty were entirely different. We are now speaking of popular fronts, overt forces. Public, open, popular. Your function has been to remain undetected. None of this affects your own cover – you know that perfectly well, Contor. And I have further matters to tell you.'

'I expect so,' said Theo, in a tone Marcus had never heard from him before, 'and I have matters to tell you, too, Marcus. Some of them concern my friend, Desmond Dillon. As you like to know all things, you should know that I saw him last night. And had a long, a very long talk.' Theo's voice was barely audible as he said 'a very long talk'; as he thought of that talk.

Theo related Desmond's conversation almost verbatim to Marcus, speaking in flat tones as they walked round the Serpentine, walked and walked, the March winds cold. He omitted his own reactions, such as they had been. He recited Desmond's long catalogue of accusations. Marcus heard him with a grim face.

'He knew a good deal, this Dillon. How?'

Theo ignored that, and said, still without expression, 'I think the only thing he didn't know was that I betrayed Breitfall, too.' Marcus frowned at the word 'betrayed', and looked interrogative.

'He made no mention of that,' said Theo. 'He hadn't worked out that in tipping off the Nazis about the attempt to rescue Fischer, by using their informers in the German Communist underground, it was primarily intended to discredit Breitfall. You passed the word that Fischer had been warned by his nephew, Breitfall, and to get that accepted you passed useful information which might lead to Fischer's arrest: and execution, of course. It was a package. Fischer – and Dillon, for that matter – were to be sacrificed in order more credibly to discredit Breitfall. Desmond hadn't really added that up.' Theo kept one thing back. Something – was it fear? he wondered – inhibited him from confessing to Marcus that he had denied nothing to Desmond and had himself explained the motive of the Fischer betrayal. Handing over one's oldest friend to the Gestapo, who might well have caught Desmond after all, needed some sort of justification. But he did not expect this point to be found persuasive by Marcus, who muttered, 'Fischer is a bourgeois intellectual, ineradicably hostile to the Party. He would have been no loss.'

'Even now, Marcus? Even in the days of popular front politics, when the Comrades are shedding their sectarian image, teaming up with all and sundry, or appearing to?'

'Yes,' said Marcus, harshly. 'Even now. So was that all Dillon did not know about you? That you had, as you call it, helped betray Breitfall?'

'Not just "helped". You know, because I told you, that I also met that man Langenbach and made clear to him that Wieland Breitfall had saved his uncle's skin. We didn't propose to let him get away with it, did we, Marcus?'

Marcus heard the new and disturbing note in Contor's voice, and reflected that it was probably as well Contor's future had been decided and was shortly to be communicated to him by Marcus. He said curtly, 'Anything else?'

'Yes, one more thing. Before I went Desmond Dillon brought out a letter from his pocket and started reading it to me.'

'You ought to hear this from me, I think,' Desmond had said quietly, looking at the letter in his hand. 'It's a note to me from Adrian Winter. Presumably you'll be hearing from him or others to the same effect. It's quite short.

'"My dear Desmond –."'

Desmond, calling on the old man at the House of Commons, had told Adrian Winter everything he knew and everything he suspected. Adrian had been stunned. Such things were completely beyond his experience. Although a cultivated and travelled man of the world Adrian had never abandoned the belief that treachery, the betrayal of friends, the pursuit of revolution and the sort of duplicity Desmond described were completely impossible in an English gentleman! Adrian could comprehend such things, add up the awful construction of events very sharply. But he had great difficulty in associating them with Theo Tate. He listened. He was shrewd and perceptive and he was at last persuaded. Desmond went through every detail.

'I'm afraid, sir, he is the only person who could have done exactly these things. And now I'm sure it goes back to Cambridge. I've been talking to a great many people in the last months, talking about this man Headley, talking about one of the dons, Playfair. I know Theo very well, you see. I've come to an absolutely definite, certain conclusion. He decided, years ago, to work for the Soviet Union.'

'Still guesswork, Desmond.'

'The guesswork becomes a working hypothesis at a certain point, doesn't it, sir. And I know no other hypothesis which fits the facts. I've been thinking and thinking, going in my mind over every talk, every episode of the last years, whether here, in Germany or whatever. I – I simply *know*, sir. In my bones.' Desmond made no mention of the casual reference in Patsy's letter. Not that. Not to Adrian Winter, her affectionate and confiding friend.

Adrian said, rather unsteadily, 'You know that there is a department who should be aware of this? Even of the suspicion? Which has a responsibility, even if at present there is nothing criminal, or may not be –'

'Of course, sir. And I'd like to leave that word to be said in the right quarter by you, if you think it right. But please let me see him first.'

'And you don't think he might, instead, be working for the Germans?'

'No,' said Desmond. 'No, I'm sure it's the others. Odd how the effect has tended to be the same here and there.'

Adrian had heard it all and accepted this.

'And to think he might have married your sister! I can still hardly believe it all!' But Desmond knew that he did. Nothing on earth would have made Desmond say, 'Tate also slept with my mother, if you must know.' That would have suggested a base motive and reduced rather than strengthened Adrian's belief. For, Desmond knew, Adrian now believed, and soon thereafter he had agreed to write the letter.

He had said, 'You say you think he'll admit all this. I only want you to show him the letter if he does. Otherwise give it back to me. It will need further thought. As a matter of fact, I'm pretty sure they want Paterson anyway, and I'd have a job to persuade them otherwise even if – if all this weren't so. But I don't want you to give him that letter unless he owns up.'

'Of course.' The old-fashioned and inappropriate phrase 'owns up' showed as nothing else could the gulf between Adrian Winter's England and that of Theo Tate.

Adrian had looked at him shrewdly.

'Why the hell do you think you'll get him to admit it? They're disciplined people, spies, agents, they'll admit nothing, under rigorous questioning even. And you –'

'I think it,' Desmond had said quietly, and with perfect confidence, 'because I'm sure he's at the end of his tether. He must be. I know Theo. It will have been fermenting. The time's right. I've seen him once or twice in the last six months. He will have worked it all out. He'll cave in.'

'I'm not quite clear why you want this letter.'

'I do, sir. Very badly. Please do this thing for me.'

Desmond read the letter aloud to Theo without expression. Theo had met Adrian's condition. He'd admitted it all, as Desmond knew he would.

'My dear Desmond,

You asked about Theo Tate's prospects, as a possible Parliamentary successor to myself, a thing which has, as you know, been mooted for some time.

338

He has no prospects. The people down there have talked
to me recently, and have decided to select someone else.
There'll be a meeting, of course, but that is the way it's
likely to go. Tate will not be invited to attend. There are
too many stories current of his flirting with undesirables
on the extremes of politics. I will say no more.

Yours sincerely,
Adrian Winter.'

Theo nodded and made his last interjection.

'"The stories", presumably, owe a little to yourself?'

'Yes. That sentence owes a good deal to myself. And is fair,
don't you think?'

'So you see, Marcus,' said Theo, quoting the Winter letter from
memory and without difficulty, 'you see I have no future of the
kind we planned. I am known for what I am.'

'I am not particularly surprised, Contor. Nor am I particularly
sorry. The truth is you have been both indiscreet and, frankly,
disappointing. You opened your mouth so wide to that young
Fascist Breitfall that he suspected you of Party membership or
more, and we had to do what you described – but late, very late.
The word from Germany is, incidentally, that Breitfall has been
dealt with. The word also is that some of the German Comrades
who were told by the Gestapo to check you out, Comrades the
Gestapo thought they had purchased, have been under very
thorough examination themselves, it seems.'

'Well?'

'We cannot dismiss the likelihood, in other words, that the
Nazi authorities believe you to be a Soviet agent. At present they
are unlikely to share this knowledge with the British, or to be
believed if they did, but – entirely through your own original
unguardedness, no doubt when drunk – you are likely to be
known, ever more widely, as not that which you have taken
trouble to appear. Everything you have told me of Dillon's
accusations confirms this. He may have been guessing. He may,

339

on the other hand, be well informed, perhaps through Fischer. It is unimportant.'

Theo sighed. Perhaps it was going to be easier than he had supposed. He jibbed at admitting to Marcus that he had himself confirmed Desmond's suspicions, and it looked as if it was going to be unnecessary. They, the Comrades, had clearly decided already that he was a poor investment and needed selling, losses needed cutting. It was better that the breach should come from their side. Marcus was talking in a flat, toneless voice, reminding of certain practicalities. Then he spoke more sharply.

'The truth is you allowed your personal emotions to intervene when your fiancée died, you lost your balance. Additionally, you have failed to impress sufficiently to make your way towards Parliament, which was agreed to be your function. I have discussed your case with the Comrades. You are something of an embarrassment, Contor.' And to me, Marcus thought, and to me! For I suggested this was a promising future, a promising agent of the Revolution. And now he is promising no longer, and his allegiance is known by at least one of his friends and may, for all I can do about it, soon be known to all the world. And the Comrades will not be pleased. He reflected without pleasure on his impending return home. But Contor was talking again, responding quietly to Marcus's last words.

'I felt fulfilled by my work for the Party. I hated the world as I found it and I knew the Party, whatever its imperfections – even whatever its crimes in the ordinary sense of the word – the Party held promise, the only promise, of ultimate decency. Of a world with human dignity, and rationality and intelligent direction. I knew that the path towards it would be hard, bloodstained at times, but I wanted to walk along it. And I agreed to – I welcomed – my own part in this, a secret part, a concealed life. It was hard, but I knew it was a privilege. In many ways I still feel that.

'But what has it led to? Everybody who cares for me as a person, who makes a human gesture towards me, is betrayed by me. I know you don't like that word, Marcus, but there is no other. Faithfulness to the Party for one like me means falsehood to everyone I have ever cared about. Even my Emma, my girl, couldn't have lived with it for ever. She'd have discovered. Or I'd have found it intolerable and told her. And I'd never have made her see it, converted her. She –' He turned his head away, suddenly, tears jumping up behind his eyes.

'I know I'm something of an embarrassment, Marcus. I know I'm no good to you any more. And I've lost everything, absolutely everything. Of course I've no ordinary prospects, no career except for the job I do for money – and that wouldn't last if they knew about me! But I've little right to grumble at that since what I've thought of as my career was anyway being pursued in order to betray. Again, to betray.'

'The Party demands great sacrifices for a great ideal,' Marcus said. 'You have found the sacrifices beyond you, as have others before you.' He spoke with surprising dignity, and Theo, knowing that the man believed in his words, and must fear desperately for his own future, looked at him and then turned away. He, Theo, was an embarrassment to the Party, Marcus had said. There were ways in which embarrassments could be diminished, even finally eliminated, but he was untroubled by concerns of that kind. He knew he wasn't really important. Marcus had run an agent, a 'sleeper', one of a number of which he, Contor, had proved a disappointment. Others, no doubt, were more satisfactory, would rise to high, covert rank in the organization which owned him. Theo would never know their names. Theo had very little to tell the authorities, were he ever so minded. Theo didn't matter much.

It was on the following day at seven o'clock in the morning that Theo made up his mind. He had been conscious, on parting from Marcus, of an overwhelming emptiness inside him. He found he could hardly feel, that his emotions, his reactions, needed a conscious, artificial effort of formulation. He had nothing spontaneous and nothing sincere left in him. A small resolution had begun to form, and he inspected it and then began to cherish it like a man in a dream; and went home to his rooms in Curzon

Street. He thought of telephoning his mother – he had moved out of the house in Albion Street some time ago, and saw her less than he should: they had never been particularly close. Then he put the thought away. She could contribute nothing. To make contact would probably be purely cruel in its effect.

Theo considered writing something. But 'What?' he said to himself aloud. 'What sort of epistle, or apologia, or testament? And to whom? Desmond?' Desmond knew him now, had confronted him, had exacted his due. There was nothing more to say to Desmond. Marcus? Marcus, too, knew all, could assess all according to his own dogmatic and absolute assumptions which had until yesterday been Theo's. Or was it the day before yesterday, or last week or last month or even from the very beginning that Theo had sensed but refused to acknowledge that his way was a dark way and that only in darkness would it end? A letter of farewell to Adrian Winter? Theo could almost smile, a twisted smile, at the thought of past ambitions. The House of Commons! A respectable Tory member, with a beautiful rather radical wife! Inwardly comforted by the knowledge that he was laughing up his sleeve at the lot of them, that he, alone, belonged to that revolutionary and secret élite who were on the side of history and would inherit the earth! Both the sham and the reality had beckoned most enticingly once. Now no more. Now he was simply a failed traitor, a betrayer of friends, institutions, lovers, and, they would say, country. He would be judged simplistically, with revulsion. But the intolerable thing was that he was now judging himself simplistically. And with revulsion too. He had meant every word of his miserable farewell to Marcus, but had not conveyed the depth of self-disgust. Not that Marcus could have comprehended that. He would have supposed he was witnessing Contor's psychological breakdown, and perhaps he was.

It had not begun like that. It really had not begun like that. There had been eager sympathy once, impatience with the sufferings of others, a desire to do good. Good? What did that mean? The word itself offended the rigorous materialist philosophy Theo had adopted. A desire to tidy up the lives of others, anyway, to regulate the world in a way which would, *in the end*, reduce avoidable physical suffering. Yes, I did want that, Theo said aloud, I did want something like that. And the comfort of an intellectually coherent creed, or so I thought. He let himself into his flat, and drew the sitting-room curtains.

No, it had not begun like that. Might he not, somehow, still obtain a little credit for decent motives? From whom? he said, again aloud. No all-seeing and compassionate Power was within the reach of Theo's belief. That door had been slammed by him long ago.

Theo drank a great deal that night and slept heavily. Next morning his head ached but his mind was extremely clear. He left his flat at exactly ten o'clock and walked from Curzon Street through Shepherd Market. The first press of people moving to work from buses in Piccadilly had flowed already through the narrow streets. The tarts who adorned the place later were not yet at their posts. It was a comparatively solitary walk, with no acquaintance passed, no incident. Two fashionable-looking women tip-tapped along the Hertford Street pavement, and in Down Street men were emptying dustbins. From Piccadilly came an even hum of traffic as Theo walked, looking neither to left nor right, towards the Down Street tube station. It was his nearest, and more often than not he used it if it was raining, changing stations at Holborn to reach the Bank and his office in the City. If the weather was fine, and preferably, he walked across the parks and took a District Line train from St James's to Cannon Street. Today Down Street would do well. Better, in fact, although the day was bright.

Theo bought a ticket with two pennies, descended by lift, walked to the eastbound platform and then moved to the far end of it. Several people were huddled near the entrance, but in his quarter of the platform he stood alone. After two minutes he heard the roar of the approaching tube train. Then there were cries and shrieks and yells of shuddering expostulation under the hard, hard artificial light.

Mid-April. The blossom in St James's Park was exquisite. Kitzi Fischer looked with great affection at Desmond Dillon as they walked together.

'It is a curious world,' he said, 'but you are a person who can understand the complexity of one's emotions. I have heard from Germany, from a reliable source. Wieland has disappeared, perhaps in one of their camps, perhaps dead. Because of me, of course. They knew he saved me, and that would not be forgiven. I brought this to my Wieland, whom I loved, who was like a son to me. I brought death, I expect it will be death, to him. And I brought death to dear, dear old Günther. If I had not gone back –'

Desmond heard it with pain, had heard it all before.

'I know why you went back. You wanted to help them. You didn't think it possible that things would reach the point they did. Nor did most people. Don't torture yourself, Kitzi.' Kitzi smiled at him. He loved this forceful young man, of a whole generation younger than his own, who nevertheless talked to him, if he chose, so magisterially, with certainty and authority. He smiled and then his face became melancholy, sympathetic, and he said, 'In spite of everything, I know you must feel a wrench of heart about Theo Tate. This man betrayed you. I am sure he betrayed my Wieland, although they were bound to mistrust Wieland, I suppose, when I escaped. He did something to betray me. He betrayed your Sonja. He –'

'He was being groomed to betray our country. All that. Nevertheless he was an old friend and he was once going to be my sister's husband.' And he was my mother's lover, Desmond thought, without any emotion now. Doubtless Patsy would suffer something, was already suffering something. She had recently declared that she intended never to return to England. Desmond said quietly, 'You're right, there is a wrench at the heart. I hate thinking of suicide, and he was, I suppose, pushed finally into it by me. As you know, I confronted him with all I knew – and guessed. He didn't deny a thing. I knew he wouldn't. Strange chap – lived his whole life as a lie, but would think it in bad taste to tell outright fibs to me if I were bright enough to catch him out! Odd!'

Kitzi's own view was hard, but he could understand. His voice was sad and gentle.

'It is a fanatical creed, Communism. They believe, after all, that they are assisting an inevitable historical tide. Nothing is more cruel than a conviction of that kind.'

'I could have sympathized with Theo, although it would have surprised me, about his Communism. What revolted and still revolts me was what it led him to do. It turned his life into a huge deception trick and it had to taint everything he did and every relationship he formed. It so happened that his betrayals were of people you knew, I knew – but his personality had become a sham, and the longer it went on and the more successful it became, the more vicious the sham and the greater the betrayals.'

'For a cause, Desmond. For *the* cause, your Communist, your Theo, has to believe. Ordinary trust between man and man, ordinary truth, has to be one of the prices demanded of some. The élite. The conspirators. The Theos.'

'And he found he couldn't go on paying it,' said Desmond. There was no bitterness or anger in his voice now. He added, 'And didn't your nephew find much the same? He believed in his National Socialism, believed utterly by all accounts. Then his duty to the Nazis meant letting them kill his uncle, whom he loved. He found he couldn't do that. He'd prefer to risk his life. And he paid the penalty.'

'And in a different way, Tate, too, found that he couldn't face the fact of incessant betrayals,' said Kitzi, 'so he didn't risk his life. He took it.'

'Yes. He took it.' Theo Tate's death on the Piccadilly line, formally classified as accidental, had clearly been by his own volition. Everybody who knew anything of the man realized that, and the word got round. Desmond had written a difficult, an impossible line of condolence to Theo's mother whom he hardly knew. No answer, and why should there be! Desmond loathed the picture imagination conjured up, the loneliness at the last. He'd had vengeance all right, vengeance for Sonja, vengeance for Kitzi's Wieland perhaps, vengeance for unknown others, it might be. Desmond found himself thinking, unbidden, 'Vengeance for Emma', even though Emma had died by accident. Still, as he'd realized before, what a self-defeating, futile thing is vengeance.

Kitzi was talking in a quiet, civilized way about the dangers represented by Communist enthusiasm for popular fronts against the Nazis. 'It will,' said Kitzi, 'obscure the fact that this is a moral struggle. If people allow it to be taken over by the Communists, so that anti-Nazism makes Communism respectable, then the moral basis of anti-Nazism is vitiated. Because Communism can never be respectable.'

'You would refuse them as allies?'

'I would be careful. Very careful. Or the world will find it exchanges one evil for another.' Desmond said that he understood that, but that it was surely very difficult. If there was military menace, it needed military response, however put together. Was that not so? Kitzi said it was not necessarily so and repeated his warning. They sat in silence for a little.

'Those two – Theo, your Wieland – both reckoned they'd found the key, didn't they? They both wanted to make the world anew, to smash it and rebuild it. They both reckoned that to do that is so important and so superb an object that one has to harden one's heart to all the small, human destinies that are crushed along the way. It's a dreadful attitude, Kitzi. The only decent approach is surely to be honest and humane, and never to believe that some great public – or national or world – object justifies small, private evil.'

'They were idealists, Desmond. That is the hard, true fact.'

'Then God preserve me from idealism!'

Desmond looked at this tall, lame man with his fine face, and his absolute standards, and his profound, civilized pessimism. He said, 'I gather you've decided definitely to try to settle in America?'

Kitzi nodded. He knew that the trite inquiry, answer already known, concealed, in the English manner, some other and more disturbing communication. To help his friend on, he told him how excellent he had thought Desmond's articles on the European situation. 'You put some things admirably, really admirably,' Kitzi said, 'and you put your telescope on French attitudes *most* shrewdly, my friend! I congratulate you.' Desmond said that he so enjoyed his work these days that he felt restless except when ferreting out hidden facts and concealed attitudes behind the opaque surface of events.

Then he said abruptly, 'I had a letter from Frau Reitz. The friend of Sonja's in Bamberg. She's heard, quite definitely, that Sonja's died. As you know, I also heard from Gerhardt von Premnitz, who prepared me for it a bit although his information wasn't certain. I'm glad. She was a superb girl and every day I woke thinking of her alive in one of those places I hated it more.'

'I can understand and agree. I, too, pray for Wieland's death. Desmond, I am forty-five years old and I have lived and fought in what men call the worst war the world has ever seen, from 1914 to 1918, and yet the things people are doing to each other, and I fear are going to do worse and worse to each other, make me feel I have seen nothing, nothing.'

Desmond said, with force, that he hoped Kitzi was mistaken. But he knew, without words passing, that Kitzi rejected consolation of this or any other kind, perceiving with a clarity of insight mercifully denied to Desmond that the waves would surge ever more remorselessly, and the tide rise ever higher before one day receding: leaving much smashed flotsam and many dismembered creatures upon the indifferent shore.

Hammond Innes

'The master storyteller' *Daily Express*

Air Bridge
'Hammond Innes achieves a mastery sense of urgency as the story rises to the climax.' *Daily Telegraph*

Campbell's Kingdom
'A fast and expertly-managed story . . . The Rockies, the squalid "ghost towns", the oil-boring – these are memorably presented.' *Sunday Times*

Golden Soak
Embittered and disillusioned with his life, Alec Falls fakes his own death and starts for Australia – and the Golden Soak mine. But he is not the only person interested in the derelict mine. The shadows of the past and the blistering hell of the Australian bush combine in a deadly maze which Falls must unravel if he is to survive at all . . .
'Pace, atmosphere, tension. Evokes Australia as few other books have done.' *Listener*

The Black Tide
The details of maritime fraud, international piracy and the working of Lloyd's insurance are presented with an authority that give *The Black Tide* an uncanny credibility.
'Exciting . . . credible . . . a polished novel.' *Sunday Express*

FONTANA PAPERBACKS

Helen MacInnes

Born in Scotland, Helen MacInnes has lived in the USA since 1937. Her first book, *Above Suspicion*, was an immediate success and launched her on a spectacular writing career that has made her an international favourite.

'She is the queen of spy-writers.' *Sunday Express*

'She can hang up her cloak and dagger right there with Eric Ambler and Graham Greene.'

Newsweek

FONTANA PAPERBACKS

Fontana Paperbacks: Fiction

Fontana is a leading paperback publisher of both non-fiction, popular and academic, and fiction. Below are some recent fiction titles.

- ☐ GLITTER BABY Susan Elizabeth Phillips £2.95
- ☐ EMERALD DECISION Craig Thomas £3.50
- ☐ THE GOLDEN CUP Belva Plain £3.50
- ☐ A THUNDER OF CRUDE Brian Callison £2.95
- ☐ DESERT QUEEN Julia Fitzgerald £3.50
- ☐ THE GREEN FLASH Winston Graham £3.50
- ☐ UNDER CONTRACT Liza Cody £2.95
- ☐ THE LATCHKEY KID Helen Forrester £2.95
- ☐ IN HARM'S WAY Geoffrey Jenkins £2.95
- ☐ THE DOOR TO DECEMBER Leigh Nichols £3.50
- ☐ THE MIRROR OF HER DREAMS Stephen Donaldson £3.95
- ☐ A SONG IN THE MORNING Gerald Seymour £2.95

You can buy Fontana paperbacks at your local bookshop or newsagent. Or you can order them from Fontana Paperbacks, Cash Sales Department, Box 29, Douglas, Isle of Man. Please send a cheque, postal or money order (not currency) worth the purchase price plus 22p per book for postage (maximum postage required is £3.00 for orders within the UK).

NAME (Block letters) _____

ADDRESS _____

_____

_____